BLOOD CAROUSEL
TALES OF A DARK LEGACY ~ BOOK TWO

L. ANN & L. GENE BROWN

ISBN:
ISBN-13: 978-1980804475

First Edition

Rowan Walker – young college student and coffee house barista – believes that her twin sister, Eden, has been taken against her will. The Seattle Police – based on evidence to the contrary; as well as Rowan's sister's free-wheeling, off-the-rails past lifestyle – believe otherwise. Rowan, however, refuses to let the case (or, for that matter, the SPD) rest and after a solid year of relentless badgering by the young woman a weary, and sympathetic detective gives Rowan an alternative solution.

Enter Fallon Wylde, 17th Century pirate turned vampire turned soldier-for-hire.

At first, Fallon, too, has his doubts. And there is the unignorable fact that his fee is well beyond the young woman's means. But for reasons he can't immediately comprehend, Fallon feels drawn to her. Out of sympathy or an undeniable sexual attraction. . .he isn't quite sure. But then, during the initial interview, the mention of an all too familiar nightspot sparks his curiosity. And from that point on things start to happen. . .

A very curious home invasion. . . The out-of-the-blue transformation of harmless next door neighbour to homicidal attacker. . . Scare tactics that run the gamut from the grotesque to the downright deadly.

And with the additional, eventual inclusion of elements which lead back one of most grisly and controversial murders in Seattle's history it soon becomes apparent that the kidnapping of Eden Walker is just the tip of a very large and sinister iceberg.

Return to the world of A Dark Legacy and Shadowfall with this second book in the hot new series!

DEDICATION

To the amazing "For The Love Of Books" Facebook Group, run by Kathy, whose support and excitement for this book has kept us going.

Kalli, Jennifer, Gemma and Emma – my crazy girls. This one's for you!

~ L. Ann

~*~

For my son, Michael. Hopefully his road won't be as rocky.

And for Scoopy, Tiki, and Red. I still remember.

~ L. Gene Brown

OTHER BOOKS BY
L. ANN & L. GENE BROWN

A Dark Legacy Series

Bonded In Blood

Shadowfall Shorts

Blood Carousel

ACKNOWLEDGMENTS

Cover designed by RebecaCovers on Fiver

PRAISE FOR BONDED IN BLOOD

"The plot twists in this book are amazing. I LOVED this book."

"A gripping story. I look forward to more."

"Not your typical vampire book. "

"This book was so enjoyable! I had to know what was going to happen, which had me flipping the pages even faster."

BLOOD CAROUSEL

BLOOD CAROUSEL
TALES OF A DARK LEGACY ~ BOOK TWO

L. ANN & L. GENE BROWN

PROLOGUE

Detective Lieutenant Sidney Marshall was a dick . . . an asshole . . . a 24-karat son-of-a-bitch. All of which, he learned in time, were prerequisites to becoming a successful, productive and, times being what they were, a surviving member of the Seattle Police Department. But, in addition to being a twenty-five-year veteran cop, he was a husband – happily married to his high school sweetheart since 1980. He was also the proud father of a son and twin daughters. Two aspects of his ongoing existence he was particularly proud of and would go to any lengths – lay down his life, if need be – to protect.

Career and family. Not necessarily in that order, nor exclusive in relation to one-another, as he often stated to friends both on and off the job. His cardinal rule – rules, plural – in maintaining both were simple. Number One: the job was the job and the home was the home. Number Two: he did nothing which would jeopardise and/or endanger the harmony and success of either.

Emotional turmoil, family stress, and the divorce rate in the American Law Enforcement community were legion. Facts well known to all officers of the law, as well as any civilian acquainted with the literature and the, oft-times, all-too-realistic cinematic versions of the genre. It was an occupation rife with daily challenges and dangers, all of which took their toll on those who 'serve and protect', putting a strain on the convictions, the morals, and the souls of even the strongest of men and women. Hence, his impromptu meeting with the woman, the detective, who now made her way toward the rear-most corner booth of the Gold Star Café.

Detective Lieutenant Virginia Frost adjusted the weight of her leather shoulder purse, pulling its strap more firmly into the top of her cashmere-clad shoulder – resisting the habitual urge to self-consciously comb a hand through her shoulder-length auburn hair – while keeping her gaze centred on the man in the booth to her left-front. Still, her peripheral vision registered the sudden jolts of recognition, the wide-eyed stares and quickly averted eyes.

The Gold Star – owned and operated by a retired member of the Seattle Sheriff's Department and his family; as well as a popular hangout for members of the SPD's Western Precinct – was packed, as usual. Most of its patrons were active-duty police officers, and *all* of them were aware of who she was.

Not that she gave two hoots in Hell.

"Jen," Sid greeted her, standing to offer an open-armed embrace as she approached.

"Sid," she reciprocated both the greeting and the hug, each holding the other for a period that felt mutually comfortable before releasing and stepping back.

Sid, ever the gentleman, remained standing while Jenny took off her coat, and placed it and her purse on the booth's seat. They sat as one, with Sid immediately signalling their waitress. Once he'd snagged her attention, he pointed to his half-full and steaming cup, then turned a questioning eye to Jenny.

"Just coffee," she said. "I've been swilling that burnt sludge at the station all day. I could use a decent cup."

"One and a top-off, Mary," Sid called out, then turned to give the woman across from him his full attention. "So . . . how's the family?"

"They're good," Jenny answered. "Rick's been out of town the past week. On a job in Vancouver. I talked to him earlier. And the girls," she made a mouth-twisting mock frown. "Let's just say that if tween and teenage angst caused grey hair, I'll be snowy-white by this time next year."

On the heels of Sid's cackling laughter, Mary arrived with Jenny's coffee, gave Sid a top-off and began making the rounds at the other booths with her coffee pot. Both Detectives took pause to sip their steaming brews before continuing the session of obligatory platitudes. This time with Sid, who spoke of his wife, Brianna's, recent trip to San Francisco to see her brother and *his* family; of their son's art scholarship to U.C. Berkeley; and the twins entering their Senior years at high school.

"God, where's the time go?" Sid said. "Feels like it was just yesterday we were both still in uniforms and—"

"Really, Sidney?" Jenny interrupted, with a head-tilted and eyebrow-cocked grin. "A stroll down Memory Lane before you ease into the sermon? Puh-lease! We've known each other too long for *that* dance."

Sid sucked in a quick breath through his nostrils, pursed his lips and nodded heavily. "Okay, sorry. And you're right, we have."

He paused again, taking another sip of java. "But the band's still playing, so I'm gonna dance this out.

"You and me – we've known each other . . . been friends since we were both patrol cops. Since Rick was just talking about breaking away to form his own architect firm. Since our oldest kids were still falling off skateboards or experimenting with make-up.

"And, as for the job, we have paid our dues. You're a good cop, Jen. One of the best on the SPD, so please help me to understand. Why--"

"Am I doing what everybody – including *you*, it seems – thinks is shithouse crazy?" she interrupted to finish his query, making a cautious scan around them in case her voice carried. "Let me turn that around. Why aren't *you*, Sid? You said it yourself – I'm a good cop. We both are. We took an oath to uphold the law and protect the citizens of this city. And we're not . . . *NOT!*" her voice quivered, hissing on the repeated word. "There's something screwy . . . screwy-wrong going on in Seattle, Sid. Crimes, *murders* are being committed, and they're being ignored. No, not just ignored, actively and deliberately covered up by the highest levels of our own department. How can you . . . how can *I* sit back and do nothing and still consider myself to be a good police officer?"

"Jesus, Jen," Sid whispered, and seemed to slump in his seat, glancing at the ceiling a moment as if sending a silent prayer for strength.

Jenny snorted. "So, what are you gonna say next? *Don't make waves, Jenny? Don't rock the boat?*"

"I'm neither blind nor deaf, Jen," he told her. "I've heard the stories. Hell, anyone who has been on the force here for more than six months has heard and seen. There are rumours of a vault, a basement, a bunch of locked filing cabinets – the SPD's own version of the X-Files – going back to the 1800s Gold Rush days. Bodies found drained of blood, throats and other body parts torn out . . . bitten out; reports changed, cops threatened by the brass. And the other – the *Men In Black* . . . in grey, in our case, and unmarked meat wagons showing up before our people arrive to cart off corpses, etcetera, etcetera etcetera.

"And I have also had long conversations with a few of the old timers – at P. T's, the cops bar downtown, and in this very café – who told me tales of other cops who waded around in the same mud you're dipping in. It didn't turn out well for them. In fact, it killed their careers. Don't, Jen. Don't throw all your good years into the toilet. Let it go."

Jenny flashed a quick, tight-lipped smile and reached across the table to give Sid's hand a squeeze. She then rose and collected her coat and purse.

"I can't, Sidney. I *can't*."

CHAPTER ONE

"Hey, Sid!" The Detective lifted his head at his name. "She's here again and asking for you."

Detective Sid Marshall sighed. He didn't need to ask who 'she' was or why she would be asking for him. There was only one person the other officer could be referring to and, sure enough, rising to his feet and looking out toward the public area of the Seattle Police Department, he could see the expected auburn-haired twenty-two-year-old personal pain-in-his-ass.

With a heavy sigh, he headed out to where she stood, arms folded and blue eyes like ice-chips.

"Miss Walker," he greeted her.

"Why?" She levelled a finger at him. "Why have you closed the case?"

"It's been almost a year and we've found no evidence to say your sister was taken against her will."

"*No* evidence? Her apartment had been broken into. There was *blood!*"

"Miss Walker," his voice gentled. "Rowan. Your sister has called you a number of times, telling you not to look for her. She even spoke to a police officer, do you remember?"

"She was forced . . . *coerced.*"

"You don't know that." The Detective shook his head. He'd had this argument a thousand times with the woman standing in front of him.

"I *know* my sister. She wouldn't have just taken off without telling me."

Detective Marshall gave the young woman a pitying look. She had turned up at SPD almost every week since her sister had disappeared – convinced she'd been kidnapped and, while she made a good argument, further investigation had brought up nothing at all. The fact that her sister had spoken to the police and confirmed she was safe meant that there wasn't much the department could do.

Patting his shirt pockets, he fished out a business card. "I'm going to give this to you." He held it just out of Rowan's reach. "Now, this doesn't mean I think you're right, but if anyone can find the truth without any evidence at all, it's this man." He allowed Rowan to take hold of the card but didn't release it himself. "But I think your sister just wanted a fresh start and you'll be wasting his time and your money."

Rowan tugged on the card and Detective Marshall let go. Lowering her eyes, she read the print.

"FW, A&R? It sounds like one of those taxes and accounting companies. Like H&R Block?"

"They're not. They find missing objects, and people . . . For a price."

"Like Private Investigators?" Rowan offered.

Detective Marshall raised a hand, palm-down and waggled it. "Something like that, yeah. They have a pretty good success rate – from what I hear, anyway. Let's just say they aren't encumbered by standard rules and regulations. If you really want to find your sister, give them a call."

~*~

Rowan sat cross-legged on her bed with newspaper clippings, missing persons reports, and other articles surrounding her. When her sister had initially gone missing, Rowan had been convinced the man she'd been dating at the time was involved. Researching him had taken months, but over time she'd amassed information and links hinting to his association with some small-time criminals who ran many brothels across Seattle. From that, she had dug deeper – finding other reports of missing women, but SPD hadn't been interested in looking at what she had found.

Her eyes strayed to the business card Detective Marshall had given to her earlier that day. She was still undecided on whether she should call FW, A&R or not. Would they laugh at her the way the police did? She knew they thought she was just a silly young woman who was blind to the idea that her sister had willingly cut off all contact with her. She understood *why* they thought that, her sister wasn't the most reliable person, but Rowan knew – she just *knew* – her disappearance was not through choice.

She picked up the card, looked at the number and then reached for her cell phone and dialled it before she could change her mind.

The number went directly to a recorded message.

"I'm sorry. FW, A&R are not available to take your call right now. Please leave your name and number and someone will get back to you as soon as possible. Thank you!"

Rowan hesitated for a second, then reeled off her phone number and name, and hung up. No more than a few minutes passed – long enough for someone to listen to the recorded message and jot down the number, possibly – before her cell rang. The display told Rowan it was a blocked number and, feeling strangely nervous, she connected the call.

"H-Hello?"

"Hello. Is that Miss Walker?" A slightly-accented female voice responded.

"Yes."

"Hi there! My name is Kate Chan. I work for FW, A&R. You left a message for us?" Kate Chan sounded far too chirpy, Rowan thought – one of those eternally happy types with a perfect phone voice. "Will you tell me what caused you to call us?"

"I was given your number by SPD," Rowan began. She explained about her sister's disappearance, about how SPD weren't investigating the case and had dismissed her concerns about a possible kidnapping.

"Please hold," Kate Chan said once Rowan stopped speaking and she found herself humming along to an instrumental version of *Sympathy For The Devil* while she waited. The song cut off abruptly. "Thank you for holding," Kate Chan's voice rang out. "We have an available slot this evening at eight. Would that be convenient for you?"

Rowan checked her watch. "That's only an hour from now?"

"Yes. We assume there is some urgency to your case otherwise you would not be calling us." She didn't wait for Rowan to confirm. "As that is the case, we are happy to meet you at the earliest opportunity."

"Well . . . yes. Of course. Where are your offices?"

"We find most of our clients prefer a first meeting to be held at a neutral location, Miss Walker. Do you have such a location?"

"Um . . ." Rowan cast around in her mind for a place that would fit the woman's description. "The Blue Star Diner and Coffee Café?" She named the 24-hour diner she worked at and was only a few blocks from where she lived. "Do you know it?"

"Yes, Miss Walker, we know it. My associate, Mr Wylde, will meet you there at eight." The call cut off before Rowan could ask how she would recognise him and she was left staring at the phone in her hand.

By the time Rowan had dressed, slicked a pale shade of lipstick across her lips, twisted her hair up into a ponytail and added a touch of eyeshadow, it was closing fast on seven-thirty. Dashing out of her apartment, she half-jogged to the diner, arriving there with fifteen minutes to spare. She slid into a booth, ordered a coffee, placed her file of research carefully onto the table-top and tried to check her reflection in the window to make sure her unruly hair was still tamed into its style.

When the waitress brought her coffee, Rowan thanked her and flipped open the file to read through some of the notes she'd made until a sudden lull in the conversation around her made her look up.

The man, clearly the reason for the sudden silence, stood framed in the doorway. Rowan let her eyes slide over him – noting the elegant expensive dark suit, white shirt open at the throat, and sunglasses (who wore sunglasses after dark?) and looked away. Obviously in the wrong place, she thought with some amusement, as she wrapped her hands around her mug and returned her attention to the file in front of her.

"Miss Walker?" A shadow fell across her table and Rowan lifted her gaze to find the well-dressed man standing beside her.

"Fallon Wylde," he thrust out a hand before she could respond. "I believe you were expecting me?"

"I was expecting *someone*," she took his hand and shook it, masking a slight wince at his firm grip. "*You?* Not what I was expecting."

In the process of sliding onto the bench seat opposite her, Fallon quirked an eyebrow at her words.

"I was expecting someone older. Not quite as—" she paused, looking for the right words. "Not quite as expensively dressed, I suppose."

"You would believe me better suited to the job had I turned up in combat gear? Or maybe a dirty trench coat and a more rumpled suit?" He settled back into his seat. "I can assure you, Miss Walker, I'm older and more experienced than I look." He reached up and removed his sunglasses, folded and placed them onto the table and Rowan found herself staring into a pair of vivid green eyes. "Is that all the information you have on your sister's disappearance?" He touched the file with one long finger, waited for her to nod and then drew it across the table towards him.

"The police officers you spoke to," Fallon said, after a few moment's perusal. "The ones who actually worked the case?"

"Nash and Cooleridge," she answered. "At least, for the first week or so. But the Detective in charge, who handled most of it, was named Marshall."

"Sid Marshall. A good man," Fallon murmured, with a quick and brief glance up from the file. He continued reading for a few minutes longer then looked up to catch her gaze. "It reports here that your sister – Eden – phoned you a few times? Four, to be exact. And she spoke to a police officer on one of those occasions."

"Yes, but there was something wrong. It was like she was reading from a script. Every time, *every conversation* was the same. '*I'm fine, Ro. Don't try and find me.*' She said the same thing to the police," Rowan stopped, hearing the quiver in her voice and sucked in a calming breath. "But she was lying. I know she was."

"You and Eden are twins? Are you saying you have some kind of twin telepathy?"

Rowan shook her head. "No, nothing like that."

"So, you and Eden were . . . *are* close?"

"It's complicated."

One of the shop's roving baristas – a gawky geekish collection of ragdoll blonde hair, metal-framed teeth and a name-plate that read 'Dustin' – arrived and set a fresh cup in front of Rowan. He stepped back, giving Fallon a 'geeks-rule-pretty-boys-die-screaming' look.

"What can I get *you*, sir?"

"How about coffee? French Roast, black, if you have it," Fallon smiled, holding back an amused chuckle as the barista departed. He turned his attention back to Rowan. "I take it you come here often?"

"I work here a few nights a week." She pulled the cup toward herself and blew across the top. "What else do you need to know?"

"As much as you can tell me. Eden – tell me about her. What's she like? Her habits, personality, likes and dislikes. What about places she liked to frequent? Friends?"

"Okay, well . . . like you already know, Eden is my twin sister, but we're not identical. She's a few minutes younger than me. Last time I saw her she'd dyed her hair pink, but her natural colour is similar to mine, maybe a little bit darker. Habits, yeah she has habits." Rowan's laugh held a tinge of sadness to it. "Her top three are cocaine, vodka and violent men. We argued the last time I saw her. She'd promised me she was clean, but she wasn't." She waited for Fallon to offer the same argument as the police – that Eden had simply left because Rowan was putting pressure on her to clean up her act – but he merely nodded and waved a hand for her to continue. "I didn't really know the people she hung out with. The few times I did meet them, they . . . well, I felt uncomfortable. Maybe if *I'd* made more of an effort, spent more time with her, I could have—"

"It wouldn't have mattered," Fallon cut in. "Addicts live for their next fix. How long after you last saw her did she disappear?"

"I'm not sure. I phoned her every day, but she wouldn't always answer, so it wasn't unusual to call and not actually speak to her. But after three or four days, she'd run out of money and then she'd turn up at my apartment. It was five or six days after our fight that I went to her place. The front door was off the latch. I thought she'd just left it open, but when I went in—" Rowan bit her lip, thinking back. "There was blood on the floor and it looked like there'd been a fight. Her coffee table was broken in half, the tv screen was smashed . . ." her voice trailed off.

"And the police found nothing unusual in that, regardless of the calls that came later," Fallon's words were more a statement of fact than a query.

"According to Detective Marshall, Eden most probably had a falling out – he called it a 'little love spat' – with her boyfriend. Her calls to me confirmed that, in *his* opinion, anyway."

"But not in yours." Another statement.

"No. Detective Marshall said there had been numerous calls reporting disturbances at Eden's – arguments, fights between her and her boyfriend. Sometimes with other people. It wasn't unusual for the police to be called out two or three times a month." She paused to take a sip of coffee. "The phone calls. They weren't normal. Eden *never* called me. If she wanted something, she would show up. I was the one who kept in contact, who would phone her."

Fallon nodded, scanning the open folder. "And this boyfriend of hers?"

"Taylor," she responded quickly. "Last name, first name . . . I don't know," Rowan shrugged. "That's all I ever heard her call him. We only met once, a month before Eden disappeared." She hunched both shoulders and shivered. "He gave me the heebie-jeebies.

"Eden had a type, of a sort. Lowlifes, I called them. The roughest kind of biker, bar trash, wannabe hustlers. She'd hook up with them for a while, never longer than six months, then drop them and find herself another. But Taylor, he was different. His whole manner. I mean, some men have this way of looking at you . . . of undressing you with their eyes. But with him, when he looked at me, it made me want to take a long shower afterwards to wash away the slime."

Dustin returned then with Fallon's coffee and Rowan fell silent while he paid for it and the barista stomped away. Fallon took a sip, grimaced at the taste, then slid the cup away.

"Anything else you can tell me?" he asked.

"About a month ago, I think someone was in my apartment. There was nothing missing, but something wasn't right. It felt different . . . wrong."

"Different how?"

"I don't know for sure. I came home from work, from *here*, in fact. Everything was fine until I went into the bedroom. I thought I heard a noise, the door closing. But I'd closed *and* locked the door when I got home. I went back into the sitting room and there was a smell, like cologne, and the chain was off the door." She swallowed another mouthful of coffee. "I reported it to the police, but they said I'd probably just forgotten to put the chain on in the first place."

Fallon studied the young woman sitting opposite him. Nothing she had told him so far gave him a reason why Detective Marshall would think it was a case that would interest him. Either she wasn't mentioning something important or the Detective had just wanted rid of her – either option was viable. He could tell from her posture and facial expression that she was waiting for him to discount her concerns, to tell her that she was worrying needlessly, that she was a silly girl seeing shadows were none existed but, while she had given him nothing to think otherwise, his instincts were telling him there was a lot more to this story.

From the picture Rowan was painting, and the impression Fallon was receiving, the two sisters were very different from one another. Rowan worked part time at the diner, which suggested she either had another job or something else that occupied the rest of her time. There was no smell of drink or drugs around her, nor any of the mannerisms usually associated with someone hiding an addiction. There was also genuine concern in her eyes and voice when she spoke of her twin.

"Okay," he said, realising he had been silent for too long. "So far, we know that Eden is an addict, and that it's highly likely her boyfriend is too, or he's her dealer. Do you know how they met?"

Rowan nodded. "Eden had gone to a club, some place near the Space Needle. She was excited because it was hard to get into without an invite and one of her friends knew someone who worked there. He was in her place when I went to see her the next day. I'm sure they were both high and I think they'd been doing something else," she bit her lip, clearly uncomfortable.

Fallon leaned forward and touched her hand. "What do you think they were doing?" His hunter's instinct told him this was it, this was the information he was waiting for.

"Something . . . unusual. There were teeth marks and blood on her neck. It looked like she'd been bitten, but not the hickey kind of bite. When she opened the door, I could see them on her wrists, too."

Bingo!

Fallon looked down, feigning interest in an item inside the file to conceal the sudden spark of curiosity that would have been clear in his eyes.

"Alright, Miss Walker. I think what you've given me so far should be sufficient. I'll take the case," he told her. "Now, shall we discuss my fee?" He paused, choosing his next words carefully. "I'm going to be honest with you. My services don't come cheap. And, please don't take this the wrong way. At the lowest affordable rate, it's twenty-five-thousand dollars for the investigation and search; another seventy-five-thousand if the situation calls for, shall we say, extreme measures. Can you afford that?"

"I've done most of the searching already." She waved a hand toward the file. "And I can continue the investigation. What I *need* is someone to help, not someone to take over."

"And if your search had truly been that effective, we wouldn't be having this conversation," Fallon countered her argument. "I *will* find your sister, Miss Walker, there's no doubt about that. But I'll do it my way and I work alone. That's *not* negotiable."

"Then I'm wasting my time here," Rowan reached forward to close the file.

"If that is an attempt to make me reconsider my fee, it won't work," he told her. He pulled a pen from his jacket pocket, picked up a napkin and jotted something down then slid it across the table to her. "That's my personal number. If you change your mind, call me."

Rowan looked at the number scrawled in big, bold handwriting, picked it up, folded it and tucked it into the file. "Thank you, but I won't." She rose to her feet and held out her hand, waiting for him to take it. "Thank you for taking the time to listen to me. I'm sorry to have wasted your time."

Fallon held onto her hand when she started to pull away and waited until she lifted her gaze to his.

"Save my number, Miss Walker. If you insist on carrying on with your search and you do end up in a situation you can't get out of, call me. I'd hate to have your death on my conscience."

He waited for her to nod before releasing her hand and allowing her to walk away.

Fallon watched her leave, a half-smile on his lips. First impressions, he mused to himself as he admired her hip-swaying walk. Rowan Walker was a determined, stubborn, gorgeous red-headed bundle of trouble and it was probably for the best that she hadn't hired him. He laughed softly to himself and absently took a sip of the coffee at his elbow, grimacing when he tasted it. Awful stuff, who the hell willingly bought it, let alone drank it.

He turned his head toward the window and watched Rowan as she exited the diner and walked past him without looking. Fallon let his eyes track her until she was out of sight, then stood up. From what she had told him, this *Taylor* was a vampire – possibly using a fake name – and the 'unusualness' Rowan had noticed told Fallon that he enjoyed drugged blood. A chuckle escaped him as he thought about Rowan's reaction when she had brought it up – an intriguing mix of embarrassment and horrified fascination – and wondered how she would react to some of the things he'd done over the years. With a headshake, he left the diner and headed toward where he'd parked his car. He decided to head over to Shadowfall, obviously the club Eden had been so excited to visit; and see if they had any footage from around the time the girl had gone missing. Rowan hadn't hired him, nor shown any signs of doing so in the future, he acknowledged to himself, but she'd piqued his interest and, if he was going to be honest with himself, he had nothing better to do.

~*~

Chatty bartenders. For as long as Fallon could remember, they had been in the upper tier of his list of things that grated on his nerves. Not to mention the 'Five Types He Would Most Enjoy Killing'. But, as the saying went, there are always exceptions. And, at this particular point in time, the woman presently pouring his x-teenth shot of Ronrico 151 was one of them.

Tigr – *'That's Tiger minus the e'*, as she was ever quick to correct. A permanent fixture at Shadowfall and, like most (though primarily more regarding the collection of diehard nightly regulars than staff) she came with her own unique story – one-part fact, and three-parts fiction.

Blonde, tall, big-boned, a penchant for leather, latex and mesh net apparel. Originally Swedish-born by some accounts, Norwegian by others. According to ongoing legend, she had always been associated with bars and/or alcohol. A 'saloon floozie' in the Bella Union Saloon in Deadwood, South Dakota in the late 1870s; a bootlegger's moll and speakeasy owner in Illinois in 1952 (one story even claimed she had shared a flophouse bed with the infamous bootlegger Dutch Schultz), whorehouse Madame and black marketeer . . . dealing in eggs, butter, and booze during World War Two; owner/bartender of Mickey's Bar & Grill, San Francisco, during the Korean War; and so on and so on.

As a member of a time-honoured profession known worldwide by varying and sundry designations – from barkeep to mixologist – Fallon knew of none better. As a conversationalist, she could be engaging, witty, captivating. But the one thing that made Tigr truly unique – that set her apart from her brethren, in both the Vampire and Human realms – was a gift of recall that could, without exaggeration, be called supernatural.

According to popular reports, Tigr possessed an ability Vampires called *văz notoros* – *Perfect Eyes*. In Human terminology, a photographic or eidetic memory. A gift that, for reasons unknown, only manifested itself in turnbloods and, even then, a one-in-a-million occurrence.

They said she could remember everyone she had ever fed upon, going all the way back to the very first. She could; and Fallon had personally witnessed several demonstrations; walk into a room, a club lounge, a gift shop, or restaurant and take one quick look then walk out. Outside of the room, she would then describe everything and *everyone* therein, right down to the cobwebs in the upper corners and the scuff marks on certain patrons' shoes. In Fallon's opinion, *supernatural* fell about a mile short.

The night had proved to be less gratifying than he would have liked. Although Shadowfall's normally surly Chief of Security had been surprisingly agreeable where access to the club's video security archives was concerned, for three, almost four, hours of scrutiny; not counting periodic breaks to ease the tedium of sitting on his ass with his eyes glued to a flickering tv monitor; he'd come away with only three semi-decent, though not altogether useful, hard copy photos of Rowan Walker's missing sibling.

He'd spent another two hours having dinner, drinks and idle conversation at LaDonna Roma's with the club's General Manager, Gayle Hunter, before finally finding his way down to the sub-level or, as his friend Eayann affectionately called it, *The Vampire Classic Zone*, and the Shadows of Night Lounge for, if little else, relaxing refreshment amongst his own kind.

"You look like a man with an itch that scratchin' won't stop," Tigr said, pouring him another brimming shot glass. "Or, at least, you drink like one."

"This," Fallon quirked a lopsided grin, then tilted his head and let the liquor slide down his throat in one smooth unbroken gulp, "is a slow night for me. But you are right," he placed the glass on the bar, allowing her to refill it. "Although, I don't think *itch* is exactly the right word. More like a bug bite."

"A woman?" Tigr prompted. "And don't be afraid to tell me to mind my own business."

"Don't worry about it," Fallon shook his head, toying with the rim of the glass. "And yes, a woman, kinda."

"Ah, business," Tigr excused herself and made a quick hop down the bar to tend one of the other customers. She was back in under a minute. "Wanna talk about it? Never know, it might help."

"It's okay, I—" Fallon started and stopped himself, shrugging after a beat's consideration. "You know, it just might, at that."

A jerk of his head took them both to the bar's secluded end, away from curious eyes and ears where Fallon produced a page of computer print-outs that contained the three images. One showed Eden Walker and an entourage of three entering Shadowfall's main entrance, past a pair of dark-suited security staff. The second showed the group among other patrons at the lobby's bank of elevators. The third shot was one taken by the elevator-cam.

"I'll take a guess. The one you're interested in is the girl with the Nicki Minaj do," Tigr offered.

Fallon nodded.

"Well, if it helps—" Tigr started, then stopped at the sound of Fallon's cell phone. He raised a finger to delay her and moved away from the bar.

~*~

She woke with a start, her eyes snapping open in the darkness of her bedroom; heart pounding, ears straining to hear the noise that had woken her. Sitting up, she was in the process of swinging her feet around when she heard a muffled curse and a footstep outside her bedroom door. Rowan froze, holding her breath. Slowly . . . carefully . . . she stretched out an arm and scooped up her phone from the bedside table. Pulling the covers up over it, she hit the LED display as she keyed in her passcode and navigated to her phone book. For a second or two, she hovered over the number for SPD then scrolled past it. She didn't think they'd believe her if she rang them.

Who else could she ring?

She watched as the list of phone numbers slowed and stopped at the very last entry in the list.

Wylde, Fallon, she mouthed. *Could she call him? Did she dare?* Another shuffling step sounded. *He'd said if the situation called for it to call him. Did this count?*

Decision made, she hit call. He answered on the second ring.

"Wylde."

"Mr Wylde . . ." she whispered.

There was a long pause and Rowan was about to cut the call when Fallon spoke again.

"Miss Walker? Isn't it a bit late for you to be calling?"

"I . . . yes, I'm sorry . . . I shouldn't have disturbed you," Rowan paused, listening intently to the movements in the outer room.

"You haven't disturbed me. What can I do for you?" She could hear the rich amusement in his voice and knew he thought she'd rang for an entirely different reason, one that had nothing to do with hiring him to find her sister and, despite the fact she was alone with a potential murderer in the other room, Rowan squirmed in embarrassment.

"Miss Walker?" His voice prompted her, telling her she'd stayed silent for too long.

"It's just . . . I don't think the police will come and . . . Well, you said if I needed to call you and I don't know who else to ring . . ." she realised she was babbling and sucked in a shaky breath. "I think there's someone in my apartment," she finished in a whispered rush.

"There's someone in . . ." Fallon repeated slowly, then caught himself the amusement gone from his voice. "Where are *you*?"

"In . . ." she swallowed. "In my apartment."

"And you didn't think to open with that? Give me your address," he demanded in a clipped tone. Rowan did so. "I know the area. I'm about five minutes away. Do they know you're there?"

"I don't know. I'm in my bedroom."

"Alright. Stay away from the door, keep as quiet as you can. I'm almost at my car now. Stay on the line and tell me if they try and come in to you."

She heard his car's engine fire into life and cringed, hoping whoever was in the other room couldn't hear it as well.

The next five minutes felt like the longest of Rowan's life as she sat clutching the phone to her ear and her eyes glued onto the door handle. Every so often, Fallon would ask if she was okay and Rowan would murmur an affirmative until, after what felt like a lifetime, he told her he had arrived and was parking his car.

"Stay in the room until I come and get you," he told her. "I'm heading up to your floor now." He cut the call and Rowan waited in the darkness.

Five minutes passed, then ten without Rowan hearing any noise and she was biting on a thumbnail nervously when her bedroom door swung open. Wide-eyed, she inched backwards in trepidation, only to sigh in relief when Fallon was framed in the doorway.

"Are you okay?" he asked.

Rowan nodded but didn't move from where she sat, knees drawn up to her chin, on the centre of her bed. Fallon stepped into the room and gave a quick glance around.

"Whoever you heard left before I arrived," he told her.

That got her attention and her eyes rose to meet his. "I wasn't lying."

"I know." He sat on the edge of the mattress. "Your front door was open, closed just enough so that it wasn't noticeable unless you pushed it." He tilted his head to look at her and held out a hand. "Come into the other room."

Rowan stared at his outstretched hand, then grasped it with her own. She allowed him to tug her to her feet and lead her back into the sitting room. Still holding her hand, he felt her stop in the doorway and turned.

"There's no one here but you and me." He urged her back into movement and directed her to the couch. "Sit down. Do you have anything to drink? Whiskey? Vodka?"

"I don't really drink," she replied. "But there might be a bottle of wine in the kitchen somewhere."

He disappeared into the other room and Rowan could hear him opening and closing doors. Eventually, he reappeared with a dusty bottle of wine and two glasses. He placed the glasses onto the coffee table and filled them before handing one to Rowan.

"Drink up."

"I'm not—"

"Miss Walker," Fallon eased down onto the couch beside her. "Rowan . . . I can call you Rowan, can't I?" He waited for her to nod. "You've had quite a shock. It's not every day you wake up to find an intruder in your home. Drink the wine, it'll settle your nerves."

"You believe me, then?"

"Yes. Your door had been forced and there's a footprint by your bedroom door. Since I can only assume you don't wear size eleven military style boots, I'm going to go out on a limb and say it was left by your unwanted guest." He couldn't tell her that he could also *smell* the intruders.

Rowan sagged back against the couch. "The police said I was imagining it."

Fallon lifted his own glass to take a swallow of wine and had to hold back a shudder at the taste. "No, you didn't imagine it."

She shifted beside him, curling her legs up beneath her. "How much do I owe you for coming?"

"Why don't we get into that later?" His eyes fell onto the wine sloshing around in the glass clutched in her hand, and he reached out to gently peel her fingers away from the stem and place it back on the table. "Right now, we need to make sure you're safe," he told her. "Do you have any other family, or friends maybe, who could put you up for a few days?"

Rowan looked back and forth from Fallon's face to her wine glass, her bottom lip caught between her teeth. Fallon watched her process what he was saying, and found himself alternating between worry for how vulnerable she appeared and admiration for how quickly she seemed to rally her defences.

"You think they might come back, don't you?"

Fallon didn't see the point in lying. "It's a definite possibility."

"I have a friend who works with me at the coffee shop – Lainie. We have classes together at . . ." she faltered, scanning the immediate area around her. "My cell phone. I think I left it on the bed. I can call her. I think it would be okay, at least for a day or so."

"Good. You do that. Pack up whatever you need." His eyes drifted over the flannel pyjamas she wore, frowning slightly at the dancing mice that covered them. "Get dressed. I'll wait here until you're ready and drive you over to your friend's place," he told her.

CHAPTER TWO

Rowan sat beside Fallon in his car as he navigated through the dark streets to her friend's apartment. As he drove, he cast sidelong glances at her, waiting for her to talk. But she didn't. If anything, she appeared to be lost in thought, hands loosely clasped together on her lap, her face turned toward the window.

"Are you sure you're okay?" he broke the silence when he pulled to a stop at the traffic lights.

"Fine!" Her snapped response had him raising an eyebrow. "Alright, no I'm not. I'm mad."

"Mad . . . ?" he echoed, faintly.

"Angry, then," she turned her head to look at him. "Whoever it is, I know what they're doing."

"And what would that be?"

"They're trying to scare me, to stop me finding Eden."

She was quick, he mused. Most mortals wouldn't have jumped to that conclusion so fast.

"Why would they do that?" he asked.

"Because they . . . because . . ." her eyes flashed as she glared at him. "I *don't* know!"

"I'm going to assume you know how to handle yourself?" Fallon spoke again, after a particularly lengthy slash of silence. "How to defend yourself, I mean."

"I . . ." Rowan's response came out in a near whisper.

"Have you had *any* kind of training?" Fallon continued. "Hand-to-hand or martial arts?"

Her continued silence was answer enough.

"Do you own or know how to use a gun?"

Finally, she shook her head.

"Then my next questions are simple, since I'm sure you're not going to stop trying to find your sister. What happens when they realise they can't scare you off? What will you do when they come back and decide to take things to the next level?" The lights changed, and Fallon eased the car forward. When Rowan hadn't answered after a mile or so, he glanced over at her. "Well?"

"Well, I was hoping the police would take my reports seriously before it got to that point." She chewed on her bottom lip. "I don't understand why they don't already."

An unexpected desire to comfort her threatened to overwhelm Fallon and he pushed the emotion aside ruthlessly. "Mostly because they lack the manpower and without evidence there's nothing they can do." As he spoke, he parked the car, unbuckled his seat belt and exited the vehicle. He strode around to the passenger side, opened the door and leaned down.

"I don't need your help to get out of the car," Rowan told him, glaring at his proffered hand like it was a snake about to strike.

Fallon laughed. "Chivalry isn't quite as dead as people think." He curled his fingers around her hand and helped her out, ignoring her protests. "I'll walk you to your friend's door."

"There's really no need."

"There's every need. I want to make sure you're safely indoors before I seek out my own bed." He caught her arm before they entered the apartment block. "Listen to me, Rowan. Whoever took your sister doesn't want you digging around. And they're serious enough about it to want to scare you."

"I'm not going to stop looking for her." She tipped her head back to look Fallon full in the face. "I *mean* it. No matter what, I'm going to find my sister."

"Well, I'll say this for you – you've got guts," Fallon nodded approvingly as he spoke. "But the thing is, cemeteries are filled with gutsy people."

"Now *you* are trying to scare me off. Is that it, Mr Wylde?"

Fallon shrugged. "There's no sin in being scared, Miss Walker. As a matter of fact, scared works. *If* you know how to use it."

"I don't understand," she stared up at him quizzically. "What are you saying?"

"What I'm saying, Miss Walker, is while I admire your tenacity, it's very likely to get you into serious trouble. Get you hurt or worse. Scared works both ways, and it's starting to look like *you're* scaring the people who took your sister. More often than not, where *they* are concerned, scared equals dangerous."

"Is this the part where you list the reasons why I need to reconsider and hire you?" Rowan asked, pushing the buzzer to let her friend know she had arrived.

"No, this is the point where I ask you to consider what might happen the next time you're paid a late-night visit."

"What's the point?" she shrugged, pushing the door open and walking through. "Oh, don't look at me like that! I hear what you're saying, but since we both know I'm not going to stop searching, I'm aware they'll either kill me or I'll find her." The smile she directed at him was brittle. "And *that* makes me even more determined."

"Suit yourself," Fallon said. "You've got my number. Call me if you change your mind."

They walked to the stairwell and up to the first floor in silence and slowed to a stop outside her friend's apartment. Rowan turned to Fallon and laid a hand on his arm.

"Thank you for coming tonight," she said. "You didn't have to. I'm sorry for dragging you away."

"No trouble at all." He placed a hand over hers, giving it a slight squeeze before turning to leave.

Rowan watched him disappear back into the stairwell and turned around to find her friend in the doorway, staring after him with a slack jaw.

"Wow! He's *hot!* Are you dating him?"

Her head twisted round to the now empty stairwell and then back to her friend. "*Lainie!*"

"What? Well, he is. Why did you let him leave?"

~*~

Sliding into his car, Fallon paused a moment before he started the engine. He rolled down the windows on both sides and focused his senses – primarily auditory and olfactory. There was no question from the scent he'd picked up at Rowan's place of the involvement of vampires in, if nothing else, her home invasion. At least *two* vampires, to be exact. The lingering scent of aftershave itself was confirmation. And, in the case of intruders, an unintentional identifier. A trick used by vampires in the Southern States – Alabama, Georgia, Mississippi - in rural areas during a time when some local law enforcement used hunting dogs in their investigations. With the noses of both hounds and their handlers swimming with the odour of *Old Spice* or whatever, they would assume the perpetrators were Human. Fallon's nostrils, however, homed in on the scent below the subterfuge.

The incident marked the second incursion into Rowan's residence. And, like the one before, nothing was taken or disturbed. Was it little more than a subtle attempt to rattle her cage, to warn her off? That, at this point was still iffy. It was entirely possible that they were both separate incidents performed by two individual perpetrators, both of whom were scoping out a potential victim – *a meal*. But Fallon's gut was telling him otherwise. Any vampire, no matter their age, would have heard her call him, would have known she was awake and aware. There was also the definite possibility that Rowan was being actively watched. On the other hand, the sun would also be rising in just over two hours, so it was doubtful she was in any immediate danger.

It was just past four-thirty in the morning by the time he got back to Shadowfall – *the Pumpkin Hour* – and all of those who partied to their respective limits, or who hadn't coupled off, were now in 'mad dash mode', en route to vehicles or domiciles in a race against the vampire's version of Cinderella's midnight – the dawn.

Inside, all the shops, bistros, and restaurants were closing and the clubs and bars, if not already shut down, were in the midst of 'last call'. Tigr was in fact, just turning the *Shadows Of Night* over to the cleaning crews when Fallon arrived. They met as he stepped off the elevator.

"I had a feeling you'd be back," she said, opening the denim shoulder bag riding her generous right hip to show the page of photo images he'd left behind.

"Thanks for holding on to it. You still willing to help?"

"You know . . ." she placed two fingers beneath his chin, tilting his face up and his eyes *out* of the excess acreage all but spilling over the border of her lace-front and leather bustier. "The sun's gonna be up in another hour or so. Why rush things if there's no need to?"

Not that there *was* any rush. As it happened, Fallon kept a suite reserved in the club's guest residential section for business purposes, as well as just such occasional occurrences. However, the current situation fell under Wylde's Rule #3 – *Never refuse the offer of hospitality, unless circumstances deem otherwise.*

"I'll take that as a yes." He executed a flourishing bow. "And ditto, Señora."

Like two-thirds of Shadowfall's vampire staff, Tigr lived on the premises. A one-bedroom apartment on the second-floor employee wing. Tigr's was a shade larger than standard. Most probably by virtue of the fact she'd been there since before Kane took over and first opened for business.

Tigr tossed her shoulder-bag to the floor beside the main room's round glass-topped coffee table and headed straight for the bedroom.

"There's liquor and glasses on the dresser in the corner," her voice floated back. "Why don't you pour some drinks and get comfortable. I'll be out in a minute."

Fallon took off his jacket and kicked off his shoes then made his way to the dresser. A very well-stocked dresser, it turned out. Which shouldn't have come as a surprise. She was, after all, the club's senior-most bartender.

He chose a bottle of *Admiral Nelson Spiced Rum*, found a pair of thick-base mid-sized glasses and filled a Tupperware bowl with ice from the mini-fridge next to the dresser. True to her word, Tigr was waiting for him when he'd finished – sprawled out at one end of the room's wicker couch; her pale, natural blonde, zaftig frame adorned in studded nipple rings, a warm smile and very little else. The photo page was spread out on the coffee table and, as Fallon poured their drinks, Tigr swung upright to study it.

She looked up to accept the glass as Fallon passed it across, raised it in salute and sipped.

"The girl with the pink hair. Just out of curiosity . . ." her gaze met his.

"Missing," Fallon answered, prompting a nod from Tigr.

"Human."

"Yes," he replied, though she hadn't spoken it as a query.

Tigr nodded, taking a hefty pull of rum. "The two girls with them aren't. But then I don't have to tell *you* that.

"I've seen them before. Once a week, usually weekends. I get out of the basement to work one of the top floor clubs – *Club Anubis*, or *Ravers* – the one that caters to the younger crowd. Those two are die-hard regulars. You know the type. Turned no more than ten years ago, twenty tops. The novelty of being immortal, footloose and fancy free hasn't worn off yet. Probably belong to one of the Pureblood politicians in the Capitol Hill district – secretaries or bed-warmers.

"The guy is another story," she tapped the page with one long blood-red fingernail. "See his body language and how he positions himself? He knows where the cameras are and he's avoiding them."

"A recognisable face," Fallon commented.

"Or maybe that's what he wants to avoid," Tigr offered, downing her drink and placing the glass where it could be replenished. Fallon immediately accommodated her.

"See that?" She pointed rather than tapped the page this time, her fingers touching the male's image – his head, to be precise – on all three photos. Fallon moved closer. "That ear-clip with the stone in it? A *ruby*? You might see a lot of similar imitations these days, but not the way it's worn high up near the top of the ear. That's a gang badge . . ." she chuckled into a gulp of rum. "Though they called themselves a tribe. Nowadays, it's covens. I blame Hollywood. All those cheesy TV shows, New Age crap . . . *Jesus!*" Tigr groaned, draining her glass.

"You said a gang?" Fallon nudged her back toward the topic, simultaneously refilling her glass.

Tigr nodded. "LA, back in the late sixties – between sixty-five and sixty-nine. Called themselves Hoodoo Fyre . . . fire with a 'y'. Supposedly came up out of Louisiana, Shreveport and New Orleans. They weren't that big, rumour said no more than fifty members, but for a while they gave the black and Hispanic Human gangs hell in the murder and drug trade.

"I did my thing on the Strip back then, the dance clubs. Mostly at the Peppermint Lounge. It's where the Fyre's hung out. One in particular," she indicated the photo from inside the elevator. "See the glove on his left hand? From what I heard, it was to cover up really bad burn scars that probably happened before he was turned. He went by the name Eli.

"Anyhow, the Fyre's disbanded, or so I heard, in seventy-one. The next time I saw him was San Francisco in seventy-eight. I was working in one of the Punk-Goth clubs in North Beach and he was a nightly regular. He called himself Martin, looked and dressed like a cross between Bowie and Jagger – long spiky red hair, no eyebrows, leather pants, the whole nine yards.

"Probably a long shot, but did you happen to pick up anything about disappearances or kidnappings?" Fallon asked. "Human girls in their early to mid-twenties, about the time this Eli/Martin was around?"

Tigr heaved a short laugh. "You kidding? You know what it was like in those days. The Hippie/Free-Love generation for one, the

Disco and mosh-pit monster crowds. Los Angeles alone had always had the biggest runaway population in the country – a literal smorgasbord meat-market. San Francisco was no different."

She was silent for a long moment, her eyes still on the photo page. "But . . ." she finally spoke, touching his leg suggestively as she sat upright. "If you wanna know if I think this guy *could* be involved in something like that. Well, him and his former tribe weren't called *Hoodoo Fyre* for no reason. Word on the street was they were heavy into voodoo. Black Magic and that Pagan ritual shit. It's probably not much of a stretch to say they'd grab a Human girl or two for something like that, if it helps at all?"

"It did," Fallon smiled, hefted his glass and downed it in a single gulp.

"Good . . ." Tigr glanced over her shoulder at the fading darkness beyond the window, then let her hand slide upward, along Fallon's inseam. "It's getting late, don'tcha think?"

Fallon reached out a long-fingered hand and tugged at one of the bars piercing Tigr's nipple, using it to force her to move toward him. "Oh, I think the night's just getting started," he smiled.

~*~

Rowan stayed with Lainie for two nights after Fallon left her there. Two nights with no unusual happenings, no break-ins, and no feelings of being watched. She arranged with her landlord to have all the locks changed on her doors and windows and, by the third night, she had moved back into her own apartment.

She had received a couple of texts from Fallon – one checking she was safe and checking if anything further had happened, and another to tell her he expected no payment for coming to her rescue, but that he was still very interested in investigating her sister's disappearance. He added that if he was able to dig up any further information he would contact her, and they could discuss the case further. Rowan had replied to the first text and ignored the second, still a little embarrassed by her friend's appraisal of his looks.

Standing in the kitchen at the back of the diner, Rowan washed her hands and then untied the apron she wore as part of her uniform, folded it and placed it on the countertop. While Lainie and Trevor – the cook – reported to the shift-change manager, she poured three mugs of coffee and took them through to the public dining area. It was a ritual they all performed each night after their shift ended. A 'wind-down' drink together where they could relax for a little while before going home for the night.

As she settled into a booth to wait for her colleagues, her phone's ringtone burst into life. She fished it out of her pocket, tapped 'call' and held the phone to her ear.

"Hello?"

"Miss Walker?" A cool female voice responded. "This is Koo from FW, A&R. I have a message for you from Mr Fallon Wylde."

"Oh . . . okay?"

"Mr Wylde would like you to know that he has uncovered some information with regards to your case and would like you to meet him as soon as you can," Koo said.

"Where? I'm still at work."

"We can send a cab to collect you from the diner and take you to Steria Supplies Warehouse in the Georgetown District."

"Will Fallon . . . I mean . . . Mr Wylde be okay with that?" Rowan asked.

Koo laughed. "Of course he will, Miss Walker. He wants you to meet him at a location that isn't our offices or your apartment. We will foot whatever expenses that incurs."

"Why does he want to meet me there?"

"I'm afraid he didn't give me that information, Miss Walker, although I do believe it's because there is something in the warehouse that relates to your case and Mr Wylde seems to feel that you would rather see for yourself than have him explain it to you later," Koo paused. "Shall I arrange for the cab?"

Rowan thought it over for a few seconds but knew she couldn't afford to ignore the chance to move forward on her sister's disappearance. "Yes, thank you."

"You're quite welcome. The cab should be with you in approximately twenty minutes. I will inform Mr Wylde of your imminent arrival."

The call ended just as Lainie and Trevor arrived and sat in the booth opposite her.

"Who was that?" Lainie asked, with a grin. "Tell me it was that hunky PI!"

Rowan shook her head, smiling faintly at her friend's look of disappointment. "It was his office. They're sending a cab for me to go and meet Mr Wylde."

Her friend clapped her hands, her eyes dancing. "Late night meetings, how exciting!"

"I doubt it'll be that exciting," Rowan smiled. "I don't even know why he's making such an effort."

Lainie gave her a sly smile. "Maybe he likes you?"

"You think he's looking for an excuse to get me in a warehouse in the middle of the night?" Rowan rolled her eyes. "I don't think he struggles for female company, Lainie"

She finished her coffee and went in search of her coat. With a promise to call Lainie when she got home, Rowan went outside to wait for the cab.

~*~

Rowan's phone rang as she slammed the door shut on the cab. She answered it and heard the same woman's voice from the earlier call.

"Miss Walker? Are you at the warehouse?"

"I've just arrived," Rowan replied.

"Excellent. You will find the entrance door unlocked. Mr Wylde is waiting for you inside. Go through the reception area and you will see a door marked 'Staff Only'. Through there, you will find yourself in a corridor. The third door on the left is the one you want." Koo cut the call before Rowan could respond.

With a sigh, Rowan slipped her phone back into her pocket and walked toward the front entrance. She opened the door and crossed the carpeted reception to the Staff Only door, which opened smoothly at her touch. As she stepped through, she paused and looked down the darkened corridor. The entire place was eerily silent, and she briefly wondered if it was a good idea. She squared her shoulders and walked forward, passed two doors and paused at the third.

Should she knock or walk right in, she wondered. Her hand hovered over the handle, then she took a steadying breath, grasped the handle and turned it. The door opened easily, and Rowan entered the room beyond.

"Mr Wylde?" Her voice sounded loud in the silence. As far as she could tell there was no one in the room with her, but the light was almost non-existent. She pulled out her phone and scrolled through the apps until she found one for the torch and tapped the screen. Light flared out from the back of her phone and she used it to look around the room. As she thought, it was empty.

"Mr Wylde?" She spoke again, louder this time, in case he was in an adjoining room – even though she could see no other doors.

She turned around to open the door back into the corridor, only to find there was no handle on the inside.

"What the hell?" She tried to prise the door open with her fingers, then banged on it with her fist. "Hello?" she shouted. "Mr Wylde? Are you out there?"

No reply.

In fact, no noise at all could be heard, other than the sound of her own breathing, which was rapidly speeding up along with her heartbeat. Why would Fallon Wylde ask her to meet at a warehouse and then not be there when she arrived? No, the woman on the phone – Koo, wasn't it? – had said he was waiting for her inside. So, *where* was he?

She banged on the door again, the noise echoing around the room, as her pounding became more frantic, until eventually she admitted to herself that she wasn't achieving anything other than hurting her hands. She turned to survey the room, slowly sweeping the torchlight around.

What was that?

She swung the torch back toward the far corner. It looked like . . . she froze, her breath catching in her throat.

Was that . . . ?

No, it couldn't be . . . could it?

She swallowed, her throat suddenly dry, and forced herself to step away from the door and walk across the room. She kept her torch aimed at the shape – a shape that grew clearer the closer she got.

"E-Eden?" she whispered her sister's name as the shape formed into a body – a body Rowan knew wasn't breathing. She closed her eyes and swallowed again, then turned and threw herself back at the door, banging it harder with both fists and screaming Fallon's name.

When the door still didn't open, she let her hands fall to her sides and stood still, breathing heavily.

Where was Fallon Wylde?

She looked down at the phone still clutched in one hand, found the contact log, located his cell number and dialled.

"Wylde." He answered on the first ring, his voice crisp and business-like.

"Where are you?" Rowan screamed down the line. "Is this your way of trying to teach me a lesson? Do you think this is *funny*? It's not! When you're done laughing at me, *open the door!*"

There was a long loaded silence, and then, "Miss Walker?"

"Don't you '*Miss Walker*' me," she shrieked. "Who the hell else did you think it would be? If you thought this would convince me to hire you, then you should have done your homework about me more thoroughly."

"I—" he paused, and she heard him take a deep breath before he resumed speaking. "Where are you?"

"What do you *mean* where am I? I'm right where you told me to be."

"And remind me where that is again, exactly." He sounded far too calm to Rowan's ears.

"Steria Supplies," her voice sounded shrill to her own ears and she tried to breathe slowly to keep the panic that was threatening to overwhelm her out of her voice. "You already know that! You had your secretary send me here to meet you."

"Okay . . . and the door you need opening?"

"There's no handle on the inside. I can't open it. And . . . and . . . and there's a *body* . . ." her voice broke on a sob. "I'm stuck inside this room with a body."

"Steria Supplies. That's SoDo, the Georgetown District, isn't it?" Fallon's voice remained calm, business-like. "The body. Is it—?"

"I don't know. I *can't* look!" Rowan's voice rose again. She knew he was asking if it was her sister. "It wasn't you, was it? Who set up this meeting? Please tell me it was you and you just forgot!"

There was a long pause before Fallon replied, and when he did his voice was carefully controlled. "No, sweetheart, it wasn't me. But I'm heading there now." He cut the call before she could say any more.

Wasn't him? Then who the hell was it? Rowan almost laughed aloud. *Stupid question.* Who else could it be – if it wasn't Fallon Wylde, then it had to have been the person – or people – who had broken into her apartment, the ones who were warning her away from finding Eden.

At that thought, her eyes slid to the body. Had it moved?

Don't be ridiculous. This isn't a zombie movie!

~*~

"Body?" Fallon vaguely heard the query as he cut the call. "Fallon . . . ?" The sound of his name, however, prompted him to focus on the person speaking to him.

Across the living room, framed in the kitchen doorway, in a frilly pink morning gown and fuzzy slippers – both of which had Fallon raising an eyebrow – Katie Chan stood with a teacup and saucer poised at chest level.

"Trouble?" she asked.

"Apparently," he answered, slowly turning toward the door to the right. "I'm going out."

"You've got that thing tonight. House Senior Members dinner at the Needle's Eye," Kate reminded him. "Your Sire—"

"Marjean can carry on just fine without me," Fallon interrupted as he moved. "Besides, she's always been a junkie for political schmoozing."

He stopped just short of the door, glancing at his watch before turning back to face her. "If you don't hear from me in an hour, call Lady M. Tell her I'm at Steria Warehouse in SoDo."

He walked out of the kitchen and into his bedroom, kicking the door shut behind him before she could reply, then crossed to what appeared to be a wardrobe on the room's left side. A nudge with his foot at the wardrobe's base triggered a small rectangular panel to slide open in its upper right quadrant and a beam of pale blue light shot out to scan his face – specifically, the retina of his right eye.

"Retinal Security Scan Confirmed," a disembodied female voice said. *"Vocal and Password Required."*

"Sobre el alma mi madre – Isabella," Fallon said, softly.

"Confirmed – Fallon Wylde." A series of clicks followed, and the wardrobe opened outward in two halves, revealing a cache of weapons – revolvers, semi-automatics, and shotguns; as well as a variety of weaponry associated with martial arts. Fallon chose a stack of throwing stars, an aikuchi – Japanese dagger – and a Smith &

Wesson 9mm. Not that it was a certainty he would need them, but better safe than sorry.

~*~

"Rowan?" Fallon's shout from somewhere beyond the door broke the silence and had Rowan scrambling to her feet.

"Open the door!" Rowan hadn't meant to shriek the words quite so loudly, but they had the desired effect with the door being opened a few seconds later.

Fallon barely managed to holster his gun before Rowan crashed into him. One arm automatically wrapped around her waist as she struck his chest with her fists.

"There's a body in there . . . a *dead* body! Who does that? Who locks someone in a room with a *goddamned dead body*?" Fallon could hear the hint of hysteria in her voice and smoothed his other hand down her spine, feeling the slight tremors that shook her frame.

"It's okay," he murmured. "I'm here, you're safe now." As he spoke, he scanned the room over the top of her head and paused when his eyes caught on the body slumped in one corner. "Stop hitting me." Fallon caught her wrists with one hand. "I need to go and look at the body." Rowan froze, then sucked in a shaky breath. Fallon waited a second, then released her hands and unwound his arm from her waist. "Wait here," he instructed her, and moved across the room.

"Wait!" Rowan caught up to him and clutched at his arm with one hand. "You're not leaving me on my own."

Fallon quirked an eyebrow. "You're scared now, but someone creeping around your apartment while you were in bed was absolutely fine?"

"It's a *dead body!*" Rowan retorted, and Fallon's lips twitched into a faint smile at the *'isn't that obvious'* tone in her voice.

"Sweetheart, it's not the dead who should scare you," he told her, angled his arm so she could hook her hand around his elbow and continued across the room.

When they reached the corner, Fallon broke Rowan's death-grip and gave her hand a reassuring pat before he bent down to give the body a more thorough examination.

The deceased girl was propped up, her back against the wall, with her head lolling to one side clothed only, and just barely, in bra and panties. Both garments were stained with blood. The rest of her body looked as though she had been used like a human piñata. There were bruises and wounds - probably from a blunt object and a blade – from hairline to ankles. On closer scrutiny, Fallon could see it wasn't Eden Walker, but with her height, build, and hairstyle – even the pink dye job – Hollywood movie casting couldn't have chosen a closer stunt double. Definitely no accident, Fallon knew.

"Is . . . is it . . . ?" Rowan struggled to get the question out.

"Eden?" Fallon finished for her, reminded of the fact the warehouse's interior would be too dark for her human eyes to see clearly. "No, it's not your sister. But someone wanted you to see it looks like her in the dark."

There was something familiar about the body. Something Fallon had seen, no, *heard* about before. One thing was immediately certain, though. There had been no attempt to conceal their scent, it was unquestioningly the work of vampires. The area around the body alone reeked of them. At least three – two males and a female. Which brought him to the second clue – the state of the body. Although the poor girl was covered in bruises, the wounds were more pronounced at her throat, breasts, wrists and the area of the femoral artery. Prime locations for feeding. The police would call it 'forensic countermeasures' – using the wounds to disguise the bite marks. In this case, however, Fallon had the sense that it was not only a long-standing procedure, but that the perpetrators were doing it to hide something that ran much deeper. Something that made the body before them just the tip of the iceberg.

"We need to leave. Now!" Fallon stood upright and took Rowan's arm, moving them purposely toward the exit.

They had driven several blocks from the warehouse in heavy silence when Fallon pulled into the parking area of a Wells Fargo Bank, and shut off the engine. He took a quick breath before swivelling to face her.

"What about the body? The dead girl?" Rowan spoke first, sitting stiff as a statue, face pale as she stared through the windshield. "Are we just going to leave her—"

"I'll put in a call to SPD later," Fallon said, then gave a soft laugh at the sound of sirens. "Or not. It seems someone has done *that* duty for us." He paused, waiting to see if she would question him further. "In the meantime," he continued when she said nothing, "why don't you tell me how you wound up at the warehouse."

Rowan nodded, drawing a deep ragged breath before launching into an account of the events leading up to Fallon meeting her at Steria Supplies.

"And the caller, supposedly from FW A&R, she introduced herself as?"

"As Koo," Rowan answered, finally turning her head to look at him. "Is that significant?"

Fallon nodded, offering a tight-lipped grimace. "Very. It's my associate, Kate Chan's, pet name. Only *I*, and very few others, call her that."

"What does it mean that they used her nickname, then? How would they know that?"

"There are ways," Fallon replied. "The important thing at this point is that they *do* know. And that means they, whoever *they* are, sent us both a message. They know – at least they *think* -I'm working for you and they want us to back off. Which brings us to the next big question." He made eye contact with her. "Are you?"

"Backing off?" Rowan responded, her expression stony and resolute. "What do *you* think?"

"What *I* think is secondary, Rowan. It's you. You need to be very sure about this, because from this point on things are probably going to get very very nasty."

Rowan sighed and the look in her eyes made her appear older than her twenty-two years. "Be honest, Mr Wylde. Whether I stopped now or not, whoever it is isn't going to rest until I'm completely out of the picture – one way or another. It's gone too far for them to be sure I would never pick it up again."

"Shall I take it for granted that it means I'm officially on the case?"

"It does if . . ." Rowan hesitated, biting her lower lip. "I'm going to be equally honest with you. I'm really not in much of a position, financially, to afford your fee."

"That warning we got was for both of us," Fallon told her. "For better or worse, we're in this together now. In some ways, that's my fault for going ahead and starting to dig before you hired me." He gave her a grim smile. "We'll work something out."

CHAPTER THREE

Detective Sergeant Valentino Greenwalt was a fifteen-year veteran officer, ten of which he'd spent with the Seattle Police Department. He braced himself against a resurging wave of nausea as the boys from the City Coroner's Office wheeled the sheet-shrouded body of their latest Jane Doe through the door, and down the ramp of the deserted warehouse's loading dock.

He'd seen quite a bit, things both gruesome and infuriating during his time as a police officer. Things that gradually, eventually, cemented the personal opinion that he'd seen it all. That nothing could ever surprise him.

Until tonight.

Erasing the images of the carnage perpetrated against the victim, the things some twisted monster had done to her young body, wouldn't be easy. Another time – two and a half years ago, in fact – a half-dozen or so stiff belts after work, going home for a good wrestle-between-the-sheets with the ol' lady, and spending a few hours with the kids would have been a viable option. Sadly, his twice-weekly AA meetings and the divorce put a ROAD CLOSED – DETOUR sign on both of those routes. These days, and in most cases, it was maybe a stopover at the little diner across from the precinct for coffee and a wedge of one of their pies and even maybe-er (was that even a real word?) the sexual version of a 'we-who-are-about-to-die-salute-you' with Beth, the divorcee from down the hall. And even then, the best he could possibly hope for was a haze in the clarity of those sickening images.

A flash of headlights to his left turned the Detective's attention to an approaching vehicle beyond the barricade of police patrol cars and crime scene tape. The return of his partner . . . *correction*, temporary replacement for Detective Glenn Rittenhouse, now on emergency leave of absence – whom he'd sent off to the nearest Starbucks and/or convenience store for a sorely needed cup of java.

The temp, a fairly new Goldshield named Lopez, met him just outside the yellow tape, a white-lidded Starbucks cup in each hand.

"Here ya go," the young Detective offered the cup in his left hand as Greenwalt approached. "Black, two sugars. And the real stuff, not that Splenda crap."

"Good man." Greenwalt took the cup, hoisted it in a 'thank you' gesture, then took a small test sip. Satisfied with the taste and the temperature, he tilted it up for a full-on gulp. And that's when he noticed her.

A woman, medium-height, slender build, semi-short dark hair hanging to just above her shoulders, light-coloured suit – most probably grey, although it was hard to be certain in the area's available light.

She stood in front of a dark Ford SUV, parked beside and slightly behind his own vehicle, which made further identification difficult. Not that he actually needed confirmation. He'd been around the block enough times to know a police car – marked or unmarked – and a police detective when he saw one. And, in this case, both vehicle and driver virtually screamed SPDSC.

Special Crimes Unit.

Noting that she'd snagged his attention, she pulled her jacket to one side to flash the badge clipped to her waist and hoisted a coffee cup of her own.

Greenwalt nodded in response.

"Lopez," the veteran Detective nudged his partner, gesturing toward the activity behind them. "The unis said there were a couple of on-site witnesses. Two transients. Why don't you check to make sure we've got their statements?"

"Will do!" Lopez replied, gulping down the remainder of his coffee and placing the cup on the ground before he departed.

They moved almost as one, slowly, as though the air between them had suddenly gained a kind of viscous resistance, fighting to impede their progress. Greenwalt knew, of course, that it was tradition, all part of the dance as instinctive and as integral to the sexes as to the organisation in which they were both a part.

In plainer language, they were feeling each other out. Each taking the other's measure. They came to a stop at the rear passenger door of Greenwalt's car.

"Detective." Detective Jenny Frost spoke first, and thrust out a hand which Greenwalt accepted, despite the reluctance evident in his eyes.

"Since when does a simple 10-100 rate the presence of Special Crimes?" Greenwalt asked, using the universal police code for 'dead body', before taking a quick sip of coffee.

Jenny pursed her lips in an effort to camouflage a sympathetic grin, knowing all too well that the acrimony on the fringes of the Detective's enquiry wasn't personal. Cops could be territorial where their cases, and specifically their crime scenes, were concerned. It was just the nature of the beast.

"It doesn't. This isn't official, just personal curiosity," she assured him in a tone that, hopefully, was successful in smoothing his ruffled feathers. "Especially where this particular district is concerned."

"Curiosity," Greenwalt repeated, rolling the word around in his head to test its flavour. The coffee cup rose toward his lips and stopped as, for the first time since their exchange was initiated, his eyes focused on her.

Jenny's smile emerged, unbidden, as the flare of recognition blossomed on Greenwalt's features, like sunlight breaking through the veil of a cloudy sky.

"You're Detective Frost, the—"

"Crazy Lady Vampire Chaser?" she chimed in with a smile, leaving him with his bottom lip hanging. She offered her hand again. "Jenny Frost. And *you're* Detective Greenwalt," she paused as he took her hand again, shaking it now as if he thought he would break it. "I've heard good things about you."

"I'm not sure how to take that, coming from you," he chuckled. "No offense."

"None taken," Jenny said, with a dismissive wave. "I'll tell you a little secret. I'm not crazy. I'm well aware of how it looks . . . and I know how what I believe sounds. Call it cop instincts or feminine intuition. Hell, whatever you please. But I know what I know. And I know what my gut is telling me. Even though most people who laugh and call me a nutjob won't admit it, they feel it too."

They both fell silent, avoiding direct eye contact as each navigated the roughhewn and multi-shaded terrains of their thoughts. Each struggling for, and in all likelihood, against their next words. In the interim, Detective Lopez reappeared, beckoning to his partner from behind the tape barricade, and Greenwalt excused himself.

Jesus, Jen. Jenny bit back a self-recriminating groan as she tracked Greenwalt's course toward his waiting colleague. *What the hell are you doing?*

If Greenwalt hadn't seen you as a babbling whack-a-doo before, she thought. *What was he thinking now after that pathetic rant?*

What everyone else she worked with was thinking, most likely.

Thinking being the operative term, of course.

Never anything overt or obvious.

Whispers out of earshot.

Laughing up their collective sleeves.

All the second-hand jokes.

"Jenny Frost – she's got Mulder and Scully on speed dial."

"Frost and her Vampire X-Files conspiracy."

"Wonder if she parties with the Winchesters at the weekend."

"Yo! Delivery for Detective Frost – Wooden stakes and a case of pampers!"

"Everything okay, Lieutenant?" Greenwalt's return and query caught her unaware, snapping her back into the moment with a jolt.

"Long day," Jenny gave a non-committal, hopefully believable, reply. And, once again, the veil of silence descended over their little enclave. A moment that might have continued indefinitely had Jenny not cued in on the distinct shift in the other Detective's mood.

"Your partner," Jenny said to hook his attention, nodding to the spot where the other, younger Detective had stood moments earlier. "Bad news?"

Greenwalt didn't respond immediately. Instead, he leaned back against the car's side with his arms loosely folded across his chest staring, first, down at his feet then over to make brief eye contact with Jenny, then a quick scan of the activity beyond the yellow tape.

"Get in," he finally said, rapping his knuckles against the passenger door, then skirted the car's front en route to the driver's side.

Once they were both inside, he took a moment to pull out his cigarette pack and rolled his window down a crack.

"Something my partner, Detective Lopez, told me," he started. "He got it from one of our witnesses, a couple of homeless who sleep in the building. Something one of them says he saw . . . off the record. It reminded me of something. Something that happened a few years back."

He took a pause, then nodded and began again.

"This was something I was involved in after I transferred to the Tacoma PD from Sacramento six months after I got my gold shield – early 2005. A case that was already in motion before I was brought into it." He paused to tap a Morley from the pack and placed it in the corner of his mouth before continuing. "Seven victims, both male and female, all homicides. Identical M.O.'s. All the bodies were discovered in motels off Interstate 5. All had wounds to their femoral arteries. The artery had been literally torn open and they died of severe and fatal blood loss – exsanguination."

"Evidence was non-existent or confusing, I take it?" Jenny prompted.

Greenwalt's response was an eye-twitching nod. "it was shit, actually. Logically, there should've been more of the vic's blood at the scene, but there were only a couple of drops on the bed and on the carpet. No fingerprints. Hair on the bed, on the victim, and in the drain of the bathroom's wash basin turned out to be from a wig, and lipstick on the victim's body . . . specifically, around the wound. Vaginal secretions on the sheets and, where the vic's were men, on their sex organs, but nothing that revealed anything other than the fact the perp was female."

Greenwalt paused long enough to accept Jenny's offered lighter for his cigarette, to puff until the cherry glowed deep red in the car's dim light and exhale the smoke before resuming.

"A canvas of the area gave us her M.O. She'd pick up her victims in a local bar or restaurant, take them to a motel where they'd have sex, and then . . ." he drew a forefinger across his throat. "Descriptions we got from witnesses were just as useless. She was tall, short, medium height. She was blonde, brunette, red. She had long hair, short hair, shorter than most guys. Blue eyes, brown eyes. She wore shades. She dressed in long skirts, short skirts, shorts, blue jeans. She looked like a hooker, a soccer mom, a punk-rocker with two-toned hair. A goth with black hair and nose and eyelid piercings . . ."

"She knew how to work a room," Jenny offered.

"She knew how to work *us*," Greenwalt said, with a snort of begrudging admiration. "With all that, and after four more murders. It was pretty obvious she was well-practiced in staying a step or two ahead of us.

"And then, finally on victim number twelve, we caught a break." He paused to take a pull off his cigarette, found it had gone out and placed it on the lid of his coffee cup. "This time she hit a club in downtown Tacoma, one of those trendy combo pub, café, dance types that drew the under-twenty-five college crowd. And this time luck was with us because it was host to two parties – a group of women who hadn't seen each other since high school and guys from a local softball team celebrating their recent win. And there was someone in each group with a camera – the digital type.

"And that was when the whole thing flipped, ass over elbows." Jenny couldn't help but smile at the swell of satisfaction in the Detective's demeanour, like a pro-athlete whose previous bottom-of-the-heap team suddenly began showing signs of upward mobility. "For weeks she'd had us playing catch-up, eating her dust, and now it was like her game sprang a leak. She got sloppy.

"It wasn't just the way she dressed and operated that night which seemed to deliberately call attention to herself – a porn star outfit that attracted the attention of the softball group's photographer and, most likely, jealousy among the ladies of the reunion – but it was almost like she was daring us to catch her. First of all, on vic number twelve, she didn't bother with a motel room. A pair of uniformed officers on the Foss Waterway found the poor S.O.B. still sitting in his car, pants around his ankles and his throat ripped out. Second, she left a coaster from the 1055 South Club on the passenger seat, with a set of four perfect fingerprints on it.

"We put the print and a couple of the best photos on the wire, through NCIC, and *pow*," his face lit up like the proverbial Christmas Tree, "less than a day later we got a hit. We got *THE HIT*. Turns out our serial killer was, get this, a cop – ex-cop, I should say. One of LAPD's first female . . ." he cleared his throat, amending himself quickly, "undercover policewomen, Vice Unit."

He paused to inhale deeply through his nose, exhaling through his mouth while shifting uncomfortably in his seat. "Now, this is where it gets weird. According to what they sent us, her name was Janet Kaiser, a native of San Jose, California, born August 10, 1935 . . ."

"I take it that wasn't a typo?" Jenny commented.

"Oh, it gets weirder," Greenwalt heaved a laconic chuckle. "Aside from that, everything started to make a little more sense. Kaiser was a damn good cop. Highly decorated, exemplary arrest record. She had a knack for undercover work. Good with disguises, characteristics, street savvy. She and her team were working a drug-prostitution sting in the area of Sepulveda Boulevard. On the night of June 5, 1965, on or around 1AM, Kaiser – who was wired, according to the report – spoke of suspicious activities in a nearby alley. Moments later, she used the code phrase for requesting backup and gave her location. But when her team, who were no less than a block away, got there, they found nothing. No suspicious activity, no Kaiser, *nothing.*"

Jenny listened with an intensity, a focus that seemed to transcend fascination. As if she were plugged into him on some empathic level that felt every dip, swirl and loop-de-loop, every high and low of the emotional rollercoaster ride Greenwalt experienced as he relived the memories he now related to her; feeling, more importantly, the rise in the level of excitement in both speech and the beating of his heart as he approached the climax of his tale.

It levelled off for just a moment as he spoke of the LAPD's procedural response to the disappearance of one of their own. The APB (All Points Bulletin) to all of the city's precincts and surrounding counties; canvassing of the neighbourhood her team had been working; hauling in any and all felons with a past and current crimes related to the team's operation.

"They didn't really go into a lot of detail. Just standard procedure. After a couple of weeks with no results, the file was stamped Open and filed away under MIA – Missing in Action. After seven years she was, by law, officially presumed dead.

"As far as what the SPD sent, they had mixed feelings. First, even though fingerprints don't lie – from the photos we sent, there was one other thing that matched Kaiser's description. A tattoo of Minnie Mouse on her left inner ankle. Second, Janet Kaiser was thirty-years-old at the time of her disappearance and our suspect didn't look a day over that. In fact, she looked a hell of a lot younger. And finally, until we could come up with some concrete, indisputable proof to the contrary, they would treat it as some kind of hoax on the part of the suspect to throw us off."

He stopped, though only momentarily, as both noticed Detective Lopez through the windshield, standing near the crime scene and throwing impatient glances their way. Greenwalt nodded to acknowledge his presence but kept talking.

"Anyway, about that time, some genius in the higher up echelons finally decided to use what we had to put out paper –

strategic countermeasures, they called it. We passed out posters with photos of Kaiser and her tattoo that asked, '*Have you seen this woman?*' And since the last thing the people upstairs wanted was the press to get wind of what was going on and stir up a big *mad female serial killer* stink, they set up a telephone tip-line through the gang taskforce. We also took the precaution to add a warning telling people not to attempt to detain her if they saw her. Whether or not we should've is debatable because that's exactly what happened. But it also brought it all to an end.

"A pair of eager beaver patrol officers," he continued, staring into the distance as if watching it all unfold on the view-screen of his mind, "saw her enter an AM-PM mini-mart out on Puyallup Avenue, and decided to go for the glory. According to the checkout clerk and four people inside, the two officers entered the store and approached the suspect with weapons drawn.

"I didn't find out the detail, the exact sequence of events that took place until much later. But I was working that night, and my partner and I picked up the Code 999 call and the location around 9.30PM. We were across town, about a quarter of a mile away and, by the time we got there, the place was almost surrounded by patrol cars."

This time his pause was accompanied by a roll of head-shaking laughter — the kind of laugh one might make after witnessing someone fall off a twenty-story building then rise without a scratch and calmly stroll away.

"There was a film . . . a TV movie that came out back in the seventies," he said, catching Lopez's eye through the windshield and tapping his wrist-watch, as if to say, 'hold on, just another minute'. "One of those cheesy so-called real-to-life horror things called 'The Stalker' or 'Night Walker' or something, about a newspaper reporter tracking down a vampire in Las Vegas. And there's this long two-part scene where the LVPD show up after this vampire tries stealing blood from one of the hospitals and it's total chaos. That's what it reminded me of.

"All the action was taking place in the mini-mart entrance and the gas pumps. I saw these officers — some of them like line-backers for a pro-football team — being thrown around like sacks of feathers by this little brunette who couldn't have been more than a buck-ten.

And they were going at her full-bore, with everything from fists to nightsticks to Tasers.

"Nothing, absolutely *nothing* stopped her. It didn't even slow her down!

"Guns came into play next. There'd been two or three guys on the fringes, circling, trying to get a clear shot. And when it came, they opened up on her full force. I could see her body jerk as the rounds hit her, but she didn't drop. Not until one of the guys brought out his shotgun – a pump action Remington. He was standing about two or three feet from her and let go a blast that hit her in the shoulder, just above her right breast. It spun her around, knocked her a good ten feet and onto her back.

"And that was it, or so we thought. We – me, my partner, and the cop that shot her – were moving up to check the body and I'll be damned if she didn't get up. I mean actually *jumped up*. And then she made this growling, hissing sound and bared her teeth. And I'll never forget it as long as I live. She had fangs – as big and long as any wild animal. It was enough to stop us cold. For a minute, at least.

"The officer with the shotgun – Hal Jenkins, I think his name was – he pumped another round into the chamber. I heard her, she actually said '*fuck this noise*,' took a couple of steps and *whooooosh*! She jumped straight up like she had wings on her ass," he threw a sheepish glance at Jenny. "Excuse my French."

"S'okay," she replied.

Greenwalt resumed. "Twenty feet, at least, before she hit the ground again. And at a dead run, across the road and into a nearby field and *pffft* . . . gone.

"A few guys tried following her, but she vanished – not even a blood trail. And, like I said, that was the end. No more sightings, no more murders. It was like she opened up a patch of thin air and crawled into it."

He went into the wrap-up then, going back to the incident's casualties: two deaths, the police officers in the AM-PM with snapped necks, and the others with a collection of broken arms, ribs, concussions. Then he spoke of how, in the days that followed, everyone seemed to avoid talking about the case as a whole. How, after a week, he was called upstairs to see the Chief of Police, who gave him a round of verbal pats on the back for a job well done, but also cautioned him on speaking of the case to outsiders (namely the new media), not just for the 'good of the department' but for his career.

"After my little 'atta boy' veiled threat session with the Chief, and out of pure curiosity, I went back and checked out the filed reports of the case – starting with my own."

"I've had experience on that score. Let me—" Jenny edged in. "Your report wasn't yours. Completely bogus."

"Not entirely," Greenwalt said. "Let's say it was noticeably altered. As were all the others. Any and almost everything pertaining to the former Los Angeles undercover policewoman, Janet Kaiser, was omitted. She was included as, quote-unquote, the 'unidentified perpetrator'. Her files from the LAPD, the photos and the coaster with her fingerprints . . . missing. The coroner's report on the victims. No mention, whatsoever, of them being drained of blood. Under cause of death, it listed severe blood loss due to wounds inflicted. The officers she killed in that final battle, according to *official* reports, the perp was more than likely *'hopped up on PCP, giving her abnormally heightened strength; which also explained why she appeared to be impervious to bullet wounds'*. And then there were the eye-witness reports." Both officers groaned in unison. "Yeah, just what you'd expect from civ's," Greenwalt said. "But the cops who were on the scene, especially the ones who saw what *I* saw. It was like they were . . ." his words trailed off, with a wobbling shake of his head.

"Like they suddenly developed a case of convenient amnesia," Jenny finished for him. "Been there, seen that. Hell, I'm there *now*."

Greenwalt continued. "Both the Chief and my Captain strongly suggested I schedule sessions with the department's headhsrink to deal with my," he made a curled fingers quotation sign with one hand, "stress-related hallucinations. And there it is. My introduction to the SPD.

"And I told you all that to tell you this," he continued before Jenny could respond. "A lotta people on the force would, and probably *do*, laugh at you and your theories. I just wanted you to know that I'm not one of them, Detective."

~*~

After rescuing her from the warehouse, Fallon insisted on taking Rowan back to Lainie's for the night and, before leaving, he requested a copy of her college timetable and her diner shifts. He asked Lainie to make sure she stayed close to Rowan while they were both at classes and told Rowan he would pick her up early the next evening, so they could discuss and come to a fair agreement on him working the case.

While Lainie had agreed to everything Fallon said with open-mouthed wonder, her eyes eating him up, Rowan had refused and argued against his instructions not to go anywhere alone. She had a routine she followed and the thought of some unknown person forcing her to change it made her furious.

He'd left the apartment after firing off a demand she do as she was told, and Rowan was left wondering if he actually thought she would listen to him. She said as much to Lainie, who looked horrified at the thought of going against what Fallon said.

Upon returning from campus the following afternoon, Lainie had changed into her uniform for the diner and dashed back out of the door to start her shift. Alone in the apartment, Rowan made herself some lunch and planned to catch up with her coursework, only to find she didn't have her laptop, only the notes she'd made that day. A quick glance at the wall-mounted clock told her it was two in the afternoon – five hours until Fallon had said he would come to collect her. She chewed on her bottom lip as she considered her options, then came to a decision.

She would take the bus back to her own apartment and grab her laptop. She would be back at Lainie's long before Fallon arrived but, just in case, she'd send him a text, so he knew where she was.

After sending a short text 'Gone home for supplies, will see you at Lainie's later', she pulled on her shoes and slipped out of the door.

CHAPTER FOUR

Fallon didn't bother knocking on Rowan's apartment door when he arrived. He simply gave it a hard shove. The ease with which it opened, along with the fact she hadn't even put on the security chain, turned Fallon's annoyance from the low simmer that had started the moment he'd received her text to a full-on boil. Had the girl listened to *nothing* he'd told her? He stalked through the door, scanned the small living room and then made a beeline for her bedroom.

"I know you're in there," he snapped. "You might as well come out." He didn't wait, but threw the door open himself and strode inside. "What was so important that you couldn't wait for me before coming back here?"

Rowan didn't answer him straight away, instead she bent to zip up the bag laying on her bed and then straightened and turned to look at him.

"I needed my laptop. I have a paper due in soon."

"And you needed it right now? It couldn't have waited until I got to you?"

"No, it couldn't wait. I have a life, commitments. I finish school, then study at home. I also have a job and my coursework has to be written around it."

"If something had happened to you before I got here—"

"Well, obviously it didn't. And I don't know whether you noticed or not, but all those things have only happened at night, not during the day."

Fallon felt a flicker of admiration for the girl glaring so defiantly at him. He was more than aware that all the situations she'd fallen foul of had been at night for obvious reasons – not that he could explain them to her – but he was impressed she'd picked up on it.

"So, let me guess," he said. "Because nothing has happened during the day so far, you figured it was safe to ignore my warnings and wander around alone anyway?"

"Oh, they were warnings, were they? And there I was thinking you were making demands. Well, as you can see, I'm not doing much in the way of wandering around. I also sent you a text, so you knew where to find me *if* you arrived at Lainie's before I came back which, to be honest, I didn't think would be the case." She lifted the bag and hooked it over her shoulder. "Now I have my laptop and some more clothes, so I won't have to come back here for a while." She walked past him, her whole body radiating disdain. "Are you ready to leave?"

Fallon's anger gave way to amusement when she stalked past him. "Actually, no." His lips quirked into a satisfied smile when she stopped and spun to face him. "Since it appears I can't stop you sneaking off when my eyes are closed and, while the idea of putting you on a leash does hold some appeal," he paused and swept his gaze from her head to her toes and back again, noting the drab beige pants and blouse she wore did nothing for her colour nor successfully hid her curves. "Although, not for the same reasons, I'll admit. I suppose I need to come up with some way to make sure you can protect yourself."

"What is *that* supposed to mean?" Rowan demanded, her cheeks turning pink.

"Which part?" he enquired, silkily, as he reached into his inside pocket and pulled out a small pistol. "Have you ever fired a gun before?" When she shook her head, he held the gun out to her. "See how it feels."

"Why do I need a gun?" She took it from him and held it awkwardly in her hands.

Moving forward, Fallon covered her hands with his and adjusted her grip, showing her how to hold the pistol properly. "It won't do much damage from a distance, but if someone gets close enough, it'll do the trick. Just point and press." He explained how to operate the safety and then had her practice flicking it on and off a few times, before nodding. "Keep it on you at all times. That way when you feel the need to sneak off again, at least you have some protection."

"I don't have a licence—" she broke off at his arched eyebrow. "Fine! Should I tuck it into the back of my pants for the full-on rebel look or are you okay with me putting it in my bag?"

Fallon laughed. "Just put it in your bag, Rowan. We don't want you shooting yourself accidentally." Shaking his head, he walked past her and paused at the front door. "Come on. We'll go get some dinner and work out a game plan."

As they headed out of her apartment, a man close to Rowan's age was walking along the corridor toward them. Fallon tensed, resting one hand on Rowan's arm and she angled her head to look up at him and rolled her eyes.

"Hey, Floyd," she said brightly, as they drew level with the young man, who grinned and went a deep shade of red.

"Hey Rowan, not working today?" he cut a quick nervous look at Fallon looming silently beside her.

"No, just off to grab some dinner."

"And we're running late," Fallon added darkly, tugging her back into movement.

Muttering a quick apology to Floyd, Rowan trotted to keep up with Fallon. "Are you always so unsociable?" she burst out as they exited the apartment block.

"Careful," Fallon corrected.

"Rude," she countered.

"Protective," Fallon denied, squashing a smile.

"Overbearing."

"Get in the car, Rowan." Refusing to let himself be enchanted by her teasing, he pushed the button on his keys to open the door.

"And bossy. Very, *very* bossy," she muttered as she bent to enter the car, then paused. "Damn it, I need to go back up."

"What for?"

"I left my research file on the bed. I'll run back up and get it."

Fallon leaned over the roof of the car. "Give me your bag but take the gun with you."

"Mr Wylde, we've only just come out. There's no one up there," she argued, handing the bag over to him.

"Rowan, just humour me. Please? Take the gun." He opened the bag and pulled out the pistol, sliding it across the roof to her.

"I hired you to find out what happened to Eden, not to be my surrogate father!"

"You haven't hired me for shit, sweetheart, not until money changes hands."

They glared at each other, then Rowan snatched up the pistol and tucked it into the back of her pants. "I'll be quick." She spun round and jogged back inside

Fallon watched her go, enjoying the visual delight of the way she moved as she hurried away and wondered what the story was behind the way she dressed. She disappeared through the entrance and Fallon slid into the driver's seat, resting his hands on the steering wheel.

Rowan entered her apartment and went straight into her bedroom to pick up the file she'd left on her bed. She tucked it under her arm and stepped out of the room, only to stop when she saw Floyd standing in the doorway.

"Floyd? What are you doing here?"

"Rowan! I thought you'd gone out," he scuffed a foot against the carpet. "I . . . uh . . . heard a noise and came to investigate. Saw your door was open, thought you were being burgled or something."

Rowan relaxed. "Well, as you can see, it's just me."

Floyd sighed. "Yeah. A shame, really."

Before she could ask why, Floyd lunged at her. "All you had to do was stay away, Rowan. Why couldn't you do that?" He grabbed her arm and dragged her back into the bedroom. "I tried to stop you."

"Let go of me!" Rowan struggled to free her arm, twisting and turning in his grip.

"And then you go and find *him!*" Floyd ignored her and continued to rant. "Of all the people you could have gone to, you end up with Fallon Wylde." He threw her backwards and she slammed against the wardrobe doors. "*Fallon fucking Wylde*, Rowan! He's more dangerous than anything else you could get mixed up in."

"I don't know what you're talking about, Floyd," Rowan tried to inch toward the bedroom door, only to find her way barred.

"Six months I've lived next door to you, trying to stop you getting involved. But you just wouldn't listen, would you? And now it's not enough to just scare you. No, now they want you dead. You should know when to quit!" He caught her as she made to dash past him and shoved her back again. "Oh no you don't!"

Rowan managed to let out a scream before he got her mouth covered with his hand. Throwing her head forward, she slammed her forehead into his nose and scrambled back out of his reach while he covered his face, swearing. She backed against the wall and felt the pistol dig into her back and, while Floyd was still distracted by the blood pouring from his nose, she took two attempts to flick off the safety and then pointed it at him.

"Stay away from me. I don't know what you want or who you are working for. But you stay away from me!"

"You bitch!" Floyd's head came up and then he was moving toward her.

~*~

Fallon was out of the car and running the minute he heard Rowan scream, but even with his preternatural speed he'd heard two gunshots before he reached the apartment. Another went off as he ran inside, followed by a fourth when he came to a halt in the bedroom. A quick glance gave him a good idea of what had happened, and he kicked the door shut behind him, just in case any passer-by became curious.

"Rowan." He caught hold of her hands just before she squeezed off another round and took the gun from her unresisting fingers. "Rowan, look at me."

He didn't need to check the body on the ground to know the young man was dead – three shots to the stomach and a lucky hit to the head had ensured that. He made sure the safety was on and threw the gun on the bed, then cupped Rowan's face between his palms, forcing her to look away from Floyd's body.

"Talk to me, honey." He kept his voice low and gentle.

"He . . . he . . . " she tried to turn her head to look at Floyd again, but Fallon held her firm. "No, don't worry about him, sweetheart. Look at me." He tipped her head up, forcing her to meet his gaze. "I don't think I've ever met anyone as hellbent on finding trouble as often as you do. You should come with a warning label." He bent his head to press a comforting kiss to her forehead, only to find she'd moved.

The feel of her lips on his startled him, and he started to lift his head only for Rowan to chase his mouth when he went to draw away. He felt her rise up on tiptoes to keep the connection. The tension radiating from Fallon's body at her move was palpable, but Rowan ignored it in favour of exploring his mouth with hers.

Fallon was torn. He was aware that shock was the biggest driving force behind her action, a need to ground herself in something recognisable. But the way her lips glued themselves to his, and the way her tongue was making quick exploratory swipes in search of access to his mouth was impossible to ignore. No stranger to casual intimacy, Fallon was disconcerted by the speed of the hunger and arousal the feel of her mouth on his caused. When she stepped closer and her breasts pressed against his chest, he was even more concerned to find himself in definite danger of erupting like a school boy on a first date. In an attempt to slow things down, he dropped his hands to her waist to ease her away, only for her to raise eyes glassy with unshed tears to look at him.

"Don't."

One word. Just one whispered word combined with raw need and horror battling for precedence in her eyes. Both emotions he recognised – horror at what had taken place and a desperate need for something to push it from her mind. In another time and place, Fallon would easily have stopped things from progressing further, but right at that moment he found he couldn't deny her. Instead of pushing her away, he let his hands continue their movement to slide around her waist. He lifted her up, so their faces were level and set her down on top of the waist-high dresser against the wall. Stepping between her legs, he lifted his hands again to cup her face and lowered his mouth back to hers.

Their lips met, and Fallon tasted the strawberry flavouring of her lip-gloss. That thought held for a second, then splintered when her tongue slid between his lips to tangle with his own, while her hands reached up to clutch at his shoulders. Reining in his natural instinct to dominate, he allowed Rowan to set the pace, followed her lead as her hands roamed across his shoulders and up into his hair, dragging him closer so she could hook her legs around his, bringing his burgeoning erection flush against her stomach.

When her mouth briefly left his to snatch in some much-needed air, Fallon ran his tongue along her jawline to her ear and nipped at the lobe gently. Her fingers dug into his shoulders as a shudder rocked her frame.

"Like that?" he breathed against her ear and she gave a ragged laugh in response.

He changed direction and nibbled a path down her throat. Rowan tipped her head back to expose more of the soft fragrant skin of her neck. For a second, he was tempted to relax his grip on the inner beast and *really* taste her but, before temptation could take hold, she touched his cheek and guided his face back up to hers and kissed him again before she inched back slightly to meet his eyes.

"We should . . ." she left the sentence hanging and let her eyes slide past his, over his shoulder, to where Floyd's body lay.

"I'll deal with it." He stroked her cheek with the back of his fingers. "Feel better now?"

"Not really." She dropped her head against his shoulder and took in a shuddering breath, then lifted her head again. "I'm sorry. I shouldn't have kissed you. It wasn't very professional."

Fallon pressed a kiss to the top of her head, smiling as he thought about how that particular action had set off the most recent chain of events.

"It's fine, understandable considering the circumstances." He reached behind him to unwind her legs from around his waist. When Rowan raised her head to watch him step away, he found himself tempted to capture her mouth again and see where it led. Willpower alone kept him moving until he crouched beside Floyd's body.

"I thought he was my friend," she offered, sadly.

"That was the idea," Fallon replied, as he examined the body.

Human, he determined after carefully stripping off Floyd's heavy plaid top shirt and checking the bared flesh below his shirt sleeves. In addition to the fact the body hadn't begun to decompose, there was a tattoo – a glyph (another example of life imitating art; probably inspired by one of the vampire films) on his left forearm. One Fallon hadn't seen before, but the meaning was clear. Floyd was a *skiv*, a thrall, a willing human slave to a single vampire or group.

There was a single soft tap on the door, followed by two more, a bit harder. Then a voice.

"Rowan, dear? Is everything alright in there? I heard noises."

"Oh, no!" Rowan half-whispered, eyes widened in surprise and dread. "It's Mrs Levesque, the old lady next door. What do we do—" she faltered in response to Fallon's raised hand.

"First, stay calm. Second, you'll have to go out there and stall her."

"Stall?" Rowan's voice, though still lowered, gradually gravitated toward squeaky. "*How*? What am I supposed to say?"

Fallon shrugged. "Anything. Make something up." He lifted his head to smile at her. "Find out if she called 911."

"And what are *you* going to be doing while I'm lying to Mrs Levesque?

"Don't worry about it. Just go."

"Rowan?" As if to expedite her departure, Mrs Levesque called out again, this time jiggling the doorknob.

With a growl of exasperation, which drew a chuckle from Fallon, Rowan slid off the unit and made her way to the door. Fallon watched her leave, ran his tongue across his lips – he could still taste her – then grinned to himself and wondered how the conversation between the two women would play out. *Oh, to be a fly on the wall.*

A moment later, he took out his cell and hit speed-dial for the pre-programmed number for E-SAN – Seattle's communal vampire emergency cleaning service. After a brief recorded prompt, Fallon gave his name, House designation, description of circumstances and situation, and finally the address of Rowan's apartment.

Mrs Levesque – curly white hair, grey cardigan, wrinkled slacks, and a four-pronged cane – was still standing in the hallway when Fallon emerged. When her narrow-eyed disapproving gaze landed on him, he immediately knew what kind of story Rowan had spun and couldn't resist wrapping an arm around her waist and pulling her close against his side. Rowan slanted a look up at him through her eyelashes but didn't resist. Instead, she took it a step further and wound her arm around his waist, playing the part of besotted girlfriend to perfection.

"Ready to go, darling?" he asked her, and hid a grin at the old woman's sniff of disgust as she turned and walked back to her own apartment.

Once the old woman had disappeared inside, Rowan dropped her arm and took a step sideways. Fallon pressed his palm to the small of her back and moved them along the corridor. Out of habit, Rowan angled toward the elevator, but Fallon quickly maneuvered her to the stairwell door. They were halfway down before Rowan spoke.

"What about the—"

"Body?" Fallon finished her question. "Don't worry. Floyd will be taken care of. Let's just hope Mrs Levesque was the only one who heard noises, and nobody called the cops."

"The other apartments on this floor are empty." She stopped on the stairs, one hand covering her mouth. "I killed someone," she whispered. "I had that gun less than ten minutes and I killed someone."

"And if you hadn't had the gun, you'd be dead."

"Maybe."

"You really believe that?"

Rowan's response died on her lips. She froze, staring at Fallon for a long moment as pieces of her violent confrontation with the young man she'd known as Floyd replayed in her head.

"He . . . Floyd . . . said some things," she said. "He said '*now it's not enough to scare you, now they want you* . . . me . . . *dead.*'"

"And I thought finding the body last night pretty much covered that," Fallon replied, dryly.

Rowan continued as if she hadn't heard him. "And he said that *you're* more dangerous than anything else I could get mixed up in. *You're* dangerous. What did he mean by that?"

"Simple enough," he shrugged. "I *am*. It's what I get paid for." He took her elbow and started moving down the stairs again.

"I haven't paid you yet," she reminded him.

His lips twitched. "I'm well aware of that."

"Of course, had you let him kill me, you would never get paid."

Amusement fled, and Fallon frowned. "Are you saying the only reason I came to your rescue – and this is the third time, by the way – was because I was safeguarding my as-yet-to-be-paid fee?"

"No," she shook her head. "I'm not stupid, Mr Wylde. Just because I don't always agree or do what you say, it doesn't mean I'm not listening. And since you've been around, things have escalated. That says to me your presence is worrying someone." She waited while he opened the stairwell door and looked out, before indicating she follow him. "And those people, people who seem to think nothing of killing and leaving bodies lying around – are scared of you. You obviously have some kind of reputation."

Fallon shrugged, waiting until they neared his car before speaking. "Those people are just getting started and next time they won't be sending someone like Floyd, so I wouldn't be quite so quick to appreciate my presence."

"Appreciate your presence?" Rowan gaped at him. "*Appreciate?* I wish I'd *never* made the phone call that brought you into my life in the first place!"

In the process of taking his key fob from his pocket, Fallon stopped and raised an eyebrow. "You *appreciated* me just fine a few minutes ago."

The sound of her palm hitting his cheek rang out down the quiet street.

Neither moved for a long moment, both surprised by her action, then Fallon smiled and lifted a hand to rub his cheek.

"I deserved that." He opened the Ferrari's passenger door and held it until she was seated inside. "Your call. Dinner or home?"

"My neighbour's *dead body* is in my home," she snapped.

"I meant—"

"I *know* what you meant." Rowan chewed on her bottom lip, then sighed. "I'm not hungry."

They didn't talk again until Fallon had pulled up outside Lainie's apartment building. Rowan threw the car door open and bolted across the sidewalk and into the building before he could speak. Fallon stayed put for a few minutes, fingers drumming on the steering wheel while he debated whether to follow her or not, then with a headshake pulled away from the kerb.

Rowan was halfway up the stairs before she realised she'd left her bag in Fallon's car. She hovered in the stairwell for a second, then raced down and outside in time to see the taillights of his car disappearing into the distance.

"Damn it," she muttered. As she pulled out her cell phone from her pocket, intent on calling Fallon, she didn't see the two men come up behind her until it was too late. They grabbed her and covered her head with a dark foul-smelling hood before she got the chance to see their faces. She tried to scream, but a hand clamped firmly over her mouth, muffling the sound, then there was a sharp sting in the side of her neck followed by blackness.

~*~

How did they – the mysterious *they* – do it, Fallon wondered as he drove his Ferrari 458 Spider down the rapidly darkening streets. The fact that someone out there knew about FW, A&R, or about *him* for that matter, was no major shocker. Despite the size of Seattle's vampire community, they would've had to have been either newly turned, lived in a cave in the wilds of the Amazon Rainforest or be Human to have never heard the name Fallon Wylde. And FW, A&R had been a name associated with him – albeit with a couple of slight alterations over time – for the last hundred years alone. But Koo . . . there was the rub. As he'd told Rowan earlier, it was a pet name of his associate (and long-time friend) Kathryn, Kate Chan. In point of fact, it was Fallon who had coined the nickname on the day they first met – two hundred and fifty plus years ago – in a back-alley gambling den in Old Hong Kong. Koo – the shortened, abbreviated form of Katie Coo Coo, because she'd waded into a swarm of hatchet-wielding turnblood thugs armed with only a straight razor and a broken bottle and somehow managed to come through it with only a few minor scratches. Not to mention the fact that she'd probably saved the lives of himself and their other long-time associate, Eayann Ó'Beolláin, at least a dozen times over.

It was doubtful that *they* knew the entire story, however. The thing most crucial at that point was how they had gotten her pet name and, not as crucial but equally important, how they knew he was working with Rowan. Three possibilities.

One: someone had physically breached their hi-tech, quadruple-redundant security perimeter and managed to get in and out without detection. Very highly doubtful, if not totally impossible.

Two: the use of a parabolic microphone, which *was* possible – even though the house was equipped with soundproofing the CIA would envy.

Three: the old fashioned 'bug' and/or wire-tap. As to that, it was possible they had tapped into the house landline from the outside. And just in case, he took a moment to call the O'Bannions (the human family who served as beards for Fallon and his comrades at his home) and asked them to instigate a sweep of the grounds for errant listening devices.

A slow cruise around the block, twice, confirmed beyond a doubt that securing a parking place in any of Shadowfall's three public parking areas was a hopeless cause.

Understandable, Fallon admitted to himself. Shadowfall, over the last decade or so, had become one of the city's five-star entertainment venues. Extremely popular with both tourists and locals – especially the current under-thirty crowd. On any given night the club played host to a large party, a corporate dinner/conference, more than a few themed-weddings, a comic-con, or celebrity from the music or Hollywood realm. Meaning that crowds started to arrive the minute the sun set, and which took Fallon to the underground car park, normally and predominantly used by the club's employees and VIP residents.

That worked out nicely, he had to admit. It wasn't much of a stretch to think that if the mysterious *them* had indeed tapped his phone or bugged his house might they not also be watching? Maybe even have an operative staked out inside the club?

Waiting until he was sure there would be no one around to see, Fallon quickly exited the car and made his way along the rear-most wall into the far corner, beneath the club-proper. Known to a very rare few, it was the location of a false wall, marked by a wall-mounted fire extinguisher. A latch below the extinguisher opened a doorway onto a staircase which led upwards to another door, which opened beside the wet bar in the office of the club's owner . . . and right into the muzzle of a SIG Sauer. Fallon instantly froze as the cold metal pressed into his temple.

"Oops. My bad. This isn't the visitor's Men's Room?" he quipped, keeping both hands where they could be seen by the gun's owner.

"Cute, Diego," Kane let the SIG, and his arm, drop. "What? Your fingers stopped working? You've got my number. You couldn't have called rather than sneak in through my *supposedly* secret escape route?"

Fallon released a quiet sigh of relief and smiled. "I was here last night, and I have it from a pretty reliable source that you'd be out of town for a while."

"It's what Gayle tells everybody when I tell *her* I need some private time," Kane smiled back, turned and went behind the bar to take out two glasses and a pair of crystal decanters. "And the last I heard you were somewhere down South, in Panama or Venezuela," he poured both glasses half-full and slid one in Fallon's direction.

"Try Peru," Fallon raised his glass in thanks and knocked back a quick gulp. "Six . . . no, seven weeks ago."

"Kind of a long stretch for you. From what I hear, the few conversations I've had with your sire, Marjean, your jobs have been running pretty much back to back over the last year."

"True enough," Fallon took another pull of his drink. "A week, sometimes two between assignments. It finally caught up with me. There's a Shaolin Monastery in the Henan Province of China. Eayann took me there the tenth year I was—" he faltered and concealed the sudden onset of emotion behind a long swallow of rum, "after I was turned. It's what initially got me interested and started my training in Asian philosophy and martial arts. We had planned to go back there, take a few months off, as soon as he returned from his own business in Ireland."

"But . . ." Kane anticipated, with a grin.

"Yeah, but . . ." Fallon polished off the remains of his drink and slid his glass down the bar to be refilled, which Kane did immediately. Fallon gave a raised-glass salute when it was returned.

"A new job, I imagine?" Kane said, also replenishing his own glass. "Also, the reason you're here?"

Fallon nodded.

"And there I was thinking you'd dropped by to catch up with an old friend," Kane chuckled. "A friendly drink and a few laughs."

"Who knows. We might just get a few laughs in before the night is over."

"I feel a story coming on. Maybe we should get comfortable?" Kane slid his glass to Fallon, grabbed the decanters and made his way to the scattered sofas and coffee table at the office's centre, with Fallon in tow.

"A couple of questions for you first, if you don't mind," Fallon said as soon as they sat. Kane inclined his head in agreement.

"Back in the days you were a PI, you worked in both LA and San Francisco, right?"

"Not at the beginning," Kane answered. "After my *thing* in '41, I hooked up with an agency run by an old friend, Richard Blessing, in New York. I was primarily East Coast until I went solo and relocated to LA in 1965. Then San Francisco from '70 through to '79, and finally here in Seattle, in 1980."

"Good enough," said Fallon. "In LA and 'Frisco, did you ever run into a group . . . our people – a gang that called itself Hoodoo Fyre?"

Kane thought for a moment then shook his head. "Doesn't ring any bells."

"How about a turnblood? Eli or Martin or Taylor?"

"Nope," Kane shook his head again.

"Okay, it's just a hunch, but I've got a feeling they're connected to my latest job," Fallon said, then laid it all out – from first meeting with Rowan, to the security cam photos and his first conversation with Tigr; Rowan's phone call about the intruders and the return to confer with Tigr; his two days of legwork that turned up nothing; and finally the events of the past twenty-four hours.

"The body?" Kane said, and Fallon definitely noted a decided change in the older vampire's demeanour. "Where did you say you and your client found it?"

"Georgetown. An abandoned warehouse."

"Tell me more about the body," he replied, and this time Fallon was sure something in his tale had struck a chord with his old friend.

"This wasn't just a kill after feeding," Fallon began. "And there was a lot more to it than *them* using her to try and scare us off. I'm no medical examiner, but I've seen a few things in my time. The signs were obvious. Whoever she was, she'd been with them for a while. Months, maybe. There were marks other than the wounds. Healed scars. They'd been feeding on her, abusing her for a long time. But what really got me was how they finally killed her. Underneath the ways they tried to cover up the bite marks. It was alike a gangbang fang frenzy. I'd say at least three vampires were on her at once, and they were like a pack of hungry dogs. No control whatsoever."

There was a long slash of silence between them, during which Kane topped off his glass and downed more than half of it before topping it off again.

"Those bells I hear, old friend?" Fallon broke the silence.

"Could be. *Old* bells." Kane knocked back another swallow, then placed the glass on the coffee table and combed a hand through his hair. "I'm going to tell you something, Diego. Part of it is old news. History. But there's another side of it. It *can't* leave this room. And I need your word on that."

"You have it," Fallon replied, without hesitation.

There was a thick, encased humidor on the coffee table and Kane took a moment to open it, revealing two rows of long, dark cigars.

"Never acquired a taste for them," Fallon shook his head in response to Kane's offer. "But I wouldn't say no to a cigarette – if you've got any."

Kane smiled and gestured across the room as he took possession of a cigar. "In my desk. Bottom right-hand drawer."

Fallon followed his friend's directions and found an opened carton of Marlboro 100s, one pack missing.

"They're Pantera's. She usually takes her breaks in here," Kane explained.

Fallon bit back an amused smile. It was rumoured amongst the club's inner circle and a few select friends that Kane and his sultry raven-haired Head of Security shared a special relationship, the truth was entirely different – and Fallon was one of the few who knew the real story.

"One of the perks of vampire physiology," Kane smiled, blowing a large, expanding smoke ring. "No worries of lung cancer, emphysema, heart attacks or, if you buy into the crap they've been spouting the last few years, impotence."

"The gods forbid," Fallon shuddered. "I can agree that we've definitely got the market cornered on upsides over being mortal," he agreed, settling back onto the couch. "But then your average Human doesn't have to worry about instantaneous cerebral haemorrhage and exploding intestines from exposure to sunlight."

"Remember that masquerade ball in Copenhagen, back in 1889?" Kane asked.

"The one we crashed?" Fallon laughed.

"And the two Pureblood noblewomen – Ladies Signe and Astrid of the House of Machiavel. *Wonder Woman and the Energiser Bunny*," Kane pulled a salacious grin. "Tell me *that* night wasn't worth giving up long walks in the sun."

"I also recall that we left town with a pair of angry husbands and sunrise blazing at our heels. But you're right," Fallon raised his glass in salute. "It was worth it."

Both men touched glasses at their base and took deep pulls.

"I'll tell you something, my friend, five thousand plus years? I'd be lying to you if I said there weren't times on the other end of the spectrum," Kane searched their surroundings for an ashtray. He spotted one on the bar and rose to retrieve it, continuing as he did. "On *both* ends and all points in-between. I've seen things of incredible beauty and ugliness; done things that would significantly impact the lives of Humans and Vampires. I could give seminars. *Hell*, I have spoken to rooms of people – *our* people – on the benefits and drawbacks of our lives. But the truth in it all? The thing – two things, actually – that vampires and mortals share in common are their capacities for kindness, compassion and cruelty – especially the latter."

Back on the couch, Kane flicked off the ash from his cigar and resumed. "As I said, I moved to San Francisco in 1970. April, I think.

And, over the years that followed, I built up a good relationship with one of the street cops, or at least he was at first. Phil Magnussen. He eventually made Inspector and worked Homicide. And yes, he knew what I was . . . *am*," he said in response to Fallon's eyebrow twitch.

"Long story, but the short version is he and his partner answered a domestic disturbance call in the Fillmore District. Some biker just released from prison at Pelican Bay walked in on his wife and her drug-dealer boyfriend. The boyfriend and two friends of his own were there, both packing. I was in the building, two doors down on . . . well, let's not go into that," Kane cleared his throat and laughed. "Things were heated up way out of control by the time Phil and the other officer arrived and they walked into drawn guns and hot tempers. The other officer took a bullet in the knee, Phil took one in the shoulder, almost two. He saw me take a .357 round in the chest, practically at point blank range, but still put one of the shooters through a wall and the other through a window. I went to see Phil at his home the next night and explained. Actually, I confessed and I'm sure you know to *what*. We've been friends ever since."

"From what I understand of the PI business, having a friend inside the department must've been a plus."

"That it was," Kane replied. "As it turned out, beneficial for both of us. And on *that* note . . . Phil's wife, fiancé at the time – Rhonda," he continued, "was a caseworker in Social Services. It was her who brought the situation to light. There was a young girl she'd been working with for about two years. Seventeen years old, parents died in a car crash when she was fourteen, no other relatives. Rhonda said the girl, Melissa, was really starting to turn it around. Cleaning up from a bout with drugs and alcohol, working on getting her GED, she even had a part-time job at one of the fast food places.

"Anyway, Rhonda got her set up with a foster family, a group home in El Cerrito. It was the heads of the foster household who called Rhonda when Melissa didn't return home from school. After waiting for three hours, the mother called the fast food restaurant and was told Melissa hadn't shown up for work either.

"The girl had been missing for more than eighteen hours by the time the story had passed from her foster parents to Rhonda to Phil and another three hours by the time Phil caught up with me. Seventy-two hours is the prescribed time-period for the police to officially call it a missing-persons case, but Phil had already done a preliminary investigation, for his fiancé's sake and, in his opinion, a few more hours wasn't going to make much difference. The thing was, according to Phil, the cops would only give the case as much attention as budget and manpower concerns allowed. *And* there was also Melissa's record. Turns out she had run away twice before when she was first put into the system, so unless they got immediate results, that's how the missing-person's unit would treat it."

"But you and Magnussen were sure it wasn't a case of a runaway?" Fallon interjected.

"One of the first things I did was get permission to check out the house and the girl's room," Kane said. "And Phil wasn't wrong. Everything I saw gave indications that Melissa was, just as Rhonda put it, getting things together in her life. Like a very happy girl. There were clothes, jewellery, a pretty well-maintained guitar, record albums, even eighty dollars and change in one of her drawers. People don't just skip out and leave stuff like that behind." Kane paused to knock more ash off the end of his cigar, take another puff or two, and sip his drink. All done, most likely, to collect his thoughts.

"Not to rush or anything, "Fallon prompted. "But I'm gonna take for granted there's a vampire element in this case, correct?"

"Oh, most assuredly," Kane answered. "But I didn't find that out for a week or so. Not until the second girl went missing.

"I turned up zip on Melissa. Four, five all-nighters and I was almost ready to believe the phrase 'vanished into thin air' wasn't a myth after all. And then Phil called me. Rhonda got an alert from one of her co-workers that another girl was missing. Same city, same situation. In fact, when I was finally showed a photo of the second girl, she and Melissa could have been sisters. Eighteen years old, petite, blonde, blue-eyed, even similar backgrounds. Melissa didn't have anyone she was particularly close to, but in the second incident I got a break. The girl's name was Lauren and one of her younger foster brothers had a crush on her. Watched her to the point of stalking. I questioned him and learned that the night before Lauren disappeared she had a visitor in her room. He – *Josh* – called her a goddess. *'Insane hot'* he described her. Black-black hair and purple eyes. Violet eyes. Other than that, he couldn't remember much else. Which didn't matter because I knew the moment I walked into

Lauren's room what Little Miss Black Hair and Purple Eyes was. Her scent was all over the room. That sent me back to Melissa's and—"

"Connection?" Fallon wedged in.

"Oh, yeah. One of the other girls in her foster family recalled hearing voices coming from the living room the night before Melissa vanished. She thought it was strange because of the time. It was sometime around 1AM, when everyone was normally asleep, so she got up to investigate. She heard two voices and when she peeked down the stairs she saw Melissa talking to another girl – short dark hair, dressed in ripped jeans and a sleeveless denim jacket. Too far away to see her features, but it sounded like the same one who'd been with Lauren. And I finally had a lead – even though it was one I wasn't altogether thrilled with." He held up a hand in response to the confused look on Fallon's face, then refreshed both of their glasses.

"We're talking about the Bay Area," he started again. "San Francisco – like Seattle, Los Angeles, Dallas, Washington D.C. to name a few – open cities, claimed by no one Clan or House. Even in 1977, every House had a represented consulate with their officers and Purebred families spread out to Hell and back, and that's not counting the Rromas and unaligned Covens. On the one hand, there was my reputation and the feelings toward me in the Vampire Nation at large. And, on the other, me being a one-man operation. I was looking at a lot of long, frustrating hours trying to track down who Little Miss Violet Eyes belonged to." Another pause, a cigar pull, followed by a swallow and then he resumed.

"And I didn't. At least, nobody claimed her, but it didn't take long for me to catch strong hints that something was in the wind. Something they weren't willing to talk to me about, which really got my juices boiling. So, I took a leap. Got Phil and Rhonda to navigate through all the red tape of jurisdictional rivalry, and a pattern took shape. From as far down as Monterey, all the way up to Napa, going back two months, girls of a specific physical and domestic profile were disappearing. Seventeen or eighteen-year-olds, blonde, blue-eyed and petite, wards of the city/state, in foster homes and with police records of drug/alcohol abuse. Girls few people would raise a fuss over – at least not for very long – if they were taken. And the pattern was a limit of two from each city before the culprits moved on; and, in at least ninety percent of the cases, the victims were seen with the girl with violet eyes. An organised effort, no doubt about it.

"At that point, Phil had no choice but to let the case drop. Two and a half months had passed since the start of the original incident, Melissa, with no leads as to her whereabouts," he quirked an eyebrow. "Needless to say, I never let on to Phil about the vampire aspect, for both our sakes. Phil gave what information we had to the respective police departments, and to the field offices of the FBI in San Francisco and Sacramento, along with our or rather, *Phil's*, theory of a sex slave operation. But I wasn't willing to give up on it.

"I had Phil and Rhonda keep doing their phone liaison thing and a week later they got a hit. It was in Oregon, a little town on the border of Washington State called Tillamook. Not only did they have a girl missing but, as with all the others, two were taken and, this time, one managed to escape her captors.

"I took off on a Tuesday, a ten-hour drive to Tillamook. Phil called ahead and arranged for an interview with the survivor for the Wednesday evening."

"Let me guess," Fallon stepped in again. "She told you about meeting the girl with the violet eyes, but her memory was fuzzy about what happened next." Fallon paused to await confirmation, Kane's nod, and then continued. "She didn't remember being taken away, they kept her blindfolded, bits and pieces of where she was. She caught parts of a conversation, naming a place . . ."

"You're getting ahead of me, but yes, that's pretty close," said Kane. "A conversation that talked about 'going back to Tacoma'. So, another three-and-a-half-hour drive, a short stop to see some people, friends I'd met years ago in Los Angeles; they ran a vampires-only club in Tacoma's Hilltop District. I hadn't fed in almost twenty-four hours and my energy levels were bumping the E-mark. After that, I found a cheap motel on the interstate and, after a near-wrestling match with the middle-aged over-sexed blonde desk clerk, I checked into a room as far into a corner, away from *any* chance of sunlight exposure, and had both blinds and curtains, and settled in for an early night. Two hours later, there was a knock on my door. *Persistent* knocking and, believe me, I tried ignoring it. I went to answer it – half-expecting to find the bleached blonde Dolly Parton-clone from the front desk – and lo and behold, I'm staring into the face of someone I hadn't seen or heard from in over thirty years – my sire, Pashet. And she was all over me. All smiles and hugs and kisses and apologies, and begging my forgiveness for abandoning me for so long."

"All bullshit, naturally," Fallon commented.

Kane snorted. "You know it. Spread thick and deep."

"Also begs the obvious question," Fallon said, allowing the statement to hang between them unfinished.

"How she knew I'd be there, after three decades of no contact?" Kane voiced the unspoken query, shrugging. "Believe it or not, her finding me in Tacoma didn't raise any red flags. I know now it should have, but there's one thing, among countless, you have to understand about my late sire. She was *never* predictable. There was always an alternative motive, a hidden agenda, a quadruple precalculated chess strategy behind *everything* she did. It wasn't the first time we had been out of contact for a long period – thirty years, fifty years, a century-plus at one time . . ." he paused, his eyes growing dark with a memory, before he gave himself a shake. "For all I knew she'd been keeping tabs on me since the day I left the House. So, no, I wasn't immediately suspicious. Not even after her predictable attempt to tempt me into bed. But I did start to feel that something was . . . off-centre, even for Pashet.

"She talked me into checking out of the motel, had one of her people take my car while *we* were picked up in a private limo, and took us to Seattle where I was checked into a top floor suite at the Sorrento Hotel. I got the five-star red carpet treatment, a string of lovely, young functionaries; dinner, five courses, including chilled Perrier Jouet Champagne; and finally, the *coup de grace* – the offer of a position in her organisation. Luxury accommodations, stylish car, limitless expense account. If I agreed, I could start immediately. As a matter of fact, it would work out wonderfully if I did, she told me. And *then* the red flag shot up. She had a job . . . a task perfectly suited to someone of my worldliness and experience. The overseeing of security at her exclusive retreat in Prague. *Prague.* Overseas – away from the case and out of their hair.

"It all started to come together then. I didn't know whether she was the front woman or the go-between or really how deep she was involved, but there was no question of her involvement. And it also explained how the girl in Tillamook allegedly escaped. A set-up. They knew I was on their trail and they reeled me in.

"I told Pashet that her offer was tempting, and that I would seriously consider taking her up on it, but only after I finished the job I was currently working on. She didn't twitch, blink or give any indication that my answer wasn't to her liking. Instead, we finished dinner, played at catching each other up and then she said goodnight. She made a date to pick me up around eight the next evening for a night on the town and then she was gone. I called it a night myself right afterwards.

"What I got the next night, at seven, was a phone call. Someone who claimed to be Lady Bianca's personal secretary telling me that Ms Manx – Pashet – wanted me to meet her as soon as possible. She was supposedly having a problem only I could assist her with. And the address given was the Georgetown District." Kane paused a beat to note Fallon's reaction and nodded. "An abandoned garage less than two blocks from where you and your client discovered the body. Where I discovered one of my own half an hour later.

"It was the young girl from El Cerrito, Melissa, hanging from the ceiling by her ankles like a side of beef in a slaughterhouse, with wounds, gashes and bitemarks covering every inch of her body. Underneath was a cassette player with a note attached that read *Play Now*. The message on the cassette was simple – *This is a warning. You won't get another. Back off. Take this little dead bitch back to California. If you refuse, we will kill another girl each night you remain in town.*" Kane stopped there, staring at a point somewhere beyond Fallon's head for an instant, then down at his glass.

"Hell of a story, amigo," Fallon said, taking a moment to down the last of his rum and stamp out his cigarette. "A TKO for Pashet and her crew."

"Not really. It was her round, no question there," Kane said. "But the fight wasn't over. Not by a long shot.

"Pashet – Bianca Manx – didn't know it but the beams in the roof of her little operation had just started to sprout cracks. After I set arrangements in motion with Phil Magnussen and the SPD to have Melissa shipped back to El Cerrito. I got in touch with Zuron. The Nikaran consulate was in London in those days," he heaved a short cynical laugh. "I was surprised to find out he knew all about my sire's activities. And he wasn't alone. Apparently, it was old news – to everyone but me, that is. Most, if not all, were aware of it; none of them liked it, but neither were any of them willing to step forward and speak out against it. Or, in many cases, they didn't give a shit. I mean, it wasn't as if she was taking *vampire* women. They were mortals – *vite – food on the hoof.* And there was also the fact Pashet and her mother, Hezarae, were very very old blood with associations and connections in very high and dangerous places. I'd seen her destroy entire families just because one of the women dared to dress better than her. She was very vain, vindictive and psychopathic. They were all scared shitless of her. Zuron, on the other hand, let's just say he had the sense to stay off her radar. More cautious than afraid.

"But, to a large degree, Zuron and I have always been kindred spirits. It was his opinion, and one I shared, that Pashet's arrogance would one day prove damaging, maybe even catastrophically fatal to our kind. So, he advised me to step back and bide my time, while he started to do a little networking and politicking behind the scenes. He painted the eventuality, a worst-case scenario, where Pashet's actions exposed our existence to the world-at-large and provoked a repeat of the first war with Humankind that very nearly wiped out the vampire race. And he came close to being right.

"Did you ever get told about the Teresa Bennion murder?" Kane asked, then.

"Teresa Bennion . . ." Fallon's gaze turned inward a moment, head cocked slightly as the wheels turned. "Bennion . . . Bennion . . ." he snapped his fingers, eyebrow rising as the memory took hold. "I remember hearing about it from my sire and from Eayann. But I was away on a job for most of it. I got back to Seattle a few months after things cooled down."

Kane took a deep breath before starting. "Teresa Bennion. *Tracy* to her friends and family. She was a young Mormon girl from Salt Lake City. She and her friends – Virginia Coombs and Miriam Higbee – were runaways, living off the streets. They were approached one night by Pashet's mother, Hezare or Hezarae or her favourite alias, Justine Manx. She offered them food and a place to stay – a place she called Shadow's Fall. The mistake that shook the rafters, as it turned out.

"Miriam and Virginia said later that they were creeped out by Justine and they refused the offer. But Tracy agreed. Two nights later her body was pulled out of the water near Pier 66, in the same shape as the body you described and Melissa's. Still, the condition of her body notwithstanding, the SPD – probably overseen by Pashet's paid stooges in the department – were ready to pass it off as a drug-related killing perpetrated by drifters, until Tracy's parents showed up. Her father, Joseph Bennion, was an investment banker, a man with a lot of weight in Utah and on Wall Street. Both Tracy's parents were also long-time friends of the families of Miriam Higbee and Virginia Coombs. Evidently, Joseph had spoken with the girls – who had run back to their parents when Tracy disappeared – and wasn't buying the cops homicidal druggies story. Even less so, and I'm going on a rumour here, after he talked to a never-identified someone in the coroner's office.

"The story goes, he was told that several of the wounds on his daughter's body were made by teeth and *'animal-like fangs'* and, regardless of how long she'd been in the water, as well as the extent of her wounds, there should have been some blood left in her remains, and there wasn't. Both these titbits were mentioned in the dozen-plus news reports and the press conferences given by Joseph and Margaret Bennion. And *bam*, before you could say Bram Stoker, the word *vampire* started popping up in news articles – vampire murders; vampire slayings; kinky sexual drug-crazed vampire ritualistic slaughter – and on and on and on.

"In a matter of two weeks, it was a full-tilt media wildfire, getting hotter with every passing day and bringing in everybody. Joseph Bennion, of course, pursued it like a rabid bear, the TV media, the papers – especially the *Seattle Post-Intelligencer*, who were on the SPD like coke dealers backstage at a Stones concert – wanting to know why the woman identified as Justine Manx from Shadow's Fall had neither been questioned nor arrested in connection with the girl's murder. Local citizen groups and churches started demanding action and, of course, there was Zuron fuelling and fanning the flames from the other side of the fence. He added to his 'worst case scenarios' with a few *'what ifs'*, as in all we'd need is for a vampire to be cornered or, worse yet, arrested, jailed and have his or her cellmates on-hand when the sun rose to witness their screaming deaths and decomposition. Then, in the third week, the local Lycan community made *their* concerns known, knowing that if we were outed they wouldn't be far behind. But what finally drove the knife in and twisted it was a communique to the Parliament from the Vatican."

"Ouch," Fallon grimaced.

"Ohhh yeah. The Treaty of Oradea. A not-so-subtle reminder of the condition that so long as we remain invisible – aka non-existent to the general Human populace – the Church's hunters would remain inactive. *That* alone was enough to have the Powers That Be pissing their Pureblood pantaloons. It sparked an emergency session with the Lords-Elders Collective and a vote, which overruled certain parties who were patrons of Pashet's clubs. And the word went out - Pashet's organisation was to be stopped, by any means necessary. And, because he had been the first one to speak out against it, Zuron was appointed to get the job done." Kane checked his cigar, saw it had gone out from lack of attendance and set it back in the ashtray.

"Now we get to the part that *has* to stay in the box," he told Fallon. "Call it fate, destiny, whatever. I wound up in Seattle when the shit was still poised to hit the fan – sometime after the V-word first showed up in the Post-Intelligencer, as part of a classic PI job that started out in Reno, chasing down a rich Pureblood's run-around wife. The job was finished, and I stuck around. I'd been in town for two or three days, in fact, when Zuron tracked me down through my answering service, caught me up on the situation and then invited me to sit in on a meeting between himself and Pashet. My first inclination was to say no, couldn't figure out why he'd want *me* there since, at that point, Pashet was more than likely going to fly into one of her homicidal tantrums and shoot anyone and everything in sight. But then he said that inviting me was *her* idea, which I have to admit was both intriguing and scary as hell.

"We were both brought in through the front and escorted to Pashet's inner sanctum through the lobby, which was a lot smaller back then and pretty much filled up – three or four groups here and there. One of the groups featured someone I flagged on instantly. A youngish looking female turnblood with short black hair and big violet eyes. Eyes, I couldn't help noticing, that tracked me like a radar until Zuron and I were out of sight. Which is where I'll leave this for now.

"Suffice to say, for all intents and purposes, she's supposed to be dead. I am one of two – now three, counting you – who knows she isn't. Her name, back then at least, was Holly, and we couldn't have taken Pashet's operation down without her. I haven't seen her since, nor do I have any idea where she is. But I do know someone who does and *can* reach her. We set it up that way in case she ever needed to contact me again. If there *is* someone out there picking up where Pashet left off, maybe she knows things that can help you. I'll get the ball rolling, but it will be up to her whether she wants to talk to you or not."

"Fair enough," Fallon said. "And I appreciate it, amigo." He thrust out a hand and Kane took it, shaking firmly.

"Now," the older vampire grinned. "it's been a while. Too long, in fact, since the two of us were free to get together. What say we take advantage of it? Dinner? Drinks at Club Anubis? Some scintillating female company?"

"Lead the way," Fallon pulled his cell out of his pocket. "Let me just check for messages."

The screen lit up, displaying six missed calls from Rowan's number. Fallon frowned and dialled his voicemail service. The shrill female voice it had recorded was unrecognisable to him and he shared a look with Kane, who could hear every word.

"OH MY GOD! This is Rowan's investigator guy, right? Where are you? Please, quick! Someone grabbed her off the street. I saw it from the window. She dropped her cell. Call me!"

The second voicemail was recorded a few minutes later.

"It's Lainie again! Did you get my message? Why haven't you called? Should I call the police? Rowan's in trouble!"

The third and fourth contained similar messages, the voice of Rowan's friend growing more and more strident. While the cell was against his ear, it bleeped to notify him of an incoming text. Fallon cut off the voicemail and opened his messages.

UNKNOWN NUMBER
Chinook Beach Park. ASAP

Attached to the message was a picture. Rowan -arms raised above her head and held by the hands of an unseen male, legs splayed and displaying the tiny pair of panties she wore, breasts full and bare. Her head lolled sideways, and her eyes were closed. She clearly wasn't conscious and closer inspection showed her wrists were bound with duct tape.

He closed the image and raised his head to look at Kane.

"I have to go."

CHAPTER FIVE

Rowan woke up shivering, legs drawn up to her chest, arms clamped around her knees and tape binding her wrists together. She tried to move and whimpered. Her head hurt, her body hurt. In fact, *everything* hurt.

She waited for the pain to ebb and then tried again, carefully lifting her arms up and over her knees, so she could straighten her legs. The small movement had her gasping, sucking air in big gulps from forcing her cold seized muscles to change position, but she pushed through until she had her legs down. It took another few minutes of sobbing breaths to reach up and clutch at the hood covering her face with frozen fingers and pull it off her head.

Blinking, her surroundings came into focus and Rowan realised she was alone, naked (or might as well have been) and outdoors. She knew her hands were bound together, the tape biting into her wrists and making her fingers numb. Further inspection found her ankles and knees had also been bound, taped so tightly she would have struggled to peel it off if her fingers had been working properly.

Panic rose. She couldn't breathe, her heart was racing, and a choked cry forced its way from her throat.

Calm down, she told herself. *Breathe slow. In through the nose . . . out through the mouth. There's no-one here and you're not dead . . . at least, not yet.* She continued whispering to herself, while her eyes darted back and forth, trying to see more than vague shapes in the faint light.

She studied the tape around her wrists, then raised her arms and tried to bite through it, to no avail.

"Come *on,* you can do this!" Teeth chattering, she tried again.

The tape had been wrapped around her wrist so many times, and was so thick, she couldn't tear even the slightest bit out of it. Sniffing and fighting the desire to cry, Rowan tried to lift herself to her feet, only to fail at that too – her feet and legs too stiff, tired and numb to hold her steady and she landed back on her bottom with a yelp. Struggling back into a seated position, she froze when the roar of a car engine broke the silence.

Fighting rising terror, she watched as the headlights drew closer and closer until the car drew to a stop a few feet away. Rowan shrank back, trying to avoid the flood of light washing over her, and desperately attempted to shield her semi-naked body. She heard the car door open over the idling engine and the crunch of gravel beneath shoes as the driver walked toward her. Rowan was torn between keeping herself covered and scrambling backwards across the ground – no easy feat with her arms and legs bound.

Hands reached out to grasp her arms and panic overwhelmed her. She threw herself backwards, rolled onto her knees and struggled to rise to her feet, sobbing in frustration when her legs refused to hold her weight and sent her crashing back down to the floor, skinning her palms as she landed.

"Hold still." Hands caught her again, lifted her off the ground and, ignoring her futile attempts to escape, carried her toward the car.

"No . . . no . . . no," she chanted, her voice rising with each repetition. "Let me go!"

Rowan twisted and turned until her captor almost dropped her. She heard him mutter an exasperated curse, then felt the world spin as he threw her over his shoulder into a fireman's lift and swatted her bottom with the palm of his hand. "Stop struggling, Rowan!"

The familiarity of his voice finally broke through her panic and she stilled, her heart racing. "Mr . . . Mr Wylde?"

He grunted a response which could have been a yes and strode back toward the car, her stomach bouncing on his shoulder with each step.

The world tilted again when he swung her down and into the passenger seat of his Ferrari and crouched down beside the open door, revealing his face.

"Lean over," he instructed her, while he shrugged out of his jacket. Rowan tilted forwards and he dropped the jacket around her shoulders. "I'm going to free your hands, okay?"

She gave a jerky nod and a knife appeared in his hand. He sliced through the tape, peeled it off her wrists and threw it to one side. With gentle fingers he lifted first one hand, then the other, and turned her arms this way and that as he checked for bruises and broken skin. Once he was satisfied she hadn't been marked, he cupped his hands around hers and lifted them to his mouth to blow warm air across her fingers.

"You're freezing," he said in response to the question in her eyes. He told her to flex her fingers, and squeeze her hands into fists, then nodded. "Alright, let's get the rest off you and get moving." He bent his head and made quick work of the tape around her knees and ankles, sprang upright, slammed the passenger door shut and headed around to the driver's side.

Once he was settled behind the wheel, Fallon cast a worried glance at Rowan, who sat shivering in the seat beside him.

"Rowan . . ."

She didn't respond, staring fixedly forward through the window. He reached out to touch her arm and she jerked, startled, and turned her head to look at him.

"You need to—" he stopped and shook his head. "Never mind, I'll do it." Fallon leaned across and tugged his jacket closed around her, closed the buttons and pulled the seatbelt over and clicked it into place, then gunned the engine and drove out of the parking lot.

~*~

"You can leave your stuff in here." Fallon opened the door to a decidedly masculine-looking bedroom and held it open for Rowan to enter.

It was quite ironic, he thought to himself as he watched her look around. The first time he brought a woman back to his own private domain and it wasn't for fun and games of the sexual variety.

"This is your room?" The question was the first time she'd spoken since he'd found her. She stood beside his bed, one hand stroking the cover, her eyes on him.

Fallon nodded, relieved she'd finally said something.

"It's a big house. There must be another room I can use."

Fallon masked a frown, disliking the exhaustion and fear he could hear in her voice. He was used to her being emotive, quick and sharp. This quiet tired little mouse he was seeing didn't fit with what he'd learned about her.

"There are a lot of rooms, but this is the only one I can guarantee your safety in," he told her. "Anyone wanting to get to you is going to have to get through the whole house to reach you."

"But where will you sleep?"

An innocent enough question, but one that made Fallon smile, nonetheless. "The couch in the sitting room pulls out into a bed. I'll sleep there."

"You don't have to give up your bed. I can take the couch."

"The whole point is that in the unlikely event someone *does* make it through the house and get up here, they have to go through *me* to get to *you* – not the other way around," Fallon pointed out gently.

"Oh . . . right . . . of course." A blush turned her cheeks pink and she dropped her eyes to study the bed cover.

"Come on, let me give you a quick tour." He motioned for her to precede him out of the room and resisted the urge to wrap an arm around her shoulder as she brushed past him. "As you can see, there's the main living area; TV, DVD player, stereo are all workable via the universal remote on the coffee table. There's a small kitchenette through that door," he pointed to a door on the left of the huge TV screen. "The bathroom is through the other door. "Another pointing finger, this time to the right.

"I need to call Lainie and let her know I'm okay," she interrupted him, spinning around.

"I sent her a text and let her know I'd found you and that I had you with me." He paused, then waved a hand toward the kitchen. "Are you hungry?"

She shook her head. "I'm sorry."

"For what?"

"Disrupting your evening . . . again."

Fallon smiled faintly. "I'm getting used to it."

He watched as she turned back to his bedroom. She was still wearing his jacket, and it emphasised how much smaller than him she was with the way the sleeves hung down over her fingers, and the hem fell just above her knee. He dismissed the sudden surge of possessiveness and told himself he had no business liking the idea of her wearing his clothes and being wrapped in his scent.

On the surface she appeared calm and in control, the only hint of distress being the periodic clenching of her fingers into fists and, as he watched her fingers curl once more, he couldn't help but step up behind her and settle his hands onto her shoulders. She tensed beneath his touch.

"It's been a rough couple of days, why don't you get some sleep? You're safe here." He wanted the firecracker back, a selfish thought possibly, but honest.

Rowan leaned back against him briefly before straightening and nodding tiredly. "Yes, okay." She headed back into the bedroom and shut the door behind her.

For a long moment, Rowan stood gazing down at the bed, but not really seeing it. She thought back over the evening. Who had grabbed her? Was it connected to Eden's disappearance? She didn't believe it was a coincidence, that was a certainty. She raised her hand and rubbed her forehead. Not surprisingly, she could feel a headache coming on. With a sigh, she let Fallon's jacket slide from her shoulders and drop to the floor, opened the bag he'd left on the bed and pulled out a pair of flannel pyjamas. Once she was dressed, Rowan slid between the sheets and lay her head on the pillow. She thought sleep would have been easily found, but instead, she spent the next hour tossing and turning uneasily. Part of it must have been sleeping in someone else's bed – if she buried her face into the pillow, she could smell *him* – Mr Wylde . . . Fallon – a mixture of expensive cologne, with undertones of a dark, earthy scent that weaved around her. Another part was fear. Fear of closing her eyes and waking up back in the parking lot.

At some point she must have drifted off because she woke with a start, jerking upright into a seated position, one hand over her own mouth to stop the scream that was lodged in her throat. She slipped out of bed, padding across the floor and out into the sitting room. The wall lights had been dimmed down, so there was just enough light to see the couch had been pulled out into a bed and, her mind still reliving the remnants of her nightmare, Rowan made her way over to it and perched on the edge of the mattress.

The movement woke Fallon, who rolled over. His eyes flicked over her form, seated stiffly with her hands folded neatly on her lap and he wondered what had brought her to his bed. His lips twitched into a smile when his eyes registered the pink elephants on her pyjamas – clearly, it hadn't been seduction.

"Is everything okay?" he asked and saw her stiffen further.

"Yes . . . no . . . I don't know!"

He leaned up on one elbow. "Can't sleep?"

She shook her head but didn't speak.

"It's no surprise after what happened. Do you want to talk about it?" Another head shake. He studied her rigid form – the set of her shoulders, the shadows under her eyes, and the fingers twisting in her lap. "You can stay there, if you like," he offered, abruptly. "This bed is big enough for six." He didn't wait to see what she did, simply rolled back over and lay with his back to her . . .

. . . and woke up what felt like minutes later but was more likely a few hours to find Rowan had taken him up on his offer. Not only was she in his bed, she was burrowed against him, her head buried into the crook of his neck and one arm wrapped around his waist. He ran a palm lightly down her flannel covered back and vented a soft chuckle.

Rowan stirred at the sound, mumbled something unintelligible and moved closer, her lips brushing across his throat, and Fallon felt his own body stir in response and shifted slightly. Rowan tensed, eyes flying open and she jerked backwards, unsuccessfully trying to untangle her limbs from his.

"Stop wriggling and go back to sleep," he told her.

Her hand came into direct contact with the evidence of his arousal and she gasped.

Fallon laughed. "Rowan, you crawl into my bed in the early hours, wrap yourself around me like a second skin, then start rubbing yourself against me. I'd have to be dead to stop myself reacting to that."

"I know . . . I know! I'm sorry!" Her face went red as the memory of his mouth on hers blazed in her mind, and she knew he thought about it too when his eyes dropped to her lips. "If you let go of me, I'll move," she mumbled, dipping her head to avoid looking at him.

"Or . . ." he waited until her eyes lifted. "We could go back to sleep."

"I can't. It's after seven. I should get ready to go to class."

That statement brought Fallon to a seated position, tumbling Rowan onto the sheets next to him. With a speed that took her by surprise, he had turned and was poised above her before she could draw a breath, arms braced either side of her shoulders.

"You can't go anywhere until we find out who took you last night."

"I can't just drop off the face of the earth," she protested.

"Rowan, you were *attacked* last night. You can't act like it didn't happen. Ring campus and tell them you're ill. Do the same with the diner."

"And then what am I supposed to do? If I hide, doesn't that mean they've won?"

"No," Fallon shook his head. "It means we take the time to go over what we know. But I can't do that if I have to spend all my time shadowing you while you're playing at a normal life." He couldn't tell her that it wasn't *possible* for him to shadow her during daylight. He stretched out an arm, picked up his cell phone and held it in front of her. "Call them now."

Their eyes clashed, and Fallon realised he'd got his wish – the firecracker was back. The atmosphere thickened between them and Fallon thought she was going to refuse, then she lifted a hand and snatched the phone from him. First, she rang her campus and left a message to let her tutors know she was feeling unwell and would not be back for a couple of days, then she repeated the process with the diner. She ended the call and glared up at Fallon, who still loomed over her.

"Now what?" she demanded.

"Now?" Fallon repeated silkily, and his eyes dipped down to watch her tongue snake across her lips. "Now we go back to sleep for a few more hours." He lifted himself off her and moved to the side.

Rowan didn't think she *could* fall back to sleep, but she rolled onto her side, her back to Fallon and tried to slow her rapidly beating heart. Fallon propped his head up on one hand and watched her. When she showed no sign of relaxing after ten long, silent minutes he gave in to temptation, reached out, wound an arm around her waist and tugged her backwards.

"What are you doing?" Her tense question was immediate.

"The way I see it, three times now when you've been in trouble, I was the first person on your speed dial."

"I didn't call you last—" he nipped her earlobe, breaking her concentration and her heartbeat sped up again.

"Hush, I'm talking," he chided, his breath warm against her cheek. "This morning I woke up to find you trying to wear me like a coat. That suggests you feel safe with me, so you might as well relax." He moved both of them around until he was satisfied with the way they were lying – his longer body curved around hers, with his arm draped across her stomach. "I've only had a few hours' sleep, so let's see if we can grab a little more, okay?"

~*~

When Rowan next awoke, she knew where she was immediately. She could feel one of Fallon's arms beneath her cheek and the other was still wrapped around her waist. She felt warm and drowsy and, yes, safe – *there*, she admitted it to herself – so burrowed deeper beneath the covers and then froze. She was pretty confident, she thought in sleepy embarrassment, that what she felt wedged between her buttocks was *not* a gun.

"What time is it?" Fallon's voice was a husky whisper close to her ear.

"I don't know," she replied and cursed the breathlessness in her voice. She felt Fallon move, and knew he'd realised how intimately he was touching her. Twisting round to face him, she found he'd shifted onto his back, an arm curved beneath his head. "It's got be at least noon." The arm under her cheek flexed and she felt his hand settle onto her shoulder and draw her closer.

"Still early, then."

"Noon is hardly early," she protested and sat up, needing to distance herself from the warmth of his body. "You can sleep the day away if you want. I can't lie still any longer." With that said, she swung up and out of the bed. Fallon watched her make her way across the room to the kitchenette, then grunted something that sounded suspiciously like '*suit yourself*' before rolling onto his stomach and going back to sleep.

Rowan paused in the doorway and looked back at him. He lay face down, one arm tucked beneath the pillow his head was resting on, black hair loose. Her eyes caught on what looked like scars crisscrossing the broad expanse of his back and she wondered what he'd been caught up in to receive them, then shook her head. It wasn't her business. She retreated to the kitchen to make coffee and find food.

~*~

Fallon woke abruptly a couple of hours later when his phone dinged once, twice, then a third time. He leaned across to pick it up and the pictures which greeted him sent him upright, all traces of sleep gone. He swore profusely, and dialled Koo's cell to summon her up to his suite.

Throwing the sheets to one side, he stood up and reached for his pants. Pulling them on, he folded the linen away and turned the bed back into a couch, then headed into the kitchen to find Rowan. The kitchen was empty and silent. Fallon stood in the centre of the room, head tilted, listening, and he followed the faint sounds he heard to his bedroom and raised his hand to rap on the door.

Before his fist made contact with the wood, he heard the main door to his suite open. He sighed and turned to face Koo.

"I need a drink. Coffee . . ." he shook his head. "Second thoughts, make that rum."

"Coming right up boss, take a load off," Koo said cheerfully, waved toward the couch and made her way to the lowboy cabinet across the room. Fallon took her suggestion and plopped down in a position that gave him an easy view of his bedroom, vaguely aware of his associate's ministrations as he mulled over recent events – specifically, the young woman in his bedroom.

He jumped, startled, when Koo returned to place the bottle and glasses – actually, she just let them drop – onto the coffee table's surface with a clatter.

"You're out of rum. You and Eayann killed off the last of it before he left for Ireland. How about Scotch?"

"Whatever. Just so long as there's a little less talk and a lot more pour," he groused.

Koo inclined her head, biting back a grin as she poured both glasses and slid his along the table. "What life or death matter had me dashing up here before breakfast?"

Rowan chose that moment to open the door and exit the bedroom, a towel and toiletries over one arm. She threw a narrow-eyed look toward them both when she spotted Koo pouring drinks before disappearing into the bathroom.

Koo picked up the glass she'd slid closer to Fallon and held it out. "You brought a *woman* here?" she gaped at him in shock. "Please tell me that wasn't the look of a jealous lover?"

Fallon pinched the bridge of his nose between forefinger and thumb, accepted the drink with a grunt of acknowledgement, then dropped his head back against the sofa's headrest.

"No" he sighed. "It's . . . never mind." He waved a dismissive hand and took a quick swallow.

"Wait!" Koo froze with her own glass halfway to her mouth. "Is *that* the girl whose sister is missing?"

"Something went down in her apartment a few nights ago, then another something last night. Two something's actually. To be honest, the past week has been . . . *gnarly*," he explained, took another swallow of his drink and gave Koo a thumbnail recap of what had been happening. After finishing, he knocked back the remainder of his drink and slid the glass back to Koo for a refill.

"I think blowing away that asshole in her apartment affected her more than I realised . . . or maybe it was the kidnapping and abandonment," he confessed.

"Ya think?" Koo asked.

"Alright, okay. So, I'm a little clueless sometimes!" Fallon said. "I'm a vamp—" he cut himself off, lowering his voice and threw a self-conscience glance at the bathroom door, "a vampire and a merc, not Dr. Phil."

"You were human once, Fallon," Koo turned to face him. "Or are you so drenched in blood and violence that you've forgotten how it affects normal people?"

"And *you* know what my life was like before I was turned," he countered. "I was a pirate. The *son* of a pirate. I *grew up* around pirates." He threw his arms up in disgust. "As far as *I* knew, killing people was normal."

"Excuses and you know it."

They both fell silent as the girl in question opened the bathroom door and returned to the bedroom briefly, clearly having forgotten something. Both tracked her movements to and from the bedroom until the bathroom door closed behind her again.

"That girl needs 'trouble' tattooed across her ass," Fallon muttered.

"Her ass?"

Fallon's grin was crooked. "It's a nice ass."

Koo shook her head. "So, what was that life or death thing?"

Fallon's amusement fell away, and he tossed his cell phone into Koo's lap. "Check the photos I just received."

Koo opened the images and sucked in a breath. "That's the girl, right? Who's the other one?"

"Her sister," Fallon gave Koo a grim smile. "Whoever snatched Rowan last night is the same one who has her sister. And they're taunting us with the information."

"Rowan?" Koo questioned, sharply. "You're on first name terms?"

"At least those photos give us proof of life," Fallon ignored Koo's question. "Which means we're looking for a living girl, not a dead body."

~*~

In the bathroom, Rowan had stripped off her clothes and lay in the bathtub, water up to her chin and her eyes closed. She didn't know who the woman she'd spied waiting on Fallon was. The way he'd been sprawled on the couch allowing her to pour and serve his drinks like he was master of all he surveyed had irritated her, and she had embraced that feeling. It was better than torturing herself with thoughts of how the bullets had sounded when they'd hit Floyd, or the thud as the body hit the floor, or the smell of the hood that had been over her head . . . or how it had felt when Fallon kissed her, or the way his warmth and scent had wrapped around her when she had slept in his arms. She physically shied away from *that* train of thought, sloshing water over the side of the bath.

The last few days had been non-stop crazy, she thought. What had started out as a simple demand for answers had turned into a psychotic nightmare. In the year since Eden had disappeared, she'd hit dead end after dead end and, if the police hadn't closed the case when they did, she would have soon reached the point where she had nowhere left to look. But with finding out they'd stopped looking, followed by receiving the contact number for Fallon, the whole situation had taken a dramatic turn – one she hadn't expected.

Sighing, she pushed herself upright in the water and washed her body, then her hair before pulling the plug and wrapping herself in a large towel.

~*~

"So, is that why you brought her here? Because she's got a nice ass?" Koo asked Fallon.

"She's in danger. Whoever is behind this broke into her apartment *while she was there*, trapped her with a dead body, organised having someone move in next door to her *and* stripped her naked and left her in the middle of a deserted parking lot," Fallon replied. "Then there's the photos. Proof her sister is still alive. Taunting me with the fact."

"Even so, we have safe houses, Fallon. She could have stayed in one of them."

"I needed to move her quickly. Here made the most sense."

"Obviously you and I have different definitions of the word *sense*," Koo said, pointedly. "Fallon . . . she's *Human.*"

"Do you see a white cane and seeing-eye dog anywhere?" Fallon countered. "Yes, I *know* she's human. And yes, I also know how risky it is bringing her here. But there was a greater risk that she was being watched and we could have been followed. Taking her anywhere *but* here was too dangerous. I made a judgement call."

"With which head?"

"Excuse me?"

"Oh, don't twitch those eyebrows at me and give me that 'how-dare-you-accuse-me' look," Koo chuckled. "I saw that look on your face when she came through the room." Her voice softened as she reached out to touch his cheek. "Fallon, she's a very pretty girl and *Lord Buddha* knows you are a lot more human than you care to admit. I can understand it to a point."

"And I'm waiting to hear what the *point* is," Fallon responded flatly.

Koo nodded. "You know what it is. You're on a slippery slope here. At the tamest, she'll find out what you are – and she *will*, you know that. On the other end, she could get you – *both of you* – killed."

"I'm hungry." He deliberately side-tracked the issue. He could deny he knew what Koo was saying, could say he wasn't attracted to the redhead currently ensconced in his bathroom, and he *could* agree that bringing her to his private home hadn't been the most logical choice. But *then* he'd have to admit that pulling into the parking lot and finding her mostly-naked and terrified had released emotions he'd long buried. He would have to admit to the demanding desire to hunt down the men who'd done it and kill them, and it was only the driving need to make sure she was safe that had kept him from starting the hunt right there.

He rose to his feet. "I'll be back. Keep an eye on her."

At any other time, Fallon would have voiced his usual displeasure, either outwardly or to himself, on the tiresome inconvenience of accessing his attic office. In light of recent events, however, he couldn't deny its location, and far from easily noticeable entrance, couldn't be more advantageous.

Its location, amongst other things, had been Koo's suggestion. One point of specific strategic importance – it was the place where he kept a personal blood supply in a modified freezer unit (in addition to the cache hidden in a secret compartment behind the refrigerator in the second-floor office) capable of storing up to a full months' supply of blood. *It never hurts to have a spare . . . or some place that is exclusively yours*, she'd said. Dead right on both counts.

He was just starting on the second bag when his cell rang. Fallon switched it over to the loud-speaker function and sat it atop the freezer.

"Fallon here. Speak."

"You're in luck, amigo," Kane's voice sounded through the speaker. "The lady's in a dating mood."

Fallon couldn't help but smile at his friend's choice of terminology. Understandable, however. The technology to track and sometimes monitor cell phone conversations was out there and the people he was dealing with could, conceivably, have that capability.

"It's been a while since she dated, and she's a little nervous," Kane continued. "Got a pen and paper handy?"

Fallon moved quickly to his desk and collected both. "I'm ready."

"Capitol Hill. Cherry Street Coffee House. The clock's ticking and she's looking forward to spending time with *you*," Kane said and cut the connection.

Koo was in pretty much the same position when he returned.

"Keep Rowan here, keep her safe," he told her. "I have something to deal with." As he spoke, he scanned the room. The bathroom door was slightly ajar, which made it easier to determine Rowan no longer occupied it. He crossed to the bedroom door and rapped loudly on the wood.

"I need you out here, Rowan . . . *now!*"

There was a moment of silence, followed by the clang of the door's inner lock and a slight creaking sound as the door eased open. Fallon stepped away, moving back into the room to allow the younger woman to enter.

"First of all," he began, gesturing as he spoke. "Rowan, this is Kate . . . Koo. Koo, this is Rowan. I'm going out. *You*," he nodded to Rowan, "stay here with Koo, understand? And here means *here*. Not back at your apartment, or the diner, or your friend's place. *Here!* Got it?"

"Right here?" Rowan pointed down at the spot where she stood. "Or am I allowed to sit down over there? Or go to bed? Or shall I just take root here until you come back?"

Her sarcastic retort caught Fallon off-guard, and in that brief moment Koo nearly lost it, covering her chuckle by coughing into her cuffed hand.

"Sit, sleep, grow a *fucking sunflower* out of your ass for all I care. So long as you *don't leave this house!*" he fired back, then turned his attention to Koo. "Our defences should keep you two safe up here. You might want to give the O'Bannions a heads-up downstairs. Nobody gets in after I leave. If need be, they can fall back here. If things get too hairy, call Kane . . . or Taz."

"Aye, Cap'n," Koo quipped, throwing him a comic military salute.

"Did we go back in time a couple hundred years while I was bathing?" Rowan asked. "Are you expecting a siege? Defences . . . falling back? You sound like a bad dark-ages movie."

Koo laughed before catching herself. "S-sorry," she choked out at the dark look Fallon threw at her.

Fallon wrapped a hand around Rowan's upper arm and pulled her back into the bedroom.

"Rowan, this is serious."

"You think I don't know that?" she snapped. "After yesterday, I can't imagine looking at anyone I know and not wondering if they're really who they say they are. How do I know I can trust *you?*"

That was the moment Fallon realised Rowan wasn't angry, she was *scared*. Terrified, in fact. And the barbed comments and aggressive stance she was displaying was an attempt to deflect the shock of the past few nights, and his own posture softened. He relaxed his grip on her arm, pressed a forefinger under her chin and lifted her head.

"You can trust me, you know you can," he told her softly, holding her eyes with his. "You can trust Koo. But I *need* you to promise me that you'll stay here tonight."

"Fine! Yes, I won't go anywhere."

"Good."

For a moment, one that rapidly approached awkwardness, neither moved or broke eye contact. Fallon still held her chin with a finger, her face tilted up to within inches of his, while he waged an inward battle. The slightest move forward was all it would have taken . . . just a nudge.

"Good!" Fallon repeated, breaking the spell. "I . . . gotta . . . in here," he muttered, gesturing to something over her shoulder before he skirted around her.

Rowan had already exited (and out of habit he had checked) by the time he ran through the wardrobe security protocols to access his arsenal. He exchanged his Smith & Wesson for a Glock 17, grabbed a few spare clips, and let the wardrobe close of its own accord as he strode away.

~*~

Choice of transport – a black 1967 Ford Mustang Fastback. About as inconspicuous as Fallon's collection allowed. And, in light of the current situation and taking into account the night's little foray into the city could get – to put it mildly – *messy*, the last thing he wanted to do was call attention to himself. Or, at least, as little attention as possible.

Fallon gave himself three blocks to test the waters, remaining relatively within his own neighbourhood. He wasn't sure at first, but a couple of right turns, a quick left and a slow cruise along West Highland Drive and, within seconds, the same cloud-grey Lincoln Town Car tooled in behind him. There were two heads visible in his rear-view mirror and maybe two more in the back seat. Fallon pulled into a curb near one of the sidewalk paths leading up to the Kerry Park overlook section and allowed the car to roll past him.

Only one in the rear seat, he confirmed to himself. Still, two too many for simple surveillance, which left only one purpose: they were head-hunters and *his* head was the prize.

It wouldn't take them long to circle and return, he knew. A quick check of his watch showed the time was 8:15PM, forty-five minutes before the coffee shop closed its doors for the night.

"No time for this shit," Fallon muttered. He checked first to make sure the Town Car was out of sight, then shut off the engine and waited.

A lot depended upon their level of experience. The average thug – Human or Vampire – would make a U-turn and approach from the front, going for the simple drive-by hit. But pros would drive around the block, first reconning the area for potential witnesses and police patrol cars; coming at their prey from his blindside – the rear. When the passage of five minutes showed no sign of them down the block, Fallon knew how the scene would play out.

The headlights appeared briefly in his rear window, then went dark. They approached slowly, carefully. Fallon waited until the car was twenty feet away, then popped the hood release and casually exited the Mustang. Unable to see him, they would have to assume he was occupied, bent over face-first in the engine. Following standard procedure, two would emerge and approach the front of the Mustang from opposite sides; the third, the driver, would remain behind the wheel, ready for a quick get-away.

Pros, Fallon smiled to himself. Evidently not professional enough. Or maybe they were *too* professional – too many jobs, too many successes, over too long a time. In any case, they made three fatal mistakes.

The first was that the hitters chose knives – Special Forces combat daggers, opting for the silent, close-up kill. The operative words being *close-up* – close in this instance. They came abreast of the Mustang's front end simultaneously, blades pointed and ready, and froze. Both expected their target to be bent over, unsuspecting, vulnerable and defenceless. Neither thought to look on the ground, parallel to the front bumper.

Fallon sprang up into a crouch and shattered the kneecap of the man on the sidewalk side with a powerful hammer fist strike, which threw the hitter off-balance and forward. As the man's body dropped, Fallon continued upward, burying one of his throwing stars into the hitter's forehead. Fallon spun and flung three more stars at hitter number two, whose reflexes caused him to lurch away from the commotion – away from the car and out into the open. The first star found purchase in its back-pedalling target's chest, two inches short of dead centre. The second thudded home in his heart, and number three smack-dab between the eyes.

Which brought Fallon to the third hitter and their second and third vital mistakes.

Their second mistake was the driver had parked much too close to the Mustang's rear, giving him a very obstructed view of his companions' activities. He was also much too preoccupied with the body that had fallen into the street and failed to notice Fallon's swift approach on the Town Car's passenger side.

Their third mistake was leaving the passenger side door unlocked. An understandable mistake as they had thoroughly expected to return to the vehicle after fulfilling their contract. Unfortunate, however, for their comrade who, in the man's defence, had the presence of mind to, at least, attempt to draw his own weapon when the door was jerked open and Fallon slid into the front seat beside him.

A quick punch to the bridge of his nose dazed him long enough for Fallon to extract the man's gun – a 22 Ruger – and jam the barrel into the man's skull through his right eye socket.

It was 8:35PM by the time he'd piled the bodies of hitters one and two in the Town Car's back seat, while swearing beneath his breath profusely, and gotten underway again. At 8:47PM he was seated at one of the tables farthest from the coffee house's windows. A tiny Asian girl in black slacks, apron and a t-shirt emblazoned with the restaurant's logo arrived within seconds, her demeanour hinting at having worked a shift she couldn't wait to end.

"If you want food, you have about five minutes before the grill shuts down," she informed him.

"Coffee, I guess. French Roast, black," Fallon replied. "Actually, I was supposed to meet someone here."

Her expression brightened a notch. "Oh . . . *Oh!* Is your name Mallon?"

"Fallon," he corrected her.

"Hold on a second," she zipped away, going to the end of the restaurant's L-shaped counter and to the cashier's station, then disappeared below it for an instant. In a minute or so she was back, carrying a standard-sized white envelope.

"There was a girl in here earlier. She showed me a picture of you and tipped me a hundred dollars to give you this." She placed the envelope on the table. "You want that coffee in a regular or to-go cup, sir?"

"To go," he managed to get out as the envelope began to ring. Opening it, he found a prepaid cell phone, a *burner*. With a quick look around him, he thumbed the TALK button. "This isn't exactly what I was expecting."

"Are you sure nobody followed you?" a youngish female voice asked.

"Would you believe me if I said yes?"

The slash of silence was so lengthy Fallon thought she might have hung up. "You still there?"

"You didn't answer my question," she said.

"Yes, I'm sure."

"I can see you," she said. "The waitress is coming with your drink order . . ."

Sure enough, Fallon spotted the waitress as she exited the break in the counter and made her way to his table. He took out his wallet in anticipation of her arrival and placed a ten-dollar bill on the table.

"The change is yours," he told her after accepting his cup, and the waitress departed with a nod and a smile.

"Your move," he spoke into the phone.

"Pioneer Square. Park anywhere – I'll find you," she said, and the connection went dead.

~*~

Pioneer Square.

It was both ironic and nostalgically appropriate that, on the one hand, it was only a few blocks, less than a quarter mile away from the warehouse he and Rowan had been sucked into. And, on the other, it was the area where he, Eayann, and Koo had first settled when they came to Seattle. The first headquarters of what was then called *Wylde Company* was, in fact, just two blocks east of where he now sat. Of all the places in Seattle, mundane or historic, the Square was Fallon's favourite. He loved the area's look, its late nineteenth century brick and stone buildings, one of America's best surviving collections of Romanesque Revival style urban architecture. It brought back a slew of good memories. Two years after the entire area was destroyed in the Great Seattle Fire, it was a time of restructure, of reconnection and, strangely enough for the Vampire community, it was a time of reconciliation. When local Clans and Houses agreed to put aside long held grievances, mistrusts and feuds, and work together for the benefit of all.

It was a whole different place these days. As the town grew and spread outward, the Vampires flowed with it. The Square was now home to art galleries, internet companies, cafes, sports bars, nightclubs, and book stores. The very epitome of mainstream commercial.

A tap on the passenger side brought Fallon out of his reverie, and called his attention to what he, at first, thought was a shadow. The shadow, however, sprouted an arm, whose pale, glossy-tipped fingers again tapped the upper edge of the Mustang's window. Fallon stretched over and promptly popped the door lock, allowing his awaited guest to open the door and drop into the seat with all the grace of a leaf on the surface of a still pond. Neither spoke. Nor did the newcomer move for at least fifteen seconds, which gave Fallon the time to determine that the shadow effect had been caused by the heavy, hooded black cloak she wore. One that covered everything, save the fact she was barefoot.

Finally, a pair of hands appeared from within the cloak to undo the ties at the hood's bottom, then push the garment back and away from her. The girl beneath it sported a long, below-the-shoulder fall of tendril-thin dreadlock braids – honey-blonde – festooned with multi-coloured beads. Her lips, like her nails, were painted a deep, glossy black. And on her small lean frame was a black t-shirt and a short bib-front denim dress, also black. A slight departure from the description he'd been given earlier. With one exception. He noticed, as she turned her head to look at him, her eyes – deep, violet, enchanting.

"Holly," Fallon greeted her.

"Nobody's called me by that name in a long time." She moved so that her back rested in the small space between the seat's outer edge and the door and folded her legs beneath her. "That's not who I am anymore. But what does it matter, anyway?" She smiled, wryly. "How many of us still go by our birth names? I'll bet your name's not really Fallon Wylde."

"And you'd be right," he replied. Then, after a beat's pause. "So, if not Holly . . . what?"

"For now, Holly's good enough," she answered, shifting again and stretching out her left leg. "So, what did Kane tell you about me?"

"Not a lot," Fallon said. "I know you helped him take down the Manxes slave operation. But he didn't go into much detail."

"The way *he* put it, I was helping *all* our kind," Holly said, with a grin playing at the corners of her mouth. "I found out later that it was Lord Zuron who took credit for breaking up Bianca and Red Carousel."

"Red Carousel?"

"That's what they called it. It was kinda like a secret order fraternity, something like the Masons. And they had chapters all over the world. Bianca and her mother, Justine, were the leaders – top of the pecking order. They called themselves Matriarchs, and the ones below them – the guys – were reverends, bishops, cardinals. Just like the church." She tilted her head and smiled at Fallon. "Anyway, I told it all, *everything* I knew to Kane, and I guess he passed it on to Zuron." Another pause, and those violet eyes studied him. "We wouldn't be having this talk if that was all Kane told you."

"He told me what happened in '77," Fallon twisted in his seat to face her more comfortably and felt something in his jacket's inner-breast pocket. A reflexive pat and he remembered the pack of Marlboros he'd snagged from Kane's office. Holly's gaze zeroed in on them the minute the pack came into view and Fallon placed it within her reach.

"Thanks." She took one, leaning in as he flicked his Zippo. Both smoked in silence for a minute or so.

"If you don't mind my asking," Fallon started, rolling down his window for ventilation. "How'd you get *recruited*, if that's the right word?"

Holly's sudden, short laugh produced a gust of blue-white smoke. "It wasn't that simple. I was in school – college – UC Berkeley, eight months into my Freshman year. Christmas Eve, 1976. I was with my family – my mom and little sister, Jessica – in Petaluma, for the Christmas Break. Me and my best girl friend were going to a movie. I think it was A Star is Born – I had this thing back then for Barbra Streisand.

"I never got to see the movie. I left Karen in the lobby to go to the restroom and the next thing I know I'm waking up in bed, tied up, gagged and blindfolded. I didn't think there was anybody there with me, not for a long while. But when someone did come back, the blindfold was taken off, they set me up against the headboard, and there was this guy standing over me – black, muscular, lots of tattoos and a shaved head. He told me I had only two choices – either do what I was told, or they would kill me, and then kill my mom and sister. What could I do but give in?"

"And that's when they turned you?"

"Not right away," she said, rolling her window down to toss out the half-smoked cigarette. "Later, after a day or so, I think. They kept me drugged. I was in and out for most of it. Then he showed up – the guy in charge. I didn't see his face at first – he wore a leather mask that covered half his face. But he was dressed like a businessman – a suit and tie. He had an accent. I thought it was French in the beginning, but it kept changing; sometimes it sounded more German. He told me he had been watching me for a very long time. That I had this special quality he was looking for and, if I cooperated, life would be very good for me. He said I was going to work with him. I didn't have any choice there. But, as long as I did as I was told, my family would be safe. And *then* he turned me.

"They left me alone in the room for days. A whole week, maybe. Long enough, anyway, for me to be climbing the walls from the thirst. And then . . ."

"Let me guess," Fallon interrupted. "They brought in someone you could feed on. Someone you knew."

Holly nodded, turning her gaze toward the windshield. "It was Karen. They brought in my best friend. And . . . and I was *so* hungry. I didn't want to. I *tried* not to, but . . ." She left the sentence unfinished and, even in the car's dimly lit interior, Fallon could see the wetness in her eyes.

"I did anything, *everything* they ordered me to after that," she resumed. "I worked with a couple of others at first, until I learned how to *choose* . . . you know, pick up the right girls. Then they let me go solo. And I got pretty good at it. Though, I know now it's nothing to be proud of."

"Something changed, didn't it?" Fallon asked. "It turned you around."

"It was the one that caused the big blow up. Tracy . . ." she told him.

"Teresa Bennion."

"Normally, I didn't get any more involved than finding them, researching their background, and setting them up to be grabbed," she said. "But that time it was different. Don't ask me why 'cause I don't have a clue. I started talking to her. Though more like *she* tried to talk to *me*. And I tried my best to ignore her. She told me her name, where she grew up, and about her high school, her friends, her parents . . ."

"She turned herself into more than just an object," said Fallon.

"But that wasn't the worst of it," Holly swallowed loudly. "I was supposed to be gone, out on another run. And I don't know what it was that made me stick around. But I was there, inside their playroom the night she died. I heard her screaming and begging for her life. And I heard those bastards laughing and hooting like animals.

"You're right – it turned me around. I was never the same after that. I had to force myself to keep doing it, as much for myself as to protect my family.

"When things started getting crazy over Tracy's death, the Manxes acted like it was no big deal, business as usual. I started picking up whispers that they might have to start 'trimming the tree', getting rid of all the excess baggage. And, I might have been a new-turn . . . young . . . but I had brains enough to realise I wasn't that important in the grand scheme. So, I started looking for a way to escape. When Kane showed up one night with Zuron for a meeting with Bianca, I saw my opportunity.

"I remember hearing his name from back in '77. He was the Vampire investigator tracking us from California. I also heard that Bianca was his sire and that there was bad blood between them. There was something about him – something in his eyes – a lot different, *kinder* than I'd seen before. So, after he left the club, I followed Kane back to his hotel. I made a deal with him – immunity from what I was sure was about to go down in exchange for information on the Manxes and Red Carousel. And he agreed. I gave him names, dates, places; told him how the girls were chosen, how they were taken and transported; where they were kept; the whole nine yards. And the rest is history."

"He kept quiet about your involvement . . ." Fallon prompted.

"That wouldn't have been enough," she said. "Somebody in the bunch, as soon as things heated up, would've ratted me out. So, Kane helped fake my death. He gave me stake money and set me up with a friend that helped me disappear.

"Okay, I told you *my* story. What's yours?" She turned the tables. "Kane said I might be able to help *you*. With what?"

Fallon took a quick breath, collected his thoughts, then gave her a condensed, trimmed-down version of the past week, putting hard emphasis, however, on the description of the man in the glove and ruby-stud ear-clip.

"I should have known he'd slip through like a greased rat," Holly said when he'd finished. "Your Taylor. I knew him as Dorian. And I should know him very well. He was the one who recruited me . . . our crew boss. And he's the one who turned me.

"And it would make sense that he's still around. He took off just after Tracy was killed. Rumour said Bianca sent him off on some special job overseas."

"Tell me about him," Fallon said.

"He's old. Used to talk a lot about the French Revolution and how he was a servant to Marie Antoinette. But I also heard he was a soldier for one of the Caesars. He is one sick, twisted son-of-a-bitch. He doesn't just like giving out pain and torture, he gets off on watching other people watching it. You know, Fallon. You might want to consider this. The girl you're looking for *might* still be alive. Sometimes, Dorian would find one he liked and hold onto her for a while. But she's been gone a year, you say?" She waited for Fallon's nod. "By this time, then, *alive* is all she might be, if you get my meaning."

Not something her sister would be thrilled to hear. Or understand, for that matter.

"Thanks for agreeing to talk to me," Fallon said, holding out a hand across the space between them. Holly took it and nodded.

"Kane called, and I answered. I owe him," she replied. "Thanks to him, I've got a life. I'm with someone and she's good to me. She doesn't know anything about my past," she shrugged. "I'm happy."

In the spate of silence that followed her statement, Holly redonned her cloak.

"Can I drop you somewhere?" Fallon offered.

"Thanks, but my car is just around the corner." She opened the door, started to step out and stopped, twisting to look back at him. "If the guy you told me about *is* Dorian, take my advice. The Humans claim our kind don't have souls. In Dorian's case they're dead right. If you threaten him, he'll do whatever it takes, *anything*, to get to you. He'll go after the people you care about and kill them. So, do yourself a huge favour – if you get the opportunity, put the son-of-a-bitch down like the sick dog he is before he can get to you."

~*~

With no lights showing in the third-floor windows when he approached, Fallon was mildly surprised to hear voices coming out of the main room when he stepped off the elevator. Voices, laughter, and cheerful chatter immediately recognisable as coming from Koo and Rowan.

He entered the room and was greeted by the sight of the two women, curled either end of the couch, glasses of wine held loosely in their hands as they chatted animatedly. Rowan was in the middle of telling Koo a story about a drunk in the diner, her hands gesturing expansively, while she mimicked the customer's words and actions. Koo was snorting into her glass, begging Rowan to stop because she couldn't take a sip without choking.

Fallon stood, unnoticed for a few minutes, watching the pair of them. His eyes tracked over Rowan; the riotous tumble of flame-red hair framing her face, her lips curled into a mischievous smile and he licked his own lips, remembering the kiss they'd shared and felt his body harden at the memory. He cleared his throat and both women reacted instantly, twisting around.

"Koo, I need to talk to you," he said roughly, into the silence.

Placing her glass down onto the coffee table, Koo stood and followed Fallon out into the hallway.

Left alone, Rowan let the look of unconcern slip from her face and sighed. Wherever Fallon had been, she knew whatever he was sharing with Koo couldn't be good news – his face had been an expressionless mask while he'd waited for Koo to reach him, and good news didn't require a blank mask, Rowan knew.

Fallon and Koo had been gone ten minutes and Rowan was starting to doze off when her cell phone started to vibrate. Blinking her eyes, she scooped it up from the arm of the couch and peered at the screen. The number displayed was unknown, which made her frown, but she connected the call anyway.

"Hello?"

"Miss Walker," Rowan felt she should recognise the female voice, but couldn't quite place it. "We have your sister, Eden. If you meet with us, we'll bring her to you."

Any sleepiness Rowan had been feeling dropped away. "Where? When?"

"The warehouse you were sent to in Georgetown. As for when, as soon as you can get away. Come alone. If Wylde is with you, you won't see your sister alive."

"How will you know when I get there?"

"We'll know," the voice replied and disconnected the call.

Rowan was left staring at her phone, teeth worrying at her bottom lip. She should tell Fallon, she knew. But what if the woman was right? She would never see her sister again. She glanced at the door Fallon and Koo had exited through and rose to her feet. She couldn't take that chance. Rowan moved swiftly into the bedroom, grabbed her jacket and pushed her feet into a pair of sneakers, then eased open the bedroom window.

She had managed to balance on the small ledge beneath the window and was stretching across to reach the drainpipe when a hand clamped around her ankle and hauled her backwards.

"What the hell do you think you're playing at?" Fallon snarled as he yanked her unceremoniously back through the window and dumped her on the floor.

"I had to go out!" Rowan glared defiantly up at him.

"You agreed to stay put." Bending slightly, he pulled her to her feet, ignoring her attempts to break his grip. "If you needed to go out, what was wrong with using the door?"

"You were in the way of the door!"

"Oh, I see. You wanted to go out without me knowing . . . *again!*" His voice rose, along with his temper, and Rowan could see Koo hovering in the doorway, a concerned expression on her face. "Have you already forgotten about Floyd? How close he came to killing you? What about being grabbed and stripped?" He shook her, fingers biting into her arms and launched into a blistering account of what could have happened to her if she'd left the house without protection.

Rowan stopped listening to him after the first two minutes of his tirade, her eyes shifting sideways to look briefly at Koo over his shoulder before returning to his imposing figure. He towered over her, green eyes blazing with anger, mouth moving with words she didn't hear. Tension and anger radiated from his entire frame, and she could see Koo was nervously watching from the door way, but he didn't scare her. In fact, the more he snarled and snapped, the more her fingers itched to reach out and touch.

"Are you listening to me?" His aggressive snarl snapped her attention back to his voice and she glanced at Koo again before replying.

"Honestly? No, not really. After you mentioned murder, potential rape, kidnapping, blackmail and death for the third time, I switched off."

"You're . . . not . . . listening?" His voice went flat and the abrupt change in tone brought Koo further into the room.

"Fallon—" she said, her voice panicked.

"Get out." The words were softly spoken, but Koo blanched.

"I don't think—" she tried again.

"I said *get out*."

Rowan felt Koo's eyes on her and nodded. "It's fine, Koo."

Koo cast one last troubled glance at Fallon and retreated from the room, pulling the door closed behind her.

He was talking again, Rowan realised. No, not talking, *shouting* and Rowan knew she should be scared; scared of the fact Koo had looked worried; scared by how Fallon almost blazed with anger, and yet she wasn't. She found him fascinating, found herself drawn to his fire and was curious to know what it would take for him to go up in flames. Not really thinking about the action, she reached out and pressed a finger to his mouth.

"Stop yelling at me."

"Stop . . . yelling . . . ?" he repeated slowly, softly, and then his temper finally snapped. "You could have slipped and broken your neck!" he roared at her.

"But I didn't."

"That's not the point! You're acting like a child with no thought for the consequences."

"I'm hardly a child," she replied.

"No?"

"No."

"Then please tell me what *possessed* you to climb out of a *third storey* window?"

Rowan tilted her head and considered her options. Her thoughts drifted back to kissing him at her apartment and, before she even knew she was doing it, she stretched up the required inches and touched her lips to his.

Fallon responded to the feel of her lips against his by jerking backwards.

"Is *that* your plan? Kiss me until I forget about what you were doing?" he spat out.

Rowan adopted a hopeful expression. "Do you think it would work?"

"Rowan!" Exasperation and unwilling amusement at her attempt to diffuse the situation replaced his anger, and he raked a hand through his hair. "Where were you going?" he asked in a more reasonable tone.

Rowan sighed, then told him about the call she had received.

"And you believed her?" He shook his head when she didn't reply. "Rowan, they *won't* give her up. That was just a lure to get you somewhere unprotected."

"I couldn't let the chance go by," she argued. "Even the slightest possibility! I *had* to take it."

"At the risk of your own life?"

"Where did *you* go tonight?" she challenged. When he didn't answer, she nodded like it proved a point. "You won't tell me *anything!* You leave me with no choice but to risk my life to find answers. I told you from the outset, I'm not going to stop looking!"

"That was before—" he cut himself off, with an audible snap of his teeth.

"Before what?"

"Never mind, it doesn't matter." He waved a hand toward the door. "Go and show Koo you're still alive." He stepped to one side, so she could pass him. "Oh, and Rowan?"

As she slowed, he caught her arm, spun her around and into his arms. "If you're going to use seduction to bend me to your will, put some effort in," he said, and brought his mouth down on hers.

This kiss was nothing like the one they'd shared in her apartment. Unlike then, Fallon gave Rowan no opportunity to set the pace, he was in control from the start. He parted her lips for his tongue to invade and explore her mouth with an ease that startled her. It hinted at something stronger, *hungrier*, something more than just trying to make a point. And, as it continued, as she found herself wrapped in his arms, and his tongue stroked and tangled with hers, she found herself thinking '*I could get used to this*'. Her own arms lifted to wind around his neck, arching her spine when his hand pressed against the small of her back to fit her closer against him.

There was a soft knock at the bedroom door, followed by a louder one. With a growl, Fallon broke their contact, lifted his head and held her gaze for a moment before taking a few steps sideways to open the door. Koo stood framed just beyond it, one arm raised, and fist cocked, as though she'd been caught just short of knocking again. Her gaze touched Fallon momentarily, then quickly leapt beyond and behind him until they located Rowan. She didn't try to conceal the look of relief that jumped to her features.

"No, I didn't kill her," he declared impatiently.

"Good, because I had a thought," Koo said, making eye contact with both. "It seems   you're having a hard time keeping Rowan under lock and key . . ."

"I would say that's obvious," Fallon interjected.

Koo's gaze focused solely on Rowan for a moment, eyes dipping to look at her lips with a twitch of one eyebrow. "Look, before you came home, Rowan and I were talking. We're both starving. There's squat in the fridge or the cupboard, and I've been stuck here to the point of climbing the walls. Eayann's busy for at least another few days; Coop's in Australia, somewhere in the Outback where we couldn't find him, even if we wanted to, and I'm pulling triple duty 'til they return. I haven't seen my own apartment in—"

"Koo, get to the point, please," Fallon interrupted.

"My point is – why not kill two birds with one stone. Aduna's."

"Aduna's . . ." Fallon repeated, raising both eyebrows.

"What's Aduna's?" Rowan asked, eyes jumping back and forth between the two.

"Aduna's is –" *the Vampire Old Tongue word for 'gathering' – Right, Fallon, tell her that!* "-a place. Kind of a club, a watering hole for people in various fields of unique self-employment."

"It's a networking thing, more or less," Koo jumped in. "It's where people get together to eat, drink, swap stories, and catch up on gossip." Her eyes caught Fallon's on the word *gossip*. "I mean, it's a way to draw them out, too. We know they're watching and they'll follow. But even if they don't, chances are better than good they've already been there. I'd bet big money somebody there has heard something about them. That alone is enough reason to go."

"I'm not sure that's a good idea," Fallon said, slowly. "There's a certain hierarchy and code."

Koo waved a hand. "It'll be fine," she replied, airily.

Rowan listened to their exchange with interest. "What kind of code?"

They both looked at her. "Because of the type of clientele Aduna's attracts, it's developed a certain type of character," Fallon paused, thinking. "We work hard, and we play hard," he tried again.

"It's a BDSM club, Rowan," Koo explained, rolling her eyes at Fallon's hesitancy.

Rowan's eyes widened slightly. "I've never been to one of those. Eden used to hang out at a few though, Aduna's, you say? Maybe she went there."

Koo and Fallon exchanged a look. "That's a good point, actually. Maybe she did. Koo, why don't you help Rowan pick out something suitable to wear?"

CHAPTER SIX

"Where is this place, anyway?" Rowan voiced the first words spoken in the last five minutes. Specifically, since Fallon had turned the SUV off the relatively smooth pavement of Interstate Highway 5 and onto an unlighted dirt road that felt as though there were potholes every three feet or so.

"Not quite within the city limits of Renton," Koo answered from the front passenger seat. "Works out better for all concerned. These people like their privacy." She twisted to look past her seat's headrest with a grin. "You'll soon see why."

Moments later they rounded a corner onto a sudden smooth patch. Behind a sparsely wooded knoll, several feet to their left, they arrived at a left turn, which took them to a barrier-blocked gate. A pair of dark-suited guards, both armed, approached the vehicle from either side.

"Three," Fallon announced, after lowering his window. The guards on both sides peered in to confirm the count and nodded.

"Mr Wylde. It's been a while," said the guard on Fallon's side.

"Yes it has, Orson. Good to see you."

"Same here. Have a good one, sir," Orson replied, and made his way to the small booth a few feet away. A moment later the barrier rose, and Fallon took them through.

"Let's go over things again, so there are no screw ups," Fallon said as they continued on. "Never make eye contact with anyone."

Rowan nodded. "I speak only to you and Koo. I don't go anywhere with anyone else. I take no drink or food from anyone other than you. I *get* it."

"Curb the mouth," Fallon cut in. "Things can, and *do*, get a bit rowdy at times. If someone tries to take liberties, let one of us handle it. You snap at the wrong person and things could get nasty."

"I'll do my best."

"You'll do more than your best, Rowan. If you don't think you can do this, say so now. If you don't get this right, they'll tear you apart and I won't be able to do a damn thing to stop them. The rules are in place to keep everyone safe, make sure you follow them." Fallon's voice was tense as he brought the SUV to a stop in a parking space and twisted around in his seat. "Are you *sure* you want to do this?"

Rowan took a deep breath, then nodded. "If it means we might find something out, yes. I'll do whatever it takes. Let's do this."

With a nod, Fallon stepped out of the car, then opened the back-passenger door for Rowan. Leaning in, he pulled a red silk choker from his pocket.

"You need to wear this," he told her, reaching with one hand to scoop up her hair, placed the choker around her neck and clipped it shut. "The colour means you are a guest and not available to anyone." He wrapped a lock of hair around his fingers and tugged at it until she slid across the seat and swung her legs around in the doorway. Fallon released her hair, dropped his hands to her thighs and eased them apart to step between them. He reached into another pocket, pulled out a red leash and smiled at her look of embarrassment.

"I see you remember my comment about putting you on a leash," he laughed softly at her blush. As he clipped one end to her choker, he dipped his head and murmured, "Last chance to change your mind and go home."

When she shook her head, he wrapped an arm around her waist and lifted her out of the car to stand between him and Koo. "Then put on your acting head and get into your role." He held the leash loosely in one hand and raised his voice. "Leave your coat in the car," he told her, then turned his back on her.

Rowan threw a quick glance at Koo, who gave an imperceptible nod, then shrugged out of the coat and threw it on the back seat. Koo closed the door, patted Rowan's arm and stepped ahead to walk beside Fallon. Rowan, tugging down the hem of the short skirt, followed them one step behind.

"Mr Wylde!" Another dark-suited male greeted them at the door. "It's been far too long. And who is *this* delightful creature?" He reached out a hand to touch Rowan's shoulder, only for Fallon to catch his wrist before it landed.

"Mine." His growl had Rowan glancing at him from under her lashes.

"Ahhh." The man froze and quickly dropped his hand. "Red collar. I didn't see it underneath all that glorious hair."

Fallon glanced back at Rowan, expression unreadable. "I like her hair down. Make it known she wears red."

"Yes . . . yes, of course!" He opened the door and held out an arm. "Welcome back to Aduna's, Mr Wylde. Stay in peace."

The light inside the club was muted and, from the sounds Rowan could hear, she was mostly glad Fallon had told her to keep her head lowered. She felt a hand settle between her shoulder-blades and glanced sideways to see Koo had fallen into step beside her. The touch on her back directed her movement, so she wasn't caught by surprise when Fallon turned left and slid into a curved booth.

"It's almost max capacity tonight," Koo said, raising her voice so Rowan could hear her above the rumble of commingled conversations. "Maybe that's a good sign."

Once they were seated – Rowan sandwiched between them – Fallon leaned over to reply to Koo's observation.

"We're attracting a lot of attention. Too much, really, because we haven't been here in a while and Rowan's a new face." He paused to scan the crowd, then addressed Koo. "I'm gonna hang here with Rowan. Why don't you mingle a bit? And see if you-know-who is here."

Koo grinned. "Oh, you *know* he will be." She slid around to exit the booth's opposite side but paused before leaving. "Fallon?"

In the process of shrugging out of his jacket, he glanced over at Koo. "Yes?"

"Don't forget why we're here." She smiled and disappeared into the crowd.

Fallon placed his jacket on the seat beside him and turned to face Rowan, who sat close beside him, her head bowed and her hair hiding her face. He knew exactly what Koo had meant. She had dressed Rowan perfectly for the part she was playing – a part they had been 99% honest about with her, the 1% being vampire-related – short skirt, strapless top, no nylons and strappy high, high heels; the perfect outfit for the Aduna Club and a temptation that was hard to resist.

He felt Rowan shift beside him and, anticipating what would come next, he turned so that his back faced the crowd, blocking her from the view of any potential onlookers.

"So, what happens next?" she didn't disappoint him.

"Next, we wait," he answered. "Once the novelty wears off, once they get used to your presence, we'll mingle a bit. Eavesdrop, interact . . ." his eyes slid down her body. "To a point, anyway. If we're lucky, we'll pick up a lead or two on the people who have Eden."

"And if we're *not* lucky?"

"Patience," Fallon chuckled.

"What do we do until then?"

Fallon leaned back in his seat and grinned. "Look around. What do *you* think we should do?" He toyed with the end of the leash he held while Rowan took a slow look around the club, eyes growing wider and wider as she did.

At a table nearest to them, two scantily clad girls were draped over one man – one kneeling at his feet, rubbing her cheek against his thigh, while he stroked her hair. The other girl had her face buried in his lap. Similar positions were repeated, by both males and females, at various spots in her line of sight, interspersed with spanking sessions, group sex, and . . .

"Are they using that girl as their dinner plate?" she asked in a strangled whisper.

Fallon followed her gaze. "Yes," he replied. He didn't tell her the girl herself was the meal and the food placed on her body was merely for fun and decoration.

"And she's okay with that?"

"Everyone here is willing, Rowan. They're here because they *want* to be, not because they have no choice. Some live here and earn a lot of money fulfilling the desires of the members. Some come here because," he paused, a half-smile on his lips, "because their turn-ons run a little differently from the norm."

He stretched his arms out across the back of the curved seat and gave in to temptation, letting one hand fall in amongst the long red curls of Rowan's hair. His touch was light, winding the silky strands around his fingers and letting them fall, taking pleasure in the way it felt on his skin, and the way her cheeks flushed.

He allowed his amusement at her fascination with the antics of the club show on his face, noting when her gaze lingered on a young woman being spanked, and mentally filing away the way her teeth caught her bottom lip and her breath hitched as she watched. He was aware they were being watched by many of the club's other clientele and didn't give any indication that he knew their table was being approached by two men.

"Fallon," the taller of the two greeted him in a jovial tone, his eyes on Rowan.

"Marcus," Fallon replied, inclining his head.

"Your pet appears to be a little bold."

Fallon gave the leash he was holding a sharp tug at her intake of breath, cutting her off before she could retort. "She's never been here before. I'm letting her see what we may do tonight."

"You've never brought a pet with you before," Marcus said. "Tobias and I saw you arrive. She looks to be a splendid creature and we thought maybe we could partake in—"

"She's mine," Fallon's voice was light. His hand dropped the leash and he reached out to stroke a finger down her neck and over the curve of her shoulder.

"Yes, we don't want ownership, Fallon, just one night."

Fallon's eyes lifted, landing first on Marcus, then on the silent Tobias standing beside him. Whatever Tobias saw in that gaze made him step back.

"I don't share."

"We didn't mean to offend," Tobias murmured, pulling at his friend's arm. "We'll leave you to your evening."

"You do that," Fallon murmured softly, visibly dismissing them from his attention.

He twisted toward Rowan, curved his hands over her hips and lifted her onto his lap. He ignored the two men, who still hovered, while he adjusted her position to his liking then leaned back to survey his handiwork. Her hands lifted to clutch at his shoulders, eyes wide as they darted to meet his, then her lashes dropped to shield her expression.

Her legs straddled his thighs, the already short skirt riding up to show more expanse of leg, and he ran one palm up from knee to thigh. Disguising his quick check to make sure Marcus and Tobias had moved away from their table by burying his face into Rowan's throat, he wound an arm around her waist to drag her closer until she was flush against him.

He felt her tense and tightened his hold, his mouth nibbling along the line of her collarbone.

"By struggling, you're giving out signals that you need to be disciplined and I'll be forced to act accordingly," he whispered against her throat.

"Mr Wylde!" she hissed his name, freezing in the process of arching away.

"Fallon," he corrected, lifting his head to smile at her.

"What?" she frowned.

"My name is Fallon."

"I know what your name is!" She braced her hands against his shoulders, forcing some distance between them.

"Good. Now say it," he said, ignoring her attempts and running a finger over the curve of her breast.

Rowan scowled at him and he laughed.

"Come on . . . *Fallon*," he coaxed. "It's not a difficult name." He dipped his head again. "They're watching us closely to see what we do," he told her, his lips hidden by the column of her throat. "It would raise questions if we just sat here in silence." His mouth reversed direction until she could feel his breath against her ear. "Good job you practiced your seduction routine on me earlier, huh? It might have worked if you'd called me by my name." He chuckled at her gasp of outrage. "Let's change position. I need you to take a good look around and see if you recognise anyone. We need to make this look natural, so follow my lead."

He moved quickly, lifting and settling her onto the table in front of him and rose to his feet. Placing his hands either side of her, he leaned over her and caught her mouth with his in a kiss that demanded an immediate response. His hand went into her hair, wrapping it around his palm and he gently tugged her head until it tilted sideways, baring her throat. His lips left her mouth to trail a path down her neck and, for a full two minutes, Rowan forgot why they were there, her attention welded to Fallon's touch – his mouth nipping, a disturbing mixture of pleasure and pain.

"Concentrate, sweetheart," he whispered. "Get your game face on." He ran his fingers lightly over her thigh, then stepped back and lifted her to her feet. "Turn around," he instructed, and directed her with his hands on her waist until she stood with her back to him. He slid an arm around her waist and pulled her backwards against him. "Look around, Rowan."

Rowan forced herself to focus on the things going on around her, fighting to ignore the devastation Fallon's mouth and hands were dealing to her emotional defences. *We're roleplaying*, she thought to herself, repeating it over and over in her head as she looked through the crowds for familiar faces.

The club's interior had gone more than a little hazy since they'd first arrived, almost like pea-soup fog in some places; easily explained by the number of tables and booths with plumes of smoke curling up from ash trays. It took a concentrated effort, three or so passes, in fact, to finally get clear looks at faces close by, let alone in the distance.

After the fourth pass, however, her eyes finally located Koo, who stood in a small clutch of leather-clad patrons, near the centre of Aduna's U-shaped combination bar and danger's runway. Koo was, in fact, gesturing in their direction to a tall, portly man on her right in an Arab Sheikh's costume and dark glasses.

On pass number five, her eyes settled on the back of the two men who had just visited their booth – Tobias and Marcus. Both stood a few feet to Koo's and the Sheikh's right, facing a booth like the one Fallon and herself occupied, in conversation with the booth's occupants.

Rowan's eyes lingered there for a moment and was just about to move her scan leftward again, when Marcus and Tobias parted, taking up position on either side of the booth and giving Rowan a clear and unobstructed view of who sat there.

"*There!*" Rowan announced, sharply. "It's him. Right there! To the right of where Koo is standing."

"Who?" Fallon asked.

"*Him!* The guy Eden was with before she disappeared . . . *Taylor!*"

"And you're sure? One hundred percent positive?"

In her excitement, Rowan started to spin around to face Fallon before catching herself. "That is one face I will never forget. It's him."

"Be very, very certain," he replied. "Take a longer look."

"I'm certain. I couldn't forget him if I wanted to."

Fallon recognised the surety in her voice and nodded. He turned her around to face him. "Let's take a walk over to Koo." He curved a hand over her hip and moved her to walk in front of him.

Rowan knew that Fallon's looming presence behind her as they moved through the crowd was responsible for the quick, darted glances from both men and women. No one kept their attention on either of them for longer than a second or two, eyes dancing away as soon as Fallon's own gaze touched them. His hand stayed firmly pressed against the small of her back, leash held loosely in his other hand, as he guided her through the milling groups until they reached Koo, who greeted Fallon with a smile.

Noting their imminent approach, the Sheikh retrieved his drink from the bar and departed, leaving Koo alone, more or less. Her gaze touched them both, though it centred on Fallon.

"Something's wrong," she said, when they stopped. "What happened?"

"Just made an iden—" Fallon's eyes covertly eased toward Taylor's booth, his words cutting off abruptly upon the discovery the booth had been vacated. "Shit . . . one of our friends was here," he continued. "And we've probably been made." He caught Rowan's elbow, jerking his head toward the door. "Time to go."

"Leaving so soon?" The man who had welcomed them hurried over as Fallon swept Koo and Rowan through the door.

"A prior engagement I'd forgotten about," Fallon said shortly, not stopping.

He helped both women back into the SUV, settled into the driver's seat and pulled away. A movement just on the edge of his vision caught his attention, and he glanced into the rear-view mirror to see Rowan sliding her arms back into the coat she'd left there. She froze, catching his eye, and he gave her a slow smile, openly running his eyes over the body she was hastily concealing.

"If you're cold, I can turn up the heater," he offered.

"Not cold," she replied, tying the coat shut with a firm tug and unclipping the collar from her throat. Fallon laughed and returned his attention to the road ahead.

Koo twisted to look at Rowan, then back at Fallon and pursed her lips.

"Fallon—" she began, softly.

"It's not your concern, Koo."

Koo shook her head but didn't reply, and silence fell between them as Fallon drove back toward the city.

~*~

Back on the top floor of the house, Koo had gone straight to the bar and poured three glasses of wine. Handing one to Rowan, she took the other to Fallon where he sprawled on the couch, watching

Rowan with hooded eyes. Rowan sipped her wine, avoiding his gaze by heading over to the bay window and looking out over the city.

Koo looked from one to the other and shook her head. Fallon caught the movement and swung his gaze toward her.

"Disapproval, Koo?" he asked.

"Concern, my friend," she replied, quietly.

Rowan glanced over her shoulder at them and set the wine glass down on the windowsill. "I don't know how you two can look so wide awake," she commented. "I'm exhausted. I'm going to bed."

With *goodnights* passed between the three, Koo and Fallon watched their auburn-haired house guest until the bedroom door closed softly behind her. As a precaution, they kept their places, as well as remaining silent, for an additional five minutes. After which, both used their heightened vampire senses to pierce the bedroom door and zero in on Rowan's soft, rhythmic breathing, to confirm she was asleep.

Fallon rose to pour himself another glass of wine. "Alright, spit it out," he said, without turning. "I'm not going to hear the end of it until you do." He turned and took a sip before he continued. "And I know you, if you don't get it out now, you'll just wait until Eayann gets back, turn it over to him and *he'll* start on me."

"You're making me feel like a nag," Koo replied.

"If the shoe fits . . ." Fallon left the rest of the time-honoured idiom unspoken, flashing a crooked smile as he took another sip of wine.

Koo sighed. "I love you, you know that. We're the only family we have left in this world. And, if that justifies me being a nag, then so be it. There's a reason we don't mix with Humans, Fallon. Our lives are too dangerous, *your* temper is too volatile."

"Yeah . . ." Fallon said, in a near whisper, wine glass poised just below his lips. Her words had hit him right where he lived – somewhere in the recesses between nostalgia, guilt, and loyalty. "Yeah," he repeated, placing his glass on the bar before going over to sit beside her. And then, it suddenly it him. "You like her, don't you? That must have been some talk you two had earlier."

"Yes, we did. She's quite a girl, Fallon." Koo picked up her wine glass, looking into it as she idly swirled its contents and seemed to speak more to the glass itself than Fallon. She spoke of what she'd learned from the talk she'd had with Rowan.

"Her middle name is Giselle. She was one of three children, born to Sigrid and John Scott Walker. Eden, her and there was a brother, Peter, two years younger than the twins. Her mother was German, a high school Calculus teacher. She met John, who was career military, Air Force, when he was stationed at Ramstein. And the whole family was stationed in Northern California, at Travis Air Force Base, when Sigrid and Peter were killed in a car crash on I-80 near Oakland. Rowan and Eden were fifteen at the time.

"For a few years, it was just John and the girls," Koo continued. "And then life dealt another tragic hand. Two days before the twins nineteenth birthday, John was killed in Iraq when the Humvee he was riding in hit an IED. From that point on it was Rowan who took on the adult role. Eden rapidly went off the rails – drugs, alcohol, a marriage that went from bad to divorce in three months.

"Rowan did her best to hold things together. There wasn't much in the way of money after their father's death. The insurance award paid off by Uncle Sam and her savings. But that was gone after the first year. She had her college scholarship and a few jobs here and there to keep her going. But dealing with her twin, in and out of bad relationships, drug and alcohol rehab, and a short stint in jail . . . her life hasn't been easy. The poor girl never really had much of a childhood, or anything that could be considered normal in the way of romance. Eden being such a party-girl seems to have put Rowan off the whole dating game. She's still pretty naïve and vulnerable—"

"And you're worried I'll add to her hurt," Fallon cut in.

"I see the way she looked at you tonight, the way she responded to you," Koo paused pointedly. "*But*, I also see how *you've* been looking at *her*. I'm just as worried about you."

"Don't worry. It'll be alright," Fallon interrupted, and left the couch to return to the bar. He took up his wine glass again, started to sip, then placed it back on the bar, going around to find something stronger.

"I did manage to pick up a few things I think you'll like, though," Koo started again, joining him at the bar. "While I was poking around, looking for Mister Eyes and Ears, actually. I found out, first of all, that Knox hasn't been to Aduna's in a long time – months, as a matter of fact."

"Odd," Fallon commented.

"Even odder – none of his people have, either. And that place is like his . . . *their* second home. On top of that, he hasn't been seen anywhere else. People are wondering if he's even still in town."

Fallon grunted acknowledgement and poured himself a tall scotch as Koo continued.

"There's something going on out there, though. Everyone's got their own take on what it might be, but it's mostly speculation. But here's an interesting point. The guy I'm sure you saw me standing next to," she paused to await his response and, when he merely sipped his drink and waved a hand at her, she continued. "Morris Ramsey. He's a . . . *the consigliere* to the Deevers Brotherhood family. Flan Deevers' personal attorney."

"A vampire lawyer?" Fallon laughed. "Now there's an oxymoron, if I ever heard one." He frowned. "He's a long way from Manhattan Island. And while we're talking about that, what the hell was counsel to the boss of all bosses doing in a place like Aduna's?"

"I asked him the very same thing," Koo chuckled. "He said everybody needs to walk the dog now and then. And then he told me the big man himself sent him out here. Someone's been stepping on the Brotherhood's toes in the Five Boroughs. And though he didn't come right out and say it, I'd say it's fairly obvious – the Brotherhood's stock in trade is white slavery."

"Still, that's New York. This is Seattle."

"Ramsey says whatever's going on was traced back here. He also said word on the street is you're looking for a missing girl and that your search is making someone very agitated. He believes you and they might have a common interest. So much that the big man in Seattle, Cokie Donaghy, would like to have a few words with you."

"Would he now?" Fallon grinned, taking a large swallow of scotch. "Well, why the hell not? Who knows, I might even pick up something useful. If nothing else, we can come to some kind of understanding. Last thing I need on this is to be tripping over Brotherhood street soldiers.

"And, on that note . . ." he downed the remainder of his drink and placed the glass topside-down on the bar. "Time for my beauty sleep. Something tells me tomorrow's gonna be a long night."

Koo watched as he headed toward the bedroom. "You're already sleeping with her?"

"With emphasis on the *sleep*, Koo." He paused just before opening the door and smiled over his shoulder. "Don't worry, little sister. I simply want to make sure she doesn't decide to go out of the window again."

Koo watched as he disappeared into the bedroom, a worried frown tugging her features. She waited until she heard the bed creak, a murmur of voices and then silence.

"I hope you know what you're doing," she whispered, then exited Fallon's apartment to seek her own bed.

~*~

Rowan woke up to the strangest sensation. In her half-sleeping state, it felt like there was a heavy but not uncomfortable weight between her shoulder-blades. Her eyes fluttered open, and she discovered she was lying on her stomach, her face inches away from Fallon's – whose green eyes watched her steadily.

Rowan blinked, fighting to keep her eyes open, and stretched, realising as she did that the weight she felt was Fallon's hand on her back. She could feel the warmth radiating from his palm.

"What time is it?" she mumbled.

A brief smile touched his lips. "Later than you think, but too early to get up."

His hand smoothed down her spine, slowed when it reached the waistband of her pyjama bottoms, then followed the material's path around her side before stroking back up, his fingertips brushing the outer curve of one breast, before returning to its original position between her shoulders, then repeated the action; each circular sweep lingering longer on her breast.

"Fallon," she murmured his name, voice heavy with sleep and turned onto her side, her back to him.

"Finally, you say my name." His hand slid over her stomach and upwards, beneath her pyjama top, to cup her breast fully in his palm. "I wanted to do this last night, at Aduna's," His thumb brushed lightly over the sensitive peak of her breast and, at the same time he closed the gap between them to bury his face in the curve between her throat and shoulder. He ran his tongue up her throat and nipped her earlobe.

"Turn over, Rowan," he whispered.

Rowan rolled onto her back and Fallon propped himself up on one arm to lean over her. He pulled his hand from beneath her top and unbuttoned the first two buttons, parting the material just enough to show the valley between her breasts.

Rowan gazed up at him. A part of her knew she should sit up, get out of the bed and walk away – stop the intimacy between them before it went too far – but another part of her admitted to herself that she was tired; not just tired from the last twenty-four hours, but tired from everything – the search for her sister, being her sister's keeper before she went missing, tired of being the responsible one, but mostly tired from being alone.

"Rowan?"

She knew what he was asking. Wordlessly, she reached down and pulled her top over her head, then wound her arms around Fallon's neck and tugged him down so she could reach his mouth.

Their kiss started out gentle, but rapidly became frenzied – tongues slid along each other, teeth bit into lips, nipping and tasting until Fallon pulled away to kiss and lick his way down her body. She moaned when his lips closed over one hardened nipple, her fingers spearing into his hair as she arched up to offer more.

And he would have taken it – happily, eagerly, willingly – if Rowan's cell hadn't started to ring.

"Ignore it," Fallon muttered against her soft, heated flesh and continued his assault on her stiffened nipple.

Rowan nodded, jerkily. She wanted to. *God*, how she wanted to ignore it, to lose herself in the electrifying sensations caused by Fallon's questing tongue. But the combination of habit, pre-conditioning, curiosity and a deeply-imprinted obligation, refused to be denied. The latter manifesting in the form of a nagging inner voice: *it might be important. What if it's them again? Or even Eden? Can you really afford to take that chance?*

"I'm sorry," she brought a hand up to lightly touch the crown of his head before pushing up into a seated position. "I have to," she told him, and swung her legs off the bed.

Visibly frustrated, Fallon came to rest on his side, watching as she quickly scooped the cell from atop the nightstand, glanced at its screen and raised it to her ear.

"Laini-"

"*Ro? Jesus H!*" Rowan jerked the phone away from her ear in reaction to the caller's – to Lainie's screeched response. "*What the hell, girl? Where are you?*"

"Lainie? Calm down. What's the matter?"

"The *matter*? I'll tell you what's the matter! There's yellow tape on your door and then . . . and then . . ." Lainie babbled. "I was worried about you after those guys grabbed you, then some strange woman came for your cell and said you were staying with her and your PI Guy and then you called in sick, and Dustin said I should go check on you and I did and the . . . and then . . ."

"Lainie, slow down," Rowan jumped in. "What did you mean there's yellow tape on my door?"

"Hold on. I'm still at the diner and there's too many people around." There was a moment's pause. Rowan could hear the familiar sounds of clinks and clatter in the background, then Lainie returned. "We – Dustin, me, everybody – we were worried about you. I recorded the session in computer science for you. Claire and Megan did the same for your other classes and gave the videos to me. So, when Dustin suggested I go and see if you were alright, I was gonna kill two birds . . . you know?

"Our places aren't that far away from the diner, so I checked out for a break, went by my place to pick up the flash drives, then went to yours," she stopped to snatch a quick breath. "That's when I saw the tape across the door – like what the police use on those TV shows that say 'Crime Scene, Do Not Cross' . . ."

"Crime Sce—" Rowan faltered at the touch of Fallon's hand. He caught her eyes and gestured to indicate she put the call on speaker. "Crime scene?" she repeated, once she'd done so.

Lainie continued to babble. "And then, as I was leaving, the old woman in the next apartment came out and stopped me. She told me there had been a murder! The cops found a dead body in your apartment. He was shot, she said. And she said she heard gunshots and saw you leaving with some guy. When I got back to the diner, the police were here, and they were asking everyone all these questions about you. Jesus, Ro. *What did you do!?*"

"I . . . nothing, I didn't . . . I'll call you later," Rowan said and broke the connection, sagging as she turned to rest against the bed's headboard. "Now I'm a murder suspect *and* a fugitive."

Fallon laughed. "Listen," he shifted to sit beside her and placed a hand on her forearm. "Maybe it's not as bad as—"

"Don't!" Rowan jerked away and twisted to glare at him. "You said it would be alright. *You* said you would fix it! So, what happened?"

Fallon shrugged and smiled. "Nothing is ever perfect. Don't worry, we can deal with this."

"We?" Rowan repeated, flatly. "*Now* it's we?"

"It's always been we," Fallon replied, a hint of amused exasperation in his voice. "Take it easy, sweetheart. This is only a minor bump in the road. Easily rectified. "

"Don't '*sweetheart*' me," she grumbled.

Fallon ignored her. "We'll go down and see Sid Marshall. You tell them you heard they were looking for you. When they tell you why, act shocked. Tell them you've been staying with a friend – haven't been back to your apartment in a day or so. If they bring up what they were told by the old lady, laugh it off. After all, she's old and could be wrong about the time."

"And it's that simple?" Rowan shot him a sceptical look.

"It should be."

"What if it isn't? What if," Rowan thought for a moment, then looked down at her hand. "What if they decide to give me one of those tests to see if I've fired a gun recently?"

"Then I'd get used to the way you look in one of those orange jumpsuits," Fallon deadpanned, then grinned. "I'm kidding!" He ducked the pillow she slung at him, laughed and pulled her onto his lap, nuzzling her neck. "They won't even suggest a test, unless you give them a reason to." He kissed the curve of her shoulder. "You're going in voluntarily, as if guilt of any kind is furthest from your mind." His fingers returned to her breast, stroking and teasing her nipple until it hardened beneath his touch. "Just stay cool and let them come to their own conclusions as to what happened."

Rowan sighed and let her head drop against his shoulder. "That's what worries me."

Fallon's hand dropped away, and he ran a finger down her cheek. "Okay, alright. I'll tell you what . . ." he set her back on the mattress and climbed out of bed, checking his watch. "It's four-thirty. That gives us about three, maybe three and a half hours to work with." He went to where he'd stacked his clothes, retrieved his cell phone and dialled Koo's number.

"Yes . . . hello?" a sleepy female voice sounded down the line.

"It's me. Something came up. I need you," he told her.

"*Now?*" Koo whined, then loosed a drawn-out sigh. "Fine! Give me five minutes." She broke the connection.

Fallon held out a hand for Rowan, and tugged her up off the bed, gave her half-naked body a heated lingering look, and picked up her pyjama top. "Get dressed, we'll pick this back up later."

True to her word, a few seconds over the five-minute mark, there was a knock on the suite door and a bleary-eyed Koo entered.

"This had better be good. That was the best sleep I've had in days."

Fallon took a moment to catch her up on the latest development. "What we need to do – in the time we have – is get Rowan coached and ready for what the police interrogators might throw at her."

"Oh, is that *all*," Koo said, with an eye-roll. "No problem."

~*~

"So, what do you think?" Koo asked, with a note of audible pride, as she centred Rowan before the bedroom's full-length mirror and stepped away.

Rowan gave her reflection a studied up and down inspection and flashed a nose-crinkled frown. "It's okay, I guess." Her shoulders twitched in a faint shrug.

"We're going for a specific look here – visual suggestion." Koo explained. "Most of the detectives are married. They have teenage daughters – or grew up with younger sisters – and even the unmarried ones have this Kodak picture in their subconscious of sweet, innocent youth. That's our frame, our focus. Even if they're not fully aware of it, we want them to look at you and instinctively believe there's no way in hell this sweet young thing could shoot someone."

Rowan shrugged again. "Okay. What about Detective Marshall?"

"What about him?" The counter-query turned the attention of both women to the bedroom door where Fallon leaned against the frame, his arms folded across his chest.

"He knows me," Rowan said. "I've been to see him quite a bit over the last year and I didn't look like *this!*" She waved a hand down over the pink t-shirt and black skirt Koo had provided, and Koo didn't miss the way Fallon's eyes followed the movement. "My attitude and language weren't always what anyone could call sweet . . . *or* innocent. If he's the one who'll question me—"

"That's true enough," Fallon anticipated her. "Marshall's no idiot. If he *is* the one who questions you, then so much the better. As you said, *he* knows you. Be yourself," he amended his instructions, with a chuckle. "To a point – and you *know* the point, I mean. Curb that straight razor tongue of yours. I might like how deep it cuts, but others won't." He ignored the question in Koo's eyes at his words and carried on. "Stick to the script. Don't give them any more than what they ask for; don't fidget, keep your hands folded on the table in front of you; set your eyeline on a point between and above the questioner's eyes – making it look like eye-to-eye contact."

"Chances are you'll be asked some of the questions more than once," Koo re-entered the exchange, still frowning at Fallon, "but in a rearranged manner. When that happens, resist the urge to let them know you realise it. Just answer the question and let that *sweet, innocent* image do the work."

Fallon snorted at Koo's emphasis and disappeared into the other room.

"Alright," Rowan nodded, took a deep breath, then nodded again. "Okay. Let's do this."

~*~

The 'interview room' for Seattle PD's West Precinct was set up more like a small break lounge with a long table that could easily accommodate four people, bolted to the wall at one end, a large mirror (two way, of course) on the left side wall; a counter at the right that featured a small microwave oven and coffee-maker; and a security camera in its upper righthand corner.

For the sake of appearance, it was agreed that Koo accompany Rowan to the station. On the surface, the petite Eurasian looked only a year or two older than Rowan's twenty-two years – when Rowan had asked Koo her age, she'd murmured something about being older than she looked and having good genes – and, whether anyone would enquire or not, they would more readily be perceived as peers, even schoolmates.

They had been met in the third-floor elevator alcove by Detective Van Nash – a pudgy, nondescript man with a brush cut military haircut and a suit that looked at least one size too small. After the introductions, he directed Koo to a waiting area and escorted Rowan to the interview room. That had been an hour and forty-five minutes ago.

"Okay, I'd like to go back a bit, if you don't mind, Ms Walker," Nash said, attempting a smile that failed miserably. "I – my partner, that is – spoke to your co-worker at the Blue Star Diner and Coffee Café – a Ms Lainie MacAfee. You spent several nights with her, two weeks ago, after someone attempted to break into your apartment. Is that correct?"

"That's right," Rowan answered.

Nash paused, waiting to see if she would volunteer more. When she didn't, he resumed. "And why didn't you report the break-in. Excuse me – *attempted* break-in. May I ask why?"

"If you would care to recall," Rowan immediately checked the icy temperature in her tone. "I said I wasn't certain. I thought I heard noises in my apartment. But nothing was disturbed or missing." A small untruth. "There was no actual evidence of a break-in. But I didn't feel comfortable staying at my place, so I went to Lainie's for a few days. Three, to be exact."

"I see," Nash said, staring down at the notepad in front of him for a moment. "And after the . . . incident in your apartment, you informed your employer and your college instructors that you weren't feeling well, that you would be taking some time off."

Rowan nodded, Nash continued.

"You are looking very well at the moment, if I may say so, Ms Walker. A twenty-four-hour virus?"

"I needed some personal time. My . . ." she hesitated, caught her bottom lip between her teeth and angled a look up at the Detective through lowered lashes. "Our . . . *my* birthday is coming up. It's . . . hard. I've never spent it alone before."

Nash suddenly looked as though he'd found an ant colony in his donuts and cleared his throat before restarting. He quickly flicked backwards in the notepad.

"Ah yes, that's right. A former . . ." he cleared his throat again, ". . . case. Your twin sister, Eden Walker, presumed missing. I'm . . . uh . . . sorry if I reopened an old . . ." his words trailed off apologetically, then leafed back to the pad's top page.

"There's a thing with the times, a contradiction," he began again. "You said you had been staying with Ms MacAfee, and you visited your apartment earlier in the day. But according to your neighbour, a Mrs Beatrice Levesque, she spoke to you outside the apartment after hearing gunshots, on or around eight that evening. And, you departed the premises in the company of a male, described as tall, swarthy complexion, late-twenties, early thirties."

"I *did* go to the apartment, around two-thirty," Rowan said. "And yes, I did see Mrs Levesque. I have no knowledge of any guns being fired while I was there. I was accompanied by an associate, Mr Fallon Wylde. Apparently, Mrs Levesque got her times mixed up."

"Ah yes, Fallon Wylde. Have you known Mr Wylde long?"

"Not really. He was referred to me by Detective Marshall, concerning my sister's disappearance." Rowan's name-drop rated a twitch of the Detective's eyebrow. "I can have Mr Wylde contact you for confirmation, if you like?"

"I don't think that will be necessary," Nash said. "Just one more thing, Ms Walker. The deceased – Floyd Behring – you had a relationship? A friendship?"

"Relationship, no. We were neighbours, and we were friendly. Which is to say, we spoke to each other in passing."

Nash twitched both eyebrows. "Can you think of any reason then, why he would be in your apartment?"

"He had a set of keys for emergencies. He had Mrs Levesque's spare set as well. I don't know why he would go into my apartment."

"Emergencies . . . I see," Nash scanned the notepad for a few minutes, then finally closed it and met her gaze with a tight-lipped smile.

"Well, I think we've covered everything, Ms Walker." He pushed away from the table and stood up, holding out a hand. Rowan rose with him, accepted the proffered hand and shook it.

"If there's anything else, we'll contact you. Thank you for coming in."

~*~

Fallon headed downtown after dropping the girls off at SPD's West Precinct. There were two things on his docket – two possibilities of gaining information and a valuable lead in establishing the fate, and the whereabouts of Eden Walker. Though it was early, there was only time to thoroughly pursue one. So, to prioritise, the first order of business was putting out the word to Seattle's chapter of the Brotherhood that their desire to meet with him was mutual.

As with their Human counterparts, there were clubs, one particular on the A-List as a watering hole for the *vampire haiduc* – vampire wise guys. It was called *Beth Bathory's* – someone's clever idea of an inside joke, no doubt. Not one of Fallon's usual, or preferred hangouts, but he'd visited enough times to become a recognisable face, as well as being on a first name basis with one of its co-owners – Sandrine, an expatriate Pureblood from the House of Belaur. She joined him three minutes after he'd settled into a booth in the far rear corner.

"Frenchie," he smiled, using her pet name, and reached across the table top to grasp and raise her hand to his lips. "*Vous êtes comme beau* – as your perfume is intoxicating, chéri."

"Ah. *De tells conneries*, Spanish," she reciprocated. "But you bullshit with such sincerity." She gave his knuckles a squeeze before he released her. "Your usual? Rum straight?" She waved to catch the bartender's attention.

"Love to, but I'm afraid I can't stay." He reached across the table to give her hand an apologetic pat. "I need you to pass a message to Cokie Donaghy."

Sandrine frowned. "Fallon, are you sure?" She leaned closer, lowering her voice. "In the last few days, I have heard your name exchanged between some, as the Humans would say, very nasty people. There are still bad feelings for your part in helping Lord Zuron's son in San Diego."

"I'm sure," he told her. "Tell the capo that I'm open to a meeting."

"It will be done," she said, and took *his* hand as he rose to depart. "I had an aunt from the Old Country who had a warning appropriate for someone like you, Spanish. *If you cannot be careful, be quick.*"

Fallon gave her a nod, and quickly slipped away.

The next thing on his list, and the one that had been nagging at him since the past night's visit to Aduna's, was to find out the disposition of everyone's favourite 'backstreet reporter', Knox.

Knox. Fallon couldn't help but smile to himself. The man was king of the one-name identity. If everything people *thought* they knew about him was true he was *Gaius*, a slave trader-auctioneer-turned minor politician during the reign of Emperor Caligula in 38AD; *Marcel* in Constantinople during the spread of the Black Plague; *Caleb*, a dubious nobleman in Italy during the reign of King Charlemagne; a flamboyant travelling performer-carnival impresario called *Ivo* in Sweden during the time of Queen Christina in 1655; a flashy Belgian pimp on London's East End named *Dante* from mid-1888 to late-1895. And *LeGuin*, the owner-operator of a small, but popular hostel/brothel in New York City in 1910. All of which, as Knox himself loved to admit, danced back and forth along the spectrum from fifty percent fact to fifty percent fiction, with a ton of deliberately glamorised bullshit in-between. But there were a few golden nuggets of truth amongst the glitter-painted stones of fabrication. For one, he was *Old Blood*; although few vampires knew exactly *how* old. Two, he was, without a doubt, the vampire world's *'Prince meets Madonna meets the Marquis de Sade'* – flamboyant, frequently gaudy, charismatic, vulgar but charming, incurably materialistic, and perverse in a style all his own. And three, though his vocations over the centuries had been as numerous as his aliases, they were all merely camouflage for his true trade: the gathering and sale of information. A commodity that many in the Vampire Nation would agree shared the top spot in the hierarchy of imperatives with feeding and staying alive. And *nobody* was better at collecting that commodity than Knox. If there was anything worth knowing; if there was *anything* happening *anywhere* Knox knew about it. A few more of the truths which supported that – though little known and rarely considered – being his longevity, the countless contacts he'd made over the millennia, and the multitude of those he employed as his 'eyes and ears'. It was said, both jokingly and deadly serious, that if a mosquito hatched in a stagnant pool anywhere on the planet, Knox knew about it. Which, in light of current events, made the allegation Fallon picked up at Aduna's both highly suspect and disturbing.

There were two more stops on his impromptu itinerary. The first, and nearest to his current location, was a posh vampire-exclusive venue called *The Power Ascendant*, located in the city's second tallest building – the 65th floor of the Corinthia Commerce Tower. Membership by *Invitation Only*, of course. It catered to Seattle's Pureblood, cultured, filthy rich and sophisticated elite. Founded and (secretly) owned by a consortium of members of the House Machiavel and L'élite, its roster of patrons featured the *crème de la crème* of Old World blueblood royalty and corporate society. And one imposter. All modesty aside, a *very* talented imposter.

Duke Diego de la Serra, alias Fallon Wylde.

Fallon stood patiently, seemingly unconcerned as the club's 'man at the front entrance', *the herald,* took time from staring past his turned-up nose to peruse the leather-jacketed notebook on the desk in front of him.

"Are you sure . . . *sir?*" His query was preceded by a deliberately pronounced and disdainful sniff. "There doesn't seem to be a reservation for a," he paused to give Fallon another disapproving look. "Mr de la Serra."

Fallon flashed a condescending smile. "Then try under membership, the House of Sasul. My sponsor is the Lady Marjean Sălbatica, and *I* am Diego de la Serra, the Duke Castille de Vigo Barcelona."

"Of course, sir," the herald blanched, then turned to the laptop computer at his left. After a few seconds of finger-dancing on the keyboard, the colour returned to his features and he rose out of his chair with an ear-to-ear smile.

"Please forgive me, Your Grace," he waved toward a set of brass-knobbed double doors a few feet to the desk's right. "If you would follow me."

"It's alright . . . ?" Fallon cut in, his tone questioning.

"Forrester, sir."

"Forrester, okay. Before we go in, I was wondering if Count Franz von Zumbusch is present this evening?"

The herald's smile deepened. "As a matter of fact, sir, yes, the Count is here tonight."

"Very good." Fallon moved closer and lowered his voice conspiratorially. "I would be eternally grateful, Forrester, if you could find me a table as far from the general populace as possible, then ask the Count if he wouldn't mind joining me. Business, *you* understand," he added, winking as he laid a friendly hand on Forrester's shoulder. "You never know who might be listening."

The herald winked back. "Oh, yes sir! I understand completely."

Fallon tightened his grip on Forrester's arm, stopping him as he attempted to move forward to the door. "Don't bother announcing me. Low profile and all that."

"Of course, sir!" Forrester nodded, finally leading Fallon to the entrance.

Although a head popped up here and there or swivelled on necks as stiff as steel columns – momentarily tracking his progress like surveillance cameras – Fallon gauged the overall consensus as something several levels below curiosity. Something more akin to catching the tail-end of a bout of barely concealed flatulence and wondering who the culprit was. Fallon stationed himself in the booth's centre, allowing a panoramic view of all exits, windows, and the club's interior entrance. A habit born out of a number of bad experiences and too many close calls. When his waiter appeared, and in keeping with his masquerade, he ordered a snifter of Hennessy Beauté du Siècle cognac, struggling against the impulse to wince as the waiter departed. At $200,000 a bottle, even a half-snifter of the stuff wasn't cheap. And, even though it wouldn't put so much as a bruise on the wallet of Duke de la Serra *or* Fallon Wylde, it was the principle that gnawed at him.

"The cost of doing business, my ass," Fallon whispered to himself. When weighted against the reason for his visit, and what he *hoped* would come out of it, it was like buying the most powerful and expensive hunting rifle on the market to catch butterflies.

The waiter was back within minutes with his brandy, and with a stony-faced Count Zumbusch right on his heels, a snifter of his own in hand.

"Well . . . Well. If it isn't the Duke of Death and Destruction himself!" Zumbusch quipped after the waiter's departure. "Believe it or not, I'm honoured, and surprised, to tell the truth." He threw a quick glance around, and slid into the booth at Fallon's left, executing a welcoming salute with his glass before sipping slowly.

"I wonder what they would say if they knew you'd killed the *real* Duke de la Serra," Zumbusch chuckled, toying with the rim of his glass. "A gentleman's duel, wasn't it? Rapiers? Or was it pistols at dawn?"

"Neither. Although it was *supposed* to be pistols at midnight," Fallon answered, with a self-satisfied grin. "Actually, I gutted the son-of-a-bitch just as he was getting out of his mistress's bed. Two hours after he sent a couple of third-rate hatchet men to ambush me."

"Oh believe me, I *know* the story. Weren't you with *his* wife at the time?" Zumbusch laughed. "The very same woman whose honour you were accused of defaming, incurring the good Duke's wrath and sparking his challenge. Humans . . . they can be so foolish."

Fallon nodded, sipping his cognac. "Stupid, inane, no argument there. But also mercenary. The Duchess Antonia was a trophy, a beard to camouflage the fact that the Duke was a flaming paedophile. She'd fall into bed with anyone, from the town drunk to the royal stable hands just to get back at him, and *everybody* knew it. He knew about me, about our kind, and the price the Church put on our heads, and he was looking for an inroad with the district diocese . . ."

"Ah yes. Bishop de Guevara, the pig," Zumbusch frowned, seeking to eradicate the offending taste of the name and the memory it had sparked with a long quaff of his drink.

"You see? That's one of the things I've always admired about you, Franz, my friend," Fallon smiled, tapping the edge of his forehead. "That super sponge intellect of yours. Memory like a computer. The way you soak up, absorb and store things," he paused to swirl and sip his brandy. "But then, you learned from the best, right?"

Zumbusch flashed a smile of his own. "And so, we come to the meat of the matter – the reason I've been graced with your presence. Hence, as I also said, my surprise that you didn't show up sooner." He paused, then asked. "Knox?"

Fallon nodded.

"We were partners, like brothers actually, for a very long time. An entire century," the Count waxed nostalgic. "And you're right. I learned most of the art from him. Although, I've learned to work in a much narrower and much more specialised field in recent times."

"The pure and the privileged, you mean," Fallon tipped his head to indicate those assembled around them. "Knowing where all the bodies are buried, which closets contain the bloodiest skeletons. Your focus of interest may not be as wide as Knox's, but that doesn't necessarily place you in the number two position. I happen to know that, while there are things that happen in *your* area he knows little or nothing about, the same can't be said for what *you* pick up in his."

"I've always said you were much smarter than people give you credit for, Spaniard," Zumbusch chuckled, and raised his snifter. Fallon did likewise and the two touched rims. Both downed the remainder of their drinks and Zumbusch signalled for the waiter.

After their respective preferences had been replenished, Zumbusch settled comfortably against the booth's plush leather upholstery.

"Preliminaries first," he said. "*Both* your names have been making the rounds lately. Primarily from two separate groups. And your actions have been cause for much curiosity, anxiety, and agitation. Concerning the latter, much more so in *your* case. There's a kill on sight order out on you.

"I know the answer already. But I need you to confirm," he added. "Knox . . . is he missing?"

Fallon nodded.

"You wouldn't have come to me if he wasn't," said Zumbusch, and took a deep breath to collect himself. "Several weeks . . . five or six months ago, actually, I started to pick up stirrings in, as you so aptly put it, *my* arena. A few of the corporate people from the Houses of Machiavel and Paladé and their L'élite offspring who dabble in business ventures. Whispers of 'human trafficking' and the words *red horse* and *carousel*."

The last word raised an eyebrow on Fallon.

"Strike a chord?"

"Maybe," Fallon answered. "Go on."

"You know what they say – hear something once or twice, it's just a whiff, but hear it a dozen times and it becomes a solid odour. And, believe me, after a few weeks the grapevine literally reeks of it. And then one day" he made a hacking gesture with knitted fingers across his throat, "nothing. It went completely silent until a month ago.

"The whispers started up again. This time they were saying something big was in the wind, and lots of people – big people – were interested. People like the Purple Brotherhood, the Outfit, the West Coast families of House of Maggio, and at least three clans from the European Rroma Alliance, Knox's playground. No one was exactly sure what was truly going on, but I'm sure Knox put it all together. That's part of his talent, finding the pattern and knowing how to connect the dots.

"About the time I started hearing the human trafficking thing again, I also heard there were two groups with designs on Knox. One group wanted to know what he knew, the other wanted him to keep quiet about it. And neither wanted to pay for the privilege."

"So, you think Knox is just in hiding?" Fallon asked.

"It makes sense. You know as well as I do that with as much profitable information around out there, there's no way in hell Knox would shut down unless he absolutely had to. Which leaves only two possibilities. One being he's dead, which is unlikely knowing Knox. I don't think even Lucifer himself could catch him off guard. Which leaves the second option – he shut *himself* down."

"True enough," Fallon said.

"Hope that helped," Zumbusch told him, pausing to drain his glass in a single gulp, "because that's all I have for the moment, and," he threw a glance beyond the booth, toward a pair of approaching young women, "all the time I have to spend with you, my friend."

He exited the booth and moved out to meet and link arms with the two beauties without so much as a backward glance.

~*~

Answers? Of a fashion. A couple of strong possibilities. The Human girl – human trafficking bit – was a very strong nod in the direction of Eden Walker's disappearance. And then there was the hint of a connection in the conversation he'd had with Holly – *red horse, carousel. Red Carousel?* Maybe, but it was just that, a possibility. No solid answers, just another bagful of questions. And the one person who could answer any, if not all of them, was himself playing hide n' seek.

Parking on the street rather than the Tower's underground garage was not something Fallon normally did. Not what anyone with half a brain and drove a Ferrari *would* do – especially in downtown Seattle at night. But the plan, his intention, had been a simple one. Initially, the possibility that he'd actually connect with Zumbusch was slim. He'd planned to leave a message. To be away from his car no longer than fifteen minutes, then be on his way to Shadowfall for a straight-from-the-vein feed at *Andre's* upstairs. But Zumbusch *had* been there and the exchange had taken quite a bit longer than he had estimated. He knew it had been a mistake a second before he reached the car.

There were two of them – both dark-haired and Human. Kids, probably no older than eighteen. The girl – the distraction – was perched on the curb near the car's rear. She stood up when Fallon appeared, flashing a suggestive smile as her coat opened to reveal an outfit far out of character with Seattle's after-dark climate.

"Hey man, got a light?" she produced a long filter-tipped cigarette, placing it at the corner of her red-stained mouth.

"Give me a break," Fallon said under his breath, almost laughing.

The boy, a broad-shouldered bruiser in a Seahawk's baseball cap and ratty U.S. Army field jacket, came out of the shadows of the storefronts behind them. He bolted out at a quick jog, almost crouching.

Fallon's mistake was in not taking the situation seriously.

He ignored the girl and didn't see the boy or his weapon – a box-cutter – until it was almost too late. It cost him an undeniably painful slash across his right bicep and the ruin of one of his favourite jackets.

"Gimme the car keys, motherfucker," the boy growled, holding the box-cutter out in front of him and pointed threateningly at Fallon. "Or the next one's gonna be a lot worse."

"Oh, give me a fucking break," Fallon repeated, louder this time, and glanced back and forth between his damaged sleeve, bleeding arm, and the boy's pathetic weapon.

"I'll give you more than . . . *aoghhhhh!*" the boy's churlish response was abruptly terminated a second later when he found his throat in the grip of Fallon's tightening fingers. He dragged the youth along with him as he covered the distance that separated them from the boy's companion and, in the blink of an eye, had captured her in an identical fashion.

He took a moment to survey his surroundings and assess the situation, thankful now he'd had the presence of mind to park the Ferrari in a spot hidden from view by the Corinthia's security cameras. And, even more appreciative of the fact that, for one thing, vehicular traffic during this time of night was at a low ebb and, for another, the area was virtually devoid of *Human* traffic – namely, potential witnesses.

"You two nitwits picked the wrong night, the wrong place, and the wrong time to play Carjack Bonnie and Clyde," Fallon told the pair of them, while dragging them to a dark recess near the building's corner where he dropped them on their collective asses.

Their predictable show of feather-ruffled bravado was cut instantly short as Fallon knelt before them and flashed a smile that displayed his fangs to maximum effect.

"Holy . . . " the boy gurgled,

'Shit!" the girl squeaked in turn.

Fallon's chuckle was decidedly sadistic in response. "Yeppers, folks. We're real, and I'm one of them. So, keep that in mind in case you thought about trying to run. I'm way faster than you are."

"You . . . are you . . . gonna bite us in . . . ?" the boy stammered, voice quivering.

"In the neck?" Fallon finished the query with a roll of his eyes. "Jesus. Fucking Hollywood! Personally, I prefer the wrist. Or the femoral artery. But all the movies, books, and tv shows have even influenced a lot of *us* to go the throat route. To each his/her own, I guess.

"But to answer your question – no, I'm not in a fast-food mood at the moment. Since the two of you have put a stain on what started out to be a fairly nice night, I think it only fair I return the favour."

He studied the two of them, his face expressionless. "Hit her," he said, addressing the boy.

"What . . . *hit?*" Wide-eyed, eyebrows raised, the youngster regarded Fallon as though he'd just been asked to unzip and expose himself.

"I'm pretty sure I didn't stutter, Clyde. Don't make me repeat myself."

The boy's eyes swivelled left and right, back and forth, between Fallon's cold, unrelenting green-eyed gaze and the blanched and gaping countenance of his cohort in disorganised crime. And, after a moment or so, he scrambled up on both knees facing the girl, and delivered a quick, though pathetically powerless right jab to the side of her head. A punch that did little more than disturb her hair and earn him a lip-biting glare.

"I wanted Mike Tyson, not Moe from the Three Stooges," Fallon said, with a dissatisfied shake of his head. "I said hit. Not love tap. Not bitch slap . . . *hit. Clock* her."

"Latifah . . . " the boy murmured woefully. "Sorry." And he cocked his elbow and fired a grunting roundhouse that connected with the girl's right eye and forehead. It didn't completely flatten her, but it took a good minute for her to recover.

"Christ, Tupac, that's gonna leave a bruise," she moaned, cupping a hand to the injured area.

"Latifah? Tupac?" Fallon snorted. "Seriously?" He shook his head derisively. "Never mind. Again . . . *Tupac*." The words had scarcely left his mouth when the boy launched a second, roundhouse assault that caught her dead centre and, this time, put her back on both elbows.

She recovered and arose with surprising swiftness, displaying a darkened and swollen eye and a split upper lip.

"Your turn, *Latifah*," Fallon directed and rose to his full height above them. He noted, with a quirk of his lips, that she didn't need telling twice, launching herself at the boy with a snarl. He took advantage of the heat of the exchange to locate the box-cutter the boy had dropped during the transport of the two would-be carjackers to their current location.

The girl, meanwhile, was tearing into her cohort like a wounded and enraged she-lion. Both were so engaged in their rage and separate struggles that it was over before either knew it.

Fallon's movements were a near-invisible blur, opening the boy's jugular vein, then forcing the weapon into the girl's hand before knocking her unconscious.

He stared down at them, trying to stem the anger coursing through his veins, spun on his heel and returned to his car.

~*~

After leaving the police station, and stopping to eat, Koo and Rowan returned to the house.

"I'll come up to Fallon's apartment with you," Koo told her as they headed to the third floor. "But I do have some work to get on with, so I won't stay. Will you be okay on your own for a little while?"

"Gee, I don't know . . . I mean, however did I survive for twenty-two years before you and Fallon came into my life?" Rowan deadpanned.

Koo snorted a laugh. "Okay, I'm sorry. I'll stop mother-henning you!"

"It's okay. I could use the time to catch up on my classwork, anyway."

Koo bypassed the security system and opened the doors to Fallon's private rooms. Even though she knew for sure no one was inside, Koo still did a quick check before allowing Rowan to enter.

Rowan rolled her eyes, but made no comment when Koo finally called her in.

"You have my number in your cell, or you can dial three on the landline, if you need me," Koo told her. "Fallon should be back soon, though."

"Stop fussing," Rowan softened the words with a smile. "Go, do whatever it is you do when Fallon isn't bossing you around." She flapped her hands at Koo and headed toward the bedroom to change out of the clothes Koo had loaned to her.

Koo stood for a moment, then exited and closed the door softly behind her.

When Fallon arrived home three hours later, Rowan was engrossed in her studies, laptop open and notes spread across the coffee table, a mug of coffee at her elbow. She didn't hear him arrive and it was only as his shadow passed over her, when he headed toward the bar, she finally lifted her head.

"You're back," she said, pushing her glasses up her nose.

"I'm back," he replied, pouring a glass of whiskey. Holding the glass between his fingertips, he turned to face her. "Can I assume your interview at the station went okay?"

"I think so. They didn't lock me in a cell, so that's a good thing, right?" she frowned, noting the red stain on his sleeve. "What did you do? Is that blood?"

Fallon glanced down at his arm and scowled. "Idiot kids chancing their luck." He lifted his head and watched as Rowan removed her reading glasses, set aside her laptop, rose to her feet and crossed the room to get a closer look.

"They attacked you?" She raised a hand and tugged the silk away from his arm, feeling it resist where the blood had dried. "Let me look. You might need stitches."

Fallon brushed her hand away. "It's nothing."

"It doesn't *look* like nothing."

Fallon couldn't have explained later how he ended up sitting on the couch, shirt half-off while Rowan knelt beside him cleaning up the cut on his arm. He could have said it was simply to save having to explain why he didn't need to worry about a small cut that would heal quickly, but in reality, the worry shadowing her eyes and the concerned expression on her face had triggered a need to soothe her which he couldn't ignore.

He watched her, his eyes hooded, as she cleaned away the blood and inspected the wound for dirt. Her fingers on his bare skin made him recall earlier in the evening, before they had been disturbed by a phone call, and the anger and restlessness he'd been feeling since the incident with the human couple dissipated abruptly.

"I'm no doctor, but I don't think it's deep enough to need stitches," she announced a few minutes later. "It's stopped bleeding already."

"I heal fast," he replied, and lifted a hand to brush a lock of hair from her cheek.

"The scars on your back –" Rowan began, leaning into his touch.

"Testimony to quick healing," Fallon replied lightly, and caught her hand as she started to move away. "Where's your phone?"

"On the table," she pointed at it with her free hand.

"Pass it to me." He released her hand and held out his palm and, although there was a question in her eyes, she reached out and picked it up. Fallon took it from her, gave it a cursory glance and switched it off before tossing it back on the table.

"Why did you do that?" she asked, her brows pulling together into a frown.

"Your phone is a distraction," he told her, shrugged his shirt the rest of the way off and reached for her.

His move took her by surprise and Rowan found herself sprawled across his lap before she could think about stopping him.

"What's the story with your clothes?" he asked conversationally, as he unbuttoned the blouse she was wearing. Rowan was too busy gaping at him to stop him, and he tugged it open and down her arms with very little resistance from her. "You either have an incredible lack of fashion sense or there's something behind your choices. I'm tempted to burn your entire wardrobe." He ran a finger along the edge of the plain white bra she was wearing. "Even your underwear is boring."

Rowan tensed while Fallon chuckled and dipped his head, replacing fingertip with tongue.

"But I know," he murmured softly, "that what's beneath all the drab is nothing short of exquisite."

"Fallon, I don't think—" she broke off with a gasp when Fallon nudged her bra to one side and ran his tongue over her nipple.

"Good idea. Don't think."

And she didn't want to think. She could feel her body humming with anticipation as he removed her bra and cupped her breasts in his palms. He buried his face in the valley between them and inhaled her scent before he turned his head to suckle first on one pebbled nipple and then the other, alternating until Rowan was arching up against his mouth.

Lost in the sensations he was arousing, she wasn't aware of him removing her skirt or panties until she felt his hand settle on her thigh. She blinked her eyes and looked down to find herself lying across his lap completely naked.

"Fallon?" He lifted his head at his name, smiled at the blush rising over her cheeks and ran his palm up her leg until his fingertips brushed against the curls nestled between her thighs, and she squirmed.

"You're so beautiful. Why do you hide it?"

"It's not . . . I don't . . . " she stammered, unable to respond while his fingers stroked through the slick wetness of her arousal.

"We'll work on it," he cut in, and rose to his feet with her wrapped in his arms.

He strode into his bedroom and captured her lips moments before he lay her on the bed and came down over her. She reached up and tugged his belt off, unbuttoned his pants and pushed them down. Her murmur of approval when his erection sprang free drew a laugh from Fallon and he guided her hand until her fingers curled around him.

When she started to stroke, Fallon's laugh became ragged and he eased a knee between her thighs.

"I wanted to bend you over the table in Aduna's and bury myself inside you," he told her, and smiled at her sharp intake of breath. "I told myself when I finally got you in my bed I'd take my time, taste every sweet inch of you." He pushed her thighs apart and used his thumbs to spread her open to his heated gaze. "But I just don't have the control or patience for that right now."

"Patience is overrated!" Rowan's words ended on a gasp as Fallon pulled her hand aside and drove himself into her. For one long minute they both lay still, Fallon's arms braced either side of Rowan's head and she lifted her eyes to meet his.

"Just . . . give me a second," she breathed. "it's been a while and you're so . . . " she trailed off with a faint smile.

"Did I hurt you?" He started to shift, to draw away and she clutched at his hips, anchoring him against her.

"No! No," she repeated more calmly and relaxed her grip to run her fingertips across his buttocks and back, her nails scraping against his skin.

Fallon gritted his teeth, fighting the urge to just pin her beneath him and to hell with the consequences. He held still as she dragged her nails across his shoulders, down his arms and up his chest, scraping over his nipples.

"Ro—" he bared his teeth, almost snarling her name, and Rowan found herself smiling, feeling an unexpected sense of power over the man holding himself so carefully above her. She let her fingers finish their journey, sliding up his throat, along his jaw and into his hair, where they stilled.

"Fallon?" she asked then.

"What?" he spoke between clenched teeth.

Rowan licked her lips, exulting in the way his eyes narrowed and followed the movement of her tongue. "Why are you just lying there?"

Fallon stared down at her, processing her words, then began to laugh, the tension easing from his frame. He dipped his head for a brief, hard kiss, then lifted his head.

"Why, indeed," he murmured.

CHAPTER SEVEN

The look on Rowan's face as they cruised by Shadowfall's main entrance, en route to the underground parking garage was more than worth the misgivings Koo had expressed earlier, when Fallon had strolled out of the bedroom reeking of sex and satisfaction and announced they were going to Shadowfall for a couple of days.

"What are all those people standing in line for? What *is* this place?" Her words, queries came out in a near unbroken stream, giving him little chance to respond. Fallon waited until they were inside and pulled into a parking space before beginning. He started with the last question she'd asked.

"It's called Shadowfall. It's owned by a friend of mine, and it's put together like . . . well, like one of the hotel resort casinos in Las Vegas, minus the gambling." He stopped until they exited the Ferrari and moved to its front, taking note of the approaching headlights of Koo's classic '74 Thunderbird.

"it's got a little bit of everything," he continued, draping an arm across her shoulders and tucking her against his side. *Why did she arouse such a protective streak*, he mused, even as he continued explaining. "A number of clubs, restaurants, a mall with several clothing boutiques and it's also a hotel."

He fell silent then, and they both watched while Koo parked in an adjacent space, exited and went to the trunk of her car. She took out an overnight bag and a zip-up wardrobe bag.

"Luggage? Am I missing something?" Rowan asked.

"Koo and I both keep suites in reserve here," Fallon told her. "I thought it might be nice to get away from the house for a night or two. Unless you'd rather not?"

"Are you kidding? After the last few days, I could do with a little normal in my life," Rowan laughed.

"Shoulda thought about that *before* hooking up with Fallon," Koo mumbled under her breath as she hefted her bags and took off at a fast walk toward the elevator.

"What's wrong with Koo?" Rowan questioned, her gaze hopping back and forth between Fallon and Koo's rapidly receding back. "Are you two okay?"

"Don't worry about it. It's nothing," Fallon assured her, dropped his arm, took Rowan's hand in his and followed along behind Koo at a slower pace.

They saw Koo again, though only once in the next hour or so, as the three of them stood at the club's Residential Registration counter to arrange for the opening of their suites. Then it was off to the shopping mall or promenade, officially called the *Çarşısı* - roughly translated, *Bazaar.*

The clothing shops and boutiques alone accounted for well-over half of the mall's venues. With names that screamed high-end – Nordstrom's and Neiman Marcus, Mario's, Alhambra, Gucci, H.E.R., Diva and on and on and on.

Initially, Rowan had baulked at going into the stores, stating the clothes were far outside of her price range. Fallon had dealt with that by telling her he hadn't brought *any* of her clothes along and it was either loan two or three outfits for their stay, wear the same clothes she had on for the entirety of it, or go naked.

All lies, of course. The truth of it was after spending the day in bed with her, making love with her and learning every curve of her body, he'd asked her again about her clothing choices. She'd replied simply and with a grin.

"They're cheap!"

He'd decided there and then that a trip to Shadowfall was in order, as well as a new wardrobe – not that he'd explained that to Koo or Rowan.

At first, Fallon had planned to just sit and wait while Rowan indulged in shopping and had, in fact, settled with a pile of newspapers while he waited for her to change into one of the outfits she'd picked up. At the swish of the curtain, he'd looked up and immediately frowned at the beige three-quarter length skirt and jacket she was wearing.

"it's the cheapest thing here," she whispered, in response to his expression.

"No," he said.

"But—"

"No. Try something else on." He met her glare with a bland expression, until she spun on her heel – flat and brown, he noted with an inward groan – and stomped back into the changing room.

The second and third outfits were no better, making Fallon grind his teeth in exasperation. He wanted to see her in something colourful, something that showed off her glorious hair and figure, something that reminded her she was young and beautiful. While she was inside the changing room, taking off the last awful selection, he waved to one of the hovering assistants and supplied her with a list of his requirements. By the time Rowan had come back outside, the assistant had returned with an armful of colourful garments.

"Try those on." He rose to his feet and plucked out an emerald green dress. "That first."

Rowan stared at the dress like he was holding a poisonous snake ready to strike.

"Take it, Rowan. It won't bite." He shook the hanger impatiently and hid a smile when she finally snatched it from him and stalked away. He was finding poking at her temper addictive.

The same scene repeated itself in every store he took her in, until Fallon simply refused to allow Rowan to choose the clothes, sending each assistant off with his instructions and then giving each outfit his undivided attention as Rowan tried each one on. At each store, he had his chosen items packaged up and sent ahead to his suite. By the time they reached the final store, Rowan was silently seething – something that, Fallon admitted to himself, had made the entire thing a thoroughly worthwhile and amusing experience.

Guiding her into the final store in the mall, Fallon counted under his breath, waiting for her to notice its contents. He barely got to three before she stopped and spun to face him.

"This is a *lingerie* shop!"

Fallon adopted a shocked expression and looked around. "Why, so it is."

"I'm not modelling underwear for you!" Rowan snapped.

"I'm not expecting you to," he paused and pursed his lips. "Well not in here, anyway. Maybe later when we're somewhere more private." He laughed as her jaw dropped and pressed a finger beneath her chin to push her jaw shut. "Close your mouth, sweetheart."

"I have underwear," she protested.

"You do, but you *need* lingerie – trust me, there's a difference," Fallon replied. "Stay here."

He left Rowan where she stood and moved further into the shop, pausing occasionally to take an item from a rack. After a few minutes he returned, handed the pile over to the hovering assistant, then retrieved a lacy emerald bra and thong set, which he held out to Rowan along with a bag he'd retained from the first store they'd visited.

"What's that?" she asked.

"A dress and shoes we picked up earlier. There's a changing room over there, go get changed and we'll go for dinner."

A pair of young women – both vampire – approached from the racks at Fallon's right as Rowan moved toward the changing room. One of them made a convincing show of losing her balance, taking a stumbling plunge toward the floor, and Fallon. He leaned out to catch her, instantly aware she'd deftly slipped something into the space between the cuffs of his shirt and jacket sleeve.

"Are you alright?" Fallon asked, helping her back upright.

"I'm sorry. Gosh, I'm such a klutz sometimes," she replied, smiling sweetly. "Thank you." She took a moment to adjust herself before moving off with her friend. Fallon tracked their departure until they were out of sight and took a careful look around before extracting the object – a scrap of folded paper – from his sleeve.

It was a note, scrawled in ballpoint blue:

Outside. Bench on the left.
Blonde, pink ribbon. NOW!

Stuffing the note inside his pocket, Fallon caught the attention of the store's sales associate and pulled her to one side. Conscious of their surroundings, he lowered his voice to a near whisper and tugged her close.

"I have an errand to run. Could you see to it that my companion is looked after?" he jerked a head to indicate Rowan's location.

"I'd be happy to, sir," the associate responded and returned to her former position.

With caution as his watch-word, Fallon stopped just short of exiting the store. As the note indicated, a blonde dressed in white – save for the pink ribbon which held her honey-coloured tresses in a loose ponytail – occupied the bench ten feet or so to the lingerie store's left. Fallon took an additional minute or two to ensure the area was threat-free, then moved toward her. When he was within a foot of the bench, she quickly rose and moved into the flow of foot traffic beyond the bench without a backward glance, leaving a cell phone on the bench's wooden slat seat. He had barely seated himself and picked up the cell when it rang.

"Boy, you take the prize, Wildman." Preferred pet name aside, the identity of he whose scratchy-throated tones assaulted Fallon's eardrum could not be denied. "Tell me somethin'," he pressed on. "How do you say self-righteous, two-faced hypocrite in *Castilian*?"

"Knox," Fallon released a faintly relieved, but nonetheless weary, sigh.

"I give you points for quality. She's as juicy as a fresh-picked peach. But she looks like high school graduation was just last week. And she's Human. At least the ones *I* corrupt have already been turned . . ."

"Knox . . ."

"And what's this crap I've been hearin' about you playin' private dick? Beatin' the streets like some low-rent Sam Spade? Boy oh boy, must *reaaaally* be good between the—"

"You contacted *me*, asshole," Fallon cut in. "I'm pretty sure you wouldn't have swallowed your pride or taken the risk of having your messenger intercepted if you didn't need me. So, let me say this in a language you understand. You've got ten seconds to get to the point or, one I hang up, and two, next time we cross paths I'll put a bullet in that shithole you call a mouth and hack off something that *won't* grow back."

Fallon jerked away from the phone on a blast of nerve-grating laughter.

"Sounds like the same old Wildman. But I dunno."

"Don't know what?"

Knox paused a beat. "Somebody says they saw that little fortune cookie you work with smoozin' it up with Flan Deevers' mouthpiece at Aduna's. They also say you showed up at Bathory's talkin' to Sandrine. Somebody might get the idea you're workin' for the Brotherhood now."

"And if you really thought that was true, we wouldn't be talking now," Fallon countered.

"Knox snorted. "But ain't that your gig, Wildman? Soldier for hire? If the money's right . . ."

"And you said it. *Soldier*, not hitman for hire. And you got five seconds, Knox. Four . . . three . . . two . . ."

"*Alright! Alright,* Wildman," Knox gave in, taking a deep, noisy breath. "I had to be sure. With the situation such as it is – and me hearin' that you were lookin' for me. I couldn't take any chances.

"Word on the wind says you and me are drawin' heat from the same people. In *your* case because you and your little sweetheart's makin' them nervous. And me, let's just say I know too much for their own good."

"Which is?" Fallon prompted.

"You know better than that, Wildman," Knox chuckled. "There's a right time for everything . . . and this ain't my right time." He took another pause, then resumed. "There's a lot more to this than what you were hired for, Wildman. A *whole* lot more. And you know me . . . I need time to calculate my piece of the pie. By the way – you'll be hearin' from Cokie Donaghy's people soon. Once you see them, and get their version, then we'll talk." The connection was broken then.

Pocketing the phone, he sighed and took a long look around before he returned to the store. A nod from the assistant directed him into the changing room Rowan occupied and he poked his head through.

"How are you—" he broke off to smile in appreciation when she spun around, hands coming up to cover breasts barely covered by the bra he'd picked out.

"What are you *doing?*" she hissed, as he stepped the rest of the way through and she backed toward the far wall.

"I knew that colour would look perfect on you," he told her, catching her wrists and tugging them away from her body.

"Fallon! There's not enough room in here for both of us." She took another step and felt her back come up against the wall.

"There's more than enough room." Still holding her wrists, he lifted her arms, looped them behind his neck and pressed forward until he was flush against her. He slid his palms down her bare arms and cupped her face, so he could tilt her head back and kissed her. She responded instantly, eagerly, rising up on tiptoes. Fallon loved her lack of pretence, loved that there were no games to be played and that she wanted him and wasn't afraid to show it.

His hands continued their journey across her shoulders, down her sides and over her hips and, if Rowan hadn't pulled her mouth from his, Fallon knew he would have taken her right where they stood.

"Fallon!" she whispered, scandalised. "We're in the middle of a public place!"

"So? They're paid a lot of money to look the other way." Fallon summoned up a smile at her surprised gasp. "Don't worry, that was just an appetiser, sweetheart." He gave her bottom a squeeze. "Finish getting dressed." A tug on her hair brought her eyes back up to meet his. "Will you leave your hair down for me?"

When she came out of the changing room a few minutes later, Fallon couldn't hide his satisfaction. The dark emerald green dress fitted her like a second skin, the material clinging in all the right places. The dress ended mid-thigh and her legs were bare, naturally tanned, with her feet encased in heels high enough to bring her head higher than his shoulder. Her hair cascaded around her shoulders in a dark red cloud and his fingers itched to touch it.

Her blue eyes, when he finished his examination of her and lifted his to meet hers, were fiery but the way she clasped her fingers together told a different story. She was as worried as she was irritated.

"Let's go to dinner," he said, ignoring her conflicting emotions. He curled his fingers around her arm and led her out of the store.

~*~

Although Rowan tried to keep her eyes centred on the back of the restaurant's graceful dark-haired hostess as she led them along the dining area's curved carpeted walkway to be seated, she couldn't help but notice the attention they were attracting. Heads turned, eyes tracked their progress with each and every step, and there was little doubt in her mind that the low murmurings her ears picked up at the passing of each table concerned the two of them.

They were taken to a booth along the circular room's leftward rim. Fallon waited for her to sit, then slid in beside her.

"Can I start you with drinks and appetisers?" the hostess enquired, after giving them their menus.

"Rum, Bacardi Gold and . . ." Fallon said, and left the order open-ended as he turned his attention to Rowan.

"Just water, thank you."

"Bacardi Gold and water, it is." The hostess flashed an amazingly white smile. "Devon will be your server, and I'll be back with your beverages shortly." She executed a bow and moved away, as though her feet trod on a cushion of air.

"Fallon . . ." Rowan said, sliding a bit closer. "People are staring."

"Yes, they are," he replied, caught her hand in his and raised it to his lips.

"Why?"

"Why *not*? You're a very beautiful woman. And they're probably wondering who you are. And," he paused to give her a dazzling smile, "the men are wishing they were me."

"Are you *kidding* me?" She looked around the well-lit room. "Have you *seen* the women in here? They put supermodels to shame."

He flicked a bored glance at the surrounding tables. "And their husbands, mates, significant others, what-have-you have seen them that way every single day. Have *seen* them like that for . . . longer than you can imagine," Fallon explained. "You're a natural beauty, no artifice, and in places like this, *that* is an unusual sight."

Their hostess reappeared with their drinks and placed them on the table, with a smile. Their waiter, a slender brown-haired male, approached as the hostess departed, his gaze settling on Rowan a little bit too long to suit her.

"Have you decided yet, folks?" he asked, order pad and pen poised as he waited. "If you need a bit more time . . ."

"It's fine, I'll start," Fallon stopped him. "Sirloin steak, rare, baked potato, no vegetables. And could you bring a bottle of Bacardi Gold run?"

"I'll have the same, only well done," Rowan added. "But minus the rum."

There was a lengthy slash of awkward, if not entirely uncomfortable silence between them following the waiter's department. Though, apparently, it felt more uncomfortable for Rowan than Fallon, who seemed relatively content to sip his rum while stroking her thigh, beneath the table, with his fingertips.

"Shouldn't we wait for Koo?" Rowan broke the quiet. "I thought she would be joining us."

"She might be along in a while. Coming here for anything longer than an in-and-out visit is a treat for us," he explained, with a smile. "A mini-vacation, you could call it. A time to leave the stresses of the job behind and relax. Everything is taken care of here. Maid and cleaning services; room service too, if you don't want to leave your suite. Actually, Shadowfall is equipped to the point that leaving the premises is completely unnecessary. Everything's provided," he smiled. "In Koo's case, even companionship. She's got a . . . friend who lives and works here, which is where I'd say she is right now."

He stopped talking when their waiter arrived with their food. Both took their time, following the waiter's departure to prepare and season their meals and take initial mouthfuls before resuming their conversation.

"Look, I'd like tonight to be a break from everything that's going on. Let's give ourselves a breather, bleed off some of the tension and worry. If it helps, I'm pretty sure now that Eden is still alive somewhere. Otherwise, they wouldn't be trying so hard to lure you away and to *kill* me." He reached over and gave her hand a reassuring squeeze. "After everything you've been through, not counting this past year, you deserve some time for yourself. Eden would understand. And we *will* find her, I promise."

Rowan nodded, slowly. "Okay, alright."

Fallon smiled. "Good girl."

When their main course was done, they both pushed their plates to one side and sipped their drinks. Fallon watched as Rowan's eyes strayed to where a few couples swayed on the dancefloor to the muted sound of music and set down his glass.

"Let's dance," he told her, and eased out of his seat, holding out a hand.

Heads turned at nearby tables, following Fallon's rise, and caused Rowan to hesitate.

"Ignore them," he told her. "They're just curious, and more than a little envious."

"Of who, though? There are just as many women watching as men."

Fallon chuckled. "Modesty compels me not to answer that."

Rowan paused a moment longer, then finally accepted his hand, allowing herself to be pulled to her feet and led toward the dancefloor. The music being played came from a small band in the righthand corner – guitars, upright bass, drummer, piano, horns. A slow jazzy tune that demanded close, intimate contact.

Fallon half-expected Rowan to keep some distance between them and was surprised when she moved into his arms. She lifted her own to drape loosely over his shoulders and linked her fingers behind his neck with a smile.

It felt good. Almost *too* good, he found himself thinking. Although he would never admit it aloud, especially to Koo who was straining at the bit to say '*I told you so*', it was highly uncharacteristic how close he'd gotten to the redhead in the time they'd known each other. But then, there was very little that could be considered standard or *normal* about both their association *and* the job at hand.

Most of his assignments called for little, if any, interaction with clients. For the most part, they were arranged through third-party intermediaries or electronic contact. In fact, the only reason he'd been the one to meet Rowan at the diner was because Koo had had a prior commitment and Eayann was out of town. But, in all cases, one rule was cardinal – no emotional involvement, it was strictly business.

Until now.

He knew that becoming emotionally involved with Rowan should concern him but, being honest with himself, it didn't.

Lost in thought, he tightened his arms, drew Rowan closer to him and lowered his head to brush his lips across her temple. One of Rowan's hands slipped from around his neck to slide down and rest against his chest. They danced in silence, enjoying the easy intimacy they were sharing and, as the music slowed to a stop, Rowan drew away a little and raised her face to look at him.

"We should," she began, her voice husky. "Maybe we should leave?"

No question there, Fallon decided. As they disentangled, he took her by the elbow and led them back to the table, though only long enough to extract his wallet and leave a tip for their waiter. At the hostess/cashier's station, they paused while Fallon signed their meal voucher, then moved out onto the causeway. Rowan took his hand as they neared the elevator alcove.

"Do you think Koo will mind that we left before she showed up?" Rowan asked.

"I doubt it," Fallon chuckled. "In fact, I doubt Koo will give much thought to you or me, or dinner for that matter, for quite a while. It's been some time since either of us could take time away from business to enjoy ourselves."

An elevator arrived almost as soon as they entered the alcove and they boarded, neither speaking again until they'd exited onto their floor. Once again, it was Rowan who initiated conversation.

"You and Koo, the two of you are very close, aren't you? More than just business partners." Fallon nodded. "You've known each other a long time then?"

"Oh yeah," Fallon chuckled again, leading her toward the corridor at their left. "Half my life and *most* of hers. She's like my little sister. And there are definitely times when she can be just as bratty." He laughed.

"And there's someone else she mentioned to me," said Rowan. "In fact, she showed me pictures. I think she called him—"

"Ian," Fallon interjected. "Only, he spells it E-A-Y-A-double N. Eayann Ó Beolláin. And there's *no way* and *nothing* I can say that will prepare you for him. He's one of a kind."

Rowan nodded.

"This is it." Fallon touched her arm, indicating she stop while he pulled a key card out of his jacket pocket. He opened the door and stepped back to allow Rowan to precede him into the room.

Light flooded the interior and Rowan came to a stumbling halt, staring down at the large collection of bags and boxes scattered around the coffee table and couch. She turned her head to look at Fallon, a questioning look in her eyes.

"What is all this?"

Fallon stepped behind her and rested his hands on her shoulders. "I don't know how long we're going to stay here, and you didn't bring any clothes." He dipped his head to press a kiss in the curve where her throat met shoulder. "And, as gorgeous as you look in that dress, I thought you'd like a change of clothes or two."

"But I can't aff—"

"You don't need to pay for any of it. *I* brought you here it's only fair I supply whatever you need for our stay."

"There's more than two outfits in those bags, Fallon."

"And we might stay here for more than two days," he told her, pressing another kiss into her shoulder before moving away to venture further into the room. How could he tell her that after hearing her story from Koo and knowing how much she'd given up to help Eden, he wanted to give *her* something. Shaking off the thoughts rolling around his mind, he continued to speak. "Actually, staying here serves a couple of purposes. One," he held up a hand, ticking off the fingers as he spoke. "We'll need some place strategically safer than the house. Chances are good our adversaries would try paying us a visit sooner or later. *I* would.

"Two. Shadowfall is literally a hotbed of intelligence. Anything that happens in this town will flow through the ears of people who frequent the clubs. And three, I've already stated, we need to unwind a bit."

"I thought you said the house was safe," Rowan said.

"I believe what I *said* – more or less – was, in the unlikely possibility someone does make it through the house and up to my suite, they would have to go through *me* to get to *you*. But I think you'll agree, so far everything about this situation has been unusual. The people we're dealing with don't seem to be playing by anyone's rule book. So, it's time we institute a few new rules of our own."

She nodded absently, her eyes returning to the bags. "This is still too much."

Stepping across to the couch, Fallon picked up some of the bags and tossed them to the floor, clearing a space. "Anything you don't wear, we can always send back before we leave . . . *if* that's what you want." He took off his jacket, draped it across the back of the couch, sat down and leaned back, watching as she lifted one of the bags and looked inside.

"Did you buy *everything* I tried on?" she asked, eventually.

"No, I didn't buy anything brown or boring," he smiled. "I also added a few extras that caught my eye." He held out a hand, palm up. "Come here."

Rowan moved to accept his hand without a second's hesitation and allowed him to pull her forward until she stood between his thighs. Releasing her hand, he slid his palm across the silken material of her dress until his fingers touched the zip, caught it between thumb and finger and tugged it down. His mouth curved up into a slow smile as the dress dipped and then fell, pooling around feet still encased in those high high heels.

"Admiring your purchases?" Rowan asked him, then blushed when he arched an eyebrow. "I didn't mean . . . you didn't *buy* me . . . I meant . . ."

Fallon's laugh was rich and deep. "I know what you meant." He tipped his head back against the couch's headrest and looked at her. "What am I going to do with you, Rowan?"

Throwing caution to the wind, she ran one hand through his hair, trailing the other down his cheek and along his jaw and she smiled at him. "I know what I'd *like* you to do."

He turned his head to press a kiss into the palm of her hand. "Is your phone switched off?"

Rowan mock-groaned. "You're never going to forget that, are you?"

"Depends," he shrugged, eyes gleaming. "What are you planning to do to distract me?"

Rowan bent forward, her fingers going to the buttons on his shirt, popping them open quickly and sliding the silk from his shoulders. Fallon didn't move, letting her set her own pace and curious to see what she would do. He contained his laughter when she realised she hadn't unbuttoned the cuffs at his wrists and swore beneath her breath.

Silently, eyes dancing, he raised first one arm and then the other for her to remove the cufflinks and tug the shirt the rest of the way off.

She climbed onto the couch, straddling his hips and let her hands run over his shoulders and chest before leaning closer to trace a finger over his tattoos, before dipping her head to do the same with her tongue. She felt his hands close over her hips and raised her head.

"I thought I was supposed to be distracting you," she said, breathlessly, as he hauled her against him.

"Too slow," he growled, meshed a hand into her hair and dragged her mouth down to his.

It took a minute or two for the sound of knocking to penetrate Rowan's desire-clogged mind, and another for her to realise it was coming from the main door to the suite and, with a crazy sense of déjà vu, she pulled her mouth from Fallon's.

"There's someone knock—"

"Ignore them." Even as he spoke, he could see Rowan drawing away from him.

"You know I can't." She reached down and pulled on his shirt, buttoned it closed, then leaned forward to give him a kiss that promised more to come. She evaded his hands as they went to grab her waist and slid off his lap to pad across to the door.

Rising to his feet, Fallon stalked along behind her. Flinging the door open, he scowled at the man on the other side.

"This better be good."

"And I can fully appreciate why," the man's reply was accompanied by a leering grin as his eyes danced the length of Rowan's shirt-clad charms.

Smecher. Rough Old Tongue translation: wise guy; rebel; thug; gangster. And, judging by the look of his jewellery (pinkie ring and cufflinks: 18 Karat diamonds), the cut of his suit and shoes, and his language, a wise guy whose pedigree placed him a lot higher up the food chain than your average street soldier. A *Sub Şeful – underboss –* more than likely. *Definitely Brotherhood.*

"And, while I can't guarantee it's as good as I'm sure the young lady is, I can at least offer my apologies for the interruption," he added into the charged silence.

There were three, all totalled. Two hidden from view to the right and left of the open doorway. And, from the sounds of their heartbeats and breathing, Fallon could tell that not only were they strapped, but they had hands on the grips of their weapons.

"So gracious. How can I do anything other than accept your apology," Fallon said, taking a step sideways to block the man's view of Rowan. "So, what do you want?"

"You requested a meeting. I'm here to escort you." The man made a half-turn away from the door, waving to indicate Fallon should follow.

"I'll need a couple of minutes." Fallon eyed both sides of the man before him, to show he knew they weren't alone.

"A couple," the man inclined his head. "My colleague doesn't like to be kept waiting."

Fallon returned the nod, took out his cell and dialled the moment the door was shut.

"*This better be very import—*" Koo's voice answered on the fourth ring.

"It is. I need you. I'll explain later," he told her. "Get over to my suite ASAP." He broke the connection and turned to Rowan. "When I leave here, you open that door for nobody. *Nobody* but Koo, that is. Do you understand?"

Rowan's eyes darted back and forth between Fallon and the door. "Who is he, Fallon? Does he have anything to do with the people who—"

"*Rowan!*" He all but barked to interrupt her, taking her by both shoulders. "Do you understand? Nobody . . . *Nobody!*"

"Yes, yes, I understand!" she answered, although the look in her eyes said, '*we'll be talking about this later*'.

Fallon hesitated, then quickly stepped into the master bedroom with Rowan trailing behind him.

In the wardrobe there were a number of shirts and jackets he kept there for emergencies. Fallon picked out one of each and threw the jacket on the bed while he pulled on the shirt. Midway through buttoning, he glanced up to find Rowan's eyes following the rapidly disappearing expanse of golden flesh.

"Don't look at me like that," he said, softly. "Don't get attached to me, Rowan."

His comment stung, but Rowan didn't let it show. She understood what he was saying – they were in enforced intimacy, and there was an undeniable attraction between them, but once the job was over, so would they be.

"Is your life always like this?" she asked instead, giving in to temptation and reaching out to run a palm down the corded muscles of his chest before taking over and finished closing the buttons on his shirt.

"Like what?"

"Always something going on." She toyed with the hem of his shirt and he reached down to cover her hand with his.

"No. You seem to be a chaos magnet." He tipped her head up so he could meet her eyes. "Will you promise me you won't leave the suite, Ro?" he asked her, softly.

"I promise," she replied, her voice barely more than a whisper.

Fallon nodded, bent to give Rowan a lingering kiss on the lips then straightened, scooped up his jacket and left the suite.

Once out in the corridor, the one who'd done all the talking stepped back, allowing his companions to finally make themselves *officially* noticeable.

"I think you know the procedure," he said, nodding to the man nearest to Fallon, who cautiously moved closer. Fallon raised both arms, spreading them outward for the traditional 'pat down'.

When he'd finished, the soldier stepped back and gave his superior an affirming nod.

"I am aware, of course, about Thoth's rule concerning weapons in his club. But there are rules and there are *rules*," the superior said, "not that you actually need a piece," he continued, jerking his head to indicate the two soldiers should precede them. Both moved as if they were connected by an invisible cord, simultaneously moving down the hallway in perfect step with one another. Fallon and the superior fell in behind them.

"I saw you once, in Berlin, three years ago. It was one of our nightspots – the Red Lotus . . ."

"A Brotherhood blood brothel," Fallon clarified.

"Nightspot . . . brothel . . . you say po-tay-to, I say po-tah-to," the superior smiled. "And, forgive my manners, I am Myrick, right hand to the *Şeful*."

"*Şeful* . . . Cokie Donaghy," Fallon offered, sensing the sudden shift in the atmosphere between them.

"Do yourself a tremendous favour, my friend," the temperature in Myrick's voice hovered just above icy. "If you know anything about American history – so-called underworld celebrities, to be exact – and the stories of how Bugsy Siegel hated that nickname – be very *very* careful never to use that name around the *Şeful*. That is, unless you enjoy pain."

"Pain has a certain amount of pleasure in the right situation," Fallon replied. "But I'll keep that in mind."

A moment later, they rounded the corner and entered the elevator alcove.

"Where was I now?" Myrick said, after a short bout of silence. "Ah, Berlin. Red Lotus, three years ago. That little altercation you had with members of the local contracting agency."

Fallon allowed himself an amused grin. "The Dietrich brothers. You say contracting, I say the Brotherhood's local recruitment gang. If you call pulling runaway girls off the street, raping and getting them hooked on smack or crack, then putting them to work as hookers and blood donors' recruitment, that is."

"You took on five men at once," Myrick chose not to respond to Fallon's accusatory observation. "At least three of them were armed with silver-bladed weapons. You're very good with that Jackie

Chan/Bruce Lee/Steven Segal stuff. Several centuries of practice, I imagine."

The elevator arrived, delivering a carload of passengers; as well as cancelling Fallon's need to respond to Myrick's commentary. The soldiers stepped aside, allowing first Fallon, then their superior to board, then followed.

The soldiers made a beeline for one of the club's security personnel the moment they exited the elevator. The latter had them stand by while she waved in the direction of the registration/security station and it wasn't long before a second S.O. joined them carrying the soldiers guns and ammo clips.

"Shall we?" Myrick waved toward the club entrance as the soldiers returned.

~*~

A black limo pulled into the curb two minutes after their exit from the club. One of the luxury stretch limo models made to accommodate eight to ten passengers, with a full wet bar and audio/video entertainment. The soldiers snapped into action. Hands inside their jackets, they raced to cover both sides of the limo – front and back – while Myrick opened the passenger door to allow Fallon inside. Everyone boarded (and, impressively, in under thirty seconds), they were in motion in less than a minute and Fallon found himself in the presence of local Purple Brotherhood clan leader Caitlin Donaghy.

A bit of an in-joke within the organisation, the so-called 'big man' in Seattle's Brotherhood cadre being a woman. But, if all Fallon had heard over the years was true, a woman in gender only. It was said that few females had what it took – guts, guile, soul (or lack of) – to earn a position of power within the *Purple*, let alone *run* a Brotherhood clan. In point of fact, or at least according to rumour, there were only four. Three of whom were chieftesses of crews and/or operations in the UK and America. Donaghy was the only Clan Boss. And her rise to power had been a brutal and bloody one.

A luxuriously well-endowed brunette in a black turtle-neck, short leather jacket, body-hugging stretch pants and calf boots, she occupied the limo's rear seat like it was a cloud-grey leather throne. Or, more accurately, as one of the Caesars might have while presiding over the commencement of gladiator combat in the Coliseum.

Attractive? In the way a hapless insect might perceive a Venus Flytrap . . . just before she ate him.

"Mr Wylde. Your reputation precedes you," she raised her wine glass in salute. "Can I offer you something? According to our mutual acquaintance you prefer rum."

"No, thank you," Fallon said, stopping Myrick as he leaned in the direction of the bar.

"Sandrine?" He gave name to the aforementioned 'mutual friend'. "I trust she's as healthy as when I last saw her?"

Donaghy quirked an eyebrow, sipping her wine. "Of course. Sandrine is an invaluable source of information. And a fantastic club hostess, as well. I would do nothing to disrupt that." She took another sip. "You should be honoured, Mr Wylde. I don't make a habit of responding in person to people who request meetings with me."

"I was wondering about that," said Fallon. "Why do I rate?"

"I'll answer that, but under two conditions, Mr Wylde. One, that you'll have a drink with me. I like things a little less businessy when I'm out of my official place of business."

Fallon nodded in agreement and Myrick moved to comply. "You said two."

"Indeed. Two, you call me Cate. And I will address you as . . . Fallon, is it?"

First name offering. As his friend and frequent Father Confessor, Eayann, might put it – warming up the butter before the scones are in the oven.

"Cate it is," Fallon smiled. Myrick returned to his seat a moment later, passing a large heavy-based glass of rum to Fallon, then saluted with his own.

Fallon stared at his drink, visibly hesitant. It prompted Myrick to retrieve the rum, salute once more and take a healthy gulp.

"It's just rum, Mr Wylde. Ron Rico, in fact. Nothing more."

"Force of habit," Fallon offered as Donaghy's nod moved Myrick to refill the glass.

"No need for apologies, Fallon," Donaghy said, waiting until the fresh drink was in Fallon's hand before continuing. "Under the circumstances, there's no reason you *should* give us your unquestioning trust. Trust is earned, after all.

"And with that said, shall we get down to business?" she continued, her demeanour making just the slightest of shifts.

Fallon knew from this point on he was under their magnifying glass.

"Tell us about the girl?" Her request was followed by a pause, albeit brief. "Or should I say plural - girls? The one you're looking for and the one you're keeping a close eye on."

Fallon twitched both eyebrows, feigning surprise. "Should I take it your interest in the girls has a connection to the reason Flan Deevers' *consigliere* is out here from New York?"

"New York is New York. This is Seattle," Donaghy answered, a little too quickly and with a noticeable smidgen of contempt. "But, for the sake of trust, let's say it's in the ballpark. You're making some very enterprising people nervous and angry. I would like to know what these two girls have to do with that. It's that simple."

Enterprising, Fallon noticed. *Interesting choice of words.* "With all due respect, Cate, I don't know which I am more – disappointed or insulted. If your ears on the street are as good as I always heard they were, then you already know the answer. And if you know, then this meeting has been set up to play me for a *debil* – a first-class idiot. Because, maybe my ears aren't as plentiful as yours, but mine are picking up that you're a lot more interested in finding Knox than figuring out how the girls fit in."

A look passed between Donaghy and Myrick, bringing a smile to the lips of the former.

"For the record, I don't think you're an idiot," she said. "Playing things close to the vest is one of *my* habits and I apologise for that. The girl you're with, we know you're looking for her sister. We know there are people out there who want you to stop. And Knox, he's got all the answers, and those same people are also looking for *him*. We'd like to fin- *talk* to him first."

"And we will," Myrick finally entered the exchange. "Knox is a businessman. And every day he stays out of the business, he's losing profit and prestige. He can't stay idle indefinitely, and when he resurfaces . . ." He made a clapping gesture, signifying the closing of a trap. "We may not be close to finding him, but the question is how close are *you* to finding your girl's sister?"

"Knox might be your best bet to finding her," Donaghy put in. "But he's off the grid. Maybe *we're* the next best thing."

"Meaning?" Fallon prompted, although he was well aware of where the conversation was leading.

"You scratch our back, we scratch yours. We're not totally clueless, Fallon. I know Knox has already contacted you. You meet with him, get him to give you the four-one-one on the situation. He'll at least tell you who's got the sister – maybe even how to get her back. You tell us and maybe we'll help you do it."

Fallon thought for a moment, or at least appeared to, and gave a shrug. "And information, that's all that's in it for you?"

"Does it matter?" asked Myrick. "So long as you get what you want?"

Fallon nodded. "Let me think about that for a while."

"The offer's only on the table for twenty-four hours," said Myrick. "We'll contact you at Shadowfall then."

Donaghy drained her wine glass and tapped the intercom panel beside her window. "Take us back now, Driver."

No more words passed between the limo's passengers on the ride back to Shadowfall. Nor were the traditional platitudes exchanged upon their arrival, as Fallon exited the vehicle. In fact, the car was in motion, more than a block away before Myrick broke the silence.

"Call me Cate?" he queried, in a tone laden with an unequal blend of amusement and disbelief. "Trust is earned? Jesus fuckin' Moses, Caitlin. No offense, but for a minute I was wondering if you were going to ask me to help him drop his pants, so you could get down on your knees—"

Donaghy's sudden laugh, a truly nasty one to be sure, cut him off and she held up her glass, shaking it to make the ice cubes rattle. Myrick took it, refilled it with her preferred blend, and returned it.

"You know, if anybody else but you had made that insinuation . . ." she left the statement unfinished, saluted and gulped. "The last time I did *that* for a man was *his* last time. But I'll tell ya somethin' – just between you, me and the ceiling, I was almost tempted. Hell, I've done a lot worse for people I liked or respected ten times less than him. Aside from the fact, he's a right sexy bastard."

"So, you respect him?" Myrick flashed a lopsided grin. "Somehow, I kinda got the feeling respect is *not* what that was all about."

"Yes, I *do* respect him. And for a few reasons. The man is good at what he does, which I'm countin' on. And you're right, it wasn't just about respect. But that's an important part of it. You see," she paused to down the remainder of her drink and pass Myrick her glass. "I got no respect for the people we're dealin' with. In fact, I despise the sonsabitches. They're a fuckin' load of backdoor politicians disguised as glorified door to door vacuum cleaner peddlers. They show up, danglin' this glorious new thing of theirs like raw meat on a hook, gettin' everyone lickin' their chops and pantin' like a pack'a hungry dogs. They dole out the odd scrap here and there, getting' the dogs all excited til pretty soon we're all snappin' and tearin' at each other, so that when they finally give us the thing . . . the big, juicy chunk of meat, we'll all be willlin' to do anything, *pay any price* for it. And that keeps *them* in control. Well, *not* this bitch."

Myrick fixed fresh drinks for them both and sat back in his seat. "Well call me dense, but how does Wylde figure into taking their control?"

"He doesn't," she smiled. "Take their control, I mean." She grinned at his look of confusion. "Look, this meetin' with Wylde served a couple of purposes. One was confirmation. The girl he's with. She's become a lot more than just a client. His feelin's are involved. And if there's one thing that's known about Mr Wylde, it's his passion, his *loyalty*, to the people he cares about. Two, I knew damn well, even before I asked, that he's not gonna cooperate with us. But he doesn't need to. Whatever Knox tells him is just fuel for the fire. And three, our friends, the salesmen, have one huge fault. They're arrogant. And arrogance leads to stupidity. And sooner or later, they're gonna commit a very fatal mistake and they're gonna have their hands full of Fallon Wylde."

"And how will that help us?" Myrick asked.

"One step at a time, my friend," Donaghy answered. "One step at a time."

~*~

It was the look on the face of the room service attendant as Fallon passed him in the hall. Lingering eye contact and a fleeting smile that said, *'Oh you lucky bastard'.* Not that the look alone was enough. The attendant was someone Fallon was passably familiar with. He'd worked at Shadowfall, out of the Dark Velvet Café, for many months. Caleb was his name, he also covered for Tigr part-time, behind the bar in the Shadows of Night Lounge. But that, coupled with 'the look' was sufficient to raise the yellow flag for Heads Up in Fallon's mind. Long before he reached the suite door and heard the peals of laughter coming from within.

"Sounds like someone's in a good . . ." Fallon spoke as he entered the suite, his words abruptly cut off by the head-on, or make that *face*-on, impact of an undefined feminine garment. *Two* garments he saw, after pulling them away for inspection – a t-shirt and silk pyjama bottoms, wadded into a single fragrant bundle.

". . .mood," he finished the observation, taking in the scene before him with an air of someone who'd just opened the door to his house and found a giraffe in the front yard. A comparison that which lent itself to exaggeration, true enough, but not by much.

First there was the mess. What had, before his departure, once been a number of parcels and clothing-filled bags placed in relatively neat, if not altogether organised clusters now looked like the aftermath of a flea market explosion. Clothes, shoes, and bags – some ripped and shredded, others wadded – covered every inch of the carpet and its furnishings. Second, the room's glass-topped coffee table was a literal swampy mess of spills, overturned glasses and champagne bottles.

Third and finally, Rowan and Koo. The former was draped backwards and upside-down over the backrest of the largest couch, legs hooked over the back, wearing . . . make that *barely* wearing a pair of panties that were wrenched and twisted low on her hips, and a strappy top that had dropped far enough to barely cover her breasts. The latter, Koo, stood just two or three feet from the door, a champagne glass in one hand, wearing an ear-to-ear smile and nothing else.

"Oh, look who's here." Her words slurred almost to the point of running into one another, and she half-turned to speak to Rowan, sloshing champagne in a wide arc that splashed the carpet, the table and the couch cushions. "Our b-b-big han'some strong protector." She swung to face Fallon again, sloshing the remaining contents of the glass within inches of his feet.

Fallon took in the scene, then reached into his pocket and pulled out his phone. Never taking his eyes from Koo, he spoke into the mouthpiece. "Call Pantera." The call connected after two rings.

"Fallon?"

"Come and get your playmate," Fallon said. "Bring a bathrobe or something."

"What?" Pannie sounded confused.

"You'll see when you get here." He cut the call before Pannie could respond. "You," he directed his words at Koo and pointed at the empty couch. "Sit there and wait for Pannie."

Fallon waited until Koo had followed his instruction, then crossed over to where Rowan had flopped back down, right-side-up, onto the other couch.

"You, up." His voice grim, he pulled Rowan to her feet and frogmarched her into the bathroom, slamming the door behind them.

Rowan didn't say a word, even when he hauled her into the shower and fiddled with the dials. When the ice-cold water hit, she gasped and flung her head back, struggling to pull herself free of his grip.

Trying to hold on to her wet and flailing arms was, for a while, like fighting an angry snake. He had to give the little spitfire her props, she was a lot stronger than he gave her credit for.

"Fallon, stop! It hurts," Rowan whined, a slight slur still on her words. "I'm al- I can do this on my . . . You don't have to treat me like a . . . a . . ."

"Drunk teenager?" Fallon finished her protest. Her response was a scowl, after which she finally succeeded in jerking her arm free.

A series of loud knocks on the outer door brought his attention back to the main room and the other inebriated party.

"You stay put until you sober up. I *mean* it," he told Rowan, lingering a second longer to make sure his words took root, grabbed a towel to dry himself off, then made his way back to the main room.

The door hadn't been locked, so it came as no surprise to find Pantera Rydell, Head of Club Security by day, had let herself in and stood, in t-shirt and suede moccasins, hands on her slender hips, a terrycloth bathrobe draped over one shoulder and was surveying the condition of the room in almost comical disbelieve. And *Koo*, naked as the day of her birth, lounged in a pose more comic than provocative on one of the wet bar's high stools.

"*Hiiii baby!*" she trilled, drunkenly, and leant forward with arms outstretched. She misjudged her balance, however, and would have kept going, face-first onto the floor, had Pannie not put on a burst of speed to catch her. Half-stooped, arms hanging limp at her sides,

Koo raised her face up to flash her dark-haired lover a droopy-eyed, toothsome smile, uttered a half-giggled '*oops*', and collapsed with her face buried against Pannie's chest.

"Is she . . . *drunk*?" Pantera looked back and forth between the top of Koo's head to the bottle-cluttered coffee table, then to Fallon. "We don't get drunk. At least *not* from what's on that table."

"Yeah . . ." Fallon replied, softly, his own gaze swinging to study the coffee table and the area surrounding it as a thought began to nag at his mind. "No, *we* don't."

The thing that nagged at him now took on the weight of a gradually forming suspicion, and Fallon was just turning to inspect one of the nearest champagne bottles when his cell phone rang. A habitual pause to check the display screen showed CALLER UNKNOWN and, for reasons he was almost certain would soon reveal themselves, the growing suspicion in his thoughts shifted to a very heavy and definite hunch status.

He barely had time to thumb the TALK button and raise the phone to his ear when a male voice, deliberately garbled, came through.

"Evenin' brother. How they hangin'?"

A frown, a glance to where Pannie still stood, now holding Koo in her arms, and Fallon replied with, "Let me take a wild guess. Taylor? Or is it Eli, or Martin? What is it you call yourself these days, Skippy?"

"I *am* flattered," the caller chuckled. "I see my reputation precedes me. But if it's a name you want, whatever rocks your clock. Anything, that is, but Skippy."

Pannie caught his attention, gesturing with a hand to indicate her desire for Fallon to put the call on speaker. Fallon nodded and did as requested.

"You're probably askin' yourself – how the hell did he get my private number? Am I correct, Fallon?" the caller said. "Okay if I call you Fallon?"

"Whatever, Taylor. And no worries, phone numbers can always be changed."

"That they can, Fallon," Taylor chuckled again, lapsing into a short silence before asking, "How's your girls?"

Fallon felt his jaw muscles tense. "I'm pretty sure you already know the answer to that. But just to satisfy my curiosity, what did you give them?"

"A sample of things to come. The wave of the future . . . *our* future, at least. Talk to your friend, Kane. From what I understand, he's had first-hand experience with it." Taylor laughed, then paused and when he spoke again, it was in a voice less technicised. "Hope you'll forgive the dramatics. I really hate using that thing. No need for it now, since you have an idea of who it is you're dealin' with."

"You said *our*," Fallon prompted, fuelling the vampire's apparently oversized ego and need to toot his own horn. "I take it that means you're organised."

"We can walk it like we talk it. That should be fairly obvious since we knew how to find your little Miss Rowan . . . *twice*. And we got someone into Shadowfall. You know, we coulda snatched her, *and* killed your little Asian friend . . . *if* we truly wanted to."

"Then why didn't you?"

There was another blip of silence before Taylor resumed. "You can thank *me* for that Fallon. You see, I like you. I *admire* you. I know your rep too, and you – my friend - are damned good at what you do. For instance, the three hitters you took out the other night. They were pros, seasoned and expensive. You are worth ten times what we paid them. I . . . *we* could use a man like you in the organisation. And *that's* why."

It was Fallon's turn to laugh. "Let me understand this. You are offering me a *job*?"

"You could say that," Taylor answered. "Although it's more like stock in a growing company. We have come a long way, Fallon. And we'll go a lot further. We are going to do big things, *great* things by putting a new spin on an old industry. You can be a part of that. Grow with us. Make history."

"History . . ." Fallon repeated the word, with a thinly veiled edge of mockery. "And the hook? The catch?"

"Nothing you don't already know," said Taylor. "Back off. Get Miss Rowan to back off, at least where the police are concerned. We'll make you a deal. Join us and we'll let you keep her for yourself. Hell, we'll even throw in her sister."

"You know, Taylor. As gracious as that offer is, it would put a very ugly stain on my sterling reputation. So, I'm gonna have to decline," Fallon answered without any hesitation. "Guess that means we can't be sweet to each other anymore, huh . . . Skippy?"

"Oh, Fallon . . . Fallon. Bad move," the tone of Taylor's voice grew undeniably dark. "The stuff we gave Rowan and your friend? That was just a taste. Just enough to make them happy little bitches. A few drops more and let's just say we'd be having a completely different conversation. But you roll the dice and you get what you get. This was your last warning, Fallon. Next time the gloves come off. Oh, and by the way," he added, "we are damn good at what *we* do, too."

"You better be, Skippy," Fallon said, in a voice that mirrored the caller's dark tone, and ended the call.

CHAPTER EIGHT

After a quick exchange between Fallon and Pantera, in the call's aftermath, during which they agreed to resume talks, including Kane within the next hour, Fallon returned to the bathroom to check on Rowan. The shower had been shut off, but Rowan remained where he'd left her, albeit sitting on the wet tiled floor, back propped up against the wall, with her eyes closed.

After stripping her out of her soaked top and panties, he towelled her off as best he could and carried her into the master bedroom, where he tucked her snugly into bed. He wanted to leave but found he couldn't. Something stopped him, held him. Some inexplicable, not-quite-fathomable something, reaching up from a place deep within. A place Fallon thought he'd closed off a very long time ago. Something that ached now when he gazed down at the sleeping woman. A feeling he wanted to deny, to wish away, but found even that to be beyond his power to control.

Admit it, Wylde, a little voice close to the surface of his consciousness spoke up. *This isn't just a gig; a mission; a case to be solved any more. And she is more than just a client. And isn't that something you've known for a while now?*

"Yeah . . . damn it, yes!" he whispered, and bent down to place a kiss on her forehead before he exited the room.

The call from Pantera came through in the middle of his third glass of rum. The meeting, she told him, would take place in Kane's suite on the club's top floor.

There were three security soldiers waiting in the outer hall when he emerged.

"The Chief wants you to know there'll be two of us here on the hall door and one man inside the suite. No one gets in or even down this corridor without being challenged and searched, head to foot, Mr Wylde."

"Thanks guys. This shouldn't take too long." He gave the group a forced grin, and the lead soldier a comradely clap on the shoulder, before making his way toward the elevators.

~*~

It was a rare occasion that anyone, who wasn't sharing his bed for an hour or two that is, was allowed inside Kane Thoth's inner sanctum. In most cases, not even Kane spent much time there, choosing to do business – social and professional – in his ground floor office. That was the first clue the incident with Rowan and Koo had touched a sensitive spot in the older vampire's life.

"Drinking?" Kane tossed his offering, his version of hospitality, like a television game show host announced the category of the next playing session, as Fallon passed over the threshold.

"Why not?" he shrugged.

"Help yourself," Kane waved in the wet bar's general direction, and plopped down on a couch that could have doubled as a king-sized bed. Pantera, already seated at the bar, set up a glass and slid the ice bucket to meet his approach.

"Pan brought me up to speed, at least on things after her arrival," Kane stated. "So how about your story?"

Fallon paused, continuing to fix up his bourbon-on-the-rocks without visually acknowledging his host. But even without seeing, his senses could hear the edge, feel the tension in Kane's demeanour. A quick glance Pantera's way told him she sensed it too. Finishing the bourbon's preparation, Fallon finally turned, hefted his glass in salute and took a long, slow quaff.

"Rowan and Koo, Pantera's update covered that," Fallon began. "The bastard got somebody inside, doctored a bottle of champagne, and got out. Slick as goose shit."

"And you can bet asses are gonna be bruised, and heads are gonna roll for that bullshit," Pantera growled.

Hers, however, wasn't the reaction that piqued Fallon's interest. It was Kane's – a tell the Egyptian hadn't exhibited in more than three centuries. His thumbnail flicking across the tip of his forefinger.

"And then the call from *him* – Taylor," Fallon went on. "He said they slipped the ladies a taste of whatever it was. And then he tossed *your* name into the pot. Said you had first-hand experience with it."

Kane made eye contact with his long-time friend, a smile slowly spreading across his features. "You trying to draw me, Spaniard?"

Draw. The word brought a reciprocating smile to Fallon's face. It was a term he'd neither heard nor used in many years. Used almost exclusively by the two of them – in the days when they were near inseparable – as part of their shorthand. Draw as in 'draw me/him/her or them out'.

"We've been friends too long for me to lie to you, Egypt," Fallon raised his glass again, noticing in the process that he only had a swallow left. A swallow he took care of and turned to pour another. "Ever since I first took this gig, your name's been bleeding into the mix. I can't help it," he shrugged. "I'm curious."

A long slash of pensive silence followed, Kane seemingly battling forces within himself that fought violently to remain contained. And then he rose, joining his guest at the bar to pour himself a glass of red wine. After an appreciative sip, he returned to the couch.

"If, and I have no reason to think otherwise," he started. "If it's what I believe Taylor referred to, it's a concoction, and an old one, created by my late sire, Pashet. She called it *Suflarea de tacere*. In Old Tongue it means 'the breath of nothingness', or 'silence'.

"It's an hypnotic compound," he took a deep breath. "Although, in today's drug culture, it would be a psychotropic. One hundred percent effective on either Human or Vampire." He fell silent, staring down into his glass, swirling the liquid within. "In any case," he continued, "depending on the dosage used, the effect can be anything from giddiness and drunken stupor to extreme sexual arousal to a total trance-like state. The latter, the person dosed becomes a prisoner trapped inside his or her body, extremely pliable and susceptible to suggestion."

"A slave drug?" Pantera offered.

Kane raised his glass in acknowledgement. "Very much so. And this Taylor . . . he was once associated with Pashet. I think it's safe to assume he's in possession of it. If that helps at all."

Fallon raised a hand, palm-down and fingers spread, waggling it from side to side. "It's starting to."

"Good, old friend. Because that's all I got for you." Kane raised a stiffened finger and drained his glass. "So, if the two of you will excuse me," his gaze strayed for an instant toward the slightly opened door to his bedroom. It drew Fallon's attention, where he caught the flicker of a shadow within.

"Moonlight communion," he murmured. Another shared term from times past.

Both Fallon and Pantera finished their own drinks and said their goodnights.

"Oh, and Pan?" Kane delayed their departure. "I expect a report on how our security was breached first thing tomorrow evening."

"I'll get right on it," she answered, following Fallon out.

They were less than halfway down the corridor when Pantera grabbed his shoulder, slowing their progress. "This is probably a stupid question but . . . moonlight communion?"

Fallon came to a stop and faced her with a smirk as he affected a high-pitched and excited rendition of a feminine voice. "*Oh God . . . Oh Yes . . . Oh Lord . . .*"

"Sorry I asked," Pantera muttered and Fallon laughed.

The rest of their journey was made in silence, with them parting ways a couple of floors below Kane's penthouse suite. Fallon continued the walk to his own suite, dismissed the guards and let himself in. Silence met him, and he leaned back against the door and closed his eyes briefly. What had appeared to be a simple case, at least in the Vampire scheme of things, of a human grab was turning into some unexpected larger-than-life conspiracy. He ran a hand over his face wearily, then pushed himself away and moved toward the spilled bottles and glasses that still littered the coffee table and floor surrounding it.

Pausing only to fill a glass with rum, he cleared up the mess left by Rowan and Koo, stacking the bottles on the breakfast bar and making a mental note to have them checked out for any residue of drugs, anything that could give him some further clues as to what the hell was going on.

Hearing a noise, he straightened and turned in time to see Rowan appear in the doorway of the bedroom.

"Fallon?"

She looked pale, Fallon noted, running his eyes over her. He felt a smile quirk up the corners of his lips at the way she clutched the oversized bathrobe closed with one hand.

"How are you feeling?" he asked, trying to stop his eyes from lingering on the expanse of thigh showing through the bathrobe, where it gaped beneath her grip.

"Thirsty," she replied, walking into the room. Fallon groaned silently as the movement pulled the gap wider.

"I'll get you some water," he told her and retreated to the small kitchenette to retrieve a bottle of water from the refrigerator. Twisting the lid off, he handed it to her, then had to fight his desire to sink his fangs into her throat when she closed her eyes and tipped her head back to drink from the bottle.

After drinking her fill, she opened her eyes and caught a look on Fallon's face that made her freeze mid-move before resuming the movement needed to place the bottle on the countertop.

They both stood, unmoving, and then Rowan slowly released the grip on the robe and let her arms fall to her sides.

"Rowan, no." Fallon was in front of her before the robe opened, catching the edges and pulling them together."

"You want me," Rowan said, her gaze dropping to where his hands gripped the material of the robe.

"Yes." *Why deny it?*

"I want you, too." She ran a finger across one of his hands.

"You're still drunk."

Rowan shook her head. "No."

"Drugged, then."

"Is that what happened?" She lifted her hands to his shoulders. "I'm not drugged, Fallon. Before you went out, you had every intention of sleeping with me again."

"And I was wrong. You're a client." He released her robe and reached for the tie at her waist, intending to knot it around her. "I shouldn't have taken advantage of you the first time."

"That's not it, and you know it." She lowered her arms and shrugged out of the sleeves, leaving him holding the robe looped over the tie at her waist.

"This isn't what you want, Rowan. You're tired, worried about your sister, lonely. What I would give you isn't what you need."

"What I need is you. What I *want* is you." Rowan raised her arms and curled them up around his neck, stepping forward until she stood flush against him. "Please, Fallon?"

She felt him let go of the tie, her robe falling around her feet and his arms closed around her.

"You'll regret this later," he warned her, then bent his head to capture her lips.

~*~

Hours later, Rowan woke with a start to find herself alone in the bed. She sat up, wrapped the sheet around her body and slid out of the bed.

"Fallon?" she opened the bedroom door and stepped through into the sitting room to find him standing at one of the windows, a glass held loosely between his fingers as he gazed out at the still dark city.

"I thought you were sleeping."

"I was." She hovered uncertainly in the doorway, unsure whether to approach him or not, and was relieved when he turned, smiled and held out his hand. She crossed the room quickly, took his hand in hers and let him draw her closer.

"Who ordered the champagne for you and Koo?"

Rowan tilted her head to look up at him. "We thought you did. Koo seemed to know the guy who delivered it, he said it had been ordered from the suite phone just before you left."

"Did she happen to call him by name?"

"Callum . . ." Rowan frowned, thinking. "No, that's not right. Caleb." She moved closer to Fallon, and he dropped her hand to curve his arm around her shoulders. "It wasn't you, was it?"

"No." He told her about the phone call from Taylor and an edited version of the information he'd received afterwards from Kane. "It's looking like Eden's disappearance is just a small part of a much larger operation," he finished.

"Do you think this Caleb is involved?"

Fallon shook his head. "That would be too easy. I'll speak to him tomorrow . . ." he paused and checked his watch, then corrected himself. "Later today, even."

"And then what do we do?"

"*We* don't do anything. There are a few people *I* need to speak to." Fallon pressed a finger to her lips when she began to argue. He couldn't help but admire her refusal to back down, even after everything that had happened. "After I hear what they have to say, then we'll talk about what we do next." As he spoke, he loosened the sheet she was wrapped in and threw it to one side, then stood back to gaze at her, catching her wrists when she moved to cover herself.

"Bit late for that now," he mocked gently, using her captured wrists to guide her backwards toward the couch and down onto it.

Raising her arms above her head, he held them there with one hand, and used the other to stroke her body, from throat to thigh.

He lowered his head to run his tongue over her breast, lapping at the soft flesh in a circle moving inwards until he reached the sensitive peak at the centre. His teeth closed over the hardened tip and he tugged and licked, until Rowan arched up with a moan.

"Fallon!" she tried to pull her arms free, wanting to touch him in turn, only to find his grip had tightened.

"Hold still," he murmured, and nipped at her sensitised flesh, making her hiss.

"I want to—" she struggled again.

"I know," he interrupted. "But if you don't hold still, I'll be forced to spank you."

At her sharp intake of breath, Fallon raised his head. Eyes gleaming, he lifted himself up to look at her.

"*Ahhhh*," he breathed. "I was right. You were watching at Aduna's, weren't you? You *like* that idea."

"No . . ."

"No?" His hand smoothed over her stomach, across her hip and down further, dipping between her legs to discover the wetness of her arousal. "You're such a liar." He gave her a wicked grin and flicked a thumb over the bundle of nerves at her centre. Her hips jerked up and she moaned.

"Fallon . . ."

"Want to change your answer?" He pushed a finger inside her, and watched her pupils dilate. "There's something to be said for a little pain to bring out the pleasure," he whispered, adding a second finger, and slowly thrusting them in and out. "Of giving control to your partner and letting them take you over the edge." A third finger stretched her, and she gasped his name. "A bite here . . . " he continued and took a nipple between his teeth and gave it a sharp nip, before soothing the sting with his tongue. All the while his fingers kept up a steady rhythm and his thumb flicked back and forth, until she was writhing beneath him.

"You're incredibly responsive," he whispered.

"Fallon, *please!*"

"So impatient," he chided, withdrew his fingers and pulled her across his lap. His warm palm smoothed across her bottom and then delivered a stinging slap.

Rowan hissed and tensed, tried to pull away but then Fallon's fingers were inside her again and she whimpered and arched her back. Another slap was followed immediately by his invading fingers and her arousal hit a feverish pitch, the pain intensifying her desire. Fallon's skilled hands issued both pleasure and pain, until she couldn't tell one from the other and, before long, she had gone from telling him to stop to begging him for more.

~*~

For the second time Rowan woke up alone. She stretched and rolled over to discover Fallon leaning against the doorframe watching her, eyes hooded.

A blush rose over her cheeks as visions of the night before flashed in front of her eyes. Until Fallon had delivered that first stinging slap, Rowan would have vehemently argued that pain of any kind would kill any passion she felt. She squirmed under his gaze, unsure what to say.

"There's coffee in the sitting room," he broke the silence, pushing himself upright and walking to stand beside the bed. "Don't look at me like that, Rowan." He placed a finger beneath her chin and tilted her head back. "I warned you that you'd regret it, later."

Her eyes lifted to meet his and her tongue snaked out across suddenly dry lips. "I don't . . . I don't regret it."

"You don't?" Disbelief sharpened his voice.

"No." With a sudden burst of confidence, she reached up a hand to grasp his shirtfront and dragged him close enough to close her lips over his.

Startled, Fallon didn't respond straight away, then he scooped her up into his arms and lifted his head, breaking the kiss.

"You are something else," he told her, striding into the sitting room and lowering her onto the couch. He disappeared back into the bedroom and reappeared a few moments later with one of his shirts. He tossed the garment to her and crossed the room to pour a mug of coffee.

"As much as I'd love to keep you naked all night and see what else you might like, we have things to do."

Rowan pulled the shirt on and accepted the coffee with a smile.

~*~

Pantera Rydell was not a happy camper. As Head of Internal Security for the flagship of Kane Thoth's global Shadowfall fleet, one of the things she was most proud of was the declaration that Club Shadowfall was not just the most safe and secure establishment of its kind in the whole Vampire Nation, but in the entire world. And yes, like all businesses of its kind, they'd had the occasional incident, flare-ups from irate patrons, bar fights, domestic quarrels which got a bit violent, and there was that *thing* a few weeks back, the shooting involving Lord Zuron and his associate, Hamish Satori. But the latter notwithstanding, Pantera and the club held true to its promise. For vampires, and its cadre of select Humans, there was no safer place for a night's entertainment or an extended period of accommodation. It was one of the things that made this latest situation so frustrating. So *infuriating*.

From stories related, after the fact, by Koo and Rowan, Caleb Townsend — a long-time and trusted employee of the club — was brought to Pantera's office for questioning. Fallon stood with Kane in the small room adjacent to Pantera's office, watching and listening to the proceedings via a two-way mirror, much like those used by law enforcement agencies around the world.

It wasn't difficult to deduce that Caleb was completely innocent of any wrongdoing as he described his actions in the matter. As per standard procedure, he explained, calls for room service were received at a small message centre set up near the Dark Velvet Café's kitchen. In these more modern times, it was a communication system integrated into the in-house phone network. A computer tower and monitor set-up.

"The minute the phone is picked up," Caleb explained, "the computer logs the call. The conversation is recorded, shows up on the monitor screen as what's ordered and which room the order is meant for.

"I didn't talk to whoever it was that took the call, but I was next in line to make the delivery. And, according to the recorded screen message, the call came from Mr Wylde. Three bottles of champagne, Perrier-Joyet Bella-Epoque Rose Cuvee '04 to Suite 347. I typed in the order confirmation and sent a copy to Accounts to add it to Mr Wylde's bill, then picked up the order and went up."

"And who set up the order?" Pantera asked.

"Depending on what it is and depending on who is working on any given night, one of five people," said Caleb. "Andre, himself, or the Head Chef take care of full meals, an assistant will do light meals or speciality sandwiches," he cleared his throat, nervously. "The other, if you know what I mean . . . the Functionary menu, Gabrielle – Mr Thoth, himself, hired *her*; and liquor and spirits, the Host or Hostess that evening. They call it in to the bar and a waitress brings it over to us for delivery."

"Gayle Hunter worked the bar last night," Pantera said, naming the club's Manager, for the benefit of those listening. "We were short a bartender. So, no help there."

"If you say so, ma'am," Caleb's response bespoke uneven, and understandable, measures of confusion, uneasiness and restrained aggravation. "If you don't mind . . . did I do something wrong? What's this about? Am I under some kind of suspic—"

"No. Nothing like that," Pantera interrupted him. "You can go back to work now." She gestured toward the door, stopping him just short of opening it. "Oh, and this goes no further than this office. Understand?"

Caleb nodded, relief evident on his features as he left the room. Fallon and Kane joined the scowling security chief a moment later.

"We have a problem," she said, making brief eye contact with both men.

"No shit," Kane remarked.

Pantera continued. "There's a fox in the chicken coop. And one who's way too knowledgeable about the way we operate. Meaning somebody that's been inside for a while."

"And, if that's the case, good luck with finding them," Fallon chimed in. "If Caleb's not the one who dosed the bottles, then it was either somebody else in the kitchen who got to the set-up before he did, or the waitress who brought the champagne over from Gayle's bar," he paused, knowing he had their full attention. "Gayle didn't – that much I'm sure we're all certain of. That leaves an unknown kitchen staffer or the waitress. So, your next move – you check to see who worked the Shadows of Night last night. I got a hunch that, if it was the waitress, she won't be here tonight. Another hunch says she's probably not even still breathing. And that leaves us where?"

"Back at square one," Pantera shrugged. "But I'll check anyway. Just to be thorough. Who knows? Maybe the bastards got sloppy."

"Don't count on it," Fallon threw in, turning to Kane. "We still on for dinner tonight, amigo?"

"We are, indeed. I'm looking forward to meeting the little lady who's causing all this trouble," Kane answered.

CHAPTER NINE

Fallon concealed a grin beneath a sip of his drink as the last — the tenth in the last five minutes, in fact — of a nearly unbroken parade of *admirers*, suck-ups and ass-kissers all, in his well-considered opinion; released Kane's hand and pranced happily away, returning to their respective situations, groups, and/or temporarily neglected paramours.

"Alright, spew," Kane shot his friend and tablemate a smirk while topping off his glass of red wine. "I know you're about to bust a gut."

Fallon straightened himself against the booth's backrest, squared his shoulders, and affected a pretentious highbrow demeanour. "*Oh, Mr Thoth! I just wanted to tell you what an honour it is to meet you . . . to dine in this, your marvellous, magnificent establishment . . . My life is complete now that I have shaken the hand of the legendary Kane . . . Mr Thoth, you are an inspiration to us all . . .* yadda yadda yadda. Give me a fucking break!"

Kane gave a conceding nod, sipping his wine, a half-smile on his lips.

"We've been in the restaurant for what . . ." Fallon continued, checking his watch, ". . .twenty minutes? Twenty-five tops. And, so far, the only ones who haven't slithered over to slurp your ass are the bartender and the jazz quartet in the corner. I don't know how you can just sit there and put up with it without losing it and telling them all to fuck off."

"They mean well," Kane said, softly. "Some of them, anyway."

"Today, maybe," Fallon countered. "But I'd be willing to bet you that ninety-nine percent of them – the trueborn Old Bloods who were around back in the day, at least – were just as willing to take a front row seat to see you crucified in the sun after what happened in '41. And the *only* reason they're so willing to kiss your ass now is because your sire made you wealthier than Gates, the Getty's and the Rockefellers combined, and if it wasn't for the stock they own in Thoth Global, they'd all still be fighting each other like rats in a bucket for pieces of the blood and flesh rackets back in Europe and Asia."

"Human nature, my friend. It's not exclusive to Humans," Kane raised his glass, as did Fallon. The two touched glasses at the rims and drank deeply.

True enough, Fallon couldn't deny it. Though their kind – trueborn and turnbloods alike – arrogantly viewed themselves as an entity apart from, and wholly superior to, Planet Earth's alleged dominant species, namely *Homo Sapiens*, the line which separated the two was, more often than not, both as fragile and transparent as a cellophane baggie.

Still . . .

"Rat droppings and cow manure come from two different animals," Fallon gave a derisive snort. "But any way you pile it, shit is still shit."

"You're preaching to the choir, brother," Kane responded, gazing into his glass while idly swirling the dark sanguine liquid. "And side-tracking the current topic, if I may," the older vampire focused his attention squarely on his tablemate. "How long have we been friends, Diego?"

"Friends? *Diego?*" Fallon's upward twitch of both eyebrows was accompanied by a wry grin. "Why do I feel a lecture coming on?"

"Devil's advocate," Kane gave one shoulder a shrug and went back to swirling his wine.

Fallon mirrored the gesture and took a hit of his drink. "Alright, and I'm going to assume the question was rhetorical . . ."

Kane nodded in response and pressed on. "Mercenary, Soldier of Fortune. Have Gun, Will Travel, and probably a couple dozen other popular tags for what you do . . . You and, at least, a dozen of *our* kind in the business – *you* being top of the A-List."

"Thank you, brother," Fallon saluted with his drink and downed the contents in one gulp.

"And there's my point," Kane continued. "Next to you, SEAL Team Six were a bunch of B-Team boy scouts. So why this . . ." he gestured with a querying lift of one hand, ". . .moonlighting as a street-beating, find-the-missing-person gumshoe? That's like . . . like sending a SWAT team out after a carjacker."

"Nice analogy," Fallon chuckled. "But the people I'm dealing with aren't exactly hijacking BMWs at secluded intersections."

"True enough. But if last night's stunt was any indication, carjackers would be a lot less personal and potentially messier. And, in case you didn't get it, that's the message this son of a bitch Taylor is sending you."

"Believe me, I get it."

. "Do you, amigo? I do wonder," Kane countered. "I'm wondering if maybe Taylor's not the only one letting things get . . .'"

"Personal?" Fallon gave voice to his friend's unspoken prompt. "If you mean am I thinking with the little head instead of the big one?"

Kane gave another head-tilting shrug. "Close but not quite, old friend. You're aim's a bit too low." He placed a hand over his heart, patting softly. "Food for thought," he said before Fallon could respond.

A shadow fell across his seat and, expecting another guest, Kane lifted his head with a fixed smile. A smile that dropped away when his eyes landed on Gayle Hunter's shaken features.

"What is it?" he asked, rising from his seat.

"I need to speak to you," her eyes slid to Fallon and back again, "*privately.*"

"Give me a minute," Kane said to Fallon, set down his glass and followed Gayle out of the restaurant.

Fallon leaned back in his seat, watching Kane and Gayle converse near the doorway. They were too far away for him to overhear the conversation, but judging by the way Gayle was clutching Kane's arm and gesticulating with her free hand, whatever she had to tell him *wasn't* good news. He watched Kane stiffen as she spoke, and when his friend turned his head and crooked a finger at Fallon, he wasn't all that surprised.

The tension surrounding Kane and Gayle was palpable, raising the fine hairs on the back of Fallon's neck.

"What's going on?" he demanded.

"There's a situation upstairs," Kane told him, as he turned to lead the way toward the stairwell. "I'll explain on the way."

"Why the stairs?"

Kane shook his head but didn't reply. Once they were in the stairwell, he stopped and turned to Gayle. "You go on back. I'll deal with this."

"But—" Gayle closed her mouth on what she was going to say with a snap of teeth and nodded. As she passed Fallon, she reached out and patted his arm. "I'm sorry," she told him, and disappeared back out into the foyer.

"What is she sorry for?" Fallon caught Kane's arm. "I'm not going anywhere until you tell me what's going on."

He recognised the assessing look in Kane's eyes as they faced each other, knew the other man was making a decision about what he should tell him, and he braced himself for what he was about to hear.

"I need you to stay calm," Kane told him. "Losing your head is not going to help anyone. Can you do that?"

Fallon clenched his fists. "Just spit it out, Egyptian."

"Someone tried to take Rowan. They got her out of the suite and were heading toward the elevator. She fought them off. They escaped but she's been hurt."

Fallon felt his stomach bottom out. "How badly?"

"I don't know. Gayle shut off the elevators and closed down the third floor."

In unspoken agreement they began to move, putting on a burst of speed that had them arriving at the third floor in seconds. The stench of blood hit them as soon as they opened the door to exit the stairwell and both men froze briefly, lifting their faces to take a breath.

"Rowan . . ." Fallon breathed her name and would have rushed forward had Kane not grabbed his arm.

"Fallon, remember, stay calm."

Fallon pulled free and they moved down the corridor. They could hear voices – first as just noise and slowly becoming clearer as they neared the elevators. Koo's voice became recognisable as they turned a corner, bringing the bloody scene into focus.

Fallon stopped, partially aware of Kane halting beside him, and took a second to let the scene sink into his brain. His eyes flicked from the open elevator to Koo, who sat cross-legged on the floor with blood coating her chest, hands and face, then down to settle on the woman who lay still and silent across Koo's lap. On the peripheral of his attention, he saw Pantera move to intercept them, and burst into movement, adjusting his pace to bypass her and reach the two women who held his focus.

"Koo?" Fallon crouched in front of her, careful not to look down at the woman across her legs.

"Koo?" He snapped his fingers in front of her face until she looked up at him, her eyes shiny with unshed tears.

"F-Fallon?" she lifted a bloody hand to grasp his fingers. "I'm sorry . . . so sorry."

"Tell me what happened." A detached part of his mind congratulated himself on the calmness of his voice.

"I . . . I'm not sure." She blinked rapidly, trying to clear her eyes. "I was leaving the elevator to come and meet Rowan. I heard a fight and came around the corner to find Rowan struggling with someone . . . a man. They saw me and Rowan t-tried to reach me. He . . . he shot her and then threw her at me. I . . . I had to choose – stay with Rowan or chase him." She looked down at the younger woman lying limply across her legs. "I couldn't leave her, Fallon," she whispered. "I couldn't let her die."

Fallon let his eyes drop down, allowed himself to look at the woman he'd held in his arms only hours earlier.

Stay calm!

She was wearing an ivory-coloured dress – now more red than white – the straps ripped. *Probably where she'd struggled to escape her captor.* He thought back to earlier when he'd told her they were going to have dinner with one of his oldest friends and she'd grinned. He'd sprawled on the bed watching as she rummaged through all the clothes he'd bought her until she'd stopped at the one she was wearing.

He reached out a hand to smooth it over her hair, then froze as Koo's words came back to him.

Keep calm.

"Koo, what have you done?"

"I couldn't let her die, Fallon," Koo whispered. "I just couldn't."

"Koo, what did you *do*?" He felt a hand come to rest on his shoulder and glanced up to see Kane standing beside him, his expression serious.

"She turned her, Diego," the other man said, softly.

"She . . . ?" Fallon shot to his feet, shaking off Kane's restraining hand. "Fuck, Koo . . ." he rubbed a hand down his face. "*Fuck!*" He spun and punched the wall, cracking plaster.

Turning a human wasn't as simple as the movies would have people believe. Many who went through the turn died without ever waking up. There was no way to tell who would survive and who wouldn't. All they could do now was wait and see if Rowan woke up – something that could happen in as quick as an hour or as long as a week.

"What in the name of . . ." a heavily incredulous exclamation turned all eyes present toward the stairwell door, and the appearance of the club's physician-in-residence.

Dr. Arlette Chambeau – in robe and pyjamas, emergency medical bag slung over one shoulder – rushed toward the scene as though the devil himself was hot on her heels. She stopped just short of the elevator entrance, her well-preserved blonde features rife with concern.

"Doc, I'm sorry you were disturbed," Kane caught the woman's arm, stopping her from reaching Koo and Rowan. "There's nothing you can do here."

"I was told someone was hurt."

Kane nodded. "Yes. But this is something beyond even your skills." He turned to Pannie. "I want to know who did this, and how they got up here."

Pantera nodded and, with a quick worried glance at Koo, dashed off down the hallway.

"Fallon, we need to move Rowan. We'll take her to the infirmary and—"

"No!" Fallon cut in sharply. "*I'll* take her back to our suite. I won't have her waking up somewhere strange."

"Fallon . . . Diego . . ."

Fallon shook his head. "She *will* wake up. She's strong, she can get through this." He strode back to Koo, bent and lifted Rowan's limp and bloody body into his arms.

"I'm sorry, Fallon. I—"

"Don't say it." He straightened. "Go and get yourself cleaned up and come back to my suite. Ro is going to need you when she wakes." He strode away without waiting for a response.

CHAPTER TEN

Of all the myths surrounding vampires, the one that really got it wrong was the claim they were undead. But there was a very good reason that particular myth had come into being. When a vampire turned a human, the human fell into a state of hibernation as the body changed to adapt to the new enzymes released into the blood. Some people were unable to handle the trauma of the change and never awoke, but for those who did survive, it could take anything from minutes to days for them to regain consciousness. Back in the days when bodies could not be stored, that meant the newly awakened vampire had to claw their way out of a coffin or crypt – resulting in the many myths and stories of corpses coming back to life as vampires.

The biggest problem any vampire considering turning someone had was no one could predict who would survive – the strongest man may never awaken, yet the frailest person would rise from their bed ready to take on their brand-new life. Even with all the technology available, the vampire clans were still unable to figure out just what it was that allowed the change to take.

Right then, that battle raged inside Rowan's frame as Fallon perched on the mattress beside her gently, almost reverently, cleaning the blood from her nude body with a washcloth soaked in a combination of hot, soapy water and a splash of her favourite scented bath oil. He paused when he reached her breasts, his hand hovering as his eyes rose to gaze down into her serene features. Despite the fact, the son-of-a-bitch who had assaulted her had delivered a shot to an area of her anatomy guaranteed to cause maximum damage – with a .357 hollow-point – and, as was wholly apparent, ultimately her death, she appeared to be resting peacefully in a sound, sweet sleep.

"Look what they did to you," he whispered, emotion constricting his throat to a point where, at the moment he could do little else. "Look what *I* did to you."

As much as he tried to suppress it, it was that emotion that weighed down upon Fallon's consciousness.

Guilt – bitter, crushing, and undeniable.

This is my fault, he mused silently. *As surely as if it were my hand that fired the gun.*

Out of the corner of his eye, he saw her hand twitch and his head snapped around. Impossible, of course. Just his guilt-ridden mind struggling for any sign of hope. His gaze moved to the ugly red and purple wound in the lower left-hand area of her abdomen. And, though he couldn't be one-hundred percent sure, it did seem as though the healing process was kicking in.

Wishful thinking?

Again, highly likely.

"I distinctly recall the mention of taking some time off while I was away."

Although the voice emanating from the bedroom's doorway was immediately recognisable to Fallon, he didn't react to it straight away. Instead, he resumed cleaning Rowan's body – specifically, the spot at her right side, just beneath her armpit, where the bullet had exited.

"A week or two, I believe you said," the figure behind him resumed. "Or was it a month? Not really sure of the exact time, but I'm at least *ninety* percent certain you promised anything to do with your usual brand of chaos would *not* be involved."

The newcomer paused then and turned slightly to gaze back at where Koo – changed out of her blood-stained dress and now wearing a sports bra and yoga pants – paced a tight circle at the living room's centre. Their eyes met for a brief moment. And, fleetingly though it may have been, it was long enough to convey a sense, beyond a doubt, that chaos was just the tip of this particular iceberg.

"Chaos, indeed," he turned back to where Fallon continued to clean up the girl on the bed. "Pantera's people are all over the lobby, guns showing. One elevator shut down," he made a fanning gesture an inch or so from his nose, "but I could smell it, even before I saw the blood splatter – *Human blood* – on the alcove wall. The same blood scent that left a trail leading right to your suite. And there's Koo . . ." He jerked a thumb over one shoulder to indicate the suite's living room. "This is probably one helluva story. And I *can't wait* to hear it."

"Uh-huh," Fallon muttered under his breath, finally returning the washcloth to the ice bucket of soapy water on the floor at his feet before standing to face the figure in the doorway. A figure who, quite literally, filled the doorway to the extent that he all but blocked the view to the room beyond him.

He was Eayann Ó Beolláin, a self-described preternatural dichotomy. Or, on those infrequent occasions when the situation necessitated a modicum of sobriety (or the wine stores gave out at his venue of the moment) it was a 'man of many parts'. An unconventional Pureblood aristocrat who gave up his privileged status to walk among the common man (or turnblood brethren, as it were), he was a former Franciscan friar-cum-theology scholar-cum-dabbler in the mystic arts; nomadic traveller and citizen of the world (though his accent carried a noticeable Scots lilt, he *claimed* his region of birth to be the Emerald Isle); Senior Elder of the Council of the House of Sasul, and personal advisor to House Leader Lady Marjean Sălbatica; though for the last five centuries, father confessor, surrogate father, constant companion and business associate of Juan Diego Velásquez de Falcone, aka Fallon Wylde. With appearances being the yardstick by which most people, vampires included, were judged, at first blush Eayann's six foot eight and a half inches, two-hundred-eighty-plus pounds line-backer brawny frame, shoulder-length fall of multi-coloured hair, and military style leather greatcoats, usually evoked terms that ran the gamut from eclectic to rebellious to downright weird. On the other hand, anyone who equated that image with anything resembling a lack of sophistication, intelligence, or that 'killer instinct', soon learned that he held his own in each of those categories. And, usually, painfully so.

"Koo," Fallon called out as he moved forward, prompting the man in the doorway to give way as he advanced and fell in behind him as he entered the living room.

Koo moved to meet him with noticeable hesitancy, arms wrapped around her stomach, features pale, and she swayed as if in fear her body would crumble to the floor before she reached him.

"Fallon . . . believe me, I—"

"It's alright," he stopped her. "It's not important now. The only thing that matters is . . ." he left the statement unfinished, placing a hand on her shoulder. "You have to be with her now. That's what's important. Understand? I want you in there," he twisted into partial profile, swinging an arm back to point at the bedroom door. "In there with Rowan until she . . ." he faltered, unable to speak, let alone think of the alternative. "Every second, every *minute*. You get hungry, call room service. You need to go," the arm swung back to wave in the direction of the room's wet bar.

"There should be another ice bucket, a flower vase. Hell, I don't give a shit. Piss in a *fucking* ash tray, if you have to." His voice rose with each sentence he uttered.

Eayann cleared his throat loudly, earning himself a quick frown from the younger vampire. "I'm fairly certain she gets the idea, Fallon," he said. Catching Koo's eye, he gave her a sympathetic nod to send her on her way and made his own way to the bar.

~*~

Silence.

Nearly a sound unto itself, disturbed occasionally by the slide of liquid-heavy glass along the bar's surface, and the gurgle of liquids leaving the opening of said bottles to fill waiting glass containers.

At last count, this had occurred at least seven times in the past ten minutes – four from Fallon's bottle of Wild Turkey 104-proof bourbon and three from Eayann's Chateau Mouton-Rothschild.

Both men occupied high stools at opposite ends of the u-shaped bar. Fallon, on the end furthest away from the suite's door, faced into the interior of the room, slouching, his back supported by the bar's cushioned rim, his body language reeking of smouldering rage, guilt and self-recrimination. And Eayann, facing his younger associate, one leg casually crossed over the other, both focused and exasperated.

"We can do this all night, if that's what you'd prefer." The older vampire finally brought their one-sided discussion to an end. It prompted just a quick sideward twitch of Fallon's eyes and a swivel to his left – or, at least, the start of a swivel – to reach for the bourbon bottle. A bottle which, just moments earlier, had occupied a space on the bar top a few inches from his elbow. A space now empty, the bottle now beside Eayann's Chateau Mouton-Rothchild.

"That too," Eayann said, drumming his fingers on the bottle's neck to emphasise the point. "To tell the truth, I've got better things to do with my time than sit here and play keep-away with you. Or sit here and watch you swill booze and brood, for that matter."

"Then don't let me stop you," Fallon slid off the stool and rounded the bar, swiftly capturing another full and unopened bottle from beneath the bar. He paused a moment, bottle held by its neck and tucked against his chest, as if daring his older companion to attempt another speedy retrieval, then popped its cap and poured himself a brimming glassful.

"I see," Eayann commented, watching as Fallon knocked the drink back by half and refilled. "If that's how you want to play this," he held back an additional moment to catch his friend's response – which came in the form of his raised glass and another deep drink – then loosed a weary sigh, "then you leave me with no choice but to make this official."

No response this time from Fallon. Outwardly, at any rate. Though Eayann knew his friend well enough to hold no doubts that his statement had penetrated his stoic façade.

"You choose to make me pull rank, then so be it," he continued. "I have yet to submit my annual evaluation to the House Advisory Council. It's up to you how it will read."

In the silence that followed, Eayann saw that his ploy had found purchase. The hand holding Fallon's drink slowed in its rise to his lips, hovering just below his chin.

Eayann seized the moment. "You know the House . . . that your Sire, the woman to whom I report, has eyes and ears everywhere. Especially here, at Shadowfall.

"I have no idea what happened tonight, nor do they I'd wager. Kane will have seen to that. But I picked up at least half a dozen circulating rumours in the lobby alone. They'll be all over the club in less than an hour. Your Sire, Lady Marjean, will hear about it before sunrise. Which version would you prefer *she* hears?"

Fallon finished his chin to mouth arc, and refilled, finally turning to face his friend. The sigh he released was one of both resignation and surrender. He refilled his glass again, took a slow sip, and rounded the bar to take the stool beside Eayann.

Turning to face the bar, he leaned . . . *slumped* forward, staring down into his glass.

"I messed up, Eayann. I fucked up big time," he said, and after a beat's pause, allowed the words, the story surrounding the past few weeks to roll out – from his first meeting with Rowan at the Blue Star Diner to the events of the past hour.

"*Damn it!*" He brought his fist down on the bar top with such force it shook the bottles and paraphernalia beneath and on the wall behind the bar. "That . . . in there," he stabbed the air with a stiffened forefinger in the bedroom's general direction, "is *my* fault. She came to me for *help* . . . and I wind up getting her shot. I fumbled. I dropped the ball."

"Oh, please. Spare me the lame sports analogies," Eayann all but groaned. "You're not some nine to five slack-jawed suburbanite guzzling over-priced beer and wolfing down pizza with a bunch of other couch cushion would-be athletes watching the American excuse for football. You're a *vampire*. As far as *that* goes, the games our kind play against each other make the Super Bowl look like bingo night at the neighbourhood Parish.

"But you *are* half-right. You did, as you so graphically put it, fuck up," he segued almost seamlessly, taking only the briefest of pauses to retrieve and sip from the wine flute beside him. "Although I would categorise it as more in the neighbourhood of stupidity. Correction. Make that *boneheaded* stupidity," Eayann added, in response to the sudden stiffness in his friend's posture, a sure indication that the fog of guilt and self-pity which surrounded him had thinned sufficiently to give the older vampire access to more malleable emotions.

Anger being the most pliable.

Fallon gave a dismissive snort. "Why do I get the feeling I'm about to get one of your famous '*I told you so*' lectures?"

"I'd curb that attitude if I were you, boyo," Eayann growled. "I'm not the one who just got his dick knocked into the dirt," he jerked a thumb over his shoulder, "and the person he was supposed to be guarding shot.

"And you're fuckin' A-right you're gonna get a lecture . . . *you stupid son of a bitch!*" Eayann's resulting open-handed slap on the bar top echoed in the suite, ironically, like a gunshot. "In case you've forgotten, your arse was already hangin' by a slender thread with the House Advisory Council after you decided to play Doc Holiday to Taz I'Ane's Wyatt Earp against House Maggio's Saviano family in San Diego a few months back."

"Taz needed help," Fallon argued. "Correct me if I'm wrong, but ain't it you who's always saying you never turn your back on a friend in need?"

"HA!" Eayann crowed and slapped the bar again. "And usin' my own crap against me ain't gonna work either. I know what I said . . . and what I *meant* when I said it. And, as far as that goes, I woulda done the same damn thing. But that's not the point and you fuckin' know it. The point is you made a boneheaded mistake in doin' it. You and your boy, I'Ane, you left *witnesses*. Witnesses who recognised you and made a complaint to the powers that be. Some of those witnesses were Human. And believe me, boyo, even with spin control and pay-offs to our people in the media and copshops, that *'shooters wore body armour'* excuse is wearin' pretty damned thin!"

"What can I say? Things went sideways," Fallon muttered, almost apologetically, and caught himself just short of a self-conscious grin.

"Sideways, arseways, what-fuckin'-ever," Eayann waved a hand up and outward, dismissing his friend's attempt at an excuse. "You're supposed to keep a low profile, be invisible. In *everything*, and I can't stress that enough. In . . . Every . . . Thing!" He formed each word carefully as he spoke. "Everything you do! For several reasons – some obvious, some not, but should damn well be!

"Which brings us to your latest disaster," he continued, sliding off his stool to pace the short gap between the back of his bar stool and the end of the bar. "And here I take off my House bureaucrat's hat and put on the one that belongs to your business partner and friend. Although, right now, more the former than the latter."

He stopped in his circular course and held up a delaying finger, pouring himself another fluteful of wine, then took a long, deep swallow, followed by a deep and energising breath before releasing it in a quick huff and roaring, "What the *FUCK* were you thinking?"

He shot a hand up between them, palm out, to block any response his friend would offer, if any. "No, don't answer that. I already know the answer. And, I'll get to it in a minute. What I really wanna know is . . . did you suffer some kind of memory lapse? Temporary amnesia? Alzheimer's?"

"I didn't—" Fallon attempted and was instantly blocked.

"Oh, I *know* you didn't! Didn't *think*," Eayann tossed a quick glance toward the bedroom, to give credence to his next statement. "At least not with the *head* you should've been using. And it's obvious why. She's a very attractive young woman. And probably a wildcat between the sheets . . ."

"Whoa! Where do you get off, Old Man—" Fallon bristled, defensively, only to be hacked short again.

"FW, A&R, one-quarter partnership. *That's* where I get off, *Mister Wylde*. And I would really like to know where the *fuck* your head was! Let me refresh your fucking memory. We are a *business* . . . an organisation that is paid a shitpile of money to perform specific, *exclusive* jobs. We *remove* would-be assholes who prey on the weak and defenceless. And, on occasion . . . and if the price is right, we rescue kidnapped girls from sex slavers. But we are *not* . . . and let me repeat that . . . *NOT* Sam Spade, Nick Marlowe, Magnum P.I., shamuses or bodyguards. We are *not* missing persons detectives. That was your first boneheaded mistake.

"And the next – you broke your own . . . your *cardinal* rules. Hells bells boy, you shattered the shit out of them!" He made a smashing gesture in the air above his multi-coloured mane with one ham-fist, then brought the hand down in front of him – unclenched fingers spread – ticking them off as he continued. "A. *Never* get close to, or involved with, the client," his eyes made a quick flick to the bedroom and back. "Obviously, you did . . . and I can see why. Like I said, she's a very lovely young woman. But that's beside the point.

"B. *Never* go into any situation without a plan – that's primary and a backup. And, unless I missed something in what you told me, you had neither. You had *squat."*

"That's not entirely—" Fallon made another attempt at an explanation.

"Bullshit!" Eayann barked, swiping the air between them, as if swatting a cloud of annoying insects. "You *thought* you did. You might even have started out with something that *resembled* a plan. But somewhere between thinking with that little head and playing Mr Uber-Cool Rico Swa-vay Private Eye, it went out of the fucking window.

"Plan, my hairy *Irish Ass*! I can cite at least a half-dozen points that left your opponent wide open and offered you inroads to track your client's sister. Maybe even rescue her, if she was still breathing. You let them *all* slip through your fingers. Which brings us to the most crucial point. C. *Never, NEVER* tip your hand to your opponent.

"This guy . . ." Eayann took a sip of wine, while tapping a finger against his cheek, as if to stimulate memory.

"Taylor," Fallon helped, earning him a mouth-twisting sneer and a vexed grunt.

"Yes, him. He's old blood . . . been around the block a few times. Meaning, for our kind, you don't get to be old blood by being stupid, careless or slow on the uptake. *You* nailed all three . . . and he tagged you. He sniffed you out, did his recon, identified your weaknesses, and hit you right where you lived." Once again, he referred to the bedroom with a glance.

Point made, he thought. *Though, hopefully, not overly done.*

Once again, the room fell into silence. This time, however, it was akin to the hushed calm before the first flash of distant lightning and the deafening crash of thunder which followed. Looking at the younger vampire sitting before him, Eayann could almost sense the dark storm of emotion building within him, a tempest of rage on the verge of release.

"He could have let it go after that little dosing stunt he pulled with Koo and the girl," Eayann resumed. "He didn't. And you know why . . . don't you?"

"Yeah," Fallon answered simply, almost whispering.

"And he's waiting for you. You know *that*, too."

Fallon's reply this time was a jerky, wordless nod.

"Then take this with you . . . Not from Eayann Ó Beolláin, elder of the House of Sasul, or Eayann, your business associate . . . but from your friend," he paused to take a quick steadying breath and a sip from his glass before continuing. "It's been a long time – much longer than I would have guessed – but, to be honest, I knew this day would come eventually. Sooner or later, it comes for all of us – those who have been turned.

"A vampire you may be – no longer Human – but whatever else you are or are not, you are still a *man*. A lingering kernel of humanity lies dormant within all turnbloods and will always . . . *always* reassert itself. In your case, the man who was once Juan Diego Velásquez de Falcone.

"It was Diego who got you into this mess. From this point on, you're gonna have to lock him back in that dark corner of you he's been sleeping in and let the other guy do what he's got to do. Do you understand me?"

Again, Fallon responded with a nod, prompting another resounding slap on the bar's surface from Eayann.

"*I SAID . . . DO YOU UNDERSTAND ME?*" the elder vampire roared.

"Dammit, Old Man, I'm not fucking deaf," Fallon answered, swivelling on his stool to meet his friend's glaring gaze head-on. "I know what—" Further exchange was suddenly disrupted by a muted buzzing from his jacket's inner breast pocket. The pocket, in fact, in which he'd placed the cell supplied by Knox's minion the day before.

He swivelled again, turning his back to Eayann, while simultaneously retrieving the phone.

"It's time, Wild Man," a familiar gravel-throated voice rumbled from the cell's speaker, almost before Fallon could press it to his ear. "Get your ass out on the street. One of my people will find you."

"On my way," Fallon's reply was delivered within seconds of a severed connection. As Fallon knew it would be. Knox was just *that* kind of guy. "Gotta see a man," he told Eayann, returning the cell to his inner pocket. "Take care of things until I get back?"

"Don't I always?" Eayann grumbled.

CHAPTER ELEVEN

The 'one of my people' Knox indicated turned out to be a girl – Human and young, fourteen if she was a day, which was typical for a guy like Knox – a homeless street rat bundled in multiple layers of filthy clothes. She managed to avoid detection until Fallon caught the stench of her unwashed body some three blocks after he emerged from one of Kane's secret entrances.

She gestured with a pair of stiffened fingers, swiping them across her mouth, then tapping her throat to indicate she was mute. She signed and jabbed her fingers at Fallon.

He nodded acknowledgement and answered. "I don't sign. Sorry."

She shrugged, then jerked her head as if to say *follow me* and took the lead.

Two blocks down, she held up a hand to stop them, removed her dirty woollen cap and waved it from left to right above her head. The headlights of a previously darkened vehicle flashed on, then blinked twice and went dark again.

The girl redonned her cap, gave Fallon a cursory glance and trotted away, back into the darkness without a single backward look. She was barely more than an after-image when the vehicle started its engine, edged away from the curb, and slowly made its way toward Fallon.

As it drew near, he saw it was a limo, solid black with highly tinted windows. Fallon took a cautious step back as it pulled to a stop in front of him. The window on its driver's side silently lowered to reveal a swarthy, bearded countenance in a Seattle Mariners baseball cap. A vampire, unquestionably. His House, indeterminate.

"Wildman, I presume?" the driver queried, with an accent heavy on London's East End.

Fallon squelched the impulse to chuckle, recognising Knox's combination at a personal dig and a coded identifier. The driver's caterpillar fluffy eyebrows bounced toward his presently covered hairline in response to Fallon's nod.

"Then get your arse into gear, mate. We got a lotta road to cover and the night ain't gettin' any younger."

Fallon quickly rounded the limo's front end and planted himself in the passenger seat of the vehicle, earning him a full-on chortle from the driver.

"The man said you'd do that."

"The *man* knows I'd turn my back on a two-headed cobra before I'd trust him," Fallon replied, meeting the driver's gaze head-on. "And you might want to take a page from *his* book, friend."

"Easy, Mr Wylde. I might work for Knox, but I answer to the same Lady . . . the same *House* as you," the driver said. "I'm just getting paid to chauffeur you. Sit back and get comfortable."

Unlike most of his particular breed, although it was standard hack cabbies rather than limo jockeys, the driver – who gave his name as 'Kass with a K' – made no attempt to continue their conversation during the drive. They drove in complete silence. Which suited Fallon just fine. It gave him time to get a handle on the emotional tempest raging within him, and to think.

As always, Eayann had played his role as the unit's strategical and emotional compass and, of course, both mentor and friend with unquestioning accuracy.

He was right, Fallon admitted to himself. *I'm a soldier . . . a mercenary, not a Sherlock Holmes or Magnum P.I.* He stormed the jungle strongholds of marauding warlords, retrieved international fugitives from countries with no extradition, and rescued kidnapped girls from sex-slavers . . . a one-man assault team, not someone who prowled the city's dark underbelly dealing with its criminal, and/or Vampire, denizens.

Especially *this* particular city. A city, the current situation forced him to realise, that in spite of the fact it had been the group's home base for over six decades, he knew damned little about it. At least, not in the ways he should.

His adversary, on the other hand, didn't labour under that handicap. A fact, he hoped, would not pop up to bite him in the ass later.

"All ashore that's goin' ashore, mate," Kass quipped, some fifteen minutes later, as he eased the limo into the dirty and partially grassed shoulder of what, at first glance, appeared to be a park area. Closer scrutiny, however, identified something markedly different.

Strewn among the sparse patches of unkempt grass and a loose perimeter of misshapen trees were uneven rows of chipped and pitted gravestones.

"You've got to be shittin' me," Fallon said, unable to hold back a chuckle. A glance at the driver was met with a hiked eyebrow and a quick shrug.

"'Fraid not, mate. He was very specific about where he wanted you," Kass slid a hand into his jacket as he spoke and produced a leather-encased flask. He unscrewed its metal cap and offered it to Fallon, who declined with a shake of his head. "Cheers, mate," Kass took a quick couple of pulls, then recapped and returned the container to his inner pocket.

"Take your time," he prompted, responding to Fallon's delay in disembarking. "He paid me for a round trip."

"Paid?" Fallon questioned, his expression leaving no doubt as to the scepticism concerning the driver's claim.

"After a fashion. Let's just say that for services rendered tonight, he agreed to keep secret certain facts I would rather a very jealous lady of the House Sasul didn't have knowledge of, if you catch my meaning."

"That's our Knox. As compassionate as a Great White shark," Fallon said, grinning as he departed the limo.

Fallon caught their scents – two of Knox's people, both Human and probably armed – as he entered the cemetery proper. They were well out of sight, near a cluster of headstones to his left and right. Neither broke cover. Instead, another girl, this one a bit older than the homeless mute who'd met him outside Shadowfall, strode out on the well-worn footpath a yard or so in front of him.

Her scent identified her as a vampire, a raw-boned and freckled redhead, no more than ten years turned. As he drew near, she jerked her ginger head in a *follow me* gesture, then turned and led him up the path.

One structure, a small A-frame mausoleum, stood at the end of the path, surrounded by a decayed and mostly broken wall. Its equally broken walkway led to a four-step stairway, which itself led to a narrow and doorless entrance.

The girl stopped just short of the entrance, taking up a guardian-like position at its right-hand side.

A full minute passed with no activity. Even the girl remained as still, and seemingly as lifeless, as a mannequin. And then a sudden flurry of movement called Fallon's attention to the stone structure's darkened doorway.

"Wildman! Good to see you, it's been too long." Recognition of the speaker, albeit voice only, was instant and undeniable, even before he stepped into the cemetery's sparse illumination to confirm his identity.

Knox. The single, and most recent, non-de guerre of a vampire whose reputation spanned as many centuries as there were cities on the face of the planet. His current persona an eclectic blend of Victorian era, '60s Carnaby Street, and modern-day Hollywood chic, from the salon-style mullet and sculpted mutton chop sideburns and moustache, dangling jewelled earrings, to a suit that would probably give Georgio Armani nightmares for the rest of his life, and the legendary black ivory, red crystal-topped cane said to contain droplets of blood from the infamous Roman emperor Caligula.

A man on whom the idiom *Larger than life and twice as ugly* fit like the proverbial glove.

"A graveyard," Fallon made a quick left to right scan to indicate their surroundings. "Seriously?"

"Yeah, I know," Knox replied with a chuckle like marbles and rusty razor blades in a blender, arms outstretched flamboyantly as he descended the mausoleum's short staircase.

"Depraved, even for me . . ." he winked. "At first blush, anyway. But, in actuality, this particular cemetery proved perfect under the circumstances."

There was a beat of silence, and then . . .

"Comet Lodge?" Knox prompted, eyebrows twitching in disbelief. "Come on, Wildman! All the years you've lived in this town and you've never heard the stories? You know nothing about *the* most famous cemetery in Seattle?"

"It's never been one of my preferred choices for scintillating commentary," Fallon answered. "Add spending time in one, too, while we're at it."

"I can appreciate that," Knox agreed, with a nod. "And, under different circumstances, take my word for it, this would be a long way down the list of places I'd prefer to spend an evening, let alone *live* in for the past few weeks. But, as they say, necessity is the mother of invention. And, in this, I'm sure even *you* would concede my genius."

A second glimmer of movement from the dark beyond the mausoleum doorway garnered Fallon's attention, putting all his senses on an even higher level of alert. As past experience had taught him, Knox was a man whose action in *every* situation were based, to a very large degree, on self-interest. Either profit or pleasure – no ifs, buts, or exceptions. It wouldn't have surprised Fallon in the slightest if the gravel-throated pipeline peddler had made a double-cross deal with the same sons of bitches that had been hurting them both. He'd made a similar attempt before. Which, though it came close to succeeding, not only failed but also resulted in the temporary loss of his right ear and most of one arm.

One could only hope that the incident had taught him a valuable lesson. But, with Knox, you could never be one hundred percent certain of anything.

The movement at the mausoleum door finally revealed itself in the form of two women – both young, lean, pale and almost glowing beneath Seattle's crescent moonlight. They wore what appeared to be ceremonial garb, gossamer white gowns and deep blue cloaks with gold embroidery.

Witches.

Attention split, but still focused. Fallon saw Knox moving closer as the two young women glided down toward them. When the two males were within three feet of one-another, each witch took a small pouch from beneath their cloaks. They began to sprinkle salt – *rock* salt – as they moved in a circle around the two vampire males.

"They're from one of the local covens," Knox explained. "We . . . help each other out now and then," he gestured to indicate their actions. "This will protect us from unwanted forces until our business is done."

"Evil spirits?" Fallon huffed a laugh.

"A vampire who doesn't believe. Now *there's* an oxymoron, if I ever heard one," one of the ladies snorted a laugh of her own.

"The Comet Lodge Cemetery," Knox chimed in. "Before 1881, it was a burial ground for the local Duwamish Indians. When the first white settlers came to the area in June 1891, they started burying their dead here.

"This cemetery is haunted. More than that, it's cursed. From the desecration of a sacred burial plot. And whether or not I . . . or *you* . . . buy into that, most of Seattle's Human citizenry – as well as our vampire brethren – do."

"Superstitious vampires?" Fallon laughed, again. "You'd think they would be more worried about the living than a bunch of boxed and decomposed bodies in a six-foot-hole in the ground."

"And, in any other case, you'd be right," Knox acquiesced. "But, a cursed Duwamish burial ground is not the only thing this particular spot is infamous for. And that, too, is moot, I'll grant you.

"I won't bore you with a commentary on local lore. But I *can* tell you because of it, whether or not you're aware of it, there is a significant absence of vampire presence in this area of our fair city. In a five-mile radius, in point of fact. They avoid it the way Humans in Constantinople used to steer clear of parts of the city infested by Black Plague. Which made it the perfect spot for yours truly to sequester himself while the city streets are so, shall we say, dispassionate concerning my continued well-being."

"One less potential pothole in the road for me," Fallon commented, with a knowing smirk. "You know, I half-expected to walk into a set-up. You double-crossing me to them to get the heat off your own ass."

"Been there, done that, you and I." Knox's reply was accompanied by a grimace and a tug at his right ear. "Besides, knowing the bastard we're dealing with, there's no doubt in my mind that he'd renege on the deal and do *me* in after he took you out."

Fallon flashed a wry smile. "That's what I like about you, Knox. You always know which side your bread is buttered on . . . so long as *you're* the one who's holding the knife."

"What can I say?" Knox grinned, twitching both shoulders in a short shrug. "I'm a pragmatist. *And* a survivor."

"Don't leave out a two-faced, backstabbing son of a bitch," Fallon said. "Survivor? The night's young. We'll see."

"Ohhh, okay. That sounded like a veiled threat," one of the witches observed. The salt circle, apparently completed, both the women stood outside, and on opposite ends of the granulated perimeter, and regarded the two men within as if awaiting further instruction.

"Are we good?" Knox asked, deliberately ignoring the witch's comment and waved a hand to indicate the circle.

"We'll let you know when we're not," the one who'd spoken answered. She and her cohort turned their backs to the circle, took up positions several paces from the circle's perimeter and began chanting softly.

Knox threw a quick glance at both women, nodded and moved closer to Fallon, stopping within a foot of him. "First of all, I think it's only fair to ask . . . are you sure you're ready for this? I mean, are you ready to get into this thing?"

"You wouldn't have brought me here if you didn't already know the answer to that," Fallon answered, without a moment's hesitation. "Besides, that ship's already sailed. It ain't like I got a whole lot of choice."

"There's always a choice, Wildman," Knox told him softly. "One, specifically, you might not have considered."

"Such as?"

"Like choosing to walk away. Cut your losses," Knox proposed, both his tone and expression carrying a shadow of solemnity Fallon had never seen before. Something that very nearly verged on true concern. "Unless . . . your stake in this has suddenly become personal. That thing, the shooting that took place at Shadowfall tonight?" the gossip peddler prompted. "That wouldn't be *your* mess, would it?"

Fallon couldn't withhold a flinch.

"Ahhh, aha, it *is* yours," Knox chortled before Fallon could speak. Not that he could have replied. "So, who got iced? That fiery Oriental you work with? That sweet little Human hottie . . . the sister you've been twisting the sheets with?" he asked, a calculating gleam in his eyes.

"You want to put your nose back in the holster and get on with it?" Fallon forced himself to counter, without bothering to confirm or deny Knox's probing questions.

Knox sighed, then took a deep breath. "Okay. You know, I got a lot of faith in you, Wildman. You have pulled things off that would make most of our kind lose their mud, not to mention their asses. Let's hope, for both our sakes, that you're *really* that good and not just lucky."

~*~

"Hey mommy."

Koo jumped at the sound of Pantera's voice and twisted in her seat to look at the woman standing in the doorway and frowned at her.

Pannie raised an eyebrow and smiled "Too soon for mom jokes?" She walked across and rested a hand on Koo's shoulder. "Are you okay?"

Koo sighed and tipped her head to brush her cheek against Pannie's hand. "I've been better, but you know me. If I'm gonna fuck up, I'm gonna go large."

"Fucking up would have been leaving her to die. You've given her a chance, one not many people get. Fallon will understand that, eventually. He just needs time to process." She looked down at Rowan's still form. "Any sign of success yet?"

Koo shook her head. "I thought I saw her move a couple of times, but . . ." she trailed off and sighed. "If she doesn't come back from this, I don't know what Fallon will do."

"Is he really that attached to her?" Pannie pursed her lips, studying the girl in the bed. "She doesn't seem like his usual type."

"She's not," Koo reached out to brush a lock of hair away from Rowan's face. "He's different with her, calmer. It's hard to explain."

They both fell silent, then Pannie chuckled. "I can't wait until she wakes up and finds out she's one of us. Does she even know we exist?"

"Not yet."

"That's going to be interesting. I don't think I've ever heard of anyone being turned without being aware of our existence before." She squeezed Koo's shoulder. "I'm sure it'll be fine."

"What will?" A third voice, little more than a whisper, joined the conversation; one that brought Koo lurching out of her seat.

"Rowan?" She grabbed Rowan's hand and placed the other against her forehead. "Oh my god! Rowan, are you awake?"

Rowan's head turned slowly toward the sound of Koo's voice and her eyes opened, wincing against the light. "My head hurts," she whispered.

Pantera dimmed the lights and disappeared into the sitting room while Koo helped Rowan sit up. "How do you feel?"

"Like . . . someone shot me," Rowan swallowed, then frowned. "Wait . . . *did* someone shoot me?"

"We'll get to that. Here," Pannie reappeared and handed Rowan a glass. "Drink this."

Koo helped Rowan sit up and lift the glass to her lips. Rowan sniffed at the thick red liquid and screwed her nose up. "What *is* that?"

"Just drink it. It'll make you feel better."

She took a sip, swallowed, and pulled a face. "It has a funny taste."

"The more you drink the better it gets. Drink up."

Rowan took another sip, grimaced then tipped her head back slightly and drained the glass. "So, what happened? Everything is muddled. I remember shouting and a noise . . ."

"Don't force the memories, just take a few minutes to wake up first," Koo suggested, hesitated and glanced toward the door.

Rowan followed her gaze to where a giant of a man stood framed in the doorway . "Who is . . . who are you?" she frowned. "You look familiar."

Casting a fleeting glance Koo's way, the giant fixed his smoky-brown-eyed gaze on Rowan, brought both hands together, fingers steepled, and executed a slight bow.

"Eayann Ó Beolláin, your servant, Young Miss," he presented himself, his gaze leaving her to touch upon Koo and Pantera while his head made a near-imperceptible nod at the doorframe.

Message clearly received, Koo gave Rowan's hand a parting squeeze and both women promptly left the room.

"You and I have much to talk about, my dear," Eayann said. "Very much, indeed."

~*~

The limo driver jumped, started and nearly dropped his liquor flask when the vehicle's passenger door opened, and Fallon slid into the seat behind him.

Kass turned to look through the window of the partition that separated them and regarded his returned passenger with an air of curiosity and a hiked eyebrow.

"You look like someone just ran over your dog *and* pissed in your favourite chair, mate."

"Drive," Fallon fired back, then twisted to meet the driver's gaze head-on. "And pass that flask back." He snapped his fingers and thrust his hand through the opening.

"There's a full bar back there, help yourself," Kass told him, shoving the flask into Fallon's waiting hand. "And fill me up while you're there . . . if you don't mind I mean."

"Yeah. Just drive," Fallon repeated, leaning toward the limo's bar set-up.

As Kass had stated, there was a full stocked mini-bar on the limo left-hand side, between the passenger door and the rear seat. Fallon identified and snatched up an unopened bottle of bourbon. *I.W. Harper*. Not one of his preferred brands, but . . .

The start of the limo's engine brought his attention back to Kass's flask and he took the bottle back to his formerly occupied seat, placing the flask between his thighs to steady it while he poured.

Once full, he tapped the frame of the connecting window where Kass immediately reached back to retrieve it.

"Cheers, mate," he piped happily. "Any place in particular you wanna be dropped?"

"I'll let you know," Fallon answered, on the heels of a deep pull from the bottle. "Just watch your speed. Trouble with the law is the last thing either one of us needs."

"Ain't *that* the truth," Kass chortled.

CHAPTER TWELVE

Rowan watched as Eayann settled upon the seat vacated minutes earlier by Koo. It creaked under his weight, and Rowan held her breath, wondering if it was going to collapse.

"Shouldn't you . . . maybe . . . get something stronger to sit on?" she asked.

Eayann chuckled and shook his head. "No, lass. This will do just fine. I've not had a chair collapse beneath me yet." He pursed his lips. "Well, maybe once or twice." He rested his elbows on his knees and leaned forward. "So, *you're* Rowan. Not quite what I was expecting, I must say."

"What does *that* mean?"

"It means, lass, that Fallon's tastes usually run to the more . . . exotic, shall we say? But you? You're a little mouse in comparison."

Rowan braced her palms against the mattress and pushed herself further upright against the headboard.

"Is this the part where you give the speech about how I shouldn't get too attached to Fallon, and gently point out how he'll grow bored soon enough and move on?" She shrugged, winced and raised her arm to probe the area where she was *sure* she'd been shot.

"Don't worry," she continued, as she touched the still tender flesh. "He's already made that more than clear. I'm his client, we shouldn't be involved, it's an aberration and once he's found my sister and brought her back to me, he'll be out of my life and on his way to somewhere else. Blah blah blah . . ." she waved a hand, dismissively. "Was I shot? I'm *sure* I was shot. How long was I unconscious?"

Eayann blinked at her tirade and snapped his jaw shut with a shake of his head. "The shooting. Well, that's one of the things we need to talk about," he told her. "Yes, someone shot you. Less than twenty-four hours ago."

Rowan laughed. "That's funny. I've watched TV. You don't get shot and heal that fast. Why aren't I in hospital? Did Koo put you up to this?" She looked around. "And where's Fallon?"

"He had to go out."

"Has something happened. Did he find Eden? I need to go after him!" She swung her legs out of the bed, only for Eayann to lean forward and push her back against the pillows.

"No, you need to stay right where you are and listen to me," he told her, which spawned a look on her face somewhere between *'get your hands off me'* and *'oh shit'*. It worked, however, and she relented, easing back onto the pillows.

Once he was satisfied that she'd stay put, Eayann leaned back on his chair, paused a moment while he pondered whether he dared to take time out and leave her unsupervised while he went into the sitting room to pour himself a glass of wine. From the look in her eyes, he was certain he was going to need it.

"Go on then, I'm listening," Rowan decided for him, the spark of belligerence he read in her eyes turning into irritation and leaving him with little doubt about what would happen if he left her unattended.

Eayann readied himself with a quick breath before starting. "Television's questionable realism aside, you are correct. Gunshot wounds do *not* heal that fast." He dropped a quick glance to the area in which hers had been. "At least not under normal circumstances. And these . . . *this* is most assuredly not a normal circumstance.

"I . . . you . . . oh *hellfire!*" He threw both hands up and rose to his feet. "The easiest way is to just show you."

"Kathryn," he called out to the presence who'd been loitering just outside the bedroom door, monitoring the exchange since her initial departure. A pale and grim-faced Koo entered, throwing a look and an attempted reassuring smile toward Rowan.

"If you would, lass," he said, garnering Koo's attention. "Assist me in a little demonstration?"

Koo nodded wordlessly and, with a second glance at Rowan, she took a small step back to watch as Eayann shucked off his greatcoat and draped it over the seat of his chair. He unbuttoned his collarless, immaculate white shirt to the waist, revealing a chest strangely muscular for a man of his girth and took a moment to smooth a hand over its whirling mass of dark hair.

One hand delved behind his back and emerged holding a knife, a *dagger*, sheathed in a leather scabbard. When it was unsheathed he presented it to Koo, nodding at Rowan, who watched him with unconcealed curiosity.

"For your inspection," he addressed her as Koo approached and placed the blade in her hands. "I want you to see for yourself that it is the genuine article, and not one of those cheap novelty shop mock-ups with retractable blades."

Rowan held the dagger by its ribbed and tapered black pommel, between the tips of her fingers, as if she were afraid it might break or shatter. Then she gripped the blade between thumb and forefinger of her free hand and jiggled it with an upward motion. Satisfied it neither moved nor retracted, she drew a single finger along the blade's lower edge, quickly jerking it away with a hissing intake of breath.

"Yes, my dear. Very sharp," Eayann said, unable to hide a smile as the young woman jammed the cut and bleeding digit into her mouth.

On some level, deep and unconscious, Rowan knew what it was all leading up to. Even as she returned the dagger to Koo, and watched her take it back to its owner, she *knew* what was to come. But knowing was a far cry from actually seeing.

Her grip on reality was jolted when she saw the man who called himself Eayann stab the dagger's blade into his chest, just below his right pectoral and draw it downwards to his abdomen, creating a wound a good six inches in length. It caused an initial gush of blood that splashed down over the back of the hand which held the dagger, followed by a rivulet that Eayann caught in the palm of his free hand. He pulled the blade free and, as Rowan watched – eyes wide in astonishment – the wound began to close; to instantly seal itself. In a matter of seconds, it was little more than a pale crimson line.

"I . . . where . . . *how?*" Rowan stammered, mouth agape, her eyes hopping back and forth between Eayann and Koo.

"It's been a few days since I last fed, so it will take a while to completely heal," he told her, while rebuttoning his shirt. "But how? I am what the unfortunately embellished mythology of our insane existence calls a vampire. And now, dear girl, so are *you.*"

"Oh . . . " Rowan responded, barely above a whisper. Then, as realisation gradually kicked in. "Oh . . . OH . . . *OH MY GOD!*"

~*~

That was the thing with vampire physiology. Their cells were in a constant state of regeneration, which was definitely a benefit when it came to ageing and healing and growing back severed limbs. But where alcohol, drugs – not that he'd had any in the past thirty years or so, marijuana, cocaine, opium, LSD, Mescaline, what-have-you – was concerned, getting drunk or stoned was next to impossible. Of course, it varied, depending on age and the vampire in question, but the best you could hope for was a large rush with the latter, and a lingering head-to-toe buzz with the former.

Hence Fallon's current physical state.

Having switched to a tall, thick-based glass after finishing the bourbon, and now on a second bottle. Scotch, this time – *Glenfiddich* twelve-year-old single malt – not that it mattered, he knocked back the remainder of glass number six, refilled the glass to just below the rim, and settled back into the limo seat's admittedly soothing backrest.

If little else, the bourbon he'd consumed had succeeded in turning the roaring firestorm that was his previous emotional climate into what was not, at least, a blazing bonfire. It put him in a mind-state better able to process what he'd learned during his talk with Knox at the cemetery.

"Let's start with the bastard we're both dealing with," Knox had said, as though the mere thought of what he was about to convey left a sour taste on his tongue. "The one you call Taylor. He's had a name, an *alias* for every letter of the alphabet – anybody's alphabet – three times over.

"He's old blood. Maybe not Kane-old or Zuron-old. Hell, maybe not even as old as *me*, but close. I think it's safe to say he's left his footprints in a few places even history doesn't remember."

"You ever met him?" Fallon interrupted. "Know what he looks like?"

"No, to both." Knox gave a jerky shake of his head. "Oh, I caught a quick glimpse of him once. Paris, during the Nazi Occupation. Doesn't make any difference, though. He likes to keep a low profile – very *low*, like almost invisible low. And he never looks the same twice. I've heard him described as tall, thin, stout, frail, dark-haired, blond, ginger and shaggy, bearded, *bald*. But . . ." He paused dramatically, a stiffened finger poised to emphasise significance, visibly savouring his moment in the spotlight, however Lilliputian. "But one thing that never changes is his mode of livelihood, his forte."

Again, the flamboyant vampire paused, as if actually expecting a drum roll from somewhere in the wings.

"He's an *Óinindi.*"

Fallon blinked, honestly thrown by the Old Tongue term and it prompted Knox to translate.

"A corruptor. A filth-maker. Someone who caters to the vile, twisted pleasures of the vile and perverse." Another pause, searching Fallon's features for a reaction. None surfaced, and Knox sighed. "Wildman, I expected you to be more worldly. He's the organiser of certain events. The man who supplies the locale, the set-up, the security, and the party favours for blood orgies and Humans-as-the-prey fox hunts. Things like starving children fighting each other to the death for scraps of food. He's supplied two-thirds of the Eastern Euro and Middle Eastern brothels with kidnapped, drug-addicted young girls." There was a tone to Knox's voice which tugged at Fallon's curiosity, but he stayed silent and let Knox continue.

"Ever hear of blood farms? Well, he's the son of a bitch who created them. Also . . . and though this won't show up in records anywhere, he's the founder and co-owner of a string of extreme SM Fetish Clubs across Germany, France, and England – Vampire Only, naturally."

"Alright, I get it," Fallon chimed in, concealing an amused grin against the image in his mind of himself as an Intelligence Agent being briefed on the crimes of Dr. Evil. "So, what's his game now? Why's he in Seattle and what does my lad . . . my client's sister have to do with his business."

Again, the finger shot out and upward. "Bear with me, Wildman. I'll get to that and try to answer at least one of your questions shortly."

"Gothenburg, Sweden, 2012. Linnea Sjöberg, the co-owner of Johannes- Sjöberg Kaffe; a café and coffee shop in the Haga District – and still damned hot for a woman in her late sixties, if the picture in the newspapers is accurate," he held up the index and middle finger of one hand, moving them from left to right, back and forth, as if scanning newsprint on a page only he could see. "The lovely Miss Sjöberg – lifelong resident of the area, and described by friends and customers of the café as quiet and reserved – emerged from the office she shared with her long-time friend and business partner, Verna Johannes, late Tuesday morning . . ." a leer materialised on his features as he continued, "completely nude and loudly announced her desire to have sexual intercourse, in her office, with any and all interested parties – male or female."

His leer exploded into a full-on laugh and the hand swung outward in a gesture that seemed to say *Voila!*

"It doesn't go into a blow-by-blow account, sadly, but reading between the lines apparently she did and there were definitely a few interested parties. It went on to say that the police were called and several of the interested parties, along with Miss Sjöberg, were admitted to the Sahlgrenska University hospital, showing all the signs of a violent hysterical breakdown. Three hours later, she died of heart failure.

"In a matter of a few hours, a quiet, demure, sixty-plus year-old – in very fit shape, by all reports - goes from a case of the monster high sweats to a screaming basket case to death by heart failure. Don't try telling me that doesn't sound a little hinky to you."

"Hinky," Fallon replied. His response was, for the most part, a partially conscious echo. He'd heard every word spoken by the man before him and while, like a sponge, there was a part of him that soaked in the gist of Knox's narrative, there was another part of him tethered to, and concerned with, the situation unfolding in a bedroom suite back at Shadowfall. With a young Human woman – correction: once Human – now adrift in the spiritual ethers between transformation and oblivion, hopefully struggling valiantly to life's physical coil.

He heard, though only half-listened, as Knox continued. Citing at least four more similar incidents, with dates stretching from 2012 to 2017 and locations that hopped from Denmark to Germany to Italy to France. And, in the current moment, took him through a good two-thirds of his second bottle.

"Red Carousel," Fallon tossed the name out, catching Knox on the cusp of another long-winded account, and completely off-guard. "Where do they fit into all this?"

"Wildman, I'm impressed!" Knox said, gawking at the younger vampire in mock wide-eyed surprise and admiration. "That's a name I didn't think anybody, other than yours truly, knew of! You may make a decent gumshoe yet."

Fallon allowed the compliment to slide over him, responding with little more than a blank stare, giving Knox time enough to reload for the next round of narrative expose.

The wait was a short one.

"Red Carousel," Knox stretched out the syllables in a tone that reeked of sarcasm. "Sounds like a seventies metal rock band, don't they? Well, believe me, that comparison is not far from accurate.

"They are, the name at any rate, the people responsible for everything I just told you about. As well as the bone of contention between their frontman and myself. The reason our Squire Taylor is so hot to shut me down.

"You see, because of *my* forte, I know that the current incarnation of Red Carousel is, for the most part, a sham. A paper tiger. The original group – the cartel when it actually *was* a cartel – was formed between the end of World War Two and the beginning of this country's Dwight Eisenhower regime, and it was founded by Pures Marisol and Celeste Santine – whom you may know as Bianca Manx and her mother, Justine." He tapped the side of his nose. "Not many people remember their born names, but I do . . . *I* do.

"Its members and supporters were amongst the crème de la crème of the influential Pureblood roster across the board – the six largest Houses in the Vampire Nation. Originally, it was the Red Horses, the Red Round, and then Carousel of Blood – clubs, brothels, sporting arenas, banks - that deal in blood *and* Human currency for investments, money laundering, stock manipulation, gambling, casinos. You name it, they had it all. Until 1979, that is."

"The Teresa Bennion incident," Fallon threw in.

"Bingo!" Knox crowed, with a loud snap of his fingers. "In the words of that old gospel song '*and the walls came a'tumblin down.*'

"These days – the last two decades, in fact – it's little more than Taylor and a handful of second-rate, wannabe turnblood gangs, scattered across Europe. Although, somehow he's managed to convince folks that they've just been underground since '79 and they're still major players. That's what this whole thing is about."

"The slave drug," Fallon prompted again.

"Slave? No, my friend, I'd say closer to *puppet*. My contacts have seen it, close-up. Even gotten some of the lesser discreet, loose-lipped members of Taylor's own associate groups to talk about it.

"The damn shit is the motherlode. One," he held up one hand, ticking off fingers as he continued. "it works on both Vampires *and* Humans. Two, it's highly and instantly addictive. Three, it works on personality, wiping out all the morals and inhibitions and produces an overwhelming sense of sexual arousal. And four, the user becomes highly susceptible to suggestions, commands and *completely* obedient.

"That's what he was doing in Sweden, and with others," he jabbed the air with the one finger that remained unbent. "They were test runs. His Human trials . . . *literally*. And the fact that the grapevine has been burning up the last few weeks about this drug of his, not to mention *who* he's been schmoozing up to about it, to me at least, it's a pretty sure indication that he's finally got it right.

"Rumour has it, he's gonna put on some kind of demonstration. A big production, knowing the bastard's ego. And he's invited some real heavyweights to see it – three of the Brotherhood's West Coast families, the *Deutsch Verein* from Hamburg, the Coalition from South Central and East L.A., and at *least* three of the Houses. And none of them would give a tinker's piss about anything he had to show if they knew Red Carousel is less than a fart in the wind."

"Which answers the question of why he wants *you* silenced," Fallon said. "But why my client? He's had her sister for over a year. And I have to assume she's still alive. But why is he now going all back-off-or-die batshit because of her?"

Knox shrugged. "No definitive answer there, Wildman. What little I know about her is that yes, she is still alive. She must be very important to him because, from what I understand, he keeps a very close eye on her. Keeps her under constant heavy guard and sequestered away from his main group of girl-toys. Not even his closest cronies know exactly where she's being kept at any given moment, when she's not in his company."

"That's just . . . perfect," Fallon groused, softly.

"You know, and this is just my theory," Knox started again. "Where the girl fits into it, I couldn't say, not exactly. But you, on the other hand . . . Going back to Teresa Bennion – the original Blood Carousel affair. Somehow Taylor, as he calls himself now, managed to escape the results of the fall. There's still a contract out on him . . . a Parliament sanctioned contract, with Kane Thoth and Zuron I'Ane as custodians." He took a step or two backwards, for visual purpose, holding up a pair of crossed fingers. "Everybody knows you and Kane are like that . . . as close as brothers. The same goes for Kane and Zuron.

"My theory is Taylor also has his people keeping tabs on your client, the sister. And when he heard you were on the case to find the sister, he figured it wouldn't take long before Kane and Zuron learned he had surfaced again. If he is successful in selling his puppet drug to the big boys, and making himself indispensable to them . . . First of all, Red Carousel will become an undisputed cartel again and, second, he'll have protection from Zuron and Kane.

"Whether you know or not, originally, they put the big Bogeyman himself, Morgan, on the case. And the Big M *never* misses. That alone is enough to scare the holy living shit out of him and make him go to any and all lengths to stay under the radar, including killing you and your . . . client. And, to tell the truth I'm surprised he hasn't done that already. To be honest, Wildman, I think *you* scare the son of a bitch, too."

"I'm flattered," Fallon quipped. "And, as always, you spin a very engaging tale. But the only thing that interests me is knowing where I can *find* the bastard – which I'm pretty sure you know. So, why don't you tell me what I need to know so I can do what I gotta do."

"Steven Segal," Knox chuckled. "Dialogue right out of '*Marked for Death*', probably his best movie. Appropriate in this case. You're our version of Segal, Bruce Lee and Van Damme. All those years your friend, Ó Beolláin, had you study under the Shaolin monks in China and the Bushido and martial arts masters of Japan, and in Thailand, Korea Philippines and Brazil. Not to mention the master swordsmen of France, and the firearms experts of Prussia. You're a fucking walking lethal weapon."

"And your point? I assume you have one?" Fallon prompted, with audible impatience.

"Think about it," Knox said. "Some of the people Taylor invited . . . They don't just deal in the vampire world. Some of their contacts are in bed with Taliban, Al-Qaeda, Hezbollah, even ISIS. What if Taylor's puppet drug gets into the wrong hands? What if an assassin or suicide bomber turns out to be a vampire . . . or he or she gets captured, locked up in a cell, and is exposed to sunlight or a medical examination? We not only get exposed, outed, we vampires will wind up on the terrorists' search and destroy list. Not just by the CIA, British Intelligence, and the Israeli MOSAAD, but the Vatican, who reactivate their hunters.

"He's got to be stopped, Wildman. And, right now, you are our best chance . . . our best hope of accomplishing that."

He was right, Fallon agreed inwardly. As much as he wanted to ignore it, to let it take a backseat to his own need for revenge, he couldn't deny that Taylor's product posed a threat to the safety of vampire-kind. And that he was the one person, by fate, chosen to deal with that threat.

Draining the remainder of his drink, Fallon rapped his knuckles against the limo's dividing window.

"I'm your man," Kass said, as he slid the window open.

"Shadowfall," Fallon said, simply.

CHAPTER THIRTEEN

Adrian the Dane, Christian. Mr Moreau. Eriq. Jean Jacques. Simon Farkas. Quinn Ó Cuinn. Giordana Mason. Darrian Van Cleef. The list was virtually endless.

Der Teufel. Janiss mentally deviated to his native German tongue, as he exited the elevator on the Hotel Tarriano's top floor and made his way to the end of the long, carpeted hallway, to the floor's luxury Superior Suite. A coded knock – two taps with his nails, a pause, and three strong raps with his knuckles – brought an answering click as the door's lock was released from the inside and Janiss entered to behold a scene, chapter and verse, from the Hollywood embellished cinematic rendition of hedonistic decadence.

A pair of stone-faced and intimidating guards on either side of the entrance, armed, and with their weapons in plain sight. Women – all shapes, sizes and situations – completely nude, for the most part, although those who wore anything at all might just as well not have bothered for what it attempted to conceal. A long banquet table, actually three joined end to end, before the suite's mock-stone electric fireplace; its linen covered surface a truly disgusting eyesore of spilled beverages, picked over food and stained napkins. And, at the very centre of it all, was Him . . . on an island of throw pillows and bracketed on all sides by attentive, naked young lovelies; a man who possessed more aliases and accompanying personas than there were snowflakes in an Arctic blizzard. A thousand, in all likelihood, even before he recruited Janiss, then barely a decade turned and known as *Jérôme*, on the Isle of Corsica at the end of the First World War.

Like some self-aggrandised omnipotent Caesar, he lounged upon a makeshift silk throne in a blood-red satin robe, his mid-back length glossy blond hair tied in a slender braid and draped over one shoulder as one of the aforementioned lovelies diligently kneaded the flesh of his upper shoulders; two others, in tandem, fed him small morsels of fruit from a deep glass bowl and sips of wine from a crystal goblet, and a fourth busied herself with affairs of a more prurient nature.

Cyprianos, Cardinal of the Cathedral, Red Carousel. And *Taylor*, his current public sobriquet. Although a look into those deep onyx-dark eyes more than justified Janiss' own personal favourite (though never uttered within earshot) . . .

. . . *Der Teufel*. The Devil. As in 'as soulless as'.

There were two additional women present in the room. One stood at the suite's tri-sectioned panoramic window, her back to the interior as she conversed on her cell phone. Someone he'd seen only three times before, in fleeting glimpses and over a period of several months. The second, located closer to the action, was all too familiar. The hostage? Slave? Sex toy? Bedwarmer? No one was really sure. No one had the *Klöten* to ask for clarification. Human, somewhere in her mid-twenties, very nicely built and attractive – again, for a *Menschlich*. Though her dual pigtailed hairstyle and its cotton-candy colouring were just a tad off-putting.

As usual, she was kept with the barest of necessities, clothing-wise. Tonight, as a matter of fact, she sported only a pair of scanty lace panties and a spiked leather dog-collar. The latter attached to a lengthy leash, its opposite end gripped tightly in Taylor's hand.

Janiss held steady on the edge of his . . . *master's* extended personal space, waiting to be noticed. Which happened, as always, swiftly and unexpectedly when Taylor cocked a leg and slammed his foot into the shoulder of the naked lovely labouring below, sending her sprawling backwards onto her naked ass.

"Give that throat of yours a break," he told her. "In fact," he raised both arms up and fluttered his hands in a shooing gesture. "All of you, take ten. Second thoughts, take a fucking hour . . . and wash off that stink while you're at it. It's time for a fresh crew."

Once they departed, he signalled with a wave for Janiss to approach and he did so with a deft determination, intent on successfully navigating the biological obstacle course of scattered incapacitated bodies, whilst being all too aware of, and averting his gaze *from*, the fact his Lord and Master didn't bother to cover that area of anatomy formerly shielded from view by the now departed lovely.

"Favourable news, I take it?" Taylor queried when Janiss stopped. "Is the," he paused, with a quick mindful flick of his eyes toward the girl in the collar before resuming, "job done?"

"Our man assures me it was," Janiss answered.

"Conclusion confirmed?" Taylor pressed.

Janiss responded with a head-tilted semi-shrug. "To put it in his words, '*I ruined her pretty party dress. Ain't no way she survived.*'"

"Party dress," Taylor repeated dryly, his facial expression a clear indication he was less than satisfied. "And by '*ain't no way she survived*', I will assume he himself made an assumption. That he failed to be certain the task was successfully carried out."

"I would have to agree with that assessment, Your Grace," Janiss replied, deliberately referencing Taylor's organisational appellation . . . *sucking up* in a bid to dodge what many past bearers of unfavourable news never got the chance to do a second time.

"That's what happens when you send in half-baked amateurs," Taylor loosed an audible sigh. "I want that asshole's head on a plate before sunrise."

Oh, Gott in Himmel, thank you! Janiss almost crowed joyously. "Consider it done, sir."

A sudden and derisive chuckle brought both vampires attention to the room's only fully-clothed female occupant who, only minutes earlier had been occupied in a quiet phone exchange at the window. She strolled toward them, giving Janiss his first clear and unobstructed view of the mysterious woman Taylor had only once mentioned and referred to as *La Signora*.

Schöne, in his native tongue. Lovely . . . beautiful. *Attrayant*, attractive as the French would gauge her. A face that would be right at home on the cover of a popular entertainment magazine or on a supermodel strolling down the runway of some noted designer's fashion extravaganza. Her midnight-dark hair was an alluring cowl of thick curls around her seemingly perfect face. A face which crowned an equally unparalleled body which complimented her cropped leather jacket, simple black t-shirt and blue jeans ensemble in a way their designers had never intended.

But the eyes . . . those were the things that caught and held Janiss' attention. Not just their look, which was both hypnotic and intense, but the message they broadcasted. They were of a type he'd seen before, in the faces of soldiers – career soldiers – specifically on the field of battle. The eyes of the warrior, the seasoned animal – both prey and predator. Seeing everything, missing nothing.

Arousing, intimidating and about a mile over the border of damned scary.

"Something you find amusing, *Signora?*" Taylor responded, finally covering himself before sitting upright.

"Just a thought," she answered, silent for a moment while toying with a large red jewelled ring on her left hand. "An old quote. If you want something done right, do it yourself. Something I, personally, can't agree more on."

"Right, wrong," Taylor shrugged. "The message was delivered. Well enough, for the time being. And there are other priorities."

"Never do a job half-assed," The *Signora* gave a contemptuous snort. "But then, it's your show. And, to be completely honest, I don't give a shit about your little cat and mouse game with Fallon Wylde. Although I will say this. For *your* sake, let's hope that move you just *half-ass* made doesn't come back to bite you. Wylde's not some turnblood punk looking to make a name for himself. His street creds are top notch – on the other side of both ponds and across the border."

Taylor hiked an eyebrow. "Why, *Signora*, that sounds like admiration."

"It is. If I didn't have my gaze set on a much bigger prize, I might have considered him instead," she shrugged. "Still, it's also good advice. Take it for what it's worth. As I said, it's *your* show. Whether you succeed or not is also something I couldn't care less about.

"Which reminds me. This is the last time you and I will be seeing each other. Our association is, as of tonight, concluded. So, I sincerely hope you have a sufficient amount of my . . . contribution . . . for your little endeavour. There won't be any more."

"So be it," Taylor executed a quasi-serious from-the-waist bow, locking gazes with the lady for a brief moment. She broke eye contact to glance at Janiss.

"I can find my own way out." She touched a pair of fingers to her forehead in salute, turned and made her way to the suite's door.

"Half ass," Taylor grumbled under his breath once the door had closed behind her. "Half ass." He fixed Janiss with a look that told him the fuse to an explosion of truly homicidal proportions was lighted and burning quickly. "I can't live with half ass, Mr J. I can't . . . and I *won't*."

Janiss, with his fear quotient at a sphincter tightening level of five-point-five, cleared his throat. "If I may say so . . . Your Grace, the situation may not be as bad as the *Signora* opined."

"And you know otherwise?" Taylor challenged.

"Know? Not exactly, sir. But then, neither does anyone else. According to our agent on the inside, the . . . incident caused little more than a ripple in the pond, in terms of normal operations at Shadowfall. The club remains open for business as we speak. But there is little, if any information at all, coming from the residential level where," now it was his turn to angle a mindful look at the pink-haired Human, "where the man in question keeps a suite. And it wouldn't. It's standard procedure. Kane's people would clamp a tight lid over it, for no other reason than to avoid alarming his guests and club patrons. For all we know the contract was successfully completed."

Taylor hiked an eyebrow. "Then find out for sure," he said. "Contact our *man* on the inside to rectify the situation, one way or another."

"Consider it done, sir," Janiss said, bowed reverently and almost scurried for the door.

~*~

She could hear them.

Hear and understand them – every . . . single . . . word.

The young Human woman who started out as a one-night-stand, then became the man called Taylor's party-girl-flavour-of-the-moment, and then his captive, then hostage and lately slave/sex toy on-again/off-again bedwarmer or, as Janiss gave frequent vocal reference to – the bitch with no name.

But she *did* have a name. One she repeated to herself every day. She had been born Hazel, a name she'd always despised, and chose to go by her middle name – Eden.

She was Eden Walker, age twenty-three, married and divorced, an alcoholic several times relapsed, a dabbler in addictive narcotics, a rebel without a clue and, for almost a year now, the captive plaything of someone . . . somet*hing* that, by all laws of reality should not exist – a vampire, a soulless, abusive monster who called himself Taylor.

She heard the words that passed between her captor, his so-called Chief of Operations, and the strange and beautiful dark-haired woman known as *La Signora* and knew that the person – the contract to whom they referred – was her sister, Rowan.

They spoke as if she, Rowan, was dead. But Eden knew better. Rowan was alive. She could feel it in her bones.

Still, the prospect that she had, at least, been seriously injured filled Eden with a bone-chilling dread.

But she didn't let on. Didn't give the slightest twitch, twinge, or blink of an eye. Physically, she might just as well have been a mannequin – unmoving, staring blankly through unseeing eyes, the sole indication of life being her measured, soundless breathing. A deception Eden had become quite skilled at over the past few months. And with good cause.

She knew only too well, had witnessed countless incidents of those girls who proved too aware. Who saw too much, protested too often, and resisted too fiercely. Some, the lucky ones, were dispatched suddenly, quick and brutally – dead within a matter of seconds. Others were made to suffer, depending on Taylor's mood or monstrous whims. Disembowelled, bled out slowly over a period of hours, or gifted to his equally monstrous ever-ravenous 'harem', who often took days brutalising their victims before finally putting them out of their misery.

Eden knew exactly what it took to survive.

Now, for example.

She braced herself, inwardly, as the exchange between Taylor and the dark-haired woman showed audible signs of concluding. Moments later, the *Signora* made her exit and Taylor began conversing with his right-hand – that elitist, superior son-of-a-bitch even his own kind called Count Brown-Nose behind his back.

Not much longer, she thought, and took a deep, quiet breath through her nostrils, readying herself as Janiss turned on his heel and all but sprinted out of the suite.

Having been placed in a position from which, after months of practice she never moved, her line of sight was over the heads of Taylor's island of debauchery, she hear the shift in his breathing, heard the rustle of flesh against fabric as he changed position on the pillows. And then came the expected, though still painful, yank on her leash.

"Come here, Pig," Taylor commanded, his voice rife with arrogance, disgust, and an air of arousal she was very much familiar with.

Eden hesitated, giving just enough resistance to pander to his ego, but not enough to evoke his anger. Giving him the sense that there was still a kernel of humanity left somewhere within her, a piece that could be tormented and corrupted further.

"I said . . . *get your ass OVER HERE!*" he snarled, giving the leash a second, more savage jerk.

Eden stumbled forward, as though at any second her legs would collapse beneath her, eyes widened and mouth agape for effect.

Terror, albeit only a smidgeon, that's what got his juices flowing and what had, so far, kept him from ripping out her throat and draining her as he'd done countless others.

"You know what to do," he said, stripping out of the robe. And Eden did.

Nodding, she dropped to her knees.

Yes, she knew. And she'd do it. Whatever it took to stay alive so that, hopefully, one day she would escape and find her way back to her sister.

~*~

Callie Ruth Johnsson. Now there was a name she hadn't heard, a life she hadn't thought about, in more than a hundred years.

She was the shy freckled blonde and eldest daughter of Swedish immigrants, Jacob and Ellinor Johnsson, a bootmaker and his young second wife, who left the overcrowded tenements of New York City in the summer of 1875 – along with her younger siblings, sister Dagmar and brother Olin – to make a new life for themselves in the New Frontier. It was a journey that took much longer and took her life in directions she could never have imagined.

It was a name, and a person, Tigr had long forgotten. Buried beneath more than a hundred aliases, through countless locales and lifestyles, from the night she was first turned to just a few minutes ago when an unfamiliar voice on her cell phone had brought it all back with, *"Callie Ruth Johnsson? It's time to honour your promise."*

A phone number was texted seconds after the caller hung up, with an additional prompt, *CALL BACK NOW.*

With the lounge's bar-back standing in for her, Tigr stood in the shadows, in the alley outside the back supply room, foot tapping in nervous anticipation as she waited for the call to be picked up on the opposite end.

"Very good, Callie," the unfamiliar male responded after a dozen rings.

"The name's Tigr," *Without an 'e'*, she almost added. *Why would it matter now*, she quickly decided.

The laughter which followed was both mocking and creepy. "Alright then . . . *Tiger.* Let's get down to business, shall we? There was an incident tonight, upstairs. Floor number three, I believe. You've heard about it, I imagine?"

"I have."

"We . . . the person to whom you are obligated . . . would like you to confirm the outcome of said incident. If the *business* was successfully completed, so much the better. On the other hand, if it wasn't . . ." he left the sentence unfinished, obviously assuming there was no need for further explanation.

"If it's not . . . *what*? You want a call back? A report?" Tigr feigned confusion. She knew full well, of course, what was being asked of her. But the pompous, superior attitude of the man on the other end rankled. She chose to gain at least a measure of respect by forcing him to state his request clearly and without question.

"Complete the transaction," he answered, after a brief silence. "I'm fairly certain you know what that means . . . *Tiger.* Your benefactor assures me that, if it comes to that, your debt will be paid in full."

~*~

Eayann and Koo left Rowan alone in the bedroom after Eayann's demonstration to, in his words, *'give her a chance to assimilate what she's discovered*. She knew they hadn't gone far, though, as she could hear the low murmur of voices through the bedroom door.

After they had exited, closing the door softly behind them, Rowan had spent some time doing exactly what Eayann had suggested. She knew Eayann and, to a less extent, Koo expected her to freak out, but after the initial shock of seeing what Eayann had done, Rowan had realised that the existence of vampires actually made a lot of what had happened make sense – Fallon and Koo's preference for working after dark, his sleeping habits and his unconcern over being hurt.

Rowan picked up the dagger Eayann left on the bedside table, padded into the bathroom, nicked her thumb and watched it heal before her eyes. She had been a little disconcerted by the pangs of hunger she felt upon seeing the blood but, with the pragmatism with which she approached most things, Rowan concluded there was little she could do to change the situation and needed to come to terms with her new lot in life. She wondered how Fallon would view this new situation and wished he would return so she could talk to him.

As she studied herself in the bathroom mirror, looking for any visible outward signs of her change, she heard the soft click of the bedroom door as it opened and closed. Rowan moved toward the door and looked through. A strange blonde woman was leaning over her bed. She appeared to be gripping something in her hand and, as Rowan watched, she raised it and slashed downwards.

Rowan was moving before she realised. She burst through the door and threw herself at the woman, knocking her onto the bed. Rowan sprung after her, straddling the stranger's back and pinning her face down. She grasped the stranger's wrist, twisting it to force the woman to drop what she had been holding, and Rowan glanced at it to discover it was a syringe filled with some kind of liquid.

"What is that?" she demanded of the woman struggling beneath her.

The blonde didn't answer, twisting and bucking until she threw Rowan off, jumped to her feet and snatched up the needle as she moved.

"I *might* be a nurse," she told Rowan as she stalked toward her.

Rowan took a step backwards. "You're no nurse."

The woman laughed bitterly. "No, I'm not." A burst of speed put her directly in front of Rowan, who stumbled backwards and hit the door. "But I'm the last thing you'll see before you die." She grasped Rowan's arm and brought up the syringe.

"No!" Rowan lunged forward, and the woman's eyes rounded in surprise before she jerked backwards, the syringe dropping from her fingers as she pressed her hands against her chest.

Both women looked down to see Eayann's dagger protruding from between her ribs, and Rowan screamed.

Two things happened, then.

The woman pulled the dagger from her chest just as the door flew open and Fallon burst into the room, Koo and Eayann close behind him.

"Ro!" Fallon had stepped in front of her, disarmed the woman and had her pinned against the wall by her throat before Rowan could speak. "Are you okay?" he asked, looking over his shoulder at her. "Rowan!" he barked, when she didn't answer straight away.

Rowan nodded. "Yes . . . yes, I'm fine."

"Get her secured," he told Eayann, his voice grim. He waited until the other man had the woman in his grip then whirled around to face Rowan. He lifted a hand to touch her cheek, fingers hovering millimetres away from her skin before he dropped them without touching her. "Are you okay?" he repeated his earlier question, his voice soft.

Rowan nodded, aware he didn't mean the incident he'd just walked in on.

"Are you sure?"

"I'm fine," she reached out and rested her hand on his arm. "Honestly, Fallon. I'm in one piece."

Her touch on his arm seemed to release the tension out of his taut body, and she watched as he threw back his head and sucked in a deep breath. Then she found herself wrapped in his arms, her face pressed against his chest. Her own arms crept around his waist and she clung to him.

"I wasn't sure . . . I hoped, but . . ." his lips brushed across the top of her head. "Gods, the past few hours have been . . ." his arms tightened their hold and he felt silent, burying his face into her hair.

Across the room, their presence forgotten, Eayann and Koo watched Fallon. Eayann glanced over at Koo, his expression thoughtful, and headed toward the door. Koo followed at a slower pace, and closed the door softly behind her, leaving Fallon and Rowan alone in the room.

Fallon held Rowan close, letting her scent wash over him, and the fear and concern of the past few hours leave his body before he lifted his head.

He knew what he had to do, and he admitted to himself that he didn't like it, but he also knew it had to be done. He dropped his arms and reached behind himself to unwrap hers from his waist, then caught her hand in his.

"Come and sit with me," he said, and led her back to the bed.

He didn't release her hand when they sat, instead drawing it onto his lap and linking his fingers with hers. His head bowed, eyes intent on their interlocked hands.

"Did Koo explain everything to you?" he asked, eventually.

"Not Koo, no. The other one . . . Eayann. And not so much explained as showed."

"Showed how?"

"He cut himself across the chest," her lips quirked into a small smile.

Fallon snorted. "Typical of him." He stroked a finger across her knuckles. "You seem to be taking this awfully well."

"It's not like I have a choice, is it?" she said, with wry amusement, and tugged her fingers free. "Fallon, please look at me."

He shook his head. "I've arranged for you and Koo to stay here for as long as you need. Bill everything you want to the room. You need a safe space while you adjust." He rose to his feet and brushed imaginary dirt from his pants.

Rowan stood, her body tensing with every word he uttered. "And *where* will *you* be?"

"When you're ready to leave . . . when it's *safe* for you to leave, Koo will set you up anywhere you want to go."

"Fallon, where will *you* be?"

"Somewhere . . . Europe, maybe. Wherever the next job takes me."

"You're running away?"

"I'm doing *my job!*" He snapped.

He still wouldn't look at her and Rowan felt her temper rising.

"Your *job* was to find my sister!" she yelled.

"My primary job was to keep you safe. I failed. You got hurt. I misjudged, let personal want get in the way of . . ." He raked a hand through his hair and tempered his voice. "You got hurt, Ro."

"Yet here I am," she replied. "Alive and well."

"You don't understand. You nearly *died*. If Koo hadn't arrived when she had, if the elevator had been just *one* minute later, you would have bled out on the floor and *nothing* could have brought you back." He raised his head and finally looked at her, his green eyes flat and hard. "And that's on me. *My* fault, *my* mistake. One mistake after another, and here we are – no closer to having your sister home and *you* almost dead."

"Fallon . . ." she reached out and he stepped backwards, his hands raised palm-outward.

"No. I should *never* have allowed anything to happen between us. It was wrong. *I* was wrong. The situation . . . we . . . *I* got caught up in it, led you on. I let you believe there was something between us when there wasn't." A part of his mind noted he was shouting again. "I'll find your sister and I'll bring her back to you. But this thing between us is *done*, it's over." He spun on his heel and stalked out of the bedroom.

Koo stood by the bar, wide-eyed and one hand covering her lips, as he emerged. He scanned the room quickly before meeting her gaze. She flinched at the expression on his face and his lips twisted.

"Where is she?" he asked.

"Eayann took her," Koo replied. "He said you'd know where. Something about cheap wine and Steve McQueen."

Fallon nodded, then jerked his head to indicate the bedroom he'd just vacated. "Don't let her follow me."

"Fallon . . ."

"Don't!" He snapped, and exited the suite, the door slamming behind him.

~*~

"*Estúpidos!*" Fallon cursed himself, pausing in the corridor outside the suite. Teeth clenched against a snarl of rage, he whirled to face the door and stopped himself scant inches short of ramming his fist through it.

No guards, dammit! Another boneheaded blunder on his part. He had assumed that a pair of Pantera's SO's would be like a neon marker to any and all – though especially to any remaining Taylor spies – that the shooter had left his work unfinished. And, as it turned out, it was another poor decision. He'd thought Eayann and Koo would have been enough, but the timing couldn't have been worse. Koo and Eayann had been standing out on the balcony, giving Rowan the space she needed, and it had allowed a second would-be hitter to walk right in, unchallenged.

Eayann was right. That, amongst others, was a mistake *Fallon Wylde* would never have made. Juan Diego Velásquez de Falcone, on the other hand . . .

He would. *He did,* Fallon chided himself. Took an innocent young woman, desperate to find and rescue her kidnapped sister, and used her to satisfy his own egotistical, self-serving, lecherous whims and, in the process, ruined . . . *ended* her young life.

Okay, technically she hadn't left the land of the living. She'd been turned and, ideally, would exist through several life times. But the young Human known as Rowan Walker was gone forever.

And it's your fault.

And there was only one way he could, albeit in the slightest sense, redeem himself. And that was by doing what he'd set out to do. What he'd *promised* Rowan he would do.

Rescue her sister.

And, no matter what it took, that was exactly what he intended . . . what he *would* do.

~*~

When Koo tapped on the bedroom door and opened it, she found Rowan standing in front of the closet, doors thrown open and piles of clothes scattered around her feet. She glanced at Koo, then frowned, eyes narrowing.

"Let me guess, the stupid man told you I'm not to follow him and you're to stop me if I try."

Koo nodded, and stooped to pick up a dress, smoothing the creases out of it.

"Stupid . . . stupid . . . *idiotic* . . . moronic . . . *egotistical* . . ." Rowan muttered, then stopped and swung around to peer at Koo. "Are you going to follow his orders?"

"That depends on what you're thinking about doing," Koo replied. She continued picking up clothes, folding them and placing them in piles on the bed.

"You know, Fallon gives off this impression that he's detached from everything around him." Rowan plucked a dress from the rail and held it up against herself. "I've got eyes, I see how people react to him. Even *you*, Koo. You all think he's unpredictable, maybe even a little crazy."

"He's not a *little* crazy, he's certifiable." A new voice entered the conversation and both women turned around.

Two strangers, to Rowan at least, stood in the doorway. The man was tall, with dark blonde hair, dressed casually in black jeans and a t-shirt which moulded itself to his physique. The woman was shorter, with long black hair in a ponytail, dressed equally as casually in similar clothes.

"Your Highness!" Koo's voice was a little strangled and, when Rowan glanced over at her, she seemed a little wide-eyed.

The woman sniggered and bumped her companion with her shoulder when he groaned.

"You'd think after a few hundred years he'd be used to the title, wouldn't you?" she said, conversationally, to Rowan.

"And . . . he's not?" Rowan asked slowly, unsure how to respond.

The woman chuckled. "He uses it *that* rarely it still squeaks if he turns around too fast." She moved forward and held out a hand. "I'll introduce us since he's still squirming. I'm Morganna. This is Taz. Fallon asked if we'd come by and babysit for a few hours."

Rowan shook Morgan's hand and turned her gaze to Taz. "He's a prince?"

Morgan gave the man beside her an unreadable look. "Clown Prince, possibly." She turned her attention to Koo. "Fallon doesn't trust that you'll stop her from following him."

"And from what we heard before we came in, he's right," Taz added. "So, why don't you get us up to date on what's been going on," he flashed a dazzling smile at Rowan, "and then we'll decide if we should help you or not."

CHAPTER FOURTEEN

Steve McQueen.

Obviously *not* the legendary Hollywood star in the flesh, but a collection of posters and associated paraphernalia gathered over the years by Shadowfall's Head of Transportation and chief mechanic, the automotive wunderkind known to one and all simply as Cameron. A temple by any other name, as Cam fondly and often put it. The large lounge-sized foyer which lead to the physically adolescent one-hundred-plus year old's motor pool inner sanctum was jam-packed – floor-to-ceiling and wall-to-wall – with artefacts and pictorial representations that spanned the iconic celebrity's entire career. A holy shrine to the King . . .

"King, my ass. The *God* of Cool," in Cameron's opinion.

Five years ago, at the end of the Mongolian job. A combination heist, assassination, and prison break that, as very rarely occurred, went off without a hitch. Fallon and his team had planned to celebrate at Shadowfall afterward with a string of primo blood functionaries. Chef André's legendary Adobo Sirloin, and a case of top shelf champagne. But, due to a miscommunication on the part of Kane's staff, an Honours ceremony and dinner for one of the local Vampire Nation's senior *consiliu* – Senators – had to be rescheduled. With the majority of the club's venues, especially LaDonna Roma's – Kane's five-star restaurant and main attraction – loaded to the rafters with local and visiting dignitaries, it left Fallon and crew with only two options, either find another location or cancel the party.

As it turned out, the end of the Mongolian job coincided with Cameron's 124th re-birthday. The celebration of which the young vampire had graciously invited Fallon and crew to join in. An occasion which included a number of fetching young vampire lasses, dancers from the House of Sybarite-owned Velvet Kitten Gentlemen's Club, Cam's own private cache of blood functionaries (not exactly primo, but willing), twenty-seven pizzas of varying compositions from Razzi's Pizzeria, and a case of *inexpensive* champagne. Not exactly the Class-A spread Fallon initially planned, but a good time was had by all in any case.

"Mr Wylde! Always a pleasure," Cameron greeted his approach as Fallon descended the short, winding staircase into the sandy-haired mechanic's notably immaculate apartment.

"Mr C," Fallon reciprocated, and the two men shared wrist-gripping handshakes.

"Mr O brought me up to speed on the situation," Cam went on, jerking a thumb over his shoulder toward the area where Eayann stood, in muted, and apparently engaging, conversation with a lovely, ginger-haired member of Cam's crew, and the couch where Tigr sat, bracketed at each end by a pair of brawny mechanics in grease-mottled coveralls. "Like I told him – *mi casa es tu casa*. Make yourself at home."

"Then maybe I should apologise now. Things might get messy."

"I live twenty feet away from a garage workshop," Cam pointed out. "We ain't no strangers to mess," he shrugged. "Do what you got to do. We'll deal with it."

Fallon nodded, and threw a quick glance toward Tigr and the couch. "I'm gonna need some privacy."

"You got it." Cam snapped his fingers and the two brawny mechanics immediately withdrew.

Fallon passed them as he moved toward the couch. A quick glance over his shoulders revealed the joint departure of Cam, the redhead and his two associates. Eayann moved toward him, slowing Fallon's approach.

"I'm not in the mood for one of your lectures on restraint, Old Man," he cautioned his friend.

"And I'm not in the mood to deliver one," Eayann replied. "If not for the need for vital intel, I'd have ended the bitch before you got here. Believe it or not, I just want to watch."

"Fine." Fallon approached the couch slowly with measured steps and stopped within a foot of Tigr, who rose to meet him.

"Look, I know what you must think of—" The words were barely out of her mouth when she was sent sprawling back to the couch cushions by a right hook to the side of her head. A punch Fallon had clearly pulled as full force would have been instantly fatal.

Tigr stayed put for a minute or two, half on the floor, half on the couch, staring up at Fallon through pain-filled eyes, while massaging the visibly bruised point of contact.

"I guess I deserved that," she said, voice slightly slurred.

"You guess?" Fallon replied, moving to stand over her.

Tigr quickly raised her free hand, as if to guard against another attack. "Okay, *yes*. I did. But it wasn't—"

"Don't you even go there," Fallon growled, cutting her off again. "You walk into *my* suite, with a hypo filled with . . ." he threw a look backward at Eayann for assistance.

"Potassium Chloride," the larger vampire answered. "Twice the dosage used by the prison systems for executions, in fact."

" . . . to kill my guest," Fallon continued. "So, you don't get to use the '*it wasn't personal*' excuse. In fact, fuck excuses altogether. I already know why, and I know who. There's only two things I need from you." He squatted over her and brought up two fingers, held practically in her face and ticked them off as he continued. "One – the girl, is she still alive? And two, where is he keeping her?"

"Okay, say I give you what you want," Tigr said, then paused, her gaze hopping back and forth from Fallon to the hulking vampire male behind him. "What happens then?"

And in the next moment Fallon's fingers were clamped around her throat. With as little effort as it would have taken a ten-year-old to pick up his favourite plastic toy, Fallon snatched the blonde bartender, a robust example of womanhood in her own right, off the floor in a steely one-armed grip that had her feet twitching in a spastic dance of desperation at least two feet above the carpet. "You are in no *fucking* position to bargain with me."

"Spaniard . . . *Diego*?" Eayann cautioned, his tone muted and mindful, not only of the circumstances at hand, but his intimate knowledge of his friend's disposition and the blonde's bulging eyes and the truly ugly shade of purple in Tigr's facial colouring.

"I warned you, Eayann," Fallon responded.

"You get no intel at all from a woman with her head squeezed off," Eayann pointed out mildly, placing a hand on his friend's shoulder.

For a moment it seemed as if Fallon would ignore Eayann and, indeed, squeeze the blonde's head off. And then, with a noise of disgust, he released her and took a step backwards. He lingered, looming above her with fists clenched, gazing down at Tigr's flushed and coughing form, then slowly backed away.

Eayann approached then, squatting down to address the bruised and distressed bartender.

"Did you think the rumours of Fallon Wylde were an exaggeration?" he asked her. "And if you don't want things to get worse, I would advise you not to make him ask you a second time."

~*~

Morgan and Taz listened to Rowan's story of her missing sister, how she was given Fallon's details and then contacted him. When she paused, Taz asked how long it was before she sought Fallon's bed.

Rowan blushed. "It wasn't like that!"

"It never is," Taz cast a sly glance at Morgan, who ignored him.

"You're important to him," Morgan told her. "He would never have asked us to come here, to even allow you to be aware of our existence, if you were just another client."

"I agree," Koo joined the conversation, her eyes still occasionally flitting across to stare at Taz. "You need to be honest, Rowan. Is he important to you? If he is, you're going to have to fight for him."

"It doesn't matter, does it? He's already told me it was a mistake."

"I've heard that somewhere before . . . *oomph*," Taz exhaled abruptly when Morgan's elbow found his ribs. "*What?*" he asked, innocently. "I *have* heard it before. And, for what it's worth, it's just denial of the truth." He dodged another dig from Morgan, caught her hand and raised it to his lips to press a kiss to her palm. She snatched it away just before his lips touched her skin and he laughed. "He's doing what he *thinks* he should be doing, not what he *wants* to do. You just have to show him the error of his ways."

"It's that simple, is it?" Morgan asked, dryly.

"You should know," Taz's grin flashed on again. "Anyway, I have a plan."

~*~

"She's alive," the bartender answered, much more cooperative following Eayann's timely intervention.

"And you're sure of that? How do you know?" Eayann asked, insinuating himself between Fallon and the bruised and subdued blonde, he assumed the role of inquisitor.

Tigr laughed, wincing as it called painful reminder to her mauled throat. "I'm friends with a couple of his favourite party girls.

He calls them *mirele* . . . like the *brides* in those old British Dracula movies. They come by every now and again for drinks.

"They've got a nickname for her. They call her the '*Boss's Blankie*' – his bedtime security blanket. The ones who've been with him the longest, they say he's got this quirk for Human women. He keeps them around for snacks after sex or something like that. But *her* . . . well, *she's* different."

"He's become attached to her, then?" Eayann offered, quickly interjecting before she could respond. "I'm going to get myself something to drink – beer, wine, whatever Cam has on hand. You could probably use one, too," he paused to shoot Fallon a conspiratorial glance. "I'm sure Fallon won't mind."

Fallon delivered a head-tilted shrug, turning away to hide a knowing smile. He had to tip his hat to the old fox. He had accomplished in a matter of minutes – with the empathetic charm of a trusted neighbourhood holy man and the wiles of a travelling snake oil salesman – what would have taken Fallon, himself, an hour of outright physical intimidation to force out of the tough-as-nails and stubborn blonde. He had her relatively relaxed and singing like the proverbial canary in a cage.

It was slow going, of course, taking its toll on Fallon's patience. Or, in this case, the complete lack of it. One of life's necessary aggravations, as Eayann would say. And one which eventually paid off.

"I would imagine your friends are more than bit antsy by now," Eayann said, delivering a second drink to the now thoroughly at ease and loquacious blonde. "Waiting for you to check in? To give your report on the assassination?"

Tigr shrugged. "Unless they think I'm dead. I'm pretty sure it was supposed to be a suicide mission."

"And wouldn't they be surprised if it wasn't?" Eayann's rhetorical query was followed by a suggestive grin and twitched eyebrows. "If, somehow, you managed to survive . . .?"

Tigr paused with the rim of her glass poised at her lips, eyes hopping back and forth between her two host-captors. "Look, I know where this is going, okay?" she said, following through with a quick sip. "And, believe me – no bullshit – I *really* don't know where the girl is. That's way above my place in the food chain, understand? I'm just a pair of eyes and ears, a low-level grunt."

"Even a grunt hears things," Fallon edged back into the exchange. "Things that might not be important to *you*, but . . ."

Tigr shrugged again. "They don't tell us much."

"*Us*?"

"Yeah, *us*. Me and the other moles." Tigr chuckled. "Did you think I was the only termite in Kane's house?"

Kane's gonna love hearing that little gem, Fallon thought.

"But if it helps," she continued. "Taylor's uber-paranoid. He's got places all over – hotel rooms, houses, renovated apartments. He doesn't like to stay in one place more than a day or two. And he *never* goes anywhere without her."

"And who, besides him, would know any or all of those places?" Fallon asked.

"Maybe . . . probably . . . just the one," Tigr answered, after a moment's thought. "Taylor's right-hand man. The girls, even some of his soldiers, call him Count Kiss Ass . . . or Brown Nose . . . or something like that. I think his name is Janiss. And I'm about ninety percent sure he's the one I report to. The one who gave me the contract."

"How would you like to get back at them?" Eayann quickly reinserted himself. "For setting you up?"

Tigr, again searched the eyes of her captors, looking for signs of sincerity. "Depends on what you have in mind."

It was at that point Fallon's cell rang, it's touch screen displaying Koo's name, followed by a text message that read '*Emergency. Call back NOW*'.

Fallon excused himself, moving a few feet away for privacy. The resulting conversation had him swearing profusely and left him with a need to wrap up the current situation quickly.

He turned back just in time to witness Tigr returning Eayann's cell. Both sported contented grins, obviously for reasons completely separate from one another. In Eayann's case, however, Fallon did not have to guess. He'd seen that expression on several occasions and knew the reason, the *message* behind it all too well.

It's time, said the gleam in the elder vampire's eyes. A gleam like the light of a rising full moon over an ice-glazed tundra, growing colder with each passing second while Eayann made vocal reference to the dwindling contents of Tigr's glass, and asked that Fallon do the honours.

No guesswork, whatsoever, as Fallon took the blonde's near-empty glass and made his way to Cameron's makeshift corner mini bar. And no surprise, finding Eayann's dagger tucked between stacked six-packs of *Budweiser* and a box of *Franzia Sunset Blush*.

Returning, Fallon stopped a step or two beyond the blonde's reach – the wine glass in one hand and Eayann's dagger hidden up the sleeve of his free hand. As he moved the glass toward her, Tigr left the couch to accept it and Fallon let the glass slip from his hand. A diversion that prompted Tigr to automatically stretch out in a futile attempt to catch the glass; also taking her attention off Fallon.

Fallon caught her by the neck, pulled her forward, and in a matter of seconds it was over.

Tigr settled onto her knees, her wide eyes registering the shock and pain of the silver blade embedded in her heart.

Her eyes met Fallon's cold green ones.

"If it wasn't for the times we have spent together, this would not have ended so quickly," he told her.

A moment later she sagged to the floor. Fallon didn't wait for her final breath. He spun on his heel.

"I need to be somewhere," he told Eayann and stalked out.

~*~

He's on his way. He's not happy.

The text from Koo was Rowan's cue to set everything in motion. Morgan and Taz had dropped her off at Aduna's, organised a private suite for her and promised to stay close by in case of any trouble. Taz's presence in the club had turned the doorman into a grovelling mess as he scrambled to meet his demands. And it was less than fifteen minutes before she found herself alone in a luxurious suite, a massage table organised in the centre, the lighting low and the smell of incense heavy in the air.

Taking a deep breath, Rowan shed the robe she was wearing and, naked, stepped over to the massage table, settled on top of it and draped the supplied towel over her bottom. She stretched out and pushed the buzzer to summon the masseur.

I hope you all know what you're doing – Koo's words whispered through her mind, and Rowan acknowledged silently that Taz's plan had every possibility of going horribly wrong. Especially if Taz had misinterpreted Fallon's reasons for wanting her protected. But she was committed to it now and had no more time to change her mind.

The door slid open and her chosen masseur entered the room. Tall, toned, dressed only in loose cotton pants, he looked more like a male supermodel – perfect for what she needed.

She greeted him with a self-conscious smile. "Just remember what Taz told you. Show no fear."

He paused in the preparation of oils. "I didn't think His Highness was serious."

"Let's hope not," Rowan replied.

He dripped the warm oil along her spine and smoothed his hands across her back. "You're very tense. Are you *sure* you want to do this?"

Rowan didn't respond, listening intently to the noises beyond the door. Voices raised in anger, a thud, a yell and then silence.

No prizes for guessing who's arrived, she thought.

The door slammed open, bouncing against the wall and the masseur flinched.

"Keep going," she murmured and, feigning a relaxation she didn't feel, she turned her head and smiled at Fallon.

"What are you doing here?" he demanded.

"Getting a massage," she arched her back against the hands running down her spine and saw Fallon's fingers curl into fists.

"You could have done that at Shadowfall."

Rowan pretended to consider his words, letting her eyes shift over the male beside the massage table. She dropped her gaze to his navel and then lower before letting her smile widen. "But I'm told they're so much more *accommodating* here."

"Rowan—" Fallon started to growl.

She chose that moment to moan. "God, that's *soo* good. *Harder!*"

"Leave!" Fallon snarled, and the younger male blanched.

"No!" Rowan caught his wrist as he started to step away. "I *want* a massage. I *paid* for a massage." She slanted a look at Fallon. "It's been a difficult couple of days, I deserve to relax." She could feel the masseur trembling as he returned his hands to her back. Watching Fallon from beneath her lashes, she gave another throaty moan, even though the man was barely touching her, and watched as Fallon took a single step forward.

The male fled.

Rowan tutted. "Now look what you've done." She reached for the buzzer.

"You will *not* call for another one. You're supposed to be resting at Shadowfall, getting used to the changes."

"You don't get to make that decision for me." She pushed the button, acutely aware Taz had paid a lot of money to make sure no one would respond to it.

Fallon stalked the rest of the way into the room, swatted her hand away from the buzzer and ripped it out of its casing.

"Why are you acting like this?" she asked him as she rolled over, sat then stood. Pausing only to pull on her robe, she headed toward the door.

"You're not calling for a replacement," he snapped.

"I *want* a massage." She opened the door, only for his hand to hit the wood and slam it shut.

"I will burn this place to the ground before I let one of them touch you."

Rowan turned around to face him. "You can't get no-contact massages. It's not a thing, Fallon," she explained slowly, as if talking to a child.

"No."

"No? *No?* What kind of answer is *that?*" She jabbed him in the chest with one stiffened finger. "You have no right! You were leaving, remember? You're going to Europe. Or have you forgotten?" She tipped her head back and looked up into his eyes. "What we did was a mistake . . . you remember saying *that?*" she shook her head. "You have no right, Fallon."

She waited, watching as his fingers flexed with each barb she fired at him. Her final chance – make or break time, as both Morgan and Taz had told her. She had to break through the walls he'd built, the excuses he told himself – all designed to keep people at a distance.

Knock him off-balance, Taz had told her. *Keep him there. If you think he's adapting, change direction. DO NOT let him see you're upset.*

Summoning every ounce of acting skill she had, Rowan shrugged her shoulders. "Well, if you won't let me call for another masseur, I suppose I could *allow* you to do it for me."

She stepped around him and moved back toward the table, dropped the robe to the floor and settled back down.

She lay with her face purposely turned toward the far wall and listened as Fallon's breathing changed. Three deep breaths, followed by the slightest whisper of sound as he moved across the room. Anticipation curled in the pit of her stomach, and she had to concentrate on keeping her breathing relaxed as she waited for that first initial contact . . . and waited . . . and waited.

Frowning, she lifted her head and scanned the room to locate him. He stood beside her left shoulder, scowling down at her.

"Can't trust yourself?" she taunted. Something unreadable flickered in his eyes and he picked up the nearest oil with a jerky motion.

"You should be grateful I arrived when I did," he informed her as his hands settled onto her spine.

"Thank you for spoiling my massage," she replied primly and felt his hands tense against her back.

"He would have touched you."

"We've been over this," Rowan sighed. "You can't have a massage without skin to skin contact."

"Massages are *never* just massages at Aduna's." A huskiness had entered his voice and Rowan fought to resist the urge to squirm as his hands smoothed over her skin, fingertips brushing against the sides of her breasts and then further down over her waist, before sliding inwards toward the base of her spine.

"Oh . . . you mean he would have *touched* me." She arched up under his touch. "Maybe I would have been okay with that." She felt him pause, then he hooked his hands under her hips and flipped her over.

"You would be okay with a stranger doing this?" He drizzled oil across her breasts and then cupped them in his palms, letting his thumbs play across her nipples.

Rowan sucked in a breath and closed her eyes, savouring his touch.

"I let you do it . . . and you were mostly a stranger."

One hand continued to play with her nipple, while the other slid down over her stomach, and down further to the small bundle of nerves hidden at the apex of her thighs.

"What about this?" he murmured, stroking, flicking and teasing with his fingers until her hips jerked up to meet his touch and a moan escaped her lips.

Rowan let him touch her as he wanted, didn't deny him access as he pushed first one, then two fingers inside her. She wanted him to remember how good it was between them. How good it could continue to be, if he'd allow it. She felt his tongue join his fingers and orgasm ripped through her, shocking in its suddenness and intensity, and leaving her limp and breathless.

When she felt him withdraw his fingers, she opened her eyes and saw the glow of satisfaction in his eyes. Taz's words returned to her – *keep him off-balance* – and she forced herself to sit up, ignoring her rapidly beating heart, and plastered a breezy smile on her face.

"Thank you," she told him, proud of how steady her voice was. She stood and wrapped herself in the robe. "That was lovely. I'll be sure to leave you a glowing review at the desk." She forced herself to walk at a steady pace toward the door, only to find him blocking the way before she reached it.

"Where do you think you're going now?" he demanded.

Rowan tilted her head to look at him. "Well, let's see. I got my massage, kind of. I even got a happy ending – that was a first for me." She flashed him an impish smile. "Now, I need to shower, change and return to Shadowfall. I'm told my new . . . state . . . " she faltered over the word, her voice quivering before she caught herself, and his eyes narrowed sharply. "My new state means I need to be indoors before the sun rises." She stepped around him and reached for the handle.

"And then what?" He caught her arm and spun her around then stepped closer, forcing her to move backwards until her back was pressed against the door.

"I have to think about things. Decide where I want to go. Consider my options."

"I have an option for you to consider," he told her, and crushed her mouth under his.

Rowan clamped her lips shut. *Do not cave . . . do NOT cave*, she told herself repeatedly, as Fallon's tongue teased at the seam of her lips.

"Let me in, Ro," he whispered, his teeth nipping at her bottom lip.

She shook her head, brought up her hands and shoved at his chest.

"You don't get to do this, Fallon," she told him as he lifted his head. "You ended it. You told me you were moving on."

"I've changed my mind." He dipped his head again, his tongue flicking against the inner shell of her ear, before he caught the lobe between his teeth and tugged gently.

"For how long?" she demanded, unable to stop her neck from arching sideways. "Until something else happens and you decide it's too dangerous again?"

He accepted her unspoken offer and ran his tongue down the side of her throat, pausing at the pulse beating rapidly at its base.

"For as long as you'll have me." He pressed a kiss to her shoulder and straightened up to look at her. "I thought I could walk away, let you move on with your life. What happened to you . . . that's *my* fault and I'll have to live with that guilt for the rest of my life. But finding you here, seeing *his* hands on you." He lifted his hands to cup her face between his palms. "Let's clear one thing up right now, I never said I didn't want you. You're mine, Ro . . . and I *don't* share."

This time when he bent to kiss her, she met him halfway.

~*~

"You're very calm, all things considered," Fallon spoke from where he was sprawled across the bed, head propped on one hand.

Rowan paused in the process of pulling on her underwear and smiled at him. "You mean for someone who was shot, almost died, discovered vampires exist, found out she was one, almost got murdered . . . *again* . . . and also thinks the man she's been sleeping with is a vampire too," she paused to take a breath. "You *are*, aren't you? You haven't actually admitted to it, one way or the other."

Fallon chuckled. "Yeah, that. And yes, I am."

She hooked her bra closed, crawled back onto the bed and curled against him. Fallon shifted until he was lying on his back and pulled her across his chest, looping his arms around her waist.

"Taylor is a vampire as well, isn't he?" she rubbed her cheek against his shoulder and continued talking before Fallon could reply. "It makes a lot of sense, looking back. Was . . . was Floyd?"

"Taylor is, Floyd wasn't. My guess is he was hired to try and keep you away from the truth. When you hired me," his lips quirked. "A fee you still haven't paid, by the way . . . well, it upped the ante, so to speak." He glanced at his watch and sat up. "We need to get back to Shadowfall."

It was Rowan's turn to watch him as he gathered up his scattered clothes, laughing softly when he frowned at the creases in his shirt and tried to shake them out. He felt her eyes on him, dropped the shirt onto the bed and tipped her head back for a kiss.

"I have a lead," he told her, when they broke apart, both breathing heavily. "I'm meeting with some people in a couple of hours. They'll tell me where Eden is. So, get dressed sweetheart, and we'll get you back to Shadowfall."

"I want to come with you to get Eden."

Fallon shook his head. "Not happening."

"Fallon, she's my *sister!*"

"I know."

"Doesn't being a vampire mean I'm stronger, faster? I can help."

"In time. You're new to it, it's going to take some time for you to learn what you can and can't do. Some things are different for all of us." He pulled on his pants and tossed her dress onto her lap. "I promise, I'll bring your sister home."

"But, Fallon—"

"No. We've had this conversation before. You can't fight, you can't shoot." He slipped on his shirt, pulled her to her feet and helped her into her dress, tugging up the back zipper. His hands smoothed over her hips and around her waist, to pull her back against him. Dipping his head, he nuzzled her throat.

"How about a compromise? You can be at the meet, *if* you do exactly what I tell you. But you stay with Eayann when we move in to get Eden."

"Eayann doesn't like me," she protested.

"Rowan," Fallon sighed. "Give him time to get to know you, then he'll love you like . . ." he broke off, frowning. "He'll love you."

Rowan turned in the circle of his arms, and gazed up at him for a long, silent minute. "This hasn't changed anything. I'm still going to keep working to find her."

"I know you will. And I'm still going to work to keep you safe. I won't compromise on that. I've made too many mistakes, already."

"Okay," she sighed. "I know you're right, I do. I just don't like sitting around to wait for news."

~*~

Fallon checked his watch as Nona, Cameron's on-loan driver, pulled their vehicle – a bogus yellow taxicab – into the curb at the unlighted end of the red brick structure; a warehouse whose stone emblazoned designation read Dunne & Elliot Storage.

A shade past 3:15AM. Fifteen minutes past the agreed upon time but, all things considered, not bad.

"You said three hours," Rowan piped up from the back seat, her voice torqued tight with a mixture of dread and impatience. "We're late. What if the guy didn't wait? What if he took off?"

"He didn't. He won't," Fallon assured her, twisting back to look at her.

"You don't know that. How do you know that?"

Fallon's mind slipped back to the motor pool, to Cam's living quarters and Tigr's interrogation.

"Trust me, I know."

Rowan leaned forward and reached between the seats to touch Fallon's arm. "Fallon. I'm new to this. What's obvious to you *isn't* to me."

Fallon held her eyes for a long moment, then nodded. "You're right, I'm sorry." He took a deep breath. "The woman who attacked you in my suite. She's been part of Shadowfall for a long time," he began, and gave her a sanitised version of events in Cam's garage.

Rowan didn't respond immediately, and Fallon settled back in his seat to wait. He didn't have to wait for long.

"You killed her, didn't you?"

"Yes."

"And . . . whoever we're meeting here . . . they think they're meeting *her*?"

"That's right."

Rowan sighed. "This guy, he's tying up loose ends. If she *had* come, he'd have killed her anyway."

Fallon masked a smile. *Good girl!* "It was a suicide mission. She wasn't supposed to survive killing you."

This guy she's supposed to be meeting," Rowan continued. "He won't be alone, will he?"

"Probably not."

"But *you* will be." The concern in her tone, at any other time, would have prompted an amused chuckle. The chuckle did come through, but the feeling accompanying it was a long way from amusement.

"I do my best work alone," he said, reached back and gave her hand a squeeze.

He opened the cab door and paused, addressing both women in turn.

First Rowan. "I'll be right back. Stay put . . . I *mean* it," then Nona. "If she tries to follow me, stop her. I don't care if you have to sit on her. *Capisce?*"

He exited the cab and Rowan's voice stopped him once again.

"Fallon?" She'd opened the window and leaned out.

Fallon stepped closer and smiled as her hand came through the window to grasp the front of his shirt and tug at it until he bent.

"Be careful!" she told him and ducked her head out of the window to press a quick kiss to his lips. "I mean it."

"Careful is not in my contract." He flashed her a cavalier smile and returned his attention to the woman behind the wheel. "Remember. Three short, then three long."

"You got it, Mr Wylde," Nona replied.

~*~

What is the essence of stealth?

Fallon remembered the question, as well as the lessons taught him during his training in the art of ninjutsu in the small village near Nagasaki, Japan, in the years between 1574 and 1625, by Master Sana Ariwa and his successor Master Anami Taro.

And the answer. *To move, to be, to see, without being seen.*

Ninjutsu. The ancient Japanese art of deception, invisibility, and the silent kill. Skills totally unnecessary in young Diego de Falcone's initial opinion, for someone of his life designation.

"True enough, young Kyūketsuki," Master Sano had nodded his head sagely. "For vampire versus mortal, there is truly no contest for someone whose physiology allows him to move within the blink of an eye. But, if what I have witnessed in my own finite lifetime, concerning your kind, is true, there are those among you whose lifespans number in the thousands and whose abilities become stronger and more acute with each passing century. If you wish to endure in the vocation for which I have been commissioned to instruct you, would it not be prudent that you acquire skills which will give you an advantage over opponents who are older, stronger, and more experienced than yourself?"

Wise words Fallon could neither find fault, nor argue with, then or now.

It was a half-century well spent, he admitted, while navigating the condemned warehouse's dark and ramshackled interior en route to his proxy-rendezvous. His vampire eardrums thundered, his olfactory senses assaulted from every direction by the scents and heartbeats from the structures populated with scattered homeless Human residents. But, as he drew nearer the building's front they became less and less noticeable, surrendering prominence to the supporting players in the night's little melodrama.

There were three, to be exact. One who stood at the northern-most end of the loading dock's cracked and trash strewn tagging platform, concealed in the shadow of a slight wall recess. And two others – driver and passenger – in a dark SUV, street-level parking lot, just below hidden Thug #1.

The classic *sucker trap*. Tigr (the intended sucker) would approach and be lulled, trustingly, into the vehicle for the meeting with her contact and *BAM!* Trap sprung. Tigr, most likely, would have barely had time to leave the imprint of her ass on the backseat's upholstery before Thug #1 swooped down to 'seal the deal' with a silver-jacketed double-tap to the heart.

Well, not tonight, Fallon thought with a smile of wolfish delight. A drastic script rewrite was in order for this scene.

"There are many ways to avoid detection," the Masters taught him. One, and the type best suited for the current situation, was called *Onsei nin* – the art of concealing yourself by the use of ambient noise. In this case, the unexpected blare of a car horn.

Six, in fact.

The first in the prearranged sequence trumpeted in a 1-2-3 succession within moments of Fallon's arrival at the warehouse front, leaving a discordant echo in their wake. Their effects were both instant and predictable. A sudden surge in the heartbeats of all three targets; which told Fallon, first of all, they were nervous and on edge. And second, they were 'first timers', run-of-the-mill turnblood house soldiers. Pros would have been more focused, less likely to give a shit about a distant car horn. Or anything other than the arrival of their target, for that matter.

Good, Fallon thought. It made the next few minutes easier.

When the first of the long horn blasts sounded, Thug #1 went as far as to chance a sneak-peek around the edge of his recessed hidey-hole. No more than a second or two before pulling back. In doing so, however, his right side encountered something that hadn't been there just a moment earlier. A bulk, a mass, that felt suspiciously like another body. Which, of course, involuntary reflex and hapless curiosity dictated that he visually investigate. His eyes barely had time to register the shape of Fallon's face and a mocking smile. And then his eyes saw no more.

At the sound of long blast number two, Fallon was sliding silently across the vehicle's roof. His soft landing at the driver's side door was as soundless as a stalking feline mere seconds away from pouncing upon her intended prey.

The driver had even less time than his cohort in the shadows. Less than a second to catch the glimmer of movement at the corner of his eye. And maybe, just for a few seconds afterwards – while his fading consciousness attempted to argue with the blade embedded in his brain – to curse himself for leaving his door unlocked.

The third and final long blast found the SUV's flustered and annoyed passenger, completely unaware of the actions which unfolded around him, in the process of reaching into his jacket to fetch his cell when the adjacent door opened, and Fallon slid inside.

Neither man spoke or moved for a long and static-charged moment. For Fallon, it was part of the strategy – knocking the mark off-balance via silent intimidation. Something which worked extremely well in Janiss' case. As he would relate to several interested parties a short time later, "In all the years I have walked upon this Earth, many many times have I faced the possibilities of Oblivion. But never before have I felt as close to death as when I gazed into that man's eyes."

"Fallon Wylde, I presume-GOTT IN HIMMELL!" Janiss' attempt at cordiality was interrupted abruptly when Fallon buried Eayann's silver blade into his upper thigh and twisted.

Coughing and writhing in pain, his body surged backwards into the space between the seat's backrest and the passenger door, as if contact with said area would somehow distance himself from the situation and the mind-numbing agony that accompanied it.

One shaky hand fluttered upward, in search of the epicentre to his agony, only to have Fallon slap it away.

"*Ah ah ah*, no touchy!" Fallon quipped, giving the embedded dagger a second twist. "Just listen . . . you know those movies when the good guy and the big villain's right hand limp dick – which I'm gonna assume is you – where they engage in punchy, stalling semi-threatening banter? Well, this is the R-Rated version. The version where the good guy – me – tells you that I got neither the time nor patience for that shit. And, by the way, neither do you.

"I wouldn't pass out if I were you," he added. "Nod or grunt if you're still with me."

Janiss did both, somehow finding the mental and intestinal fortitude to meet his antagoniser's gaze.

"Good man!" Fallon grinned. "Okay, I got bad news, not-so-bad-news-that-might-turn-into-good-news, and I got questions.

"The bad news, first. That blade, as I'm sure you're feeling, is silver. Which means that wound is never going to heal properly. And worse, it's been coated with Allium sativum, better known as garlic. And just in case you didn't know what that means, when taken the way I gave it to you, it causes blood poisoning. A very *very* bad affliction for our kind." He twisted the blade again to emphasise his point.

"Your cells are already starting to decay. In an hour or so, your leg flesh will start to blacken, to decompose. Another half hour and it'll saturate your blood stream. Your vital organs will start shutting down. The pain will be . . . Well, I'm pretty sure you get the idea."

"I . . . I . . . Yes, I . . ." Janiss' attempt at a reply ended in a forced nod.

"So, here's the thing," Fallon continued. "You got a shade over ninety minutes before it becomes irreversibly terminal. And I know a doctor at Shadowfall who can treat it. For a price, of course. You turn yourself in to Kane, give up the other moles in his club, he lets the Doc save your worthless ass, you get our version of the Witness Protection Program, and everybody wins . . . And believe me, you ain't got time to think about it.

"Now, here's what *I* want. Answers to my questions. Question one – the girl. Is she still alive?"

Janiss responded with a violent, breath-snuffling nod. "Y-y-yes. Yes, she's alive."

"Very good. Next question. Where is she?"

"She is . . . with the . . . Cardinal. With *Cyprianos*," Janiss almost vomited the name.

"I'm gonna assume that's Taylor's big boy name," Fallon chuckled and gave a satisfied nod "Okay. That gets you in the front door, at least." He extracted his dagger. "But we still got lots to talk about."

CHAPTER FIFTEEN

When Fallon slid back into the taxi forty minutes later, there was an air of satisfaction surrounding him. He asked Nona to wait until he saw a dark-coloured car pull out, then gave a nod and Nona started the car.

Rowan wanted to ask him what had happened, whether he'd found out where Eden was, but she was distracted by the scent pervading the car. A smell that made her mouth water. She shifted in her seat, sniffing, trying to figure out what it was and where it was coming from. When her stomach gave an embarrassing gurgle, Fallon's head snapped around.

"Hungry?" he asked.

"Starving," she replied. "What *is* that smell?"

Fallon's head tilted sideways, and he took a deep breath through his nose, before glancing down at the blood splatters on his shirt. "Pull over," he told Nona softly.

Their driver cast him a questioning look but did as requested and Fallon exited the front passenger door, opened the back and slipped in beside Rowan.

"Drive," he directed, then turned in the seat to regard Rowan thoughtfully.

"Did Koo feed you before sending you to Aduna's?" As he spoke, he reached out with one hand to tilt her face up.

"She didn't *send* me," Rowan protested.

A smile ghosted across Fallon's lips. "Your idea, was it?"

"Partly." She leaned forward, inhaling. "What *is* that?"

"You know what it is." He brushed a finger down her cheek. "Are you hungry, Ro?"

She licked her lips and nodded jerkily.

"The back of a cab isn't the ideal place for this," he said as he popped open the top buttons of his shirt. "But it'll tide you over until we reach Shadowfall."

"Ideal place for what?" Her eyes followed the movement of his fingers as he pulled his collar away from his throat.

"Eayann explained what you . . . what *we* are." He tapped his neck. "You need to aim for here."

Rowan's jaw dropped. "I'm not going to *bite* you!"

Fallon laughed. "You will." He leaned forward until his lips rested close to her ear. "And you'll enjoy it," he whispered, and nipped at the sensitive lobe. "It will come naturally but let me show you how it's done." He brushed his lips down her throat and settled them over the pulse beating frantically at its base.

"Fallon—" she began, then gasped as he sank his fangs deep. "Fallon . . ." she repeated his name this time in a whisper and clutched at his shoulders.

Fallon lifted his head, eyes glittering with an emotion Rowan couldn't name. Before she could speak, he was kissing her, his tongue sliding between her parted lips, his hand cupping the back of her head.

Liquid heat pooled between her thighs and Rowan shifted on the seat, trying to ease the sudden surge of desire.

"Fallon." The third time she spoke his name, it came out as a moan.

"Trust me, Ro," he whispered against her mouth. The hand on the back of her head directed her to his throat.

~*~

"Hate to break up your private party back there," Nona's dry voice brought Rowan to her senses abruptly. "But we're back."

Rowan jerked her head up, panting heavily. From the minute her mouth had landed on Fallon's throat, she'd lost track of everything around her.

"It's okay," Fallon murmured, lips barely moving. "Take a breath."

He lounged back in the seat, head tipped back against the headrest and watched her, his own eyes hooded and expression carefully blank, as she struggled to regain control. He knew the moment she realised she was straddling his hips by the way she tensed, and her eyes flew up to meet his.

"I think," he said, a smile curling his lips, "we definitely need to do this again . . . somewhere more private." His hands rested on her hips, holding her against the erection straining below the material of his pants, and he grinned at the blush rising over her cheeks. "Don't be embarrassed by what you do to me," he told her, as she hurriedly climbed off him, evading his gaze. He caught her hand and raised it to his lips. "Especially when I *like* what you do to me."

"Fallon, I—" she paused and licked her lips, her eyes touching the puncture marks on his neck and then bouncing away. "Will it always be like that?"

"With me? I sincerely hope so. But with Humans? It will take some time, but it will get easier." His teeth flashed in a quick smile. "I'll just make sure to be close by while you feed until you gain control."

There was a tap on the window, stopping any response Rowan might have made.

"Let's go finish this," he told her, opened the door, took her hand and helped her out and into Shadowfall's underground garage.

He kept a grip on her hand as they walked across the floor to the elevator bay where three people awaited them. Rowan knew two of them, but not the one who stood slightly apart talking quietly on his cell.

"I see my boy couldn't resist our plan," Taz said to Rowan, while he slapped Fallon on the back in greeting.

"Last time I ask you to watch over someone for me," Fallon responded, dryly.

Taz snorted. "You'd have done the same thing to me."

"Maybe, maybe not." Fallon glanced at Morgan, who stood beside Taz watching their exchange, silently. "We'll never know, will we?" He looked around. "Did my *friend* turn up?"

"He did. Kane had Pannie pick him up and sort out appropriate accommodation." Taz nodded toward the man on the cell, who Rowan assumed was Kane. "Pannie just called to give him the low-down on where she's put him."

Fallon nodded. "Would you mind taking Rowan back to my suite?" he asked Morgan. "She needs to feed but . . . " he hesitated.

"But she's freshly turned, not in control and you don't like the idea of her feeding without you there," Morgan finished for him, with an eye roll in Rowan's direction. "Alpha males," she added, derisively.

"Give us a minute," he said, ignoring her comment. He drew Rowan away from the group and turned his back on them. "I need to talk to Kane. I'll be as quick as I can, then we'll plan our next move."

"You still haven't told me what happened at the meeting," she said to him, softly.

"I know, and I will. I promise. But we need to move quickly." He tucked a finger under her chin and tilted her head up. "Trust me a little longer?"

When she nodded, he led her back to Morgan, who escorted her silently into the waiting elevator.

"She seems to be holding up well, all things considered," Kane said from behind him, and Fallon turned from watching the elevator doors close.

"Yeah. I'm not sure it's really sunk in yet. Once we have her sister back and there's time to slow down, we'll see what happens."

Kane chuckled and patted his shoulder. "Have faith, my friend."

~*~

By the time Fallon and Taz reached the lobby, the security storm soon to be known as *Hurricane Pantera* was in full effect. A number of gun-wielding S.O.'s could be seen herding what appeared to be small groups of both employees and guests – their expression sullen, wrists bound in zip-tie restraints – across the lobby floor, toward a door to the left of the registration and information centre. Their ultimate destination, the Security Holding and Detention area.

Minutes later, the doors to two of the lobby's three elevators cleaved open on similar scenes. Violent struggling and streams of vociferous profanity from its near-nude and lingerie clad apprehendees.

"Looks like her man held up his end of the deal," Fallon commented as the chaotic procession passed them.

"And you actually trust the bastard?" Taz challenged. "That he'll really give up all the moles?"

Fallon waited until a free elevator arrived and they'd boarded, before he replied. "Trust him? About as far as I can push this building with a wet rope. That's why, when I called ahead, I had Kane tell Doc Chambeau *not* to start the son of a bitch's treatment until after I talked to him."

Taz nodded, impressed. "And I take it that's where we're headed now?"

"Yup. I figure the fear of a slow agonising death, mixed with the pain has him at the point where he'd gouge his own eyes out with a spoon if we asked him to."

O Fortuna from the Carmina Burana opera – or, more commonly referred to as 'The Omen' music – blared out and Taz paused, patting his pockets. Fallon raised an eyebrow.

Taz grinned. "Anna's ringtone." He lifted it to his ear. "Hey gorgeous." He listened for a minute then ended the call. "She's bringing your girl back down to meet us. Something to do with her need to do somebody somewhere."

"*Do* somebody?"

Taz waved a hand. "You know, a job." He paused, then continued in response to Fallon's confused expression. "Long story. And something I can't talk about. Bottom line – she's on her way down. Which is probably a good thing, in the long run. If your girl is gonna be hanging out with you for any amount of time, the sooner you introduce her to your special brand of crazy, the better."

"Yeah," Fallon's response was a near-whisper. "I guess."

~*~

Morgan and Rowan caught up with them just as they exited the elevator. Rowan immediately reached out a hand to curl around Fallon's arm, then leaned against him.

"This is so weird," she muttered, and briefly turned her face into his shoulder. "Why do you smell so good, and why didn't I notice it before?"

Fallon chuckled. "Heightened senses – smell, taste, even your eyesight will be better," he told her, winding his arm around her waist. "You'll get used to it."

Taz snorted a laugh and looked at Morgan. "You should take notes."

Morgan arched an eyebrow at him. "If there is ever a time you smell as good as Fallon, I'll be sure to let you know." She scanned the area, then nodded. "I've got to go." She started to walk away.

"Not even a kiss goodbye?" Taz called and laughed at the raised middle finger he got in return. "I'll take that as a rain check, then." Grinning, he followed Fallon and Rowan down the corridor.

Fallon couldn't help but laugh to himself at Pantera's sense of irony as Taz, Rowan and himself arrived at the apartment at the end of the employee wing's southwestern hallway. The apartment where she had stashed their damaged stool pigeon was Tigr's, the woman he'd been sent to erase.

A pre-arranged series of coded knocks, rather than using the doorbell, allowed them entrance via one of the two S.O.'s stationed inside the apartment. Dr. Chambeau, her normally unshakable blonde countenance marred by blood-stained surgical gloves and an expression closer to exasperation than clinical concern, moved to meet their approach.

Behind her, Janiss half-reclined, shuddering and writhing in undeniable torment on the room's leather couch.

"Thank Christ Almighty, you're here! As you can see," she jerked a thumb over her shoulder. "The man's a five-star mess! I have to give the bastard credit, I'm surprised he's still conscious."

"You did a good job, Doc. Thanks," Fallon said.

Despite the situation, the doctor chuckled. "Me? That's mostly *you*. You know . . . there's not enough garlic in his system to kill him. Cause excruciating pain, yes. But not fatal."

"*He* doesn't know that . . . unless you told him?"

"I didn't," Chambeau said, and threw a quick glance back at her distressed patient. "And I don't imagine you're here to offer him any relief."

"Oh Doc . . . I'm just getting started," Fallon's smile was a baring of his teeth.

"*You!*" Janiss suddenly shouted, uttering a strained groan as he pulled himself into a sitting position, raising a hand to point at Fallon and company. "You . . . " he repeated, though not as loud. "*Komm her* . . . Come here, please."

The doctor hadn't exaggerated, Fallon saw as he approached. The man on the couch, fighting with all his might even to maintain his upright stature, was indeed a sweat drenched and convulsing mess. Not entirely where Fallon wanted him to be, but it was a good start.

"Ro," he peeled her hand away from her arm. "I need you to stay there and be quiet. Can you do that?" he asked her, softly. He waited for her nod, then spoke again.

"Taz . . . " he caught the Nikaran Prince's attention, waving toward a spot, a long wooden cabinet in the main room's rear-left quadrant. "The booze is back there. Could you get us all something? And glasses."

"Been here before?" Taz quipped, as he made his way to Tigr's liquor cabinet.

Fallon surveyed the room. He saw, first of all, the coffee table had been moved away from the couch, obviously to give Dr. Chambeau room to work. He moved it back again, turning it so he could use one end to sit on.

Regarding the man on the couch – specifically his torn and splayed open pant-leg and the blood-soaked bandage over his wound – Fallon had Chambeau straighten his leg out.

"That bandage looks saturated," he said, suggestively. "Just saying. Not telling you how to do your job, Doc."

"Well, I held back on treatment, as *you* requested," the doctor said. "Stopped the bleeding and affected a temporary closure with butterfly stitches."

"You might wanna have a few more of those handy," Fallon told her, with a wry smile and a twitch of one eyebrow.

"Uh huh," Chambeau murmured and, taking her cue from the implication in Fallon's tone, moved to the area in which her med kit was stationed.

Taz, meanwhile, returned with an armload of liquor selections and an open elongated packet of plastic cups. "Pick your poison, folks. I've got whiskey, whiskey and whiskey," he announced, placing the named items on the coffee table's opposite end.

"Please. *Mein Gott*," the man on the couch whimpered, clawing the air in Fallon's direction. "You said, you *promised* . . . ninety minutes, you said."

"What the hell do I know?" Fallon shrugged casually. "I'm no doctor, it was a rough estimate." He leaned forward, making a show of inspecting the bandaged leg. "It hasn't turned black yet, so I'd say you got time." He smiled. "Tell you what . . . how about a little liquid medication?" He twisted slightly to thrust a hand back toward the coffee table's end. Responding to the gesture, Taz half-filled a plastic cup and placed it in his friend's hand.

Three things happened.

First, the man on the couch bent forward to reach for the offered cup.

Second, Fallon launched a fist into the blood-soaked bandage, which re-opened the wound.

Third, he emptied the cup into it.

The scream which ensued was both piercing and, to all but Fallon and Taz, disturbing. It ended with the man who'd uttered it keeled over on his side, both hands clutching the affected limb.

"I'm sorry. Did you want ice with that?" Fallon said, with a dark laugh.

"W-why-*why*?" Janiss howled. "I . . . I did what you asked. Gave you the names of—"

"That's what I have a problem with," Fallon interrupted, leaving his perch on the coffee table to kneel closer. "I came through the lobby on my way here, and I saw some of the people security brought in. A handful, as a matter of fact. And there's what I have a problem with.

"You see, I think you've been playing me. I don't know a hell of a lot about your boss. But I think I've got a good handle on his personality type. He's the kind that doesn't put a lot of trust in anybody. Even the people closest to him. Meaning, he wouldn't give too much information to any one person. And that means he only told you about Tigr . . . and probably no more than a couple of others. So, here's what I think, Hoss. I think you padded the count. Bullshitted Pantera to give an over-inflated sense of your importance, so we'd cure your blood poisoning, give you time to rest up, get your shit together, then you'd sneak word out to the real moles for a rescue attempt."

"I didn't . . . I wouldn't!"

"Like *fuck* you wouldn't," Fallon cut him short again. "And you know, I can understand that. You've been with Taylor for a while. Probably a very long time. And you've got more confidence in him, or more *fear* of him than you have of us. So, let me make a couple of things very clear."

He leaned closer, and his voice dropped. "First, you may be in Kane's house at the moment, but Kane has yet to take custody. *I'm* the one that's got you. I'm the one who says when and if the doctor treats you. And if I decide on no, not only don't you get the cure, but I will help things along. I'll make things painful for you in ways that would make even the most monstrous of our kind shit their pants."

He grabbed a fistful of Janiss' hair, twisting his head up and around so they were eye-to-eye. "Bottom line, asshole. *Don't . . . fuck . . . with me.*"

"I- Yes, I understand," Janiss stammered on, nodding jerkily as he fought to sit up again. "Please . . . give me another chance."

"To do what? Feed me more shit?" Fallon clamped his fingers into the nape of Janiss' neck to prevent him from rising.

"No. Please. I . . . I will do what you asked. Give you whatever you need. Just . . . the pain. Give me something . . . for the pain."

"I'll tell you what," Fallon tightened his grip, "you give me something. Something solid, something *real*, and I'll have the doctor give *you* something to make it all better. What about that?"

Janiss nodded violently. "Yes. Alright. *Anything* . . . please!"

"Good man," Fallon said, turning his head to make eye contact with Taz. "Your Highness, want to get our friend here a pen and something to write on?"

As the Nikaran prince moved away, a flicker of motion in Fallon's peripheral vision recalled his attention or, more accurately, served to remind him of the room's additional person . . . it's fifth occupant . . . Rowan, who stepped in to occupy the space recently held by Taz.

Fallon quickly shifted his position to avoid eye contact with the redhead. He didn't fully understand it, but knew beyond question, that should their gazes lock there was no way he would be able to continue the interrogation . . . to do what had to be done.

He turned his attention, instead, to Dr. Chambeau, beckoning her with a jerk of his head.

"Can you give him something, Doc?"

"To wipe out the pain? Maybe . . . possibly," she answered, with a grimace of uncertainty. "It's tricky with vampire physiology," she lowered her voice a mindful octave, glancing past Fallon to the man on the couch. "You know yourself – the older the vampire, the higher his threshold to the effects of alcohol or drugs, medicinal *and* recreational. With his age, which I'm sure surpasses a century or so, even a dosage that would kill an average human wouldn't do much. But your garlic has most probably lowered his tolerance level. Too large a dose could put him into a coma . . . or kill him."

Fallon shrugged. "Flip a coin, Doc. The son of a bitch has got something I need, and I need to be able to trust what he'll give me."

"Alright, give me," Chambeau took a thoughtful pause, "two minutes. Three to be certain."

Dr. Chambeau set up an IV drip with a massive cocktail of oxycodone, hydrocodone, and morphine and monitored Janiss' reaction to it. Once she was sure he was stable, she nodded at Fallon and he instructed Janiss to write the names of the true Shadowfall moles on a paper towel provided by Taz.

"Alright. Time to 'fess up," Fallon said after a few minutes, retaking his perch on the coffee table's end.

Janiss gave a sluggish nod. "He . . . Taylor, as you call him . . . by now has left the country. Gone to his place, his compound in Mexico. And the girl . . . she is with him."

"Why Mexico?" Fallon pressed.

"He needed a safe place . . . to do his work."

"You mean the drug?"

"Yes. He calls it *cal roşu* . . . the red horse. The compound in Mexico is where it is manufactured and stored. And it is protected by the local crime cartel – the *Chorti Familia*."

"Territorial Mexican vampire clan," Fallon said, with a twitch of his brow.

"Worse than that," Taz chimed in. "The Chorti is one of the half dozen smaller vampire clans the American Houses don't have a treaty with. You go in there and things go south, and you get captured, you can forget about a diplomatic rescue. They'll chop you up into tiny pieces, slowly."

"Maybe . . . even worse than that," Janiss said. "Taylor expects you to come after him or to attempt to rescue the girl . . . or both. He *will* take precautions."

"Fallon?" Rowan spoke up, moving forward so the man on the couch could see her. "I want to talk to him . . . please?"

"Fine," Fallon responded after a brief and reluctant pause, stepping aside to give her room.

"So, you are her . . . the sister," Janiss, sufficiently calmed now by the IV drip, sank back into the couch cushions and addressed Rowan through drug-glazed eyes and with a distinct, though slurred, German accent. "I can see the resemblance. You are, both of you, very beautiful."

"Thanks. But fuck your compliments," Rowan responded, prompting both impressed and amused grins from Fallon and Taz.

Janiss actually laughed. "You are like her - *zäh, stark* . . . tough and strong. His people, other girls, even the guards – they call her *Käfigvogel mit rosa Haaren*. It means *caged bird with pink hair*.

"Many, many others have come before her, over the years. None of them lasting longer than two, maybe six months. But your sister . . . she is different. He cannot conquer her spirit. Cannot completely break her. She . . . endures."

"And how much of her endurance is thanks to you?" Fallon asked, with audible disdain.

"This is all new to me. I don't understand," Rowan joined in. "Why did he do it? Why does he do what he does? Why do *any* of you!"

"I . . . I . . . " Something came over him then. Something they all noticed. A change in both his facial expression and attitude as he stared up at Rowan.

"What I know is this," he told her, his voice unexpectedly gentle. "He is old. Very, very old. He has seen much, lived through much in this world and it has changed him. Made him callous and unfeeling and . . . twisted inside. He has a need, a desire for certain forms of sexual pleasure that –"

"I'm pretty sure we don't need to take it any deeper than that," Fallon cut in, in response to the look of horror and disgust in Rowan's eyes.

"In answer to your question," Janiss continued, eyes on Fallon. "I am ashamed to confess, I did nothing to aid her. I . . . I was afraid to.

"There are some things you *must* know about him. He is an extremely cruel, possessive, vindictive, and arrogant man. Any emotions that may have existed within him before he was turned, they have long since died. Taylor believes himself to be above, superior to, any of our kind. Almost godlike. So much so, he makes up his own rules, his own laws.

"I first met him during the final days of the First World War. I was a *proxen* . . . a pimp, very small-time, hiding out in a barn on the Isle of Corsica," he stopped to massage his rebandaged leg. "All truth. I was seriously wounded. Stab wounds in my chest and shoulder from a fight with a pimp from a rival House and had not fed in days. I would most likely have died had it not been for him."

"So, he saved your life and you feel you owe him," Fallon voiced a given conclusion.

"It's not that simple," Janiss immediately countered. "Everyone within the organisation, whether they be rescued or turned by him, is made to understand one indomitable truth. It is the one thing, the *first* thing he makes certain we all comprehend. He tells us *'either you are with me or you are against me. From this day on,'* he says to me, *'your life belongs to me. Serve me and live, disobey or betray me '. . .'"* he left the last segment of the statement unspoken.

"I have witnessed what happens to those who disagree with him or who fail to do his bidding. Believe me, few things are less horrific."

"So, I guess this goes without saying," Taz entered the exchange, tapping his fingers idly against the side of his plastic cup. As he spoke he shared a conspiratory glance with Fallon. "For the sake of your continued safety, you followed *every* order . . . " he paused to await Janiss' response which, in this case, was an assenting nod, " . . . regardless of how wrong, how monstrous . . . without question?"

Again, Janiss offered a wordless nod.

"Did that include the kidnap of Eden?" Rowan put to him. "And her abuse?"

Janiss hesitated, which itself was an admission, even before he spoke. "Your sister . . . she gave herself to Taylor voluntarily, you must understand that," he paused, once more avoiding Rowan's gaze. "But yes, it was my job to ensure she remained . . . amongst other things. And, for that I *am* truly sorry."

"Not sorry enough," Fallon said dryly.

Rowan's pale features and her pained sob made Fallon's next decision an easy one. He reached into his jacket, extracted Eayann's dagger, and swiftly sliced Janiss' jugular ear-to-ear. An act that caught all, save Taz, off-guard. An act that was, for at least two of the people in the room, disturbing, if for little else than the calm and seemingly detached manner in which Fallon stood and watched as Janiss writhed and clawed at the gushing wound, sputtering and choking on the blood that flooded his damaged windpipe.

Being a vampire, a slashed throat would, of course, only serve to cause the victim a lengthy period of pain and discomfort until the healing process kicked in. So, after watching Janiss beg wordlessly for a minute or two, Fallon held out a hand to Taz. A gesture the Nikaran prince obviously expected.

"Safety's off," he said, placing his Beretta into Fallon's waiting hand.

"Maybe in the next life, Skippy," Fallon whispered, and put two silver nitrate loaded 9mm rounds in Janiss' head.

"Jesus H," Chambeau muttered under her breath and quickly turned her back to the scene. "I don't get paid nearly enough for this."

"For whatever it's worth, Doc, you get no argument from me," Fallon told her as he returned Taz's piece and made his way toward the door.

~*~

Rowan moved around the bedroom, listening to the sounds of Fallon showering. After leaving Janiss, or what was left of him, he'd seemed edgy, unwilling to meet her eyes or even talk to her. In fact, he'd stalked out of the room without checking to see if she'd followed, and it was Taz who had linked his arm through hers and led her out of the room.

The trip back to his suite would have been awkward if not for the Nikaran Prince who had taken one look at Fallon's face and decided to accompany them. He'd kept up a steady stream of conversation all the way up to their floor. When the elevator doors had finally slid open, he'd touched Rowan's arm, holding her back as Fallon strode out.

"He didn't want you to see that side of him," he told her, all playfulness and teasing gone from his voice, and Rowan suddenly realised there was far more to the Prince than most people saw. "He'd keep you wrapped in cotton wool and far away from the kind of life he lives, if he could. But if you want even the slightest chance of an equal relationship, you need to show him you can handle it." A faint smile tugged at his lips. "He needs to know you can handle *him*."

"He should know that already."

Taz shrugged. "Take it from someone who knows him. Go on, before he comes back and guts me for keeping you here talking." He shooed her out of the elevator and pushed the button to close the doors.

The minute they'd reached his suite, Fallon had muttered something about a shower and disappeared into the bathroom. That had been over half an hour ago . . .

"I've ordered room service," his voice had her spinning round. She watched as he crossed to the wardrobe, opened it and pulled out a clean shirt and pants. He slung them onto the bed and dropped the towel that had been wrapped around his waist.

Rowan's eyes tracked over his back – the faint scars crisscrossing the broad expanse, the colourful tattoos – and reached out a finger to trace over his skin.

She felt him stiffen beneath her touch, then forcibly relax his muscles and turn to face her. He lifted a hand to stroke her cheek with the back of his fingers, but stopped before making contact and slid them into her hair instead. He tugged her head back and gazed down into her eyes, his own searching for something – she didn't know what – and then his mouth descended on hers in a bruising kiss, teeth biting into her lower lip, making her gasp. Fallon took advantage of her parted lips to thrust his tongue inside to tangle with hers.

Her hand crept between them to curl around the thick, hard length of his erection and he growled, pulling back.

"Clothes . . . off," he demanded.

"No." Rowan stroked him . . . up . . . down.

"Rowan . . . clothes!"

"No," she repeated, placed her free hand against his chest and pushed. He took a step backwards, surprised by her action and tilted his head to look at her, eyes narrowed.

"The blood on my hands too much for you?" he taunted.

Rowan simply smiled at him and sank to her knees.

"Row*an*," his voice broke midway through uttering her name when he felt her tongue lick his entire length, before her lips slid over the sensitive tip and sucked him deep into her mouth.

Coherent thought fled, his entire focus welded to the warm wet feel of her mouth sliding up and down, of her fingers cupping and stroking, driving him closer and closer to the edge of control.

"*Rowan.*"

There was no other word in his mind, in his vocabulary. He made the mistake of looking down, of watching her take him as deep as she could, and he could give her no more than a quick growled warning before he lost control and spilled into her mouth. Even then, she didn't pull away, taking everything he had, milking every last drop from him. He could feel her tongue, lapping at him like he was her favourite lollipop.

"Ro . . . " His voice shook, along with the hand he placed on her shoulder. She leant back on her heels and let him slide from her mouth with a final long lick, before she tipped her head back to look at him.

"You . . . I . . . " he closed his eyes briefly, and when he opened then, Rowan had risen to her feet.

Discarding words, Fallon pulled her against him. She wrapped her arms around his waist and rested her head against his chest.

"What you did downstairs," Rowan began, and felt him tense. She pressed a kiss to his collarbone. "I get it," she continued, softly. "It shocked me, but I get it." Another kiss, this time in the hollow of his throat. "It's like discovering a world within a world, one that has its own rules and ways of dealing with . . . with the lawbreakers." She raised her head, unwrapped her arms and took a step back out of his embrace. "I need you to make me a promise though, Fallon."

She watched as his expression blanked and reached out to curve her palm over his jaw.

"Don't try and protect me from what you are. For better or worse, this is my world too, now."

He was saved from responding – in actual fact, he wasn't sure he was *able* to respond, his mind still reeling from her actions and her words - by the sound of the main door opening, and voices talking . . . *bickering* . . . in the sitting room. He turned his head to press a kiss into the palm of her hand, then forced himself to move away from her and dress.

Rowan watched him. The dark edginess she'd sensed had disappeared, his movements more relaxed and natural than they had been when they'd first returned to the suite.

I did that, she realised with a start, and smiled to herself.

The voices in the other room grew louder, and Fallon threw a frowning glance toward the door.

"I'd better find out what's going on out there," he said, buttoning his shirt. "Why don't you take a bath, relax for a bit. I'll call you when dinner arrives."

CHAPTER SIXTEEN

Neither Koo or Eayann heard Fallon enter the sitting room until he slammed a hand down onto the coffee table.

"*Enough!*" he levelled a finger at Koo. "What were you thinking allowing Rowan to leave Shadowfall?"

"I . . . you had told her . . . Taz said that . . . " Koo scrambled to explain.

"You sent her to *Aduna's*," Fallon cut in. "And without feeding her."

"Also, against the decision we'd made" Eayann joined in. "Fallon had agreed to stay away from the girl."

Fallon's eyes swung to Eayann. "We'd agreed *no such thing*, Old Man." The two men glared at each other.

"We've been here before, Fallon," Eayann said, finally. "How do you know the sister even exists?"

"Why do you think she doesn't?" Fallon challenged.

"I never said that. But is the story she's spun you really what she claims it is? Last time you became involved with a girl in need, you almost died."

"Rowan is *not* Natalia," Fallon responded, flatly.

"And yet—"

"No. You don't get to throw one mistake back at me just because you don't like the choices I made here." He crossed the room and poured himself a drink. "I'm sure Koo has given you *her* opinion on what's been going down."

Koo looked away in embarrassment.

"Yeah, that's what I thought." He knocked back the drink and poured another. "I'm seeing this through to the end. You'll either join me or you won't. But know this, Eayann. Rowan is here *now*, and she will be staying. Accept it, don't accept it. I don't really care either way."

"Really?" Eayann countered, with a taunting smirk. "I wonder what your Sire . . . what Marjean would say about that."

"I wasn't aware I needed her blessing for every choice I make," Fallon retorted.

"Only when those choices could kill you."

"Oh, you mean the way *she* carefully considered *my* feelings when she took me to the brink of death and turned me?" Fallon slammed the glass down onto the countertop. "Spare me the pretend concern. We both know the only thing worrying Marjean is how my actions will make her look in front of the council."

"Clueless whelp!" Eayann spat. "If not for Marjean's intervention, the Council would have had you terminated years ago. You have no idea what a slender thread you . . . *we* . . . our little enterprise is hanging on."

"Oh, *fuck you*, Old Man," Fallon snarled just as loudly. "She knew what she was getting when she picked me."

Silence fell over the room while the two men glared at each other. Eayann couldn't deny the truth of Fallon's statement – Marjean *had* been completely aware of Fallon's character before she'd chosen to turn him, and he had warned her at the time that she would not be able to control the tempestuous young man.

He rose to his feet and crossed the room to where Fallon stood, ducked down behind the wet bar and rummaged inside to find a bottle of wine and a glass. Fallon watched the older vampire as he poured his drink and sampled the liquid, smacking his lips in satisfaction, then gulped back half the glass before refilling and returning to his seat.

"Did she now?" he broke the silence between them and looked at Fallon. "Let's take a close honest look at that, shall we?"

~*~

Pain, her constant companion, woke her. More precisely, a kick to her already-bruised, possibly even broken, ribs. Eden rolled to her hands and knees, drew in a quiet breath and carefully levered herself to her feet. Keeping her head bent, she took a moment to scan the room through lowered lashes. Bodies, in various states of undress, littered the floor. Some still lived. Some, she knew, hadn't survived the night. In many ways she envied the dead ones – at least, for them, the nightmare was over.

Last night had been the worst in a long time. Taylor had been almost out of control with rage, and Eden thought the time had come and he would finally kill her. It had been close, she knew. He'd done things to her – things she had no intention of thinking about – things she wouldn't have believed a human body could live through prior to having a front-row up-close-and-personal interactive session with them.

After he'd finished and left her on the floor covered in semen, saliva, urine, blood and who knew what else, he'd given her to his inner circle, who had fell upon her body like ravenous dogs. She'd thought, *'this is it, he's finally letting them kill me'* but as she felt her heart start to stutter and strain, he'd called them off.

She remembered him crouching beside her head.

"If only your *darling* sister could see you now, pig," he said. "Would she really want you back? Look at you – filthy, naked, used . . . *broken*. Just a toy, a whore, a bunch of holes to be stuffed, worthless. Your pretty sister would be disgusted. Even if I discarded you, let you leave. No one would want you now." She hadn't reacted, *couldn't* react, too close to unconsciousness but every word had hit home, cut her deeper than any of the fangs buried into her flesh only minutes earlier.

She had embraced the pain which exploded outward from her ribs when he kicked her, because pain meant she wasn't dead, and being alive meant her sister wouldn't be taken in her place. And Eden would do anything it took to keep Rowan away from Taylor.

~*~

"You've been on a path of self-destruction for as long as I've known you. That temper of yours, that need to take risks – do you think Marjean doesn't know *why* you let it control you?" Eayann was almost nose-to-nose with Fallon when Rowan entered the sitting room.

"I'm sure you're about to enlighten me," Fallon responded.

Neither man acknowledged Rowan's presence and she paused in the doorway to look around. Koo sat stiffly on one couch, hands clutched together in her lap. She glanced over at Rowan and gave her a nod before returning her worried gaze back to the two men. Rowan crossed the room and sank onto the seat beside Koo.

"What's happening?" she whispered.

Koo shook her head, mutely, and Rowan turned her attention to the argument going on beside the wet bar.

"It's been four hundred years! I was young and stupid. How many times do I have to pay for one mistake?" Fallon slammed his empty glass down onto the countertop. "How often are you going to throw Natalia's death in my face?"

"As often as it takes, until you *learn* from it!" Eayann roared.

"Oh, I learned from it. How could I not?" His movements jerky, Fallon poured another drink.

"Obviously, you didn't because here we are again. Another clusterfuck. Another girl, one that managed to survive this time, I'll grant you."

Fallon flinched, amber liquid spilling over the lip of his glass onto his hand.

Eayann's gaze flicked sideways, over Fallon's shoulder, acknowledging Rowan's arrival. He carefully placed his wine glass down and straightened to his full height. "Do I need to remind you how the choices *you* made led to this point? A young woman, almost dying, being brought into our world with *no prior knowledge* of it? A situation that now has Marjean scrambling to stem the calls for your blood *again!* And, for what? So you can scratch an itch with a tasty young mortal?"

The sound of Fallon's fist connecting with Eayann's jaw echoed around the room.

"Fallon!" Rowan jumped to her feet and was across the room before Koo could stop her.

Both men turned at the sound of her voice, and Fallon's arm automatically wound around her waist when she reached him to pull her in against his side.

Eayann rubbed his jaw and said nothing as he watched Fallon's attention immediately switch from him to the woman in his arms, the younger vampire's anger draining away between one heartbeat and the next. He lifted his eyes to look over at Koo, who was perched on the edge of the couch, ready to jump up and intercede, and tipped his head toward the door of the guest bedroom. Koo rose to her feet and followed him as he crossed the room.

Once they were both inside, he eased the door shut and turned to face Koo.

"Does that always happen?" he asked.

Koo frowned. "Does *what* always happen?"

Eayann waved a hand in the direction of the outer room. "*That*. His reaction to the girl . . . "

"He loses his temper with her all the time, but you know how he is. That's pretty normal," Koo began, slowly. "She won't do anything he tells her without arguing. There was a time a few days ago, I honestly thought he was going to hurt her, but . . . " she trailed off.

"But he calmed down faster than you expected?" Eayann offered, and Koo nodded. "Interesting. Why did he take this job? A favour to a bed partner? Wanted to keep her sweet?"

Koo laughed. "Gods, no! She got our number from someone in SPD. I took the call, arranged the meeting. She didn't even hire us. Told Fallon she just wanted some help, not someone to take over."

"Then, why are you so deeply involved now?"

"Fallon and his gut. You know what it's like. There was something about the story that made him take notice, so he gave her his personal number and . . . well, he's already told you how it went down from there."

"And his behaviour hasn't seemed odd to you? Out of character?"

"Rowan isn't playing him," Koo protested.

Eayann laughed. "Look, even you're protecting her." He patted Koo's arm. "I'm not claiming she is. *That*, out there," another arm wave toward the door. "We both know what happened with Natalia was out of Fallon's control. He was young, he was stupid. But he carries that responsibility around with him. We've discussed it before, tried to make him see that it was *one* mistake. In fact, everything he's just said to me is what we've been saying to him for years. Why is he seeing it now?" He didn't wait for Koo to respond. "I think she is *Liniṣti*. She calms his temper, he wants to protect her."

Koo gaped at him. "I thought *Liniṣti* were just a myth."

"No, they exist, although they're rare. It's like a Lycan pack finding an Omega wolf – a prized possession. As a mortal, she would have found people around her unusually willing to help when she was in need – which is likely why she ended up with our contact number. For Fallon, it's gone a little deeper. They have a connection now, developed from the shared experiences they've had." The older vampire smiled. "As a vampire, with some tutoring, she can tap into that talent and use it at will. A prize indeed for our House, and one that many will seek to use."

"Are you saying that what Fallon feels for her isn't real? That Rowan has made it happen?"

"Not at all. Not even *Liniṣti* can force people to feel emotions they don't have already. When they first met, she would have appealed to his desire to help on some level." He paused, thinking. "The missing sister is her twin? I wonder if she is also *Liniṣti*. It would explain why the girl still survives."

~*~

Fallon thanked the functionary who had arrived shortly after Eayann and Koo had disappeared, slipped a folded hundred-dollar bill into his hand and led him to the door.

"Who is Natalia?" Rowan asked, once they were alone.

Fallon paused, one hand resting on the door and closed his eyes briefly, before he turned to face her.

"You don't want to talk about how your first proper feeding went? No questions?"

"I have lots of questions. Like . . . how do I put these things away?" she replied and lifted a finger to tap against the fangs still protruding against her lips. "But the one I want answered most is the one I just asked."

Fallon smiled as he crossed the room and sank down onto the seat beside her. "You look cute with them poking out," he teased. "They'll revert back themselves if you stop thinking about them." He tipped her head up with a finger and ran his gaze over her face. "You were looking a little pale, I was worried we had left feeding too late, but you look better now."

"What would have happened?"

"You could have lost control and killed the functionary. Feeding from the wrist reduces the instinct for wanting to rip out someone's throat, though."

Rowan gasped and pulled away from him. "Really? I could have killed him?"

Fallon chuckled. "No, I'm just teasing." His chuckle turned into a full-on laugh when she punched his shoulder. "It *can* happen. Some do lose control and kill. But you aren't one of them." His thumb brushed over her lips. "See, fangs all gone now."

Rowan ran her tongue across her teeth. "That's so weird." She twisted on the couch until she was facing him. "So . . . Natalia."

"Natalia was a young lady, not unlike yourself, Fallon was assigned to protect. He allowed his temper to get the better of him and failed, which resulted in Natalia's death and Fallon's life on the line." Eayann entered the room and the conversation before Fallon could reply.

Rowan's eyes swung from Fallon to Eayann and back again, waiting for Fallon to defend himself. When he stayed silent, she spoke. "You were lovers?"

"Of course they were. He had been told to keep his distance, and Fallon has never done well with being told no," Eayann came to a stop before the couch and folded his arms. "Of course, Fallon also liked female companionship a little *too* much, and on the night in question, when he was supposed to be guarding Natalia from those who wanted her dead, he was enjoying the charms of a young Spanish tavern wench a mile or so away."

"I heard you say you were young . . . young and foolish?" Rowan asked Fallon.

"Yes, he was. And foolish he continues to be," Eayann replied again.

Rowan turned her head to look at the older vampire towering over them both and narrowed her eyes. "I'm talking to Fallon, *old man*. If you can't be quiet and let him speak, I'll need you to leave."

"Let him . . . ? Need me to *leave*?" Eayann spluttered.

"Yes, *leave*! The few times I've met you, I've learned one thing – you *really* like the sound of your own voice." Rowan rose to her feet and jabbed a finger at Eayann. "But I don't know you. I don't *trust* you. I *do* trust Fallon. So shut up and let Fallon explain, or go away."

Eayann turned his head to mask a smile.

"Ro," Fallon finally spoke, his voice soft. "Sit back down." He patted the cushion beside him. "If what I did downstairs didn't send you screaming for the door, I don't imagine something four hundred years in the past will." He directed his next words at Eayann. "You edited that story in a few interesting ways. Do you want to tell me why?"

"I've been told to stop talking," he replied, shaking his head and mimicking turning a key against his lips.

Fallon gave a soft laugh, while Rowan glared at Eayann before settling back down onto the couch beside him.

"Most of what Eayann said was true, if a little skewed. Natalia was a human from a family connected to the ruling family of House Sasul – you'll learn all about the Houses and the hierarchies later. I was . . . struggling with the change from Human to Vampire and Marjean, my sire, thought it would help me if I had something to focus on, something to take my mind off things I had no way of changing. Natalia had claimed someone was trying to kill her and her sister, that her sister had disappeared, so Marjean assigned me the task of investigating her claims." He sighed. "Eayann told Marjean it was a mistake to pair me with the girl, given my state of mind, and he was right.

"Natalia was unstable. I didn't see it at the time, I was too wrapped up in my own problems. She needed something I wasn't capable of giving. To answer your earlier question, yes, we were lovers. But for me, she was just one of many. For Natalia, however, we were destined to be together." Fallon paused, sharing a look with Eayann. Eayann nodded, strode to the wet bar to retrieve Fallon's glass, filled it and brought it back to him. With a murmured *thank you*, Fallon took a sip, then continued.

"I did look into her sister's disappearance, although I didn't put a lot of effort into it. It was obvious from the outset that the claim was a lie. Her sister had married a few months earlier to a low-ranking Sasul turnblood and had turned her back on Natalia.

"When I told Natalia the results of my search, she refused to believe it. She told me she couldn't marry a man who wasn't willing to believe her. As I had no intention of marrying the girl, that came as quite a surprise and, I have to admit, I didn't let her down gently. I laughed at her. The argument that followed wasn't pretty. I walked out, and she screamed after me that if I left, I would never see her alive again." Another pause while he took a drink. "I headed into the nearest tavern where, as Eayann told you, I spent the rest of the night with a tavern wench. I was woken the next night when a couple of Marjean's people dragged me out of her bed and back to Natalia's home.

"The servants had found Natalia hanging from the rafters of her bedroom. They arrived too late to save her. They had all heard the argument we'd had, and all agreed her death was my fault. Her family wanted my death in return, but Marjean and Eayann argued my defence." He shrugged his shoulders. "You asked about the scars on my back a while ago . . . a silver-tipped whip – the price of my failure." He fell silent.

Rowan's eyes jumped from Fallon to Eayann and back again. "I don't understand," she said, finally. "You think I'm like this Natalia?" she addressed Eayann. "That I'm going to . . . do what, exactly?"

"I'm allowed to talk now?" Eayann asked and smiled at Rowan's immediate glare. He settled on the edge of the coffee table in front of her. "No child, I don't think you're like Natalia. I was worried that instead of thinking clearly, Fallon was blinded by his attraction to you and because of the guilt he carries through Natalia's actions. I was concerned that he was going in the opposite direction and taking risks to make sure what happened with her does *not* happen with you. With Natalia, he missed the signs of her sickness—"

"Signs he was clearly in no condition to see!" Rowan cut in. "What I'm hearing is that he's *still* being punished for a mistake his sire made. If anyone should take the blame for this girl's death, it is *her*, not Fallon."

"It doesn't work that way," Fallon told her. "Natalia was my responsibility, whether I wished it or not."

"You said yourself that you were in no condition to have such a responsibility. It was such a long time ago, why is it even still being raised?"

"Because after that, it was agreed that Fallon should no longer be directly involved with any clients. He would be a step removed at all times, to stop such a thing happening again. By taking your case, he has gone against his sire's directive," Eayann explained.

"It means that once again, Fallon's life is on the line. Those who want him removed are using this . . . situation . . . to air their concerns once again." He leaned forward to look Rowan in the eyes. "I had to be sure that you are exactly what Fallon thought you are."

"And so you . . . what? Tested me? Tested him?"

"Stop, both of you," Fallon joined the conversation again. "It's a concern for another day. For now, we have other things to discuss."

As he spoke, the main door opened and Taz and Morgan entered the suite, each carrying bottles of wine, water and glasses, prepared for what promised to be a long and brain-taxing session.

"My contact in Mexico City came through about a half hour ago," Morgan informed the gathering, producing a sheet of folded paper, size 8x10, from her back pocket as the group set up around the coffee table. "His people made a single fly-by over your man's compound to get photos, high enough to not arouse suspicion from anyone on the ground, but his equipment wasn't state of the art, so don't expect much, detail-wise."

"Better than nothing," Fallon said as she spread the sheet out on the table.

Silence reigned for a long moment while the group inspected the sheet's pictorial content and prepared individual liquid refreshment.

Taz was the first to speak. "It's like a military outpost, or vacation retreat . . . "

"A combination of the two," Eayann observed, using the blade of the dagger – returned to him by Fallon earlier – to point out items as he spoke. "That large, long structure there is probably used as both a headquarters and residential. And there, beside it, an area for recreation . . . "

"Barracks there," Taz jabbed a finger, "and a landing strip –"

"Uh-uh," Fallon cut in. "Not large or long enough to land planes. More likely a landing pad. If you look closely, you can see those small blips at the centre are probably choppers. The large cargo types, CH-47 cargo carriers . . . Chinooks."

"Fallon," Koo jumped into the conversation, her voice barely above a whisper. Fallon turned and then followed Koo's gaze to where Rowan was curled up on the couch, her eyes closed. He smiled and crossed over to her.

"Ro?" Rowan's eyes snapped open to find Fallon crouched in front of her, one hand resting on her shoulder. She blinked, realised she was lying on the couch and pushed herself upright.

"I'm sorry. I fell asleep."

"It's no surprise, the sun rose an hour or so ago, and it's been a long night." As he spoke, he picked her up into his arms. "Let's get you to bed."

Rowan didn't argue, looping her arms around his neck as he straightened and moved toward the bedroom.

"Are we really going to get Eden back?"

Fallon lowered her to the bed. "We're going to do our best to make that happen." He brushed a finger down her cheek. "Get some sleep. We have a few more details to work out, then I'll be in."

Rowan reached up to grasp his shirtfront. "You won't go without me, will you? I need to be there. She won't know you."

"I know, love." He covered her hand with his. "I promise, you'll be on the plane with us." He pulled the door shut behind him, flicking off the light as he went.

"There's something you need to know," he started quietly once he was back in the other room. He paused to pour himself a glass of red wine and took a slow sip before continuing. "This thing we're going into has more than one objective. Rescuing Rowan's . . . my client's . . . . sister is important. Make no mistake about that. But the man who has her is involved in something equally as crucial."

He turned to Taz and made the long-standing and universally recognised 'telephone handset gesture' with thumb and pinkie finger. "If you would, my friend, I need to have your father in on this."

Noticeably reluctant and, after exchanging a look with Morgan whose meaning only the two of them were privy to, Taz extracted his cell and turned away to comply with the request.

A muted conversation between father and son ensued. During which, Fallon made eye contact with Eayann. Painful contact, to say the least. It had been a while, centuries in fact, since the two had been at odds over anything more serious than the best venue for a night of drunken debauchery. And, to say their current flap weighed heavily on him was an understatement. On the other hand, it was Eayann who always said *'When you're right, you're right. Stand your ground'*.

"Alright," Taz said, snapping Fallon into the moment, as he turned and placed his cell on the table. "We're on speaker."

"Mister Wylde," Zuron's rich baritone somehow extended beyond technology, giving the eerie impression that his voice emanated from the very walls around them.

"Lord Zuron. First of all, I want to apologise for any interruption or inconvenience my call may have caused you. But I have information that, in my opinion, will not only prove invaluable to House Nikaris, but is vital in maintaining the safety and wellbeing of our species."

"I see," Zuron replied, after a short pause. "Then I would say it is well worth any inconvenience I may have suffered. You have my full and undivided attention, Mr Wylde."

Taking a deep drink of his wine, Fallon took a moment to top off his glass and began. Pacing between the group and the suite's wet bar as he spoke, Fallon laid out the entire episode – from his first meeting with Rowan to his most recent interaction with the man called Janiss; with pointed emphasis on his meeting with Cokie Donaghy, the information he'd gotten from Count Zumbusch at the Power Ascendant, and particular emphasis on the meeting with Knox.

There was a long slash of heavy silence when he finished, broken eventually by a near-whispered curse from Eayann - "*Saints, sinners, and godless imbeciles!*" – in heavy Scottish brogue.

"To say the least," Zuron commented. "Inasmuch as myself – the House of Nikaris shares a measure of responsibility in this situation – we would not have gotten to this point had we thoroughly eradicated Bianca Manx's Carousel, abroad as well as here in Seattle, tell me how I can be of assistance in your endeavour."

"We'll be stepping on some toes, ruffling feathers with our cousins across the border," Fallon said. "I was hoping we could count on your expertise in the diplomatic area."

"Consider it done, Mr Wylde."

"I was wondering, also," a new voice entered the exchange, prompting a noticeable reaction in the way of a wry smile in Morgan. "Would the offer of a little help in the personnel area be accepted."

"Accepted and welcomed," Fallon answered. "We leave from Sea-Tac Airport at sunset."

"Understood," the new voice said, and the contact was severed.

"Well, I suppose we best get our heads together. As the saying goes, we're burning daylight."

~*~

It was gone midday before the group called an end to their discussions. They'd planned as much as they possibly could and needed at least a few hours sleep before they set out. After saying goodbye and seeing everyone out of the suite, Fallon locked the doors and headed back into the bedroom.

From the discarded clothes scattering the floor, he knew Rowan had stayed awake long enough to change or, he amended spotting her bare shoulder showing above the covers, long enough to take off what she'd been wearing, anyway. He picked up her clothes, folded them neatly and placed them in a pile, before stripping out of his own.

The plan he and the others had made was dangerous, and the chance of getting Rowan's sister out was slim. The chances of Fallon and his friends getting out alive wasn't much better, he acknowledged to himself. He slid under the sheets and lay beside Rowan. If he was going to die, then he wanted to do it with one last good memory, he thought.

He inched across the bed and nuzzled Rowan's shoulder, kissed his way across and up her throat, then smiled against her skin when she stirred and sleepily lifted a hand to reach backwards and curve it around his hip.

"Fallon?" her voice was a husky whisper.

His mouth trailed along her jaw, then up to nip the sensitive lobe of her ear. "If you're too tired . . . " he began.

"*Never* too tired for this," she told him and turned her head, seeking his lips with hers.

CHAPTER SEVENTEEN

There were two strangers standing on the runway near to Kane's private Lear jet, when Fallon pulled the SUV to a stop. Both male, both topping six four in height, but that was where the similarity ended. Stranger #1 wouldn't have looked out of place in an action movie – all big muscles, crew cut hairstyle, clean-shaven square jaw, dressed in black combat gear. Stranger #2 was leaner, dark hair short and spiked into messy points, a few days' worth of stubble covering his jaw. He also wore black combat pants, coupled with a dark t-shirt with some kind of slogan emblazoned across the front. He leaned against the steps which led up to the jet's entrance, a cigarette hanging out of his mouth, and Fallon caught the flash of something silver as he flipped it over his knuckles.

"Are they the backup?" Fallon twisted round to address Taz, who sat in the back beside Morgan. Both shifted forward to look through the window and Morgan chuckled, while Taz cursed.

"Yeah," Taz told him. He sighed as Morgan opened the door and slid out, striding across the tarmac where both men waited.

"I take it you know them?" Fallon asked.

"I know *one* of them," Taz clarified. "The cocky son of a bitch leaning against the jet is Devlin Satori – Anna's brother."

They both watched as Morgan reached her brother, said something which brought him upright away from the steps, then threw a right hook which snapped his head backwards.

"Fuck!" Taz shot out of the car, leaving Fallon and Rowan alone.

"You have some really interesting friends," Rowan said into the silence and Fallon laughed.

"I guess we should go and meet some new ones," he replied.

They caught up with Taz and advanced together. They could hear Morgan and her brother talking as they neared the jet.

"You *said* you were on the same page as me," Morgan was saying.

"The same page?" Her brother shook his head. "Acushla, we weren't even reading the same fucking book." He rubbed his stubbled jaw, and turned to watch as Fallon, Taz and Rowan approached. "We should discuss this some other time." His gaze flicked from Morgan to Taz and back again. "I see the rumours are true. You've shacked up with the Nikaran Whore Prince."

Morgan's eyes narrowed. "What did you just call him?"

Dev's smile was bland. "The Nikaran Heir Prince . . . what do you *think* I called him?"

Morgan shook her head and turned to greet the others. "Fallon, Rowan, this is Dev and Lochlan."

Dev shook Fallon's hand, then lifted Rowan's to press a kiss to hers. He grinned at Fallon's growl and took a step back. "Now that's no way to be treating your backup, is it?" There was a strong Irish lilt to his voice, which caused Rowan to frown.

"Didn't you say he's Morganna's brother?" she questioned Taz.

"The princeling told you that, did he?" Dev replied, before Taz could speak. "I'm amazed he even remembers." The look he sent in Taz's direction was cool and unreadable.

"To be clear, the Prince and your sister are my backup," Fallon pointed out. "*You* and Lochlan are *their* backup. I trust there's no problem with that?"

Dev placed his palms together, fingers steepled against his lips, and bowed reverently. Which wasn't exactly an answer to his query, but in the interest of saving time, Fallon didn't press.

A flutter of movement over Dev's shoulder called Fallon's attention to the plane's doorway, where Koo stood on the landing of the passenger boarding ramp, nodding to signal the approach of their departure time.

"Alright, let's get this show on the road," Fallon announced, making sure it was noticeable, to one person in particular, as he took Rowan's hand. "Make sure you have everything you need on board. Final briefing once we're in the air."

~*~

"Are we there yet?" Taz's attempt at humour fell miles, and most likely deliberately, short as he dropped heavily into the aisle seat beside a silently pensive Fallon, who favoured the Prince with a sympathetic smile.

"That bad?" Fallon asked.

"Nothing I can't handle," Taz's reply, though seemingly complete, contained an unspoken and wholly noticeable '*but*'.

"Dev?" Fallon offered, continuing before the Prince could acknowledge it. "There's history between the two of you. Anything I should be concerned about?"

Taz hesitated, knowing the person in question was probably eavesdropping on their exchange.

"I wouldn't worry. Kane had heightened auditory senses factored into the specs on all his aircraft," Fallon said. "You know *him* – his privacy is worth more than all his money."

"Dev's a strange one," Taz began, after an additional moment's pause. "A disrespectful pain in the ass. And if, by history, you mean are we like cobra and mongoose? Dog and cat?" he chuckled at the last comparison. "In our case, it's more like I'm a tree to his dog. But whatever else he is, he's *damn good* at what he does. And neither one of us will let our thing get in the way of business."

"Good to know," Fallon said. "Because this one won't be like San Diego, *or* that thing with the kids. We'll probably be going up against a small army. Mexican turnbloods, a lot different, tougher than ours. If this thing goes sideways, it could be the end of the road."

"Understood, amigo," Taz gave a solemn nod.

"You might want to get a little shut-eye or spend some quiet time with your girl," Fallon checked his watch. "We'll be landing in just under an hour and forty-five."

~*~

The compound, known to the denizens of several small villages surrounding Oaxaca, Mexico, as *El Patio Del Diablo* – The Devil's Playground – was a combination HQ/Business Centre/Private Hideaway of Joaquin Vidal Villarreal, current leader of *Chorti Familia*, of the Mexicana Vampire Clan Casa Salamanca. It was a virtual fortress, encompassed within a one-hundred-foot circular defence perimeter. A kill zone – i.e. the distance between the treeline and the compound's towering eight-foot thick concrete wall. The compound itself was a squarish configuration with gun-mounted guard towers at each corner, a wall of electrified razor wire between each tower, a three-ring circle of barbed wire stretching out fifty feet from the main walls, with the first containing magnetic vibration sensitive anti-personnel mines, the second with M18A1 directional mines – claymores – and the third motion sensors programmed to activate a bank of automated M-134 20mm mini-guns whose two to six thousand rounds per minute cyclic firing rate could splinter bone and shred flesh like a shower of rocks through rice paper. Certain death for anyone who sought to encroach upon the security of those who resided inside.

Anyone *human* that is.

Although his companions may have found navigating the compound's deterrents a bit tricky, for Fallon covering himself in blood and taking a swim in shark-infested waters would have been more of a challenge.

Luis Sosa, the guard in the southwest gun tower – and a turnblood of just over a decade – thought he saw a glimmer of movement at the edge of the jungle. *Imagination*, he told himself . . . a trick of the moonlight fostered by less than three hours sleep and a pitiful two-minute feeding he'd gotten in the past two and a half days. *Movement?* If anything at all, it was a monkey, *jabali* – jaguar – or wild boar.

But a wild boar, even a jaguar, couldn't scale a thirty-foot concrete wall in a single leap. Nor rip a man's beating heart from his chest with such precision and speed that the victim was only aware of said inflicted carnage when his gaze fell upon the vital organ in the hand of the man who had extracted it, a full ten seconds later. Luis Sosa was dead before the ultimate question – *How?* – had time to completely take root in his fading consciousness. And Fallon was in motion, taking the thirty-foot drop from tower to ground in an instant and moving across the compound at a dead run. He was little more than a blur and a *swoosh* of wind to the three guards at the target structure's southeast corner. A *swoosh* that opened the throats of all three men from ear to ear without breaking stride.

The intel he'd gotten earlier was, it seemed, near-perfect. The compound's expansive interior contained, not counting Villarreal's large four-bedroom hacienda, a motor pool of at least a dozen jeeps, SUVs and two and a half ton transport vehicles; a stable, with six more stalls than they had horses; a rec area with a large all-purpose sports court; a swimming pool, with attached wet bar; and, not least of all, a large barracks-like building, only recently constructed for the purpose of the most recent additions to the cartel's repertoire: kidnapping, extortion and white slavery.

After scanning the immediate area with his heightened senses to make sure he hadn't missed anything guard-wise, Fallon took pause to do the same for the building's interior then, satisfied with his findings, inserted his ear transceiver.

"This is Ghost Prime. Southwest buttoned. Sitrep," he whispered, tapping his earbud.

"Ghost One. North buttonhole closed," Taz I'Ane's voice crackled through a moment later.

"Ghost Two. Northeast buttonhole closed," Morgan chimed in. "Southeast tower is in flux. The guard is out of position – they stagger shift changes so that one tower is always in sight to cover the others. No worries . . . I'll take care of the new guard. Standing by for Phase two."

"This is you-know-who," Dev's voice crackled in with audible irreverent glee, deliberately ignoring his previously agreed upon tactical callsign. "Loch and I have ears on the landing pad. There's a whole fleet of transport trucks out here. And people loading big crates onto them. Looks like they're close to being finished. Whatcha want us to do?"

"This is Prime, Ghost Three," Fallon responded. "Hold your positions but confirm they're in completion. If they are . . . those choppers are not, I repeat *not* to leave this location. Do you copy?"

"Loud and clear, Optimus," Dev laughed.

~*~

"There's a sweet little pig. Still so tight, feels so good." His voice was deep, gravelly, and Eden had once found it sexy, but not anymore. Not after spending a year as his toy, his possession, his *thing* – there solely to meet his needs; whatever that need might be at the time.

She shoved her face into the cushion, trying to hold back a cry of pain as he slammed into her again. It hurt, it *always* hurt, but when he had given her the drug she hadn't cared. He'd stopped giving her *that* drug when he decided he enjoyed her fear and pain more than he wanted her willing to please. There were other drugs he fed her, though, to keep her compliant, fuzzy, unable to disobey.

"You like that, don't you, little pig?"

She made a sound that could have been agreement, as he grasped her hips and shifted her position, so he could thrust deeper and harder. Eden bit her lip, pain stabbing at her insides. If he had any idea how much agony he was causing her, it wouldn't stop him, it would only spur him on.

His fingers traced a pattern over her lower back and Eden knew he was following the lines of the tattoo he'd given her, branded into her skin while she'd screamed and begged and pleaded with him to stop. A wave of shame and nausea enveloped her as she thought about the words forever visible on her skin – a reminder that even if she ever got away from him, he would always own her.

A sharp yank on her hair brought her focus back to the present, to the burning soreness between her thighs as he slammed in and out, his movements jerky.

Almost finished, Eden thought and sagged against the leather couch in relief as, with a guttural groan, he spilled into her and shoved her forwards, away from him. She felt him wipe himself clean against her thigh and then a sharp pain as his fingers found and twisted one nipple.

"Look at me, pig," he demanded.

Eden turned her head and lifted her lids to look up at the man . . . the monster . . . who owned her.

Taylor stared down at her, his own eyes unreadable, then he nodded abruptly, seemingly satisfied with what he saw and turned away.

Eden waited until Taylor had left the room and carefully rose to her feet. The chain around her throat felt heavier than usual. Taylor had hooked it to the wall, leaving her with little room to move and she knew he wouldn't be gone for long. He rarely let her leave his side. She cleaned herself up as best she could then moved into position – arms behind her back, head bowed, eyes downcast, back arched so her breasts thrust forward and legs shoulder-width apart . . . and waited.

~*~

Dammit, Fallon cursed silently after a quick lift of his watchband's combat face-cover.

Thirty minutes was the estimated time limit for the operation: fifteen minutes for insertion and prep, another fifteen for execution and extraction. Granted, the operative word was *estimated*. No operation ever went exactly as planned. Things inevitably went awry and one of, if not *the* first casualty was timing.

Now, for example. He was four minutes away from the location and destruction of Taylor's drugs warehouse, laboratory, chemists and manufacturing apparatus. At this point, hopefully, Taz and Morgan would have secured the compounds inner perimeter and placed timed C4 charges at the entrance and exits to the barracks. Dev and Lochlan should have been set up at the landing pad to prevent any of the 'puppet drug' from being flown away and to secure the area for the arrival of Koo and their extraction helicopters.

Eden Walker was, without a doubt, being kept in the main house where, unless his senses deceived him, there was one hell of a party going on. Fallon's ears were detecting what sounded like at least thirty heartbeats – an uneven blend of both Vampire and Humans – the throbbing, percussion-dominant sound of recorded music, the commingled drone of excited vocals, and the sporadic clink of glassware. Swimming through all that to accurately identify a single Human female, even for a vampire of his age and talents, was not only highly difficult, but would take more time than he could currently afford.

He suddenly thought of Rowan. In another ten minutes or so, she and her recently acquired rebirth mother would be leaving the below-deck quarters of the *Diosa Azul*, a modified Suezmax-class oil tanker anchored off the Oaxacan coast, to board one of the choppers that would serve as the rescue team's escape from the compound. She'd be expecting to find him, as he'd promised her, with Eden in tow. A promise he intended to keep.

Unfortunately, Eden wasn't the mission's exclusive priority and, regardless of his intentions, there was something he had to take care of first.

~*~

Taylor stood at the railing on the upper level of Don Villarreal's party palace, a flute of red wine in hand, and gazed down at the festivities unfolding with a sense of elation, of satisfaction beyond even his own wildest expectations.

Three decades past, at the height of Carousel's international prominence, he had attempted to warn his mistress, his mentor, Pashet, Bianca, Seline, aliases ad nauseam, on the dangers of her excesses. The goings-on at the Seattle temple, he told her, were dangerously extreme. Involving locals in their games, their blood sports and blood orgies tempted fate. It all but guaranteed that sooner or later a situation would arise that would attract unwanted attention. And, of course, he was proven right. Although he would have preferred to have been wrong – on one score in particular.

Pashet's failings lay in more than the monstrous, uncontrollable appetites. Short-sightedness, he could forgive her. Strangely enough, that was a trait part and parcel of the immortality experience. For those who believed their lives were endless certain things – though they shouldn't be – were taken for granted.

In Pashet's case, and the one thing he could not forgive, it was her almost cartoonish, and ultimately fatal arrogance. Specifically, the way she not only ignored but completely underestimated the potential and very real threat of a certain Nikaran war horse. It didn't matter that she had certain well-placed officials on the Seattle City Council, on the SPD, and even the Governor's office, on her payroll. In the end, it was her own kind, *their* own kind – namely, Lord Zuron I'Ane Dasmalle – that laid her in the dirt. A mistake Taylor vowed not to repeat.

He'd been abroad, in Vienna to be exact, when news of the Bennion mess reached him. And, by some incredible stretch of luck, hell maybe even divine providence, he'd managed to escape the purge that followed. It kept him one, often *two* steps ahead of the Nikaran assassins until Zuron and company were satisfied that Bianca Manx's *Carousel of Blood* had been all but erased.

All but, Taylor loosed a sotto voce chuckle and raised his glass ceilingward in triumphant vindication.

Recovery. In truth, it hadn't been an easy road. There had been crater-sized potholes, collapsed bridges, and gigantic obstructions along each and every mile. Even recently, the threat of having the 'project' prematurely outed by that damnable *băgăci,* Knox, and of course Rowan – little sex piggy's sister – and her stubborn refusal to let go; even to the point of bringing in a vampire *soldat al norocului.* And not just any soldier. A friend and associate of the very people he'd been, up until now, successfully working to avoid the past forty years.

It was nothing short of a miracle that the Project was still on track. His people, it seemed, had been successful in scaring Knox into hiding. And, insofar as he'd received no bad news from his chief operator – no news, in fact, from Janiss at all – it would appear that his move to take out Eden's sister-dear had also worked like the proverbial charm. Which, no doubt, had her knight-in-shining-armour-turned-lover, Mr Fallon Wylde, tearing up the Seattle streets in search of the man who had ordered her death.

In any case, whatever their present activities or machinations, both were much too far away, in both time and distance, to rate more than a footnote in this historic venture. The first consignments of *'Blue Howdee'* (the puppet drug – named for the famed 1950s TV marionette *Howdy Doody*) were being loaded for shipment to the U.S. and Europe at that very moment. In another few hours individual quantities would be delivered to their buyers in the East, West Coasts and Southern states of America, Eastern and Western Europe. Nothing could stop that now.

"Gentlemen . . . *friends!*" Taylor called out, catching the attention of the drunken revellers below, then raised his glass again. "A toast. To pleasure and to profit. Shall we never want for either, ever again."

~*~

An underground bunker. Something Morgan's aerial photographer hadn't so much missed as failed to identify. Understandable, Fallon had to admit, as he would have bypassed it too had he not almost stumbled over the ventilation fan disguised as a hay bale. Closer inspection located a half dozen more situated at ten-foot intervals in a rectangular configuration at the compounds centre. No apparent entrance but from the way it was positioned, as well as its proximity to the main house, logic strongly suggested a tunnel access from either inside the house or a point somewhere near it.

"Fucking great," Fallon whispered, and checked his watch. *Five minutes into the red. Better put wings on your fucking feet,* he prodded himself, already in motion and on a beeline-stealth-conscious-be-damned-course for the main house.

~*~

First there was a feeling. Like a blip on her inner radar, a twinge on the edges of Morgan's awareness, warning that something wasn't quite right as she set the timed charge beneath the door of the last barracks. And then, as she rose, a glimmer of movement in the shadows on the sandbag-lined corridor between the two Quonset huts at her right.

Backing quickly and carefully into the darkness behind her, Morgan froze and allowed her eyes to focus on the light limited space.

Had she been spotted, she wondered? Maybe by one of the *Chorti Familia* soldiers who'd left his bed for an early evening feed, or to relieve himself; which Vampire or Human, all creatures needed to do on occasion. Or a sentry, which was highly likely. Insofar as they'd jumped into this op without the benefit of a complete intel profile, the presence of individual sentries and roaming patrols was a distinct possibility.

Imagination? She mused when, after a minute or so, nothing materialised.

"OW! Mother . . . fuckin' Hubbard," a voice, clearly Taz, growled over her earbud. "*SonofaBITCH!*"

"Could you possibly be a little louder?" Morgan struggled to stifle a chuckle. "I don't think they heard you in Cancún."

"Something fuckin' bit me," Taz responded. "Took a bite *out* of me, dammit."

"Oh poor baby," the chuckle materialised. "You're a vampire. Man up. It was probably just a mosquito."

"Mosquito, my ass. It was the size of a hummingbird."

"You'll be fine. Now hush, you're too loud."

"*Hush?* Did you just *hush* me?" Taz mock-growled, making Morgan smile. A smile that dropped away when the fine hairs at the back of her neck rose.

There was definitely someone out there and, unless her senses were lying to her, it was a Necuno.

"Dev?" she whispered her brother's name, wondering if he'd done his usual and decided to sing from his own hymn sheet. No reply. She took two steps toward the huts in the distance. "Dev, come in."

Her earpiece crackled again. "What is it, acushla?" Her brother's voice came through.

"Have you or Loch changed location?" Her eyes caught a faint movement and she padded toward it.

"No, we're still here, locked and loaded. Primed and ready to explode. Pumped and . . . "

"For fuck's sake," Taz joined the discussion. "Can't you just answer the damned question. What's going on, Anna?"

"There's someone . . . " she inched forward, keeping to the shadows. "Wait a sec." She pressed against the wall and waited. Sure enough, three seconds later a figure detached from the side of a hut and sprinted across the clearing, face lit up briefly by one of the security lights.

"No way," Morgan breathed.

~*~

Another pair of roving guards silently taken out of play and Fallon stood, shrouded in shadow, at the south-eastern corner of Villarreal's ridiculous two-story Pueblo adobe mansion, visually confirming his supposition.

A pair of dark-clothed guards – Angelo, not Latino – stood on either side of a classic pre-fab double-door cabana/pool house, both draped in sturdy leather rigs and matching sets of 9mm mini-Uzis. All sporting silver nitrate loaded hollow points, no doubt. On the one hand, as they were Taylor's people and not Villareal's *Chortis,* it made the pool house the most obvious location for the hidden entrance. On the other, and par for the course, given the level of activity as well as the calibre of company present for one of the situation's most crucial aspects, the protection of Taylor's guests.

The patio and pool area was a scene straight out of a Hollywood movie version of your average LA A-list *'Lifestyles of the Rich and Drug Addicted Customers Appreciation Party',* with a Vampire kicker. A literal horde of luscious, leggy young bimbos, sporting their well-toned and cosmeticized goodies in dental floss bikinis, accompanied by an equal number of hapless functionaries, mostly involuntary blood donors, to sate the perverse appetites of Taylor buyers; his intended future business associates.

Stretched out, or splayed out and writhing, sitting, squatting, or lounging on chaise lounges, or at tables around the villa's over-sized pool were at least four recognisable members from the Houses of Machiavelli and Maggio, Bela Hauptman from Hamburg, German's *Deutsch Verein,* two members of Philadelphia's Outfit, and a Diamond Dog Gant and Valentino Cortez from the LA Coalition, were either sowing their infertile turnblood oats or filling their nasal cavities with long, fat lines of *ka'yo* – blood-cured cocaine. All of which sat directly between Fallon and his destination.

The odds against a successful outcome were, at the very least, astronomical. On the other hand . . .

Fallon calmed himself, breathing deep and slow as he allowed his thoughts to slip backwards, deep into his past.

"To be a ninja, you need to learn to become a shadow, to blend into your surroundings and to escape the eyes of others, to conceal your identity," said the voice of Ninjutsu Grand Master Anami Taro. "Normally, this would present no

problem for someone of your kind, as your abilities in the realm of speed far surpasses those of your Human counterparts. However, this is not so with your Kyuuketsuki . . . Vampire brethren. In situations such as these, the ryu of Yonin – infiltration when in plain view – is recommended."

Recommended or not, circumstances being what they were – and with time being a critical factor – it was the only option.

~*~

Morgan was torn between following the person she'd spotted and staying in her location to follow the plan devised by Fallon. In the end, duty won, and she held her position.

"What did you see?" Taz's voice whispered through her earpiece. "Anna, talk to me."

"You remember that girl we picked up . . . she smashed one of the windows at Shadowfall and ran?"

"Raven?"

"Yeah, her. I swear she's just headed away from your location." Morgan leaned back against the wall, keeping an eye out for any movement.

"No way," Taz's denial was immediate. "Can't have been her. A trick of the light."

Morgan sighed. "Yeah, you're probably right." Her gut told her differently, though. "Fallon's late," she changed the subject.

Taz laughed, the sound making her stomach flip. "He'll catch up, chances are something caught his eye and he needed to go check it out." There was a pause and Morgan could hear him breathing through the connection. "You should come over here," he said, eventually. "We're stuck now until Fallon turns up, everything's in place, we're just waiting on his signal."

"And do what?"

"Oh, I'm sure we could think of something." She could hear the smile in his voice.

"Oh, for the love of all that is holy," Dev's voice broke the mood. "Stop flirting with my sister."

"Don't listen," Taz retorted. "Come on, Anna. You . . . me . . . the sound of the cicadas. Underneath the stars . . . " his voice had dropped to a husky whisper. "It's quiet over here, no one's around. We could take some time . . . "

"I swear," Dev cut in once again. "If you don't back off, I'm going to fucking cut your dick off."

"A little advice, asshole," Taz responded. "Bring a little more help than you've got at the moment."

"Enough!" Morgan snapped. "I don't know what history you two have but put it aside until this job is done."

"Acushla," Dev began, just as Taz spoke her name.

"No. Just stop."

~*~

If there was one thing that years and experience had taught Fallon it was that few things activated the 'stupidity gene' like drugs, alcohol, sexual excess, and boredom. All of which were prevalent in the situation going on around him. So much so, in fact, that having to use a ninja technique to ghost his way across the pool area might have been completely unnecessary, had it not been for the presence of the two sober, non-participating *armed* guards at the pool house entrance.

It was disguise and camouflage in the loosest sense of the terms, thanks to the involuntary assistance of one of the male carousers – a ginger-haired, towel-draped and robe-clad sot who made the mistake of staggering off-site to empty his bursting vampire-bladder at the corner of the house.

Stripping off his black t-shirt and tabi boots, Fallon rolled his BDU pant-legs up to the knees and folded up the essentials – throwing stars, Beretta with silencer and spare clips, combat knife and *ninjatō* short sword, along with his t-shirt and boots into the towel, which he tied around his waist like a fanny pack. The bulk of his equipment was stashed against the wall at the corner of the house where, he hoped, it wouldn't be discovered before he returned. The robe was wrapped and belted around him, from the waist-down, to conceal the suspicious bulge in the towel at the base of his spine.

Moving into play, and completing his disguise, Fallon latched onto a passing, all but naked dark-haired girl who, apparently, was more than happy to allow him to wrap her long, supple limbs around his waist, her arms around his neck, and be transported on his leisurely trek across the area's damp, tiled deck.

He caught the scent of lemon from the girl's hair and an image suddenly formed in his mind's eye, a feeling taking hold with equal swiftness.

Rowan.

Guilt?

Sparked by the brunette's scent, her warm breath on his neck, her soft lips nuzzling her throat, he felt an unbidden, helpless stirring in his crotch.

It's just business, he told himself.

Focus, dammit, focus!

~*~

There was always one, Taylor affirmed. In every group business negotiation, always one. One stubborn, cautious, cagey hold-out that required patient pampering, finessing, outright ass-kissing to assuage the icy underpinnings of their dark uncertainties.

In this case, however, there were two: Morris Ramsey, the *consigliere* to Flan Deevers, the Purple Brotherhood's boss of all bosses, and Caitlin 'Cokie' Donaghy, *Şeful* of the Seattle Brotherhood clan. Beyond any and all doubt, *the* most important potential clients of the whole shebang.

The Brotherhood had been around forever, for as long as there had been a Vampire Nation. They were world-wide, top of the food chain, and historically, the founders/progenitors of every scheme and racket known to, and practiced by, the Vampire syndicates and cartels that came along afterwards. To get them – even one of them – on board would guarantee the far-reaching successes of not only the Project, but Red Carousel, itself.

And there was the rub. The challenge, precisely speaking.

Taylor's lure – his combination, celebration, introduction to the product, and demonstration – a show of appreciation, if you would, was in full swing. The entire lower level of Casa Villarreal was a hotbed of action and prurient activities, the likes of which went far beyond what even some vampires fantasised about. Though, through it all, since it kicked off in fact, Donaghy, Ramsey and their entourage of hawk-eyed, Armani-wrapped watchdogs steadfastly remained unaffected. Untouched, either physically or emotionally. For upwards of two hours they had either skirted the perimeter or occupied a corner of the main room – currently, the bar – apparently enjoying the provided top shelf alcoholic refreshment while watching the carnal chaos play out around them.

Both made visual contact as Taylor descended the staircase and tracked his progress through the writhing sea of ravenous debauchery. Taylor could see it, their feelings toward him, as he approached. Not so much seen as sensed where Ramsey was concerned. Body language, and to a barely concealed degree, disgust. He was, after all, the underworld vampire version of a Human diplomat, well-practiced in masking his personal sensibilities. Donaghy, on the other hand, was just the opposite. Her eyes told him that she'd just as soon have her bodyguards bend him over, so she could shove a silver stake up his ass. And she'd probably have an orgasm in the process.

He nodded to both as he approached, successfully stifling the urge to grin at Donaghy's reciprocal look of unabashed loathing.

"A bit noisy," Taylor waved a hand to indicate the pandemonium surrounding them. "Why don't we retire to someplace a little less . . . distracting."

"Why? Is your bullshit any easier to swallow without the noise?" Donaghy tossed back, dryly, glaring at him over the rim of her glass as she took a deliberately long drink.

"Unnecessary," Ramsey chimed in, quickly. "We're all very comfortable here, as a matter of fact. More than a little disentranced, if the truth be known."

"And in case that word carries too many syllables for you to comprehend, try 'ho-hum'," Donaghy threw in.

"Really?" Taylor smiled, unaffected.

"I believe what the *Şeful* is saying," Ramsey stepped in diplomatically, waving to indication the action around them, "is that your demonstration is barely impressive."

"Barely impressive," Taylor echoed the *consigliere's* declaration, his gaze hopping back and forth between the two VIPs with an expression that bespoke both astonishment and amusement. "Seriously?"

"What we're saying, Taylor," Ramsey continued, "is that what you are showing us – what's going on here and all around us – while extraordinary at face value, could very well be smoke and mirrors."

Donaghy joined the exchange, then. "For all we know, the effects of your alleged miracle puppet drug we're seeing right there could be something you and your people whipped up in some rinky-dinky little basement laboratory just to get the rubes to sign on to your little circle tent revival show. How do we know that it's real? That what we'll get later isn't some hopped up batch of crack and sodium pentothal?"

Taylor nodded, after a moment's pause. "Fine. You don't trust me. I can respect that. What, then, can I offer that will rectify that?"

"I'm glad you put it that way," Ramsey smiled. "There *is* one way."

~*~

Luck or fate. Fallon didn't care which. But, whichever was the case, it was the only way to explain how, as he and his bikini-clad cargo moved beyond the two bored guards, the pool house doors opened and a lanky, apparently youthful Vampire male in a white lab smock emerged.

Fallon moved purposefully to intercept him; ever-mindful of the fact that, because of their nearness, the guards could be alerted to his intentions; and used the girl in his arms like a flesh and blood plow, blocking the lab tech's exit and forcing him back inside. To anyone who may have been watching, like the guards for example, hopefully it looked as though the drunk-with-the-party-girl-wrapped-around-him stumbled into the guy coming through the pool house and almost spilled them all to the floor. Fallon even helped things along, in that respect, by dropping the girl at the lab tech's feet, then quickly shut the door behind him.

"Whoa, brother. Looks like maybe you had a little *too much* party—" the lab tech tried, attempting to help steady what he believed to be a man on the verge of drunken collapse. His observation was cut abruptly short by a severely bruised larynx.

"Listen closely, *brother*," Fallon said, pulling the tech close as he spoke. "You got two options. One, you take me down to the lab, get me inside without a hassle or, two, I make sure you won't be a threat . . . if you catch my drift." He smiled, a baring of teeth. "Nod once for option one, twice for two."

Clutching his injured throat, the tech gave a single nod and Fallon's smile widened. He moved them away from the prostrate party girl who, thankfully, had passed out the moment she hit the floor.

A fake fireplace – very James Bond-ish, Fallon mused; Taylor *did* have a flair for the dramatic – opened outward, revealing a shiny, circular elevator compartment. On its interior, to the right of the opening, was a square translucent panel with a thin slot-like opening beneath it. Obviously a portal which required either voice or retina, as well as a key card for identification. A quick scan of the tech's smock showed nothing.

"For your sake, I hope you didn't leave the key in your other pants," Fallon told him.

"I . . . wait here . . . " the tech struggled to speak, massaging his throat while rummaging through one of the smock's pockets and moving toward the wall panel. A quick pass over the panel turned the translucent square a luminescent green. The tech then slid the card into the bottom slot and croaked, "*Production.*"

In the next instant doors, both camouflage and actual, shut and the compartment began to descend.

"Good boy," Fallon gave the tech's head a semi-playful pat and pulled him away from the panel.

"We'll . . . be down in a . . . couple of minutes," he said, still struggling from Fallon's throat blow. "You . . . are you gonna kill me now?"

Fallon shrugged. "Depends. Cooperate and . . . " he left the sentence unfinished, shrugging again. "Any surprises waiting for me down there? Like guards?"

"No," the tech answered.

"How about more coded doors?"

"No. Just the elevators."

"*Elevators?*" Fallon reacted to the tech's plural response, grabbing a tight fistful of the young vampire's smock-front.

"Yeah, jeez, take it easy, man. This ain't the only entrance. There's another one, another elevator that leads up to the house. It's private. Only the boss, Mr. Dorian, uses it."

"Mr. Dorian," Fallon sneered softly. "Okay . . . last question. How many levels to this bunker?"

"Three. Not counting up-top," said the tech. "One is storage, warehousing for the finished product, ready to be shipped out. Two is bio-material. The specimens. You know . . . the walking blood bags."

"Walking blood bags," Fallon repeated the tech's callous portrayal of the human condition with a slow shake of his head. *Charming.* "How many *specimens* are currently on hand?"

"None. The last lot were delivered to the labs more than two weeks ago," the tech explained. "The next group hasn't arrived yet."

After a short pause, Fallon poked the young vampire's forehead and he resumed. "And the bottom is the laboratories and packaging . . . Production."

A sudden jerk announced their nearness to the third level and Fallon turned to face his reluctant fellow traveller. "You've been a great help, dude. But you know, there's a problem I just can't get by . . ."

"Hey. *Hey*, you said—" the tech's eyes widened, realising what was coming just a little too late. Fallon braced himself and drove a stiffened forefinger into the young vampire's forehead.

" . . . I don't like you," Fallon said, using the tech's hair to wipe the blood and brain matter off his finger.

~*~

"A tour of your drug facilities," Ramsey said.

"We would like to know there is a legitimate process involved," Donaghy added.

"There's no secondary agenda, no subterfuge," Ramsey was quick to assure him. "This is not some backhanded attempt to try and steal your formula. We would just like to be satisfied that for the price you are asking, as well as our organisation's participation, we're not buying a pig in a poke."

Suspicious? Taylor couldn't help but be. Especially when they trotted in a trio of supposed expert professionals – members of their entourage barely seen since the two Brotherhood bigwigs first set foot in the compound; two males and a female as ill-attired for the climate as their watchdogs-in-designer-togs, who boasted academic letters from prestigious European universities.

Still, they had him over a proverbial barrel and they knew it. He needed them. Especially Ramsey. Or, more accurately, the man Ramsey represented – Flan Deevers, *Şeful tutu sail, the Boss of all Bosses*. Trying to work the Project *without* the blessing of the Purple Brotherhood would be, first of all, pretty much asking that his shipments be hijacked on regular basis . . . if, in fact, he survived past the first one. And second, that Deevers would have him delivered to Zuron and the Parliament of Lords like a trussed-up lamb, ready for slaughter.

Taylor had agreed, of course.

"There's no need to put yourself out," Ramsey told him. "Have one of your staff . . . more than one, if that's preferable. Have them escort our people. Şeful Donaghy and I will remain here with you . . . as collateral. The minute our experts give us the confirmation, we will call our people in New York and Seattle and the payment will be e-transferred into your account. *Afacere?*"

"Agreed," Taylor answered, with extreme reluctance. "If you will wait here, I will make the arrangements."

~*~

Eden stiffened when she heard the door hiss open, the sound of footsteps against the wooden floor as they crossed the room, and then a pair of black leather shoes stopped in her line of sight.

Even after all this time, it was still a struggle not to raise her eyes and she battled with the need to see who was staring at her.

"Is *this* the girl Wylde is hunting you for?" The voice wasn't one she recognised, and Eden tensed further. Had Taylor brought someone new to use her?

Taylor's chuckle froze the blood in her veins. "Oh, I think Fallon Wylde has more important things to worry about right now than a little pink-haired whore."

A finger hooked beneath her chin and tilted her face up. "Look at me, little one."

Eden's eyes flickered upwards, before dropping again. Taylor didn't like her making eye contact and she'd learned her lesson well.

"I saw your sister," the stranger continued, and Eden couldn't stop a gasp. "She was in Aduna's with Fallon Wylde. She hasn't quit looking for you."

"Talking to my little pet pig wasn't part of our deal, Ramsey," Taylor gave a sharp pull on the chain hooked to the collar around Eden's neck. "Pet her, by all means. But no conversation. Animals can't talk."

"I think she's been *petted* enough, don't you?" A third voice, female this time, joined the conversation.

CHAPTER EIGHTEEN

Fallon had seen his share of the strange, the unique and the unequalled, the extraordinary and the bizarre, things both noteworthy and unforgettable, things which plumbed the depths of cruelty and soared beyond the heights of the monstrous. But, until he entered Taylor's subterranean drug factory Fallon would have sworn to God Almighty – if He, She or It truly existed – that in all the days since he first drew breath, some 508 years past, even for Vampire-kind, that he knew the true meaning of monstrous.

What he bore witness to was a bone-chilling combination of twisted medical reality and grotesque science fiction. Looming high above him in the cavernous structure was a system of cross-beam metal rails. And from each, at intervals of four to five feet, a nude body hung from its ankles – like racks of meat in a slaughterhouse. Attached to each body was, firstly, IV apparatus, which Fallon assumed replenished body fluids to keep the bodies functioning. Secondary, a series of transparent tubes which helped in the evacuation of body wastes and the extraction of blood. Below them were two large vats, obviously for blood and bodily waste, attended to by lab workers in white Hazmat suits, who transferred the specified substances to large plastic containers and then to motorised carts.

There were at least an even four dozen of the suspended bodies. Several of whom, and which made Fallon clench his teeth against the near-overwhelming urge to vomit, were children.

"Hey. *You!* You got clearance to be here?" A gruff male voice cut into the building rage within him. "Let me see your ID badg—"

In the space of a single second, Fallon whirled and stood with his fingers embedded in the speaker's eye sockets. It took another minute or so for the man's body to receive confirmation from his brain that his life had ended, and for his legs to buckle beneath him. It was only after Fallon withdrew his blood-coated fingers from the man's sockets that he realised his victim was not alone. A second lab worker – a woman, a dark-haired Latino – stood just a foot beyond her now deceased co-worker, mouth agape, eyes wide, obviously paralysed in fear.

"You wanna live?" Fallon's voice was a low growl.

The worker nodded jerkily. *"si. Si. Claro, señor. I want to live. Yes!"*

"Good. Then don't try to be a fucking hero. Don't give me any trouble," Fallon warned, using a stiffened finger to imply what would happen should the still wide-eyed lab tech fail to comply. "The actual laboratory – the place where Mr Dorian's drug is created – take me to it."

"No lo hare. I will not. And *si* – yes, I will," the tech replied, nodding in an almost perfect imitation of a dashboard hula doll.

As promised she stood rooted to the spot, watching in cowed docility as Fallon doffed the robe and towel camouflage and unpacked his gear. Once ready, she took the lead with Fallon, within striking distance, in tow.

They moved at a moderate pace along the production area's walled perimeter, eventually and inevitably attracting the attention of other workers. Something which brought a number of crucial, inescapable, and not to be ignored facts into increasingly sharp focus. The first, and most apparent, being the lack of sufficient intel for this mission hadn't taken into account that Taylor's drug facility would be so numerously populated and the facility itself would be so large. Which led to the next problem – if the number of people he'd counted during the first two or three minutes into his stroll with his unnamed captive were any indication, he'd be in deep shit if even less than half of them decided to rush him at once. Last, but not least, not only was the facility larger than Fallon anticipated but it was, obviously, bigger than the amount of explosives he'd brought along – all of which, unfortunately, he'd left with the bulk of his equipment, topside.

Boy, when you fuck up you really go ass-deep, he silently kicked himself. *Still, a fuck up don't mean you give up.*

A crowd, growing larger by the second, began to assemble in their path and, from the looks on their faces, Fallon realised that the moment was swiftly approaching where the situation would get ugly and bloody.

"Whoa. Let's think about this, okay?" Fallon pulled the Beretta and waved it in a slow arc as a trio of coverall-clad males moved toward them. He clutched his captive companion's shoulder and turned her to face him. "What's your name?"

"I – My name . . . I'm Olivia," she stammered back.

"Alright, Olivia. That guy . . . what happened back there," he jerked his head back over one shoulder, indicating the spot where their association began. "What can I say? Shit happens. Wrong place, wrong time. But I'm not here for you," he waved the gun again, indicating the crowd. "*Or* for them. I'm here," his eyes twitched ceilingward, "for this. It can't be allowed to continue. And I'm here to burn it down . . . amongst other things," he finished, softly, then moved out to Olivia's side where he could be seen clearly by the others.

"I don't want to hurt you . . . any of you. But I will, if you force me. All I ask is that you don't get in my way. Let me do what I have to do."

"Do we have a choice?" Olivia asked quickly, also turning to regard her co-workers. "We are, all of us, not here *nuestras propias elecciones* . . . by our own choice. *Dominar* Villarreal, the *jefe* of our clan has pledged allegiance to the *vampire blanco*, Dorio. He tells us that we work here, for Dorio . . . If we do not, we will have no home, no food and, for some, no life. So, why should we risk this for you?"

"Fair enough. Okay. I'll make you a deal, and a promise," Fallon answered. "You help me – meaning you don't get in my way – and, after tonight, Dorio and Villarreal won't be a problem. For *you* or anyone else, ever again."

"And we can guarantee that promise." A new voice joined the exchange, coming from beyond the furthest group of workers. As one, all heads swivelled to greet the approach of several Caucasian newcomers.

~*~

"T'Ane?" Dev's voice broke the uneasy silence. "Is your man usually so bad at timekeeping?"

Taz curbed his natural instinct to snap at Morgan's brother. "No . . . something must have happened."

"We have movement over here. If Loch and I don't act soon, we're going to lose the chance to stop this shipment from leaving."

Taz chewed on a thumbnail, thinking. "Anna, what's your status?"

"All quiet over here. No unusual movement. Guard patrols are following a stable pattern," her response came back immediately. "But our transport is going to be here very soon, so I have to agree with Dev. We need to move."

"Okay. Dev, you and Loch make some noise. Anna, head over to me. We'll contact Koo and tell her to delay things for twenty minutes. That'll give us a chance to get closer and see what's happening inside. Fallon will make contact as soon as he's able to and we'll update him."

"On it," Dev responded, gleefully. "Time to blow some shit up. Dev out!"

Taz heard Morgan sigh. "I don't think he'll ever grow up."

He chuckled. "Get your ass over here. I'll call Koo."

His call to Koo was short. He explained the situation, asked her to delay their arrival, waited for her agreement and cut the call without further conversation. He leaned against the wall and waited for Morgan.

When her figure appeared in the darkness, he smiled and pushed himself upright. Desire unfurled in his stomach as he watched her lope toward him, so when she was within reach, he caught her arm and pulled her forwards into his arms.

Her startled exclamation was swallowed by his mouth on hers as he turned and moved them both until she was flush against the wall.

"Taz!" Her mouth separated from his long enough to gasp his name, and he pressed forward, teeth nipping at her lip.

"We've got time," he told her, his hands on the waistband of her pants.

"Are you joking?" She pulled his arms away, and planted one palm on his chest, holding him at bay. "What do you think you're doing?"

Taz growled, the sound coming from deep within, and he surged forward, batting her hand out of the way. "Come on, Anna . . ." his head dipped again, and she jerked her face sideways.

"What's got into you?" she ducked under his arm and took a step away.

Taz froze and shook his head. *What are you doing?* He asked himself. Another headshake and his mind cleared.

"Fuck . . . I don't know what happened," he said, slowly.

Morgan eyed him, staying just out of reach. "Did you breathe something in? Chemicals?"

"No, I . . . I don't know what that was." He lifted a hand and reached out to touch her cheek, unable to hide a scowl when she leaned away. "Seriously, I'm not going to grab you."

She frowned at him. "Are you sure?"

"I'm sure," he hesitated, then smiled. "But . . . rain check for later?"

Morgan laughed, as he'd hoped, and shook her head at him. "One track mind, I'Ane," she told him.

~*~

Rowan quickly changed seats, moving across the helicopter's passenger compartment to sit beside the woman who had, for all intents and purposes, recently become her de facto mother. The move was, of course, unnecessary. Since both women sported headset and microphone assemblies, they could have easily conversed with one another regardless of the distance between them. But Koo had just had a comms conversation that Rowan had been excluded from, and if the lovely Asian woman's demeanour was any indication, it was an exchange Rowan could not live without being privy to.

"Koo? What is it? Is something wrong? Is everything alright?" she pressed, almost babbling. "What? Tell me . . . *please?*"

Koo paused a moment, then sighed. "It was Prince I'Ane," she paused again, giving the young Newborn's hand a reassuring squeeze. "He wants us to delay our arrival by twenty minutes. But I wouldn't worry. Timetables are never precise with a mission like this."

"Please, Koo, I'm not a child," Rowan replied. "Don't sugar-coat it. I can take it. Is something wrong? Is Eden alright? Is . . . Fallon? He's okay?"

"As far as I know, everything is fine," Koo interrupted, hoping the younger woman couldn't detect the doubt in her voice. But then, she hadn't *actually* lied. The Nikaran Prince hadn't given her any details. As far as she *knew*, everything *was* fine.

"I'm sure your sister is just fine," *relatively*, Koo thought. "And I wouldn't worry about Fallon. The man's got more lives than a bagful of cats."

"Uh-huh," Rowan uttered, settling back against the chopper's canvas seatback. "Isn't that the same phrase people use to describe a crazy person?"

Koo turned away, concealing her widened eyes and hiked eyebrows Rowan's query had sparked. "You have no idea," she whispered, under her breath.

~*~

In the moments, and the awkward silence, that followed the newcomers' introduction, Fallon watched as they, first, stripped out of their fashionable outerwear; revealing attire more suited to clandestine military endeavours; then began to peel, unwind, detach and unpack bits, pieces, sheets, and coils of plastique from attaché cases, body parts and body cavities Fallon would have preferred he had not been witness to. When they had finished, he beckoned the one who'd introduced himself as Killian, the group leader, aside.

"Let me get this straight," Fallon said. "Donaghy had you people watching . . . shadowing me. And you followed me to Mexico?"

Killian chuckled. "We've been on you since Taylor had your girlfriend shot back at Shadowfall. We kept our distance, but we were there when you had your meeting with Knox. Listened in using a parabolic microphone." Killian paused, then added with a frown and a shiver, "and he didn't exaggerate. That damned graveyard gave me the willies."

"So, do you have Shadowfall bugged, too?" Fallon asked, wondering if they had listened in on the interrogations of Tigr and Janiss, too.

"Above my pay grade, Brother," Killian answered. "But we watched you snatch Taylor's head kiss-ass, Janiss. And our people at the Sea-Tac Airport reported your departure tonight. The *Şeful*, Cokie, and the *consigliere* from New York got their invites to this place a coupla days ago, so when they heard you and your crew were travelling, it was a pretty safe bet where you were headed, and why. The *Şeful* brought us along as a just-in-case kinda thing."

"Just in case . . . ?"

"Just in case you *didn't* show. And, if you did, to give you a hand."

Just in case, Fallon repeated the phrase silently. He held eye contact with Killian for a long moment to gauge the level of or, if nothing else, the presence of the man's sincerity. His attention then shifted to Killian's cohorts, who were diligently involved in chunks of plastique explosives and attaching charges. At first blush, it looked as though they were preparing for some serious damage. Still . . .

"Help is appreciated," Fallon said, turning again to meet Killian's gaze. "But let's make sure we're both on the same page. If you overheard my meeting with Knox, then you and your boss know what I came here to do . . . right?"

"Relax, brother. In the words of the powers that be, we don't want Taylor's shit on the streets any more than you do," Killian assured him, then threw a quick glance over Fallon's shoulder, no doubt to one of his companions.

"You don't trust us," Killian continued. "You got no reason to, and we get that. But you're gonna have to. My guess is you got this mission timed down to the minute," he flashed a wry grin, "and the clock's ticking."

He hesitated then to allow his words to sink in and gave Fallon's shoulder a comradely clap. "You got a young lady to rescue. Don't worry about this . . . we got it covered."

Still more than a little unsure, Fallon lingered a minute or so longer, searching the eyes and faces of all those around. His gaze finally settled on Olivia.

"Alright. But promise me one thing," he said, gesturing at Olivia and her co-workers. "These folks – they've got no stake in this. Make sure they get out of here clean."

"Consider it done," Killian offered his hand. Fallon accepted and shook it.

The second elevator, the one mentioned earlier by the first lab tech, was located at the far end of the facility's production complex. Fallon was joined, or more accurately, escorted there by Killian, while giving him a rundown of the layout of the Casa Villarreal's interior and situation.

"You know, you got a pair'a big brass ones on you, soldier," Killian commented, as they stopped at the elevator doors. "Your rep is pretty solid. But, to be honest, I always thought it was mostly exaggerated bullshit. Looks like I was wrong." He offered his hand again.

Fallon accepted the gesture and, as the elevator doors opened behind him, released Killian's hand and stepped inside. "Let's hope that's the only thing you'll ever be wrong about."

Confident that his message was understood, Fallon held the man's gaze until the doors closed between them. As the elevator began its ascent, he tapped his earbud.

"Ghost Prime to all elements –"

"*Jesus H, man – where the FUCK have you been?*" Taz's voice screeched back, bringing a smile to Fallon's lips despite the momentary lance of pain. "We were just about to come check on you. The choppers are on a twenty-minute hold—"

"That's ten minutes by now," Morgan jumped in.

"Getting down to the wire, Prime. What's up?" Taz pressed.

"Forgive my tardiness, Your Grace," Fallon responded, dryly. "I'll explain later. But, for right now, let's get this show on the road . . . Light it up."

~*~

Cokie Donaghy loosed an audible sigh of much-needed relief as Ramsey pulled the bedroom door shut behind them, then clutched her midsection in a gesture of revulsion, waiting until they had reached the end of the corridor to speak.

"At the risk of losing my die-hard atheist status, *thank God* he got that phone call." She made a short gagging noise, a show of disgust. "If we had stayed in that room any longer, I would have heaved up *yesterday's* lunch. The man is a fucking pig."

"I'm certain even a pig would take offense at that comparison," Ramsey concurred. "And that poor girl." He shuddered. "Did you see what he's done to her? As well as the bruises and scars, it's a miracle she's lasted so long."

"Well," Donaghy heaved a barking laugh. "Not that I really give a shit about Humans. They do worse to each other on a daily basis. But . . . " she paused as they reached the top of the staircase. "That girl, a few years back. The one whose death brought down Bianca Manx . . . What was her name?"

"Benson. No – Bennion. Teresa Bennion," Ramsey said.

Donaghy nodded in response. "They say her body had wounds that looked like those. And Taylor worked for the Manxes. I'd say it's obvious who took part in that mess," she growled and gagged again as they started down. "Regardless of what that drug of his can do, that sick *La Dracu* and his twisted habits will eventually bite us all in the ass."

"Agreed," Ramsey said. "Hopefully, that won't be a problem providing Mr Wylde does his job."

"Oh, I'm pretty sure that's a given," Donaghy laughed. "And, with that in mind," she glanced at her watch, "we had better make our exit. Things are gonna get very lively around here shortly."

~*~

"Let me understand you," Taylor said. The smartphone that, just moments ago, had been held casually in one hand, away from his ear like a serving tray, while he lounged lord-like on the end of the room's oversized bed and used the toe of one immaculate Italian loafer to toy with the bare, and severely bruised, breast of his pink-haired sex slave . . . he now gripped his cell tightly, pulling it flush against the side of his flushed face.

"Janiss is . . . dead?"

"There's no official confirmation," said the voice on the cell's opposite end. "But no one has seen him – or Vince and Trevor – since they went out last night."

"And they went where?" Taylor prompted.

"I'm . . . not sure, Cardinal. I was told he received a call . . . from one of our people at Kane Thoth's club. And the message, his parting words, I believe were . . . something about tying up a loose end."

"That would be Tigr," Taylor muttered under his breath.

"Beg your pardon, Excellency?"

"Never mind. And, of course, you cross-checked with some of our other Shadowfall contacts?"

There was a moment of audibly awkward silence before the voice spoke again. "That's the problem . . . why I'm calling, sir. I can't seem to reach them. *Any* of them."

"Bullshit! If I were you, I would try ag—" Taylor's words ended abruptly as the sounds of distant thunder were quickly followed by an ever-increasing rumble. A rumble that became a quake which shook the structure's very foundation.

"What the fuc—" Again his words were curtailed. The house rocked again, harder this time, by the unmistaken force of manmade thunder. Bone-jarring and coming from seemingly *all* directions.

"No . . ."

First, three in rapid succession . . .

"Oh no . . . no . . ."

. . . then three more . . .

"No. NO . . . "

. . . and the last shattering windows, showering the bedroom's interior with shards of heated glass.

"*Noooooooooooooo!*"

~*~

That was fast, Fallon thought in response to the first tremors that rocked the floor beneath him. He had no more than exited the house's private elevator – less than three minutes after his brief confab with the man apparently in command of Cokie Donaghy's demolition team – and had paused to make a last-minute check of his equipment.

Two minutes and fifty seconds, according to his watch. Damn fast, in fact. But then, they were vampires and he would have expected no less. Being honest with himself, Fallon's only real concern – one of them, at any rate – his *hope* was that Killian kept his word and allowed Olivia and the other *Chorti* turnbloods to get out before he destroyed the bunker.

It was pandemonium, full-tilt, by the time Fallon reached the end of the hallway, which opened onto the living room. A scene, in all truth, both comical and bizarre. With the sounds of high explosive thunder and sporadic bursts of automatic weapons fire; both near – Morganna and Taz; and distant – Dev and Lochlan – as its backdrop; men writhed, flailed, stumbled, and scurried frantically on all-fours, desperately attempting to disengage from their previous licentious activities to retrieve their clothing, and in most instances, their weapons, while their sexual partners tried, with equal ferocity, to halt their progress.

Like shooting fish in a barrel, Fallon chuckled to himself. *Just that easy.* Way *too* easy, he decided. And, after another quick glance at his watch, easier than he had time for.

Time. The most critical factor of all in that, for one thing, he was off the operation's original schedule by at least twenty minutes. A good five minutes had elapsed since the first charges were detonated. Meaning he'd lost the element of surprise where Taylor was concerned, which might very well have put Eden's life in jeopardy, making haste the first order of business.

According to Killian's briefing, she was being kept in a room on the house's upper level. The exact room unknown, but before he and his team departed for the underground, Killian had witnessed his Şeful and the New York *consigliere* being escorted upstairs by, quote-unquote, 'the Man himself'. Eden, Fallon deduced – or hoped like hell – was at least somewhere close by.

Even though the real-life combination of a Chinese fire drill and a scene from a Three Stooges film short stood between him and the stairs – though, more accurately, because of it – no one seemed to notice, or care about the armed man in black combat gear who moved among them on a determined and sporadically uneven course toward the staircase. A trek which came to a stop when one of their number, someone with clan status judging by his attitude, wrested himself from the amorous clutches of two unignorably well-endowed blondes, while simultaneously firing off bursts ceilingward from an AK-47 while barking out a stream of commands and profanities in guttural Spanish.

At least three of the near-nude and thrashing throng responded, assuming positions of reverent, if not entirely stable, attention.

"*Si mi Dominar,*" they addressed him, in tandem.

Dominar? Fallon regarded he whom the trio addressed, and who bore a very uncomfortable resemblance to a young Antonio Banderas, with hiked eyebrows and a nasty smirk as the conversation he'd had with Olivia and the promise he made resurfaced.

"*Dominar . . .* " Fallon snapped his fingers, instantly capturing the attention of the aforementioned and his reverent audience of three. "So . . . where I come from that would make you a Don . . . *Don Villarreal.* How's it hangin', Joaquin?"

The three henchmen went suddenly slack-jawed and bloodless. The Dominar, on the other hand, went bug-eyed and beet-red. "Lowly dog!" he growled. "You *dare* address me with such disrespect? I will have your *ass!*" His growl turned to a snarl and he made a very unfortunate mistake. The last mistake, in fact, he would ever make in his attempt to bring the muzzle of his assault rifle to bear on the grinning pissant before him.

In the next instance a small red hole appeared in the Dominar's forehead. Put there by the *lowly, disrespectful dog* with his silenced Beretta, and done with such swiftness not one of those who stood there saw him move or heard the weapon's near-muted *pofft* until Villarreal's body crumpled to the floor.

"Sorry, asshole, not my type," Fallon murmured, then swung the Beretta on the late-Dominar's gaping subjects. "Any hard feelings, fellas?"

Two of the trio seized the opportunity to make decisively quick backpedalling departures. The third slowly raised both hands to shoulder-level and shook his head.

"*Ninguno de mi, hombre* . . . Not from me."

"*Goood.* Good, my man. Now I want you to do me a little favour," Fallon said, gesturing with the gun's barrel to indicate the upper level. "Go up and tell the gringo . . . Taylor . . . that his old cell phone tag-buddy from Seattle is waiting to talk to him. And tell him to bring the girl with him."

Following the messenger's visibly rattled departure and stumbling sprint up the staircase, things calmed considerably. Most of Taylor's guests, the buyers of his so-called puppet drug were, as the saying went, in the wind. Mixed amongst the sounds of gunfire, shouts scream, and the occasional war whoop – Taz and Morgan mopping up . . . but mostly Taz – which reached Fallon's ears from beyond the house's sandstone walls were also the sounds of blaring horns, revving engines, and the brittle purr of gravel on rubber characterising the tumultuous execution of mass vehicular evacuations. All of which left the house, the living room specifically, virtually devoid of living presences and auditory distractions.

Not that it mattered.

Positioned well out of sight and beneath the winding staircase, Fallon had no trouble whatsoever detecting movement on the level above him.

Following the initial turn, the soft metallic slide of the bedroom door knob and the metal-on-metal squeak of door hinges, two sets of footfalls made their way along the upper corridor. While both were slow, one set moved with a timid, uncertain gait indicating someone barely in control of their motor functions. Set number two, on the other hand, were both mindfully cautious and carefully measured. Years of experience notwithstanding, it didn't take much to figure out which belonged to whom.

Predictably, they stopped at the top of the stairs – silent and moving no further.

Also predictable, Fallon thought. *Bastard's waiting for me to give myself away.*

"Hidin' my brother?" Taylor tsk-tasked after a long, drawn out moment. "I mean, you jump in like Rambo and now you go PG-13 on me? Colour me disappointed."

When his attempt to provoke Fallon failed, he continued. "A big thumbs up on your assault, by the way. For what it's worth, I did *not* see that coming," he gave a short, huffing laugh. "Havin' your girlfriend popped . . . shoulda worked. Shoulda hit you right where you live. You are as good as your rep, Brother Wylde. I'm impressed."

"*Fuck you, Óinindi,*" Fallon finally responded, employing a tactic taught to him many years earlier by his long-time friend, Kane Thoth. It was known among select members of the older vampire hierarchy as *'the umbra' - The Way of the Shadow.* The vampire equivalent of Human ventriloquism, changing the voice to give it a whispery, ghostly quality and projecting it so that it appeared to come from the very walls themselves. It was a trick that never failed to unnerve and, as Fallon himself had witnessed on a number of occasions, literally scare the piss out of its victims.

Although it had yet to elicit such an extreme reaction, Fallon *did* detect a sudden surge in his target's heartbeat.

"*Let . . . The girl . . . Go,*" Fallon said.

"Letcha in on a little secret . . . I don't scare so easy, Fallon," Taylor replied, with a laughing attempt at unaffected bravado. An attempt, however, which fell decidedly short. "I still got the trump card for this hand. The girl's in my possession. Maybe . . . I won't *kill* her. But there's other ways. Other *things,* if you know where I'm comin' from."

Fallon let Taylor's thinly veiled and undeniably impotent threat go unanswered, allowing the house's now thunderous silence to enhance the terror boiling in the older vampire's innards. But in doing so it freed his senses to detect the familiar, distant sound of approaching rotor blades.

The rescue helicopters. Still some distance away but closing fast.

"*-if you're listening, I got good news and bad news,*" Taz's voice buzzed over his earbud as Fallon activated it with a quick tap. Then tapped it twice more, giving the code-response to signify he needed to remain vocally inactive.

Taz resumed. *"Good news first. Our limo service is en-route. About five mikes out. The bad news — the pilots spotted lights and three vehicles, two two-and-a-half-ton troop trucks and an SUV, coming up on the road to the compound. ETA three mikes . . . maybe less. What's your status?"*

Sneaky son of a bitch, Fallon almost laughed. Taylor had obviously gotten a call out to Villarreal's reserve forces before leaving the room with Eden and was stalling for time.

"This is Prime," Fallon lowered his voice to the minimum level of comprehension before establishing contact, hoping to remain undetected by the man on the stairs above him. "Buy me some time . . . two mikes, minimum."

"Will do," Taz acknowledged.

Two minutes. A pitifully short time for someone like Eden Walker, whose continued life or sudden and brutal death hung on actions beyond her control within those collective increments of time. But for a vampire — a virtual immortal — a proverbial drop in the bucket. And, for Fallon, more than enough time.

CHAPTER NINETEEN

"On your knees, little piggy."

Eden felt the collar around her throat jerk as Taylor pulled on the chain. She blinked, trying to make sense of his words. The drugs he'd forced between her lips just after the windows in the bedroom had shattered clouded her mind, making it hard to concentrate.

"Do you see her, Wylde?" Taylor's voice rose and Eden frowned, struggling to focus, to see who he was talking to. He ran a finger down her arm. "Do you like my little pet pig? Another yank on the collar and she dropped to her knees. "I thought about takin' your choice little piece, you know? Seeing them play together woulda been a sight to behold."

She felt his hand rest on her head and tensed, but he only petted her like a favourite dog. "With a bit of training, her sister could be just as talented."

Sister? The word sunk into her mind and an image of her twin flashed before her eyes.

"Ro . . . Rowan?" She whispered the name, her voice hoarse from lack of use.

The hand on her head clenched and he yanked her hair until her neck bent backwards and her face was gazing upwards.

"I *never* told you to speak, pig. Your mouth is for one thing only and talking isn't it."

Fallon had to give the son of a bitch credit. Taylor was on the razor's edge, a heartbeat away from losing his shit. But somehow, he managed to stay in character. Force of habit, most probably. For someone with his longevity, and taking into account his lifestyle and chosen endeavour, this was more than likely not the first time he had faced the possibility of oblivion.

But it was different now. This was the first time he'd ever had to face it without the comforting certainty of a support mechanism. No back-up.

This time he was alone.

Fallon, however, *wasn't*. In this scenario, he had an ally. Although she wasn't completely, or entirely, aware of it yet.

Fallon kicked the *umbra* up a notch with a peal of taunting laughter.

"*Fool!* Torturing her won't help," he said, his own confidence rising as Taylor's heartbeat ramped up another two degrees. Heart attack territory if he were Human.

"Maybe . . . maybe not," Taylor replied. "But the question is . . . can *you* afford to take that chance, solider? I remember the talk we had on the phone," he continued. "How'd it go? You not wanting to stain your sterling reputation? How big a stain would it make if the world knew Fallon Wylde failed an assignment outta stupidity? Outta stubbornness?

"I'll slice her, Fallon. Cut off both ears . . . both her tits . . . then gut her like the catch of the day. And *you*, Young Blood, ain't quick enough to stop me."

Fallon smiled as the sounds of distant gunfire erupted beyond the walls.

Time, he said inwardly, and stuffed the short sword into the back of his waistband, tossed the remainder of his gear – still wrapped in the pool towel – onto the floor, and moved out to make himself visible to Taylor.

"Hear that?" Fallon allowed Taylor to see him drop the Beretta to the floor and started upwards, arms outstretched. "That's my people dealing with Villarreal's reinforcements. Your back-up's been backed up," he laughed. "It's just us now – you and me and *Eden*."

At the mention of her name, Eden looked up and made eye contact with the man on the stairs. A stranger. But there was something about him. Something in his eyes . . .

Fallon ascended the stairs with purposeful ease; not swift enough to be gauged by Taylor as threatening, but fast enough to be mindful of the time involved.

"You know it doesn't have to be this way, Brother," Taylor said as Fallon drew nearer. "Okay, so I had the piggy's sister iced. She was a *mortal*, man. Human cattle. Come *on*, Fallon. A guy like you . . . a *player* like you? You can pick up one like her off any street corner. They're a fuckin' dime a dozen. Not worth the pain, or the blood . . ." he paused to gauge Fallon's reaction. The man in question, however, showed not a single sign of being affected – good, bad or indifferent – nor did he slow in his approach.

"Why do you care?" Taylor continued. "Compared to them, we're *gods*. They're entrées on the menu and we own the restaurant. What does one steak or breadstick mean in the grand scheme?"

"Let the girl go, Taylor," Fallon said, moving ever closer.

Closer now to the top landing, two things were noticeable. The first was the glove on Taylor's left hand. It brought back something Tigr had mentioned during their initial talk in the Shadows of Night lounge.

From what I heard, it was to cover up really bad burn scars which probably happened before he was turned, she'd said.

Bad burns. Chances are it also meant the muscles and cartilage hadn't healed properly, which explained the fact that while his thumb was curled around the hilt of the blade he held at Eden's throat, the remaining fingers were straightened, knitted against it. Could be his grip on the dagger wasn't as secure as Taylor wanted it to be appear.

And two. Eden. Looking into her eyes, Fallon saw someone who may have been a lot more lucid than her captor counted on. Either the drugs he'd been pumping into her were beginning to lose their hold or, somehow, the girl had found the inner strength to resist them.

Hopefully, and for what was to come, Fallon was banking on the latter.

"Okay, alright then. Here's one for you – a win-win," Taylor attempted to negotiate as Fallon moved relentlessly forward. "How 'bout this? I had your girlfriend iced, you destroyed my business deal. We call it even . . . I give you the pig here," he yanked Eden's leash for emphasis, "and you let me walk outta here. Deal?"

Fallon stopped, three steps short of the landing, within arm's reach of the girl. Within that distance depending on Eden's clarity of mind and her resistance to the drugs in her system, Taylor's grip on the dagger at her throat and Fallon's own speed, one of two things could happen. Either a sliced jugular and immediate death for Eden or a very nasty wound and a scar that would mar her looks for as long as she lived. At least with the second option, though Fallon would rather avoid it, she would live.

Down to the wire, as Taz had put it earlier.

Now or never, Fallon thought and, with a slight vote of confidence brought on by the pressure of the short sword against his spine, he placed a foot on the step above him.

To coin a time-honoured idiomatic phrase, Taylor heart was suddenly in his throat. Another phrase wafted through Fallon's mind – *time to give the Devil his due.* Though he put up a half-convincing front, the air around Taylor and Eden swam with the smell of stomach-clenching fear.

"Even? Not even close," Fallon said, his voice soft, and brought his arms down slowly. "I got news for you, no score for the visiting team. Your right-hand man, Janiss, he's a stain on a set of couch cushions. He showed up to wrap up a loose end and I took care of him."

Eden's eyelids fluttered.

"And Tigr . . . the loose end? I tied that one up for you. Opened her up like a cheap suitcase. And your hitter?"

Eden's eyes opened, finally rising to meet his.

"He did a damn half-ass job," Fallon continued. "*Rowan* is very much alive . . . *brother*. Looks like it's Visitors zero, Home Team five."

And in the fleeting moment of silence which followed, the look of smug confidence on Taylor's face began to melt, his eyes narrowed, and his gloved fingers attempted to tighten on the dagger's hilt.

"Ru-Ro? Alive?" Eden whispered. "Is . . . true?"

Fallon nodded.

"*I told you not to speak, pig!*" Taylor growled, giving the leash a savage yank. At which point Eden answered with a snarl of her own, twisted her head sideways, away from the blade, and sank her teeth into his upper wrist.

"*BITCH!* I'll kill—" Taylor roared and attempted to break her grip. As he did so, he twisted rightward, exposing his left arm – the leash arm. Within seconds, Fallon drew the short sword and, in a move he would later confess was equal parts luck and experience, took off Taylor's gloved hand from mid-forearm down.

Taylor froze for a moment, in shock and disbelief, staring at the cleaved shirt sleeve and bloodied stump that was once his arm and lunged forward past Fallon, howling in pain as he half-tumbled half-slid down the staircase.

Eden, meanwhile, scrambled in the opposite direction. Still mostly under the influence of Taylor's drugs, she struggled weakly to rid herself of the restraining collar. She crawled into the nearest corner of the corridor, back against the wall.

Fallon took a moment, a brief glance, to ensure the girl was unscathed before setting his sights and all of his senses on the next task at hand.

~*~

It was probably a combination of the pain from his injury and his shaky attempts to apply a belt as a tourniquet to stem the blood loss that prevented Taylor from detecting Fallon's approach until he was almost on top of him. He stood at the bar, back facing the all but decimated living room, uttering low grunts and mumbling to himself while tightening the belt at his upper harm. Fallon patiently allowed him to finish the task before loudly clearing his throat.

Taylor swung around without hesitation, simultaneously delving into the waistband of his blood-splattered trousers to extract a weapon – a Beretta. *Fallon's* Beretta, in point of fact. The one he'd left behind prior to their confrontation on the stairs.

"Gonna pay for this, deadman," he croaked, indicating his bloodied stump while, at the same time, bringing the gun's muzzle up to aim in Fallon's general direction. Although his grip may have been firm, his focus was shaky. Again, the pain from his injury, plus the doubtlessly severe loss of blood detracted from the strength needed to hold, let alone accurately aim, the weapon.

Fallon gave his head a contradicting shake. "*My* gun, by the way," he jerked his chin at the weapon. "ProMag Beretta, M92F, ten round magazine, ten silver, soaked in concentrated garlic rounds. I fired off a few shots earlier, so there's less than a full clip. But all you need is one. And that said . . . " he took a step closer and to the right. "I don't have time for the classic good guy bad guy face to face final showdown banter. You got about a sixty-forty chance of getting through this alive. Meaning . . . *over my dead body*."

Fallon moved again. Faster this time. And Taylor began firing.

The first round blazed through air less than an inch from Fallon's left. And Fallon moved closer, in a zig-zagging pattern, that brought the next two rounds past his right temple. The fourth round cut a groove in the top of his left shoulder, one that burned like hell, and the fifth, an even deeper and more painful groove in his right side, almost spinning him around. And then, finally, came the distinct and all too welcome *chok!* As the slide assembly locked back on an emptied clip.

If not for the fiery discomfort of his own wounds, Fallon might have been tempted to smile at the rapidly flashing expressions of surprise, annoyance and, lastly, stark wide-eyed horror on Taylor's face following the realisation that he was out of ammo and that, more importantly, his target was still alive.

Fallon deftly plucked the Beretta from Taylor's hand and tossed it onto the bar beside him. He easily blocked the growling vampire's pathetic attempt to deliver a defensive punch, catching his wrist in mid-swing. A lightning-swift and powerful headbutt broke Taylor's nose and sent him back against the bar, flailing with his uninjured arm to hold his footing.

"You sonufabitch I'll GAHHHH!" Taylor's blood-snuffling curse was instantly transformed into a gurgling howl as Fallon slammed the short sword's pommel into his exposed stump . . .

"*Ohhhh JESUS!!!*"

. . . following through by burying the sword's blade in the man's thigh.

"I. Really. Don't. Think. He's. Taking. Any. Calls. At. The. Moment," Fallon said, punctuating each word with a head-snapping punch to Taylor's face that drove him along the bar's front surface, and closer to the floor with each one.

He stepped back after the last blow, gazing down at the red and pulpy mess he'd made of the man's face with a sense of rage-tinged displeasure. With a vampire of Taylor's longevity – even though it wasn't visually evident – his injuries were only a stopgap measure. Even now, they were beginning to heal and, in a matter of hours, his pretty boy blond features would appear as perfect as a Hollywood glamour photo. The arms, too, would have started to re-emerge.

"You know what . . . Skippy," Fallon squatted over Taylor's bloodied, prone form and hauled him up by his shirtfront so that he was propped against the base of the bar. "You know that one line in every action movie where somebody says '*nothing personal*,'" Fallon yanked the sword free, bringing a sudden, startled yelp from a barely conscious Taylor, and stood up. "Not this time."

His gaze fell upon the infamous ruby ear-clip and with an eyebrow twitching smirk the blade flashed forward, leaving a glistening red crater where the ear had once been.

"Say Goodnight, Gracie," he whispered and buried the blade to the hilt in Taylor's chest, holding it there until the body had ceased its death writhings.

~*~

"No . . . please . . . " Eden whimpered in dread, as Fallon knelt in front of her.

"Hey . . . *hey*, it's alright," Fallon assured her gently, taking her trembling hands in his. "Look at me, Eden." He waited until her breathing slowed, then carefully reached out and tilted her chin up until their eyes met. "It's over, okay? I'm a friend of your sister's . . . of Rowan. You'll see her soon."

"Ta—" she swallowed, clearly struggling to speak. "Taylor?"

"Don't worry about him. He can't hurt you anymore . . . and that's a promise," he answered. "Come on," he urged, helping her stand.

An examination of the leash and dog collar revealed that while the former was attached by a simple bolt snap and swivel ring, the collar itself was fitted with a combination lock. The kind of device which instilled both a physical and psychological humiliation on its wearer.

Fallon detached and tossed the leash and Taylor's still firmly attached and rapidly decomposing gloved hand.

The least I can do, he told himself.

The collar would have to wait until they were out of this hellhole.

Eden's first steps were unsteady. Her legs nearly buckled beneath her, in fact, and she would surely have taken a header down the stairs if not for Fallon's strong arms and vampire reflexes.

"Easy there, I got you," Fallon said, supporting her against his hip and an arm around her waist. He eased them both back to the wall, intending to sit her down again and wait until she had gained a bit more strength. And, as he did so, his fingers came into contact with something noticeably odd on her back . . . something along her spine.

Scars were his first thought. Apart from the collar she was as naked as the day she was born, and it was impossible not to notice the multitude of ugly blemishes, both old and recent, that stood out on her fair complexion and covered her body from neck to ankles.

This one, however, had both height and depth. It felt ridged, as if the flesh had been rended.

"Eden . . . " He waited until she met his gaze before he continued. "I need to see." Another long pause before she nodded jerkily and allowed him to ease her forward. And what he saw sparked a blaze of both shock and anger that filled him from the pinnacle of his conscious mind to the depths of his soul.

Etched down her back, from the top of her spine to the midpoint of her back, were branded the words '*WHORE*' and '*Urât*' – a rough translation, and in the combined Human-Vampire tongue, meant 'nasty whore'. A practice from olden times, the days of vampire robber barons who ruled entire regions of villages and regularly took their sons, wives and daughters for his/her harem. They were branded as such so they could never return to their people or be claimed by another vampire.

Fuck.

His fingertips ran across the words and he felt Eden stiffen under his touch seconds before she whirled around to face him. Her hand grasped his arm in a grip that surprised him, considering the amount of drugs that had to be swimming through her system.

"You must not," she stopped, swallowed and tried again. "Rowan must . . . not know." Her eyes caught and held his. Eyes that were so much like Rowan's, Fallon realised, that he couldn't help but imagine Rowan in Eden's place.

"Promise me," she continued, her voice low and raspy. "This is . . . my penance."

"Penance?" Fallon repeated. "Eden, are you sure it's—"

"*Promise!*"

He could have argued further, but if anyone in this world understood the need for atonement, he surely did. Their eyes held and then Fallon nodded abruptly. At his wordless agreement, Eden let loose a soft sigh and, almost as if needing his acknowledgement had been the only thing keeping her lucid, her eyes emptied and her body slumped forward.

With a lingering look at the brand on her back, Fallon made a quick but necessary trip to the nearest bedroom. The room, as it happened, was occupied by the vampire whom Fallon had sent to deliver his ultimatum to Taylor. Fallon found him cowering in a corner near the wardrobe.

The wardrobe's double doors were ajar. Fallon opened them wide and selected a man's gaudy red lounging robe, mostly probably Villarreal's, from the rack and draped it over his shoulder. He turned to regard the man in the corner.

"What's your name, *hombre?*" he asked.

"Raúl . . . Raúl Eduardo."

"Eduardo . . . it means 'protector'," Fallon said, locking eyes with the obviously terrified man. "Listen up, Eduardo. I'm taking this robe out to cover the lady in the hallway. We'll be leaving here soon, and Villarreal's people will be coming. I'm pretty sure they won't be happy with what they find. They'll be looking for someone to blame. *Entender?*"

"Si, senor, I understand, completely."

"My advice – gather up any of your people who survived and leave this place," Fallon told him. "As quickly as you can."

~*~

Taz, Morgan, Dev and – Fallon couldn't help but smile – Rowan were swiftly approaching the house when Fallon emerged with Eden in his arms.

"You're bleeding, amigo," Taz pointed out as Dev moved in to take the limp and still unconscious girl off his hands. Fallon flashed the Nikaran prince the unspoken, facial equivalent of '*duh*' before turning his gaze to Rowan, watching as she paused in front of Dev to look down at the still form of her sister.

"How bad is she?"

Fallon moved to stand beside her. "We won't know for sure until we get her checked out. She was lucid . . . for a little while."

She nodded and reached out a hand to touch Eden's cheek. "Thank you, Fallon."

"I made you a pro—" his words cut off as Rowan's fist connected with his jaw. Before he could react to the punch, she pressed her lips to his in a quick kiss.

"We thought something had happened to you!" she told him. "Don't *ever* do that to me again!" Her eyes dropped to the blood seeping through his shirt. "And you're hurt . . . oh my god, shouldn't you have healed already?"

"Silver bullet. It's fine, just a flesh wound," Fallon stroked a finger down her cheek. "Taylor managed to grab my gun and—"

"*Dude*, you got shot by your own weapon?" Dev snorted a laugh. "That's a rookie mistake."

CHAPTER TWENTY

Six hours, twenty minutes later . . .

It was a race against sunrise on their trip back to Seattle. And at 4:10AM, the Thoth Airlines private Lear jet touched down and tooled into its private docking space five minutes later.

The group were met by Pantera Rydell the Shadowfall's Chief of Security officer, who used Kane's contacts at the airport to get the group through Customs, then herded them all into limousines for the trip back to the club.

When Rowan stopped beside the car Eden was placed in, Fallon caught her arm and tugged her gently away.

"But—"

"While I'm confident nothing is going to happen, I don't want you travelling in the same car just in case Taylor made contingency plans. I think he was too arrogant to really believe we could get Eden away from him, but he was sly enough to have something in place should anything happen to him," he told her, opening the door to the next car in the queue.

"You think we might still be targeted?" she asked him, sharply.

"Truthfully? No, but if we ignore the possibility and all get in the same car, and something *does* happen . . . " he left the sentence hanging, and waited for Rowan to come to her own conclusion.

She stood, one hand on the door, her gaze looking beyond him and at the car Dev was entering. "Can he be trusted?"

Fallon glanced behind him. "Dev? Yes, for all his faults, I believe he can."

Rowan nodded. "Okay," she bent and settled onto the back seat, sliding across so Fallon could sit beside her.

As the car pulled away from the kerb, Fallon leaned forward and opened a small door which revealed a self-contained bar within the divider between front and back. He selected a bottle of El Dorado rum and poured a glass, tipping the bottle toward Rowan with a raised eyebrow.

Rowan shook her head. "I don't know how you can drink that stuff."

"I developed a taste for it over the years." Fallon smiled faintly. "It *is* the preferred drink of pirates, after all." He took a long, savouring swallow before returning to his seat beside her. Rowan immediately shifted across the seat to curl up against his side, and he draped his free arm across her shoulders.

"I still can't believe you got her out. Do you think . . . " she paused, her teeth worrying at her bottom lip. "Will she be okay?"

Fallon let his mind drift over the events that had played out only hours earlier; to the scars, bruises and marks across the girl's body and the methods Taylor had used to keep control. "Taylor is dead, she's free. I wish I could tell you everything will be fine, but I don't know, Ro."

Rowan reached up to where his hand lay on her shoulder and linked her fingers with his. "She's alive, though," she said, softly. "That's a start. Anything else is a bonus, right?"

"Right," Fallon echoed, and silence fell for the rest of the journey.

~*~

Shadowfall – two hours later . . .

A drink. A steaming hot shower. Eight-plus hours of serious sleep. These were the things that called out to him – which taunted and pushed at his inner being – as Fallon emerged from Shadowfall's Operations complex, or more accurately, Dr. Chambeau's med centre, and made his way across the club's uncommonly deserted lobby.

Uncommon in that, in all the years he'd patronised and been associated with the now pre-eminent Seattle venue, he couldn't recall a time when its virtually cathedral-like entrance hall did not contain at the very least a dozen end-of-shift employees or last call drunks or, where the hardcore vampire regulars were concerned, dawn dancers.

Now he counted two, both human and members of the dayshift cleaning crew, emptying rubbish bins and shampooing the carpets while he awaited the arrival of an elevator car. But then it was well past sunrise and anyone who had physiological issues with Sol's lethal light and UV radiation would have long since sought the protection of sun shielded accommodation and the comforts of consenting companionship and a soft mattress.

For the past two hours he had been afforded the former while having his wounds tended to by Shadowfall's fetching Cajun wunderkind of vampire ills and Chief of Medicine, Dr. Arlette Chambeau, who administered her own unpatented but never failing cure for silver poisoning and a robust feeding from one of Chef

Andre's lingering functionaries. And as for the latter, the soft mattress was waiting, minutes away and two floors above. The companionship would come later. Rowan, at his insistence, would be taking advantage of one of the med centre's guest rooms to stay close to her sister.

There were a pair of written messages waiting for him, taped to the bar, when Fallon entered his suite. One which read . . .

Fire in the hole. Call me the moment you return
E

. . . E was, of course, Eayann. And . . .

Breakfast at LaDonna's . . . 9ish.

. . . No signature, but the handwriting was instantly recognisable as Kane's.

Fallon tossed both into the trash basket behind the bar, then poured himself a brimming therapeutic glass of Ronrico Caribbean Rum Gold and downed half the glass in a single gulp.

Fire in the hole. In military jargon, it was a warning that an explosion, a detonation in a confined space was imminent. A catchphrase or warning for '*watch out!*' or '*heads up*'. In the case of his long association with Eayann Ó Beolláin, it was code for '*brace yourself, trouble coming*'.

And why should that surprise him?

In hindsight, looking back on everything that had happened over the last two days, it was Shadowfall. Unofficially the unsanctioned House of Thoth. A place constantly under the eye of the Vampire Nation's Parliament of Lords, as well as all the Houses. For varying and sundry reasons, Kane Thoth and his empire were to vampire kind what the Kardashians, Harvey Weinstein and the Trump-Russian scandal was to the mainstream media. The grapevine worked overtime, and everyone was plugged into it.

Without question, Fallon knew that everyone had heard about his quest to find Rowan's sister. There was speculation, at least, as to his relationship with Rowan herself, that she had been the intended target of an unsuccessful assassination, that she may have been turned . . . and by his business associate, no less. There was *mucho* speculation concerning the involvement of a certain outlaw vampire known only as Taylor.

Gossip was like a Kansas tornado – a powerful, whirling force of mayhem and uncertainty. Uncertain or not, it had a penchant for making certain highborn and official personages uncomfortable.

Something he should be concerned about . . . maybe.

But not for the time being.

Drink?

Fallon downed the remainder of his rum and poured himself another, downing it in a single gulp. Next a soothing, scalding shower and afterwards he'd slide between the cool sheets of his bed and let sleep overtake him.

Tomorrow would take care of itself.

~*~

Warm hands sliding down across his chest woke him and his reaction was immediate.

Grasp, twist, flip and pin.

A soft surprised exhale sounded as the newcomer was held captive beneath the weight of his body.

"You're supposed to be down in the med centre." Fallon didn't ease his grip on the wrists he had pinned above the red hair spilling across his pillow.

"Eden's asleep. They'll call me if she wakes." She tried to pull her hands free and frowned slightly when he didn't release her. "Are you going to let go?"

Fallon gazed down at the woman below him, eyes sliding over features that had become important to him in such a short time. A smile tugged at his lips when he recognised the pyjamas she wore as the same ones she had on the first night she shared his bed.

"Fallon?" His name brought his eyes back up to hers and his smile broadened.

"No, I don't think I am."

He shifted his weight onto the arm he was using to hold her wrists and brought his other hand up to brush her cheek. His fingers traced down across her jaw, stroked down her throat and down further into the shadowed valley between her breasts.

Rowan didn't say a word as he deftly flicked open the buttons of her top and pushed it aside. The breath arrested in his throat as he looked at her bared flesh, the nipples rosy and hard.

"Fallon," she murmured his name, arching her back as his eyes swept over her.

He bent his head, lowered his mouth and caught one nipple between his teeth, nipping at the sensitive peak and drawing a gasp from Rowan. His fingers circled the other nipple, stroking inwards before thumb and forefinger caught the tip, tugged upwards and twisted slightly. Rowan moaned, her hips shifting restlessly against the leg pressed between her thighs. His mouth and fingers moved relentlessly, nipping, tugging, twisting until Rowan was moaning and writhing beneath him. All the while he kept her hands pinned securely above her head.

Lifting his head, he swept his gaze over her flushed features and, for no more than a second, the imprint of the bruises, scars and marks that covered her sister's body overlaid Rowan's.

Fallon froze, icy fingers of fear slithering down his spine. *That could have been Rowan.* He shook his head, dismissing the image, but not quickly enough. Rowan's eyes caught his and when she tugged her hands, he released them immediately.

What was he doing? Holding her down . . .

Her fingers curved over his cheeks. "What was *that* look?" she asked.

"You should go back to medical," he ignored her question and rolled onto his back. "Eden needs you."

"Eden doesn't need me, Eden is sleeping," Rowan responded. She sat up and twisted to glower down at Fallon.

"Look, it's nothing," He swung his legs around and off the bed, until he perched on the bedside. A self-conscious glance over his shoulder revealed a look from Rowan that, strangely enough, partially thawed the sudden freeze within him.

"Fallon?" Rowan prompted, reaching out to stroke his back.

"The things he did . . . the things he liked to do. If I lost control, I could become him . . . "

"No!" Rowan's denial was instant. "Where is this coming from?"

"You didn't hear him, Rowan. He recognised the monster in me."

He felt the bed dip as she moved, then her hands slid over his shoulders to wrap around him from behind.

"You know that's not true."

"Isn't it? He put a collar around her neck, Ro, and led her around like a prized pet." He clenched his fists. "I put a collar on you."

"Yes, you did." Her hands smoothed down his arms, over muscles locked up tight. "But it was silk, not metal."

"I hit you."

"You *spanked* me," she corrected. "And, I'm sure, at some point you'll want to tie me up, too." She slid off the bed and moved to stand in front of him. "Look at me, Fallon." Her fingers touched his cheek. "I need you to hear what I'm saying to you." She waited until his eyes lifted to meet hers. "I'll let you spank me, tie me up, do whatever you want to do because I *trust* you. You won't do anything I don't want, Fallon, and that makes you *nothing* like him."

Fallon snaked out an arm and wrapped it around her waist, pulling her forward between his thighs and rested his head against her stomach.

"I don't deserve you," he murmured.

He felt her hand run through his hair. "No, you don't," she told him, her voice matter-of-fact. "Especially after I came up here in my sexy elephant pyjamas, which I know you love so much, to seduce you."

Fallon laughed, surprising himself. "You could wear a trash bag and I'd be seduced." He rubbed his cheek against the soft skin of her stomach. "Seriously, though, if I ever . . . "

"Stop it. You don't scare me, Fallon. You bark and you snarl, but underneath it all, you're just marshmallow."

"Marshmallow?"

"Yeah, soft and sweet, and gooey and sticky and . . . " she shrieked when he moved too fast to stop and she ended up on her back bouncing on the bed with Fallon poised above her.

"And what?" he asked.

"And addictive," she whispered, and wound her arms around his neck to pull his head down to hers.

~*~

He awoke to the sound of . . . nothing.

And how long had it been since that last happened?

Welcomed, comfortable, stressless *quiet*.

Stretching catlike, with arms and legs spread wide, Fallon discovered three things. First the bed, save himself, was empty.

Rowan was gone. Physically, anyway, but her scent lingered, permeating the entire room, in fact. Second, he was pleasantly sore in a number of places. Testament to the ferocity of the past night's/early morning's passionate romp with the aforementioned and currently absent young woman.

And he'd been worried about hurting her!

And third, upon rolling onto his side in preparation to exit the bed, he discovered the note, tucked beneath his cell on the bedside table.

`Hey marshmallow. Eden woke up and freaked out, so that's my day so far. R x`

Fallon's lips twitched at the endearment, and he knew it was something she wasn't going to let him forget any time soon. Rising to his feet, he stretched and ran a hand through his hair. Turning, he caught sight of himself in the mirrored door of the wardrobe and froze, head tilting to one side as he studied his reflection.

The little minx had certainly done a number on his throat and chest. Bites and scratches, deep enough to draw blood and need time to heal, peppered his skin and he knew, if he checked, his back wouldn't have fared much better. But he found he couldn't raise any degree of concern over her passionate display. In fact, he was hard pressed not to grin like an idiot.

The grin remained intact throughout his shower, while he dressed and sauntered, finally, out into the main living room.

"Did you misplace your sense of urgency along with your understanding of how to stay *below the radar*?"

Fallon's head jerked up from where he had been fiddling with his shirt cuffs and his eyes landed on the larger-than-life figure seated at the bar.

~*~

"Don't come near me."

"It's just a blood test, Eden. Nothing more."

Rowan could hear the two voices long before she reached the room Eden had been placed in.

"No! no more needles."

She didn't *sound* scared, Rowan thought, as she walked down the corridor. In fact, her sister sounded furious. The crash of something hitting the ground had Rowan speeding up and throwing open the door just as Eden tried to yank it open from the other side.

The two sisters stared at one another. Eden broke eye contact first, her eyes moving sideways to look over Rowan's shoulder. Her arms wrapped around her stomach and she stepped backwards, out of Rowan's reach.

"The doctor is just trying to help you," Rowan broke the silence, closing the door gently behind her. "They're trying to figure out what drugs were in your system, to make it easier to . . . "

"Clean me up, yes I know how it works," Eden snapped. "This isn't my first rodeo, Rowan."

"It's different this time."

"Is it?" Eden's eyes glittered with an emotion Rowan didn't recognise. "Why don't you tell me all about how different it is? Because you've experienced this *so many times*." Her eyes swung back to the doctor moving slowly toward her. "I *told* you no more needles."

"What do you want to do, Eden?" Rowan asked. "Are you hungry? I can get some food."

Eden shook her head. "I want . . . " her hands came up to clutch the sides of her head, and she closed her eyes. "I need everyone to stop looking at me," she whispered.

Rowan exchanged glances with the doctor, who eased forward silently and injected Eden before she could stop her.

"What did you . . . I said no more . . . " Eden staggered, one hand reaching out to grasp the bed. "I can't . . . " her eyes fluttered closed and the doctor caught her before she fell to the floor and eased her onto the bed.

"Don't worry," she told Rowan. "I just gave her something to calm her down, let her sleep for a while."

Rowan gave the doctor a tired smile. "If only that would fix everything."

~*~

Larger than life.

In this instance an understatement of the highest order.

Her Majesty Queen Elizabeth II of England, Winston Churchill, JFK, Albert Einstein, Richard Attenborough, Dame Judi Dench, Helen Mirren, Sean Connery, Morgan Freeman, Denzel Washington, Barack Obama, Marvin Gaye, Frank Sinatra – *they* were larger than life.

The woman who graced the high stool at his bar the way Leonardo da Vinci's Mona Lisa graced Paris' Louvre Museum was the antithesis of comparative scale. She was, in true essence, beyond the scope of Life and the true essence of legend.

She was Marjean Sălbatica - also known as Marjean of Anglesey – monarch of the House of Sasul and, more to the current situation, Fallon's sire. Ever the impressive mesh of regal vampiric potentate and seductive temptress, she curled one sinuous mocha limb over the other and extended one hand outward, the hand which contained the House's bejewelled signet ring.

"And have we forgotten our manners, young squire?"

She was not alone, he noticed. Just beyond her, at the bars end, Eayann stood as stiff and expressionless as a military cadet in the presence of a visiting general. And beyond Eayann, on either side of the suite's entrance, were a pair of equally ramrod straight vampires in the one-piece black, web-belted coverall and bloused booted garb which identified them as House Sasul *Archeoni* . . . Archons – police officers. And perched on a sofa, one of Fallon's least favourite people – top of the list, in fact – the Sasul Advisory Council's chief hatchet man, Aiden Gorrie.

"No, *we* haven't. But it looks like maybe *you* did," Fallon answered, throwing a look at the hatchet man, a look whose meaning no-one had to guess. "You brought that ass-biting *Feciora* into my—"

"*FALLON!*" Eayann barked loudly. "You are in the presence of the Lady! Your *sirenă*. That disrespect . . . that *language* . . ." His words trailed off as Marjean raised a hand.

"Remember Aiden, old man?" Fallon said, his tone low and strained as he slowly moved toward the sofa. "Remember what I promised I'd do if you *ever* came within ten feet of me again?"

Gorrie squirmed on the cushions, eye flitting back and forth nervously from Eayann to Marjean. "I was just . . . just doing my job. I had *orders*."

Fallon snorted. "Orders. And you enjoyed it, didn't you? A little too much from what I hear."

"He's right, Spaniard. It's done now – ancient history. Stand down," Eayann said, and moved to intercept his long-time associate. The look in Fallon's eyes, however, stopped him in his tracks. He turned instead to Marjean, his own eyes both quizzical and pleading.

The Lady, it seemed, had no intention whatsoever of intervening.

"Ten lashes with the — what did you call it?" Fallon said, getting closer with each second. "The little silver bitch . . ." Almost there — within a foot, in fact — when Gorrie leapt to his feet and began backing away. "Ten lashes was the punishment. But *you* threw in three extra . . . for good measure."

"I — I didn't mean . . . I'm sorry," Gorrie stammered, both hands raised in front of him.

"You know Aiden," Fallon continued. "You really should be more careful. Check your surroundings when you mouth-off later. How did you put it - *if it were left up to me, the little Spanish cunt would have to unbutton his shirt to shit.*"

"*Dammit* Fallon!" Eayann snarled.

"*Fuck off* Eayann!" Fallon snarled back.

"*ENOUGH!*" Marjean's husky contralto echoed through the room, catching Fallon seconds away from striking. "Diego."

Fist clenched, arm cocked, Fallon reacted slowly to her usage of his true name, head swivelling to meet her gaze.

"Believe me, you're in enough trouble. He's not worth it."

Gorrie, now beet-red faced, quivering like half-frozen Jell-O and on the verge of pissing himself, loosed an audible sigh as Fallon reluctantly eased off.

"Councilman Gorrie," Marjean said. "I think it would be . . . advisable if you retire to one of the club's café's for refreshments, don't you?"

"Y-yes, yes M'Lady. I am . . . I will. Yes," Gorrie stuttered, all but running for the door.

A door which opened before he reached it.

All sets of eyes swung to watch, both Archons stiffening and their hands dropping to the guns at their hips.

"Fallon, I'm—" Rowan walked into the room and stopped mid-sentence, stumbling back as Gorrie crashed into her. One of the Archon soldiers caught her elbow, saving Rowan from hitting the ground.

"Thank you," she said to the guard, sending a look in Eayann's direction that had the older Vampire fighting a smile. "Eayann," she greeted him. "You're back and you brought . . . friends?" She didn't wait for him to reply, her eyes seeking out and finding Fallon, where he stood fist still clenched, eyes on Gorrie. She followed the direction of Fallon's glare and looked at the man who had almost knocked her off her feet.

"What did *you* do to deserve that look?" she asked him, curiously. "If he could kill through thought alone, you'd definitely be a warm wet mess on the carpet right about now."

Ignoring the tension that had the small hairs rising on the back of her neck, she stepped around the stranger and made her way across the room to stand beside Fallon. "Are you okay?" she asked. She reached out and curved her hand around his fist.

Unnoticed by Rowan, Marjean watched in silence as Fallon slowly lowered his arm and tilted his head to look down at the redhead.

"I'm fine," Fallon's eyes briefly caught Eayann's before dipping down to focus on Rowan. "How was Eden?"

Rowan sighed. "Freaking out. The doctor gave her something, she's sleeping now. I don't know what to do, Fallon. The doctors say it's not going to be easy, they don't know what all the different drugs in her system are, so withdrawal is going to be hard. They're not sure she's healthy enough to . . ." she faltered, closing her eyes. "I just don't know."

Marjean's cleared throat instantly garnered their attention. "If I may interrupt? The person you speak of . . . the girl Fallon brought back from Mexico?"

"My sister, Eden," Rowan answered.

"Then you must be the young woman I have been hearing so much about," Marjean's gaze switched to Fallon, silently prompting.

"Ro . . . Rowan," he slid a hand to the base of her spine, directing her toward the bar. "May I introduce Lady Marjean. My sire."

Rowan hesitated, visibly wary, which prompted Marjean to smile and reach out with both hands. "It's all right. I don't bite. Come here, child. Let me look at you."

"You can look at me just fine from there," Rowan replied, making no attempt to move closer.

"Rowan," Fallon's voice held a note of warning.

"What? She's your sire . . . that means she turned you into a vampire, right?" She waited for Fallon's nod. "What does she want? A medal?" She flashed him a quick grin. "Okay, fine . . . thanks are in order for that. I mean . . . *look* at you. It would have been a waste to have not –"

"Rowan!" Fallon spoke over her, effectively cutting off her tirade. "She's also the head of our House."

Rowan looked blank and Fallon sighed.

"This is fascinating," Marjean joined the conversation. "Have you educated her in *nothing*? Is this something else we need to add to your ever-growing list of problems?"

"It's been a busy few days," Fallon muttered, defensively.

"Yes, it has. Why don't we discuss that?" Marjean rose to her feet and turned toward the two soldiers standing silently beside the door. "Please leave. Eayann, you too. Fallon—"

"No."

One elegantly shaped eyebrow rose. "No? You would defy me?"

"On this, yes." Fallon folded his arms and stepped forward, placing himself between Rowan and Marjean.

"I . . . see." Again, one sculpted eyebrow rose as the young newborn vampire woman pressed herself against Fallon's side and he wound an arm around her. "Then, by all means, stay," Marjean announced, waving a dismissive hand. "Everyone else . . . out."

~*~

"Um . . . Uh-hmm," Lord Zuron Dasmalle I'Ane grunted contentedly, very much impressed as he perused the satellite photos from the aftermath in the Oaxaca mountains, and as he finished with each one, he passed it to the man beside him, his friend and Chief of Security, Hamish Satori.

"Excellent, if I do say so myself," Hamish commented.

"I'll say one thing for Wylde," said Zuron. "Nothing I've heard about him accurately does the man justice. This was precision work."

"My people couldn't have done a better job," Hamish agreed.

"I feel like I should be offended by that."

Hamish smiled at his daughter, who sat at one end of a couch which took up half the room. "You're more of a secret weapon than an official member of my detail." His eyes dropped to look at the man sprawled across the rest of the couch with his head in her lap. "Is he asleep?"

Morgan nodded. "Yes. He . . ." she paused and frowned. "He hasn't slept very well since we got back. Says his head hurts." Her fingers stroked through his hair as she spoke, and Hamish wondered if she even realised she was doing it.

The bond between their offspring seemed to be working perfectly. Although Hamish couldn't help but wonder. No bond was every without its hitches – and they knew so little about a blood bond. For a normal bond there were always bumps in an otherwise smooth road. Why should this one be any different?

"And the drug Wylde told us about?" Zuron's query interrupted the Necuno Lord's mental musings.

Morgan paused as Taz groaned softly at the sound of his father's voice, his body shuddering for a moment, and he pressed his face against her hip. She allowed his movements to subside before she spoke, smoothing a gentle hand across the top of his head.

"Well, Dev and Lochlan took care of the finished product, the outgoing shipments and the cargo helicopters. And, according to the debrief from Fallon on the trip home, he destroyed the laboratory and production centre beneath the house."

"Then nothing got out . . . Good!"

"I wouldn't say that exactly, sir." The uncertainty in Morgan's tone sent the heads of both her father and the elder vampire swivelling toward her.

"If everything we were led to believe about this Taylor is true," she continued, "and as you know, at one time he *was* Bianca Manx's right hand – there's *always* the possibility he had a backup plan, in case something like this happened."

"A valid concern." Both Zuron and Hamish responded exactly, in unison, with identical amused smiles.

"So, realistically, shall we say the file is not closed yet?" Zuron suggested.

Hamish gave an assenting nod. "I'll alert our people, worldwide, to remain watchful . . . just in case."

~*~

"I don't like her," Rowan declared as Fallon shut the bedroom door behind them.

In the brief moment that followed the requested departure of Eayann and the *Archeoni* guards, Marjean took a smartphone from her leather purse – Gucci, of course – draped across her immortally svelte frame and dismounted the barstool.

"To be fair, all those concerned should be present to hear what I have to tell you," she said and, with a dismissive wave, tapped out a number on the cell's face while simultaneously moving to one of the suite's more comfortable couches.

It was then that Fallon seized the opportunity to get in a little private time for Rowan and himself.

"And I don't like the way she talks to you," Rowan continued. "To *anybody* . . . who does she think she is? Lady Dracula, Vampire Queen or something!"

"As a matter of fact," Fallon couldn't help but grin at the newly-turned young vampire's fiery indignation. He was flattered, in fact, knowing that she – this feisty one-hundred-and-ten-pound vampire newborn – would stand up for him against one of the most powerful entities in the Vampire Nation. "She's not exactly a queen," he continued, "but she *is* the leader of the House of Sasul. My House, and the one you now belong to. So, do us both a favour," he reached out to give her chin a playful tweak, "dial it back a bit, okay?"

"I'll try," Rowan began, uncertainly, "but with the way Eden is and everything else that's been going on, I can't promise not to say something if she starts threatening you again."

"Threatening?" Fallon queried, an amused grin gradually dominating his features. "Just how much did you hear out there in the hall before you came in?"

The beginning of a sheepish grin quickly curved into a defiant frown. "Enough . . . well, nothing really. But I've worked in retail sales and customer service long enough to become pretty good at reading faces and body language. Eayann's, your sire's, *and* yours.

"And enough to know that her being here is something to do with me being turned by Koo. I'm one of you, now. People have been talking, *whispering*, and I can hear them. Koo broke the rules and—"

"Yes. She did," Fallon interrupted her. "Rules that have been in place for a very long time. And for good reason. She's my business associate . . . and my friend, and I failed to report it. Which makes me just as responsible in their eyes."

"I was dying. Would *have* died," Rowan pointed out. "Koo saved me. Doesn't that count for something?"

"It does . . . it *should*," Fallon sighed. "Out here, in the field, things aren't always black and white. But the 'suits' – and yes, even *we* have our bureaucracy – can't see the real world with their heads up their asses. That's why Marjean is here." He stopped to pull her close, looping his arms around her. "And don't be so quick to judge her. Marjean may come off as a royal bitch, but she walks a very thin tight rope. Give her a chance . . . alright?"

Rowan stared up at him for a long moment, both holding the other's eyes in silence. Eye contact finally severed when Rowan nodded and dropped her head against his chest.

The sound of knocking at the suite door, and a peal of strangely girlish laughter prompted Fallon and Rowan to return to the living room. They discovered, first, Marjean in a decidedly less official mood and demeanour in quiet and, apparently, pleasant conversation on her cell and, secondly, the arrival of Koo in the company of Shadowfall's Chief of Security, Pantera Rydell.

As the two couples converged on the room's midsection, Marjean briefly lowered her phone into the crook of her shoulder and waved them onward, pointing to the couch, opposite the one on which she sat, at the centre of the room. While Fallon and Rowan continued, Koo and Pantera held back, carrying on a muted exchange of their own. One that ended in a short, but passionate, embrace, a quick brush of lips, and Pantera's unquestioningly reluctant departure.

"Let's drop all the cards on the table, shall we? Down and dirty," Marjean said and slid off the couch in a move so graceful it looked almost choreographed. She moved in an arc, which brought her to a point in which she faced the gathering. "I could bore the shit out of you – myself included – by reciting the law, chapter and verse. But I'd rather not. So here it is, bare bones . . .

"You," she nodded to Koo. "In the eyes of the Executive Directorate, also known as the House of Sasul's Advisory Committee and Council of Legal Protocols – you, Kathryn Chan, Sire Unknown, brought over in 1810A.D. are guilty of utilising the abilities granted you as an entity officially designated as *inrudire*, and to the world at large as *vampire*, to adopt meaning 'turn' the female human known as Rowan Giselle Walker—"

"My name. My full name," Rowan spoke up. "How do you know – "

"Ro . . . let her talk," Fallon cut her off, then took hold of her hand and squeezed gently; a gesture meant to delay, if not extinguish the spark waiting to blossom into full-fledged fiery anger in the redhead's belly.

His attention then shifted back to Marjean. There was something there – not quite materialised, camouflaged – something he couldn't quite put his finger on, but there nonetheless. Something below the horizon of his sire's masked – to all but himself, that is – features. . . as if silently whispering '*wait for it*'.

In fact, and again in ways neither Koo nor Rowan would recognise, taking a mental step back to look at her more closely, the visual package which made Marjean . . . *Marjean* was more than a tad egress off her True North. From her hair – usually pulled back into an elaborately braided bun – now down around her shoulders, the jacket of her Anne Klein sheath dress that rested atop the bar, her doubtlessly high dollar Rodeo Drive pumps and special-order panty hose in a pile on the floor beneath one of the bar stools, and the bodice of her dress gaping wide on a stylish lace-weave bra. An appearance several notches removed from her norm *and* from her station as Sovereign of the House Sasul.

That, he knew, was neither random nor a lapse in judgement.

Marjean's eyes met Fallon's briefly and the ghost of a smile crossed her lips before she returned her attention to the young woman beside him.

"Do you know what happens when an unsanctioned adoption happens, Rowan Walker?"

Fallon tensed.

"In some cases, the poor unfortunate turnblood is . . ." she glanced down at her nails, frowning, "well, let's just say the problem gets removed."

"Removed?" Rowan queried. "Does that mean like . . .?"

"She means *permanently* removed," Koo joined the exchange. "Erased. Reversed. *Death.* As if the whole situation never happened."

Marjean gave a confirming sidelong nod. "She's correct, I'm afraid. Rather harsh, but that is the penalty. Part of it, in any case." Her attention returned, exclusively, to Koo. "As the violator, you would be sentenced to serve a term of not less than one, no longer than five years solitary imprisonment in the Nation's Carpathian facility."

"The Crypt? *Jesus*, Marjean! For a *first* offense?" Fallon was on his feet in a flash, fists clenched, mere seconds away from leaping over the coffee table before he stopped himself.

"The Crypt?" Rowan repeated. "What is that?"

There was a beat of weighty silence all around before Koo answered, slowly. "It's the nickname for our version of Pelican Bay and Sing Sing – state correctional institutions, where they send all our . . . hardcore cases. It's called The Crypt for two reasons. One because it's located deep inside the Carpathian Mountains in Eastern Europe; and two," she paused to pull in a deep, shuddering breath. ". . . Two, because like a burial chamber, few who enter ever come back out again."

"Is that what you want for—" Fallon resumed, only to be halted by Marjean's raised hand.

"Oh, it's gets better," she said softly, and began to move, to *pace* while speaking. "And *you*, my beloved problem child. And, again, this comes from the Council – based on reports they have been receiving. The name Fallon Wylde has been blazing through the streets of Seattle like a wildfire. Pun unintended," She gave an unamused laugh. "Fallon Wylde is off the reservation. He's finally cracked, gone apeshit crazy . . . *crazier*. He and a human female accomplice are responsible for at least four deaths. He is the cause of gunplay inside Club Shadowfall, which resulted in the mortal injury and unsanctioned adoption of his accomplice."

"*Accomplice?*" Rowan commented with a scornful *pffft*.

"I'm not finished," Marjean snapped. "The mortal injury, and unsanctioned adoption of his accomplice, which resulted in two additional retaliatory deaths. Both of which were carried out covertly within the walls of Shadowfall."

"I wonder what Kane will do when he finds out Sasul has eyes and ears inside his club," Fallon remarked, meeting his sire's gaze with a twitched eyebrow. "Fine, alright. That much *is* true. Two persons *were* interrogated and later killed, by *me*, here at Shadowfall. But Rowan is not and has *never* been my accomplice. And yeah, gunplay of a fashion. But there was no gun battle."

"And do you truly believe that I don't know that?" Marjean's response came with a headshake and a dry chuckle. "And, as far as Kane is concerned, I'm quite certain he is aware of our position. We *all* spy on each other. It's the nature of our existence.

"As to everything else. Eayann and Kane filled me in on what really happened. But with that aside, *I* know without question there is no way you would initiate a gun battle in the establishment of a man who is as much your brother as your best friend. And *you*," she turned to Koo, then. "Although you and I have never had the opportunity to become better acquainted, I am indeed aware of your story.

"I know that you, too, were brought back from the brink of death by a sire who then abandoned you to fend for yourself in the slums of Shanghai over two hundred years ago. And I imagine the memories of those days – before you met Fallon – are what prompted you to 'turn' Rowan. And for that, off the record of course, I applaud you. The three of you, in fact. But the rules are incontrovertible."

"And that brings the circle back to me," Fallon prompted her.

"It does, indeed," Marjean nodded, snatching a quick glance at her watch before continuing. "They want you clipped, *sângele sângelui*. They want your mercenary-for-hire enterprise shut down and *you* restricted, indefinitely, within the borders of Chimera."

"And if I say no?"

"What do *you* think?"

Fallon's responding laughter was, in every sense of the word, nasty. "I think it could get very messy. In fact, I guarantee it."

"Of that I have no doubt," Marjean smiled, and came to a stop at the end of the couch on which Koo and Rowan still sat. "They know it, too. But they'll still do it. Because as scared shitless of you as they are, they are more afraid of what they *think*, what they *believe* you might do if you're not stopped."

"What are you talk—" Fallon began, and was cut short again by her raised hand.

"Oh come on, *dragă*, think about it. Your *BFF*. The one who has them all, in *every* house, pissing themselves and putting their security on high alert every time he sneezes. The Vampire Nation's most infamous rebel. Which is what they're afraid *you're* turning into.

"There are a lot of people in high places who truly believe that Kane Thoth will one day lead a coup to overthrow the current regime . . ."

"Bullshit," Fallon laughed. "Kane couldn't care less about vampire politics."

"You know that, *I* know that. But them—" she shrugged and began to pace again. "Our Council members are crapping their custom silk underwear wondering if you're going to do to *them* what Kane did to the Nikaran Council in 1941. And they're using this incident as a pre-emptive defence to ensure it doesn't happen."

"I can't believe this. I just can't," Koo said, sagging against the couch's backrest.

"And I *don't* believe it," Fallon said, skirting the coffee table to block his sire's path. "Tell me something – is it just me or you wouldn't be here, with us, alone and in, what I'm sure is an unofficial capacity if everything was really that cut and dried?"

"I . . ." Marjean checked her watch again, her dusky features rife with hurried anticipation. "Let's just say that *everything* is open to negotiation. For the two of you," she looked past Fallon to Rowan and Koo. "I spoke with Eayann earlier and the word *Linişti* popped up. I'm sure Miss Chan is familiar with its meaning. Hold that in mind. It can be used as a bargaining asset. And I wouldn't worry about death in *your* case, Miss Walker, or the Crypt in yours, Miss Chan.

"And you, my child . . . consider your value to the House of Sasul. I've heard it said on a number of occasions that your skills could be put to great use for the House, as well as several of its outside contacts. Think on that for a while."

An all too telling flush rose on Marjean's mocha cheeks as a knock sounded at the suite door. She took hold of Fallon's arm then, pulling him aside.

"Listen . . . it's been a very long two days," she said, voice lowered considerably. "A long trip from Paris, and I'm feeling a little . . . *anxious*, if you know what I mean, and I need to unwind. There was no room available when I arrived," she threw an antsy look at the suite door, "and I ran into an old friend in the lobby."

"Old *friend* friend, you mean?" Fallon teased as realisation set in.

Marjean frowned. "Don't be an ass, Diego." Her demeanour immediately softened. "Be a dear and do your sire a huge favour."

Fallon made a show of mentally struggling with the request, then gave in. "Alright . . .but give housekeeping a call when you're finished *unwinding* so they can change the sheets."

CHAPTER TWENTY-ONE

After one last admonishment from Marjean that they stay within the walls of Shadowfall, Fallon led Koo and Rowan out of the suite, nodded to the man standing just outside the door, and suggested they head to one of the café's. They walked to the elevator bank in silence, Rowan's hand clasped firmly in his and Koo walking alongside. It wasn't until they were in the elevator and heading down to the first floor that Rowan spoke.

"You don't seem very bothered by what she said they wanted to do to you."

Fallon smiled. "You need to listen between the lines of what Marjean said. It'll take some fast talking, but I'm confident we can turn this around to our advantage."

"That word she used . . lin—"

"*Liniști,*" Fallon supplied, and she nodded.

"Yes, that . . . she made it sound important?"

"It –" he broke off as the cell in his pocked burst into life. He pulled it out and scowled at the unrecognised number, before thumbing call. "Wylde."

"Wildman," the deep throaty growl of Knox blistered his ears and he jerked the phone away from the side of his head. "Rumour said you'd survived, guess they weren't wrong."

"Knox," Fallon sighed. "How did you get my private number?"

Knox's laugh was raucous. "Everythin' is available for the right price, my man. That's something you should keep in mind for future reference." He paused, and Fallon heard voices in the background.

"Thanks for the unasked-for advice," Fallon responded, dryly. "Did you want something in particular?"

"I want a lot of things, Wildman. Maybe I just wanted to hear your voice?" He laughed again. "Confirmation that you didn't die in Mexico. You answerin' your cell gave me *that* answer. Don't mean your Council won't try an' take you down, but that's nothing new, is it?"

The Council? Fallon's thoughts snapped back to the all too recent meeting with his sire and all the implications therein. There were times when Knox could be one spooky son of a bitch. And this was definitely one of them.

"I'm not gonna ask where that little tidbit came from, Fallon replied. "But while I have you on the line, you got no more worries as far as Taylor is concerned. All his Christmases have been cancelled. But then, I have a feeling you already know that."

"I do, Wildman, I do." Knox's glass-shards-in-a-blender laugh made Fallon wince. "And we're probably the only ones who know. Word from my contacts below the border say the House of Salamanca are so pissed and embarrassed by the whole thing, they're screwin' a tight lid on it. So, chances are Taylor's people in Seattle don't know what happened yet."

"Good to know. Much obliged," Fallon said. "Maybe I'll make a house call."

"Whoa. Hold up. Don't hang up yet," Knox blurted quickly. "The girl. . . your squeeze's sister. What's her status?"

"It's . . ." Fallon pinched the bridge of his nose with thumb and forefinger, aware Rowan was listening. "I got her out, but she is struggling."

"I was thinkin' that would be the case, so . . ." Knox paused.

The elevator doors slid open and Fallon's eyes landed on a familiar black ivory, red crystal-topped cane. His eyes lifted to the hand resting on the crystal, followed the line of the dark-purple silk clad arm up, until he met the unreadable eyes of one of the most infamous figures within the Vampire Nation.

". . . I thought I'd offer you some help," Knox finished, cut the call and threw him a wolfish smile.

"Wow . . ." The women beside him spoke at the same time, and Fallon sighed.

"Ladies." Knox executed a flourishing bow, angling his cane to one side and almost taking out one of Shadowfall's guests, who happened to be walking past at that exact moment.

Knox watched as the man stumbled, caught himself before he tripped and chuckled loudly when their eyes met. He straightened to his full height and tipped his head toward Koo and Rowan.

"I'll give you points for taste, Wildman," he said.

Fallon ignored his comment. "What are you doing out of your crypt?" He exited the elevator, knowing the two women would follow him, and stopped a foot away from Knox.

Knox tutted. "Harsh, my friend, very harsh. My *crypt*, as you so delightfully call it, is no longer a necessity."

"How can you help my sister?" Rowan spoke before Fallon could respond and Knox's gaze swung to her.

He opened his mouth to answer, then stopped. His eyes narrowed as he stared at Rowan, causing Fallon to shift closer to her. Knox's eyes snapped to him.

"Oh stand down, Wylde, I'm no threat to your sweetheart." For a second his jovial tone dropped, leaving something darker in its wake.

Rowan stepped around Fallon, recapturing his attention and something unreadable flickered across his features as Knox looked at her.

"I need to see her before I can make any promises, sweetness." His voice had returned to his typical amused drawl, leaving Fallon questioning whether he'd heard correctly.

"Fallon," Rowan turned to the man beside her. "If he can help Eden . . ."

"You don't understand, Ro. Knox can't be trusted."

Knox laughed. "Standin' right here, Wildman, listenin' to every word."

"*Can* you be trusted?" Fallon challenged.

"When it suits me," Knox replied. "And on this, if it's what I think it is, you *can* trust me to do what's best for the girl."

~*~

What's best for the girl.

Those words rolled around in Fallon's head as he led the way to the infirmary. Rowan had jumped on Knox's offer of help and nothing Fallon said had swayed her from accepting Knox at his word. As they walked, Fallon could hear Knox whispering to Koo. He couldn't quite make out what the flamboyant vampire was saying, but he *could* hear Koo giggling like a schoolgirl in response.

"I should go in first and see if she's awake," Rowan said, when they reached Eden's room.

Knox tilted his head to one side, eyes on the door. "She's sleeping . . . dreaming, in fact."

"How do you know?"

Knox tapped the side of his nose and winked slyly at Rowan. "Funny thing about our species, some of us develop the strangest talents."

Fallon glanced sharply at Knox. *Did he know what Eayann suspected Rowan was?*

"I think you should let me introduce myself," Knox smiled knowingly at Fallon. "Why don't you continue to wherever it was you were going, and I'll sit with Eden until she wakes."

Rowan hesitated, her gaze bouncing between Knox and Fallon. "I don't think that's a good idea."

Between one breath and the next, and before Fallon could stop him, Knox was directly in front of her. The information peddler took both Rowan's hands in his and bowed his head over them.

"I give you my word, Rowan Walker, no harm will come to your sister through me."

"Back off, Knox," Fallon growled.

Knox released Rowan and raised his hands, palm outward. "Peace, brother."

Fallon ignored him, and curled a hand around Rowan's arm, pulling her further down the corridor.

"You *can't* trust him, Rowan."

"The doctors don't know what to do," Rowan replied, softly, her eyes lingering on the vampire standing outside her sister's door. "Do you think he can help her."

Fallon wanted to say no, to deny any possibility that Knox could have any clue what would help Rowan's sister, but he knew he'd be lying. "If anyone knows, it'll be Knox. It's what he's good at. But Ro, you have to understand, *everything* Knox does is for his own agenda."

"You mean he has something to gain from helping Eden?"

"That's exactly what I mean."

"But we're out of options. The doctors don't know what drugs are in her system and aren't sure how best to help her. He says he *can* help her. She deserves that chance, Fallon."

Fallon nodded. "If that's what you want to do, then we'll do it." He left unspoken that there would possibly be consequences for trusting Knox later.

They returned to where Knox leaned against the door, arms folded across his chest, cane tucked under his arm.

"Rowan's willing to let you do this, but I give you fair warning. *If* you hurt Eden or do anything Rowan is uncomfortable with . . ."

"Yeah yeah, dismemberment, pain, torture . . .the usual," Knox cut in. He opened the door to Eden's room and stepped inside, paused in the doorway and turned his head to flash a grin at Fallon. "Trust me. What could possibly go wrong?" He let the door close gently, sealing him inside the room with Rowan's sister.

"I've got a bad feeling about this," Fallon muttered, but allowed Rowan to tug him away.

Koo tagged along until they reached the main lobby, then laid a hand on Fallon's arm.

"I'm going to find Pannie and let her know what happened," she told him.

Fallon nodded, and patted her hand before she veered off toward the security wing.

Dropping his arm over Rowan's shoulders, he smiled down at her. "Want to go grab a coffee and pretend everything is normal for a while?"

She leaned into his side. "I'd like that."

~*~

Fallon chose the Dark Velvet Café, with its dimmed lights and secluded booths, as the place for him and Rowan to settle in while his suite was occupied, and Knox lurked in the Infirmary. After ordering drinks and a selection of snacks, he leaned across the table and curled his fingers around Rowan's.

"You left without waking me this evening."

Rowan's lips twitched. "You were fast asleep, I didn't want to wake you."

He ran a finger over the back of her hand. "Yeah, you did exhaust me." His green eyes danced with suppressed humour. "My back looks worse than it did when I got a whipping."

Rowan sputtered a shocked laugh. "How can you even joke about that?"

He shrugged. "It was a long time ago."

Their drinks arrived, and both fell silent as the server placed their cups in front of them.

Rowan lifted her mocha and inhaled the scent with a smile. Taking a sip, she peered at Fallon over the rim.

"What happens now?"

In the middle of taking a swallow of his own coffee, Fallon gave her a quizzical look. "How do you mean?"

"Well, you've done what I hired you for and you said once it was done, we'd be done too."

Fallon snorted. "You *really* want an answer to that?" He reached out a finger and tapped her hand. "Also, you still haven't paid me my fee."

"Doesn't death cancel all outstanding debts?"

"That's low, Rowan," he chuckled. "Anyway, you didn't die. As for the other part of your question. It's going to take you a couple hundred years to pay off your debt, so . . ." The table shook as Rowan kicked his shin beneath it. "Ouch! When did you become so violent?"

"When did you become so annoying?" she retorted, with a laugh.

Fallon's cell began to ring. "Hold that thought," he told her and pulled it out of his pocket.

Rowan propped her chin on a hand and sipped her drink while Fallon took his call. When he started to swear, she sighed and lowered her cup back to the table.

"Break time over?" she asked, when he ended the call.

"You could say that. Knox has . . ." His phone rang again, and Fallon looked at the number. "Speak of the devil." He connected the call. "What the fuck have you done?"

Whatever Knox was saying to him, Rowan knew Fallon didn't like hearing it. His fingers drummed on the table, and his jaw was clenched as he grunted in response to Knox's words.

"I *know* I can't fucking find you," he snarled eventually into the mouthpiece. "But that doesn't mean I won't hunt you down."

Another period of silence while Knox responded, and Rowan strained to pick up his words without success.

"Fine!" Fallon snapped. "But you better keep me in the loop." He cut the call and stared down at the cell in his hand for a long silent moment then raised his eyes to look at Rowan.

"Somehow that fucking miscreant managed to get Eden out of Shadowfall without anyone seeing him do it."

"*What?*" Rowan half-rose from her seat.

"Sit down," Fallon caught her hand and waited until she'd lowered herself back onto the chair. "He insists that being here was not going to help your sister and that he knows somewhere that can.

He says he'll be in touch in the next few days and that he'll supply Eden with a cell of her own, so she can contact you if she wants to."

"*If* she wants to? That doesn't sound very comforting."

"Knox says Eden needs to feel like she has control over every choice before her right now. He believes being here, with you, surrounded by our kind was going to achieve nothing more than her spiralling into a darkness she could not recover from."

"What does that mean?" Rowan whispered. "Does he think Eden would kill herself?"

"That was always a possibility," Fallon's voice gentled. "What he's saying does make sense. If Eden feels like she has more control over her own life, she might be able to find the strength to live with what happened to her."

"*Might* be able to," Rowan echoed. "Not very reassuring."

"What can I say? Life is a roll of the dice."

CHAPTER TWENTY-TWO

"Alright, *alright*. All-fucking-*RIGHT!*" Fallon cursed, and lunged across the bed in response to his annoying, and way too loud, cell phone alarm. Scooping it off the nightstand, for a brief instant he was tempted to launch it against the wall. The fact that he'd done that very thing to two others in the past twenty-four hours was the sole reason he didn't.

He froze there for a moment – stretched diagonally on his stomach, face-down against the cool sheets – with the phone clutched tightly in his hand while he struggled with the urge to roll back into his former position on the bed's opposite side and go back to sleep. Or what passed for sleep. The last few days were more like sporadic periods of sleeplessness mixed with tossing and turning. Which ultimately killed the aforementioned urge, prompting him to place the cell back on the nightstand and roll out of bed.

He padded into the bathroom, stepped into the shower stall, and stopped. *Rowan.* Although Shadowfall's unquestioningly professional housekeeping staff had given the suite, as they did all the rooms in the massive residential complex, their usual A-1 top-to-bottom beyond the commercial norm cleaning service, her scent lingered. *Haunted* him. A ghostly testament and, depending on the situation, a blessing or a curse to his matured vampire senses.

"*Damn*," he whispered, twisting the hot water spigot to its highest setting and barely feeling the sting of its initial scalding spray.

It had been three days since she . . . since *they* left Seattle for the House of Sasul's Mediterranean compound in Calvi, Haute-Corse on the northwest coast of Corsica. As part of the agreement, mediated by his devious sire, the charges against both Rowan *and* Koo would be rescinded due to extenuating circumstances. All dependent, however, on Koo's acceptance of, and entrance into, the House's *Ordine înalte de Orgine* – also known as the *Ascendenⓩă*. Which was little more than a fancy name for Sasul's fraternity/sorority of registered sires. It was also a backdoor legal way for the political/corporate class of the House to have provisional access to Rowan's *Liniști* abilities since, by Nation's law, the talents couldn't be accessed without her sire's permission, and Rowan, as a vampire newborn, had to be a member of an established House. Hence the second part of the agreement. Rowan's death sentence was lifted in exchange for her vow, and official entrance into the House of Sasul. Meaning she would have to go through both the Vampire Nation's and Sasul's indoctrination for newborns, covering vampire history, rituals and protocol, social etiquette, etcetera etcetera, the whole nine yards. A process that would keep both Rowan and Koo busy for the better part of a year.

An old saying came to mind as he shut off the shower and stepped out of its frosted glass enclosure. *'You never miss your water till the well runs dry.'* And he did, indeed, miss her. Both of them, yes, but Ro especially. More than he thought he would.

Funny how deeply she'd gotten under his skin, embedded herself into his very essence in such a short span of time. Was Eayann right, he wondered. Was it Fallon Wylde, vampire mercenary-for-hire and soldier of fortune, or Juan Diego Velásquez de Falcone, former pirate, whose heart felt the absence and whose loins burned for the young woman, now newborn vampire, formerly known as Rowan Walker?

Time would tell.

And there was another one of those true quotes that, in times such as these, always seemed to pop up and sink its teeth in your ass like an angry alligator.

Showered and dressed, Fallon took note of a message that had come through on his cell some minutes earlier. From Eayann Ó Beolláin that read:

Still angry at me? Breakfast and drinks at LaDonna Roma's. I'm buying.

Eayann

Angry? Yes. But that was an on-again off-again thing between the two of them. They had always been a strange mesh of squabbling siblings – older and younger brothers – father figure and rebellious son, occasionally at-odds business partners. But even though the two of them frequently slid into the roles of dog and cat, it never lasted.

It was Eayann who was responsible for introducing him to the Shaolin monks, the Japanese samurais, Korean and Indochinese martial fighting arts, French swordsman, Prussian gunsmiths and, in short, helped mould him into the man . . . the soldier he was today. More than that, Eayann had been there when he needed an ear to vent in, a shoulder to lean on, and a light to guide him out of those times when the overwhelming tsunami of darkness threatened to consume all logic and release a truly monstrous murderous rage into any given situation. In all seriousness, where would he be if not for Eayann?

Or, for that matter, his sire?

Marjean. Although far from the woman who'd carried him within her womb and brought him into the world, she'd been his surrogate mother for over four centuries. A woman who knew him better than he knew himself.

Or thought she did.

Fallon couldn't help but laugh as he left the suite, en-route to the elevators, remembering the look on his sire's face during that critical moment in his own tribunal. Knowing her as he did, Marjean had had the entire situation – from accusations to alternative resolutions – worked out in advance. In this instance, however, the master manipulator failed to take into account the unexpected.

Kane had graciously allowed them the use of one of his conference lounges and, following the resolution of their action with Koo and Rowan, Fallon sat with Marjean, the visibly shaken Aiden Gorrie, his assistant and a Sasul representative introduced as Mr. de Balzac. Mr. de Balzac was a strange dwarfish and moustachioed little man who looked as if he'd been turned in his middle-age period.

"I have been ordered to inform you," de Balzac said, "that the House of Sasul has decreed that the enterprise known as FW, A&R cease and desists all operations from this point onward."

"Or?" Fallon counter queried. A response the bureaucrat obviously had not been prepared for.

"Pardone?"

Fallon snorted. "There is always an 'or else'. What's the alternative?"

Mr. de Balzac exchanged confused glances with both Marjean and Gorrie, then cleared his throat nervously. "I don't . . .I am not—"

"I believe what Michel," Marjean stepped in, ". . . Mr. de Balzac means to propose is that your enterprise comes under the exclusive purview of the House of Sasul. That you and yours work for no one else."

Fallon laughed. "How about you kiss my ass?"

And the looks on all their faces – though, mostly Marjean's – was priceless. They had all been so certain, so *convinced* that their position was so iron clad solid, and that he was defeated, they were unprepared for anything other than total capitulation.

"Diego . . . what are you doing?" Marjean stage-whispered.

"Let me inform you people of something," Fallon began. "You want me exclusively, no problem. But my organisation consists of a few hundred additional assets across the country and around the world – back-up combatants, pilots, drivers, logistical personnel, arms specialists, intel gatherers, covert operatives, and others. Informed humans and independent vampires . . . none of whom will work for free and I will be *damned* if I'll ask them to.

"So, I have a counter-proposal for you," he added. "I . . . *we* will take assignments from the House. Under provision, of course. With each assignment, you subtract my fee from my yearly tribute to the house and I will pay my people from my existing accounts. And if that's not good enough for you, as I said earlier," he raised a middle finger salute, "then kiss my ass."

They had called for a break to mull over Fallon's counter-proposal, during which time he'd opted to spend the waiting period at a little bistro/café off the lobby called the Human Bean Coffee Café. Marjean arrived in the middle of his second cup.

"You know, I almost choked on your first 'kiss my ass'," she told him. "I would have bet my long life there was nothing you could ever do that would surprise me. I was wrong."

"They went for it . . . right?"

Marjean nodded. "Gorrie, not so much. He's split between hating your guts and being scared shitless of you. But de Balzac is impressed, and his vote carries more weight than Gorrie's," she reached up to caress his cheek. "I could not be prouder, my child."

"And you," He'd met her gaze head on and with a knowing grin. "You knew things would go this way . . . mostly, before you got off the plane, didn't you?"

Marjean reached across the table, taking his free hand in hers. "Of course I did. Do you think, for *one* second, that I would allow anything or anyone to harm my boy or his friends or . . . the woman he loves. And you *do* love her, don't you?"

"Yes . . . I do," he answered, after a beat's pause. "Thank you . . . Mother."

A thought occurred to him on his way down and when he exited the elevator on the second floor, Fallon moved across the level's exclusively constructed alcove and enclosed observation deck and took out his cell. A quick search of his personal directory located and highlighted a number in the local area – one he hadn't called in quite a while, in point of fact – and after nearly a dozen rings, he began to wonder if the call would go unanswered.

"Uh-huh," A familiar voice responded – a near-grunt – finally.

"Detective," Fallon replied, simply.

"Mr Vee," Sid Marshall acknowledged with the coded designation the two had worked out in the early days of their unique relationship. *Vee for Vampire.* "You know, I almost forgot I had this thing. I keep it in the bottom desk drawer in my in-home office, where I used to keep my booze before the wife put me on the wagon. You're lucky I was close enough to hear it." A pause. "It's been a while," he threw in.

"Don't tell me – you missed the sound of my sweet voice," Fallon quipped.

"*Missed*, the man said," Marshall chuckled. "How long's it been now – since we first met – two and a half or three years? Twice for the number of times we talk to each other on this thing; which is beside the point.

"All that time and I still ain't completely used to the fact that you're a . . . that people like you exist. So no, missed is definitely *not* the word I'd use when it comes to you.

"But while we're at it, why *are* you calling?" Marshall queried on the heels of their shared laugh.

"Two reasons. First, and apologies for not checking in with you sooner, I thought you might like to know the situation with Miss Walker has been taken care of successfully. The sisters were reunited."

"Good to know. And thanks . . . again," Marshall took a brief pause before resuming. "You know – and you're probably tired of hearing it - but if I said it a thousand times it *still* wouldn't be enough for what you do. What you *did* for me.

"I mean, that dirtbag gang banger had me cold. And with my own piece. If you hadn't come along when you did, my wife would be a widow."

There was a moment of measured silence before Fallon replied. "You're a good man, Sid. More than that, a good cop. Something the city of Seattle can't have too many of."

"Now who's getting sentimental?" Marshall laughed. "And you said *two* reasons."

"I did. Thanks to this recent gig, I have decided to add something new to my dance card. Remember that TV show back in the eighties? The British actor – Edward Something – ex-CIA, advertises in the newspaper Personals section. In fact, they did a movie remake of it with Denzel . . ."

"Equalizer. Yeah, I liked that show," Marshall said.

"There we are then," Fallon said. "I'm sure there are a few cases, people you run into who need help the SPD can't legally give them."

"Interesting, Mr Vee. *Very* interesting. I will keep it in mind. And . . . I'll be in touch," Marshall replied and severed the connection.

Fallon tucked his phone back inside his jacket, thrust his hands into his pants pockets and gazed over the lobby beneath him. His eyes caught and held on a redhaired figure gliding through the crowds and, for a second, he thought he could smell Rowan's unique scent. He scowled and shook his head.

"You're losing the fucking plot," he muttered to himself, and turned to head toward LaDonna's.

"Talking to yourself is supposed to be the first sign of madness, you know." A soft voice spoke behind him.

Fallon froze. "Is hearing voices the second sign?" he asked, eventually.

"You're supposed to be the crazy one . . . you tell me."

He turned slowly, half-afraid he *was* crazy and hearing voices, to find the woman who had haunted both his dreams and waking thoughts for the past three days standing no more than three steps away.

"You're supposed to be in Corsica."

Rowan smiled. "Funny story. Apparently because I'm *Linişti* – *not* that I know how that works yet – it means that when I say I can't focus on developing that talent until I am given the things I want first, people fall over backwards to comply."

"Is power already corrupting you?" He arched a brow.

"Absolutely!" She took a step forward. "They hustled me out of that meeting room so fast and onto a plane, I didn't realise what they had planned until they were telling me to buckle in for take-off."

Fallon snorted a laugh. "Did you try and climb out of the window?"

"I told them that if they wanted me to go along with their plans, they had to bring me back here so I could make sure you were still alive. I told them I don't trust their word, especially that greasy nasty little man, Gorrie."

"Good instincts," Fallon murmured. "So, what were your demands?"

"I don't want to go to Corsica," she paused and scrunched up her nose. "Actually, that's not true. I'd quite like to visit but not with a bunch of people I don't know."

"And they agreed?"

"Well," she hesitated. "That really depends on you."

"Me? I'm fairly sure I'm the last person whose opinion they want right now."

"Marjean suggested they could possibly set up a House Consulate in Shadowfall. She said someone else has one here, too? And that Koo and I could do everything we need to do here instead . . . but only if you agree." She caught her bottom lip between her teeth and looked at him. "Fallon, do you want me to stay here?"

Fallon's brows pulled together in a frown. "Why do you even need to ask me that?"

Rowan sighed and glanced at the space between them. "Because you're still all the way over there and I thought that maybe—"

She didn't get to finish the sentence before Fallon's arms were around her, and his mouth was on hers.

"I've killed two fucking phones and nearly gone crazy," he told her between kisses. "Where have you been for the past three days?"

Rowan leaned back in his arms, her eyes dancing away from his. "That's another funny story . . . kinda."

Fallon recognised the stubborn set of her features and vented a mock-sigh. "What did you do?"

"I overheard Gorrie talking about you to one of the others. About how he was the one to give you those scars." Her lip caught between her teeth again. "I might have punched him in the mouth. . . just a little bit." She laughed softly. "I'm not sorry, either! Marjean made me stay in her rooms as punishment, to learn to control my temper."

Marjean, Fallon laughed inwardly. Knowing his sire, as well as the councilman in question, it was probably something *she* had been itching to do for years. And confining Rowan to her room would have been a precaution, in case Mr. Macho Asshole decided to do something petty in retaliation to save face.

"Wish I could've been there to see that," Fallon smiled, then leaned his forehead against hers. "I cannot even begin to explain what it means to me that you would do that," he told her softly. He pressed another lingering kiss to her lips, then straightened. "I'm supposed to be meeting Eayann at LaDonna Roma's."

"Ahhhh, no. He sent you that so I could find you. So, unless you *really* want to go and have breakfast . . ." She threw him an arch look and he laughed.

"You know, I believe I'm hungrier for something else now that you mention it," he said, wrapped his arm around her waist and headed back to his suite.

EPILOGUE

There were days when, with everything, all the shit – the whispers, mumbled comments, snide remarks, the giggle-up-the-sleeve jokes – Detective Virginia Frost had to put with during the course of her 8:30AM to 5:00PM shift, she seriously began to wonder if it was truly worth it.

And today had been one of those days.

It started with the necklace of garlic bulbs and a wooden cross some overly literal comedic asshat had left on her desk with an attached black and white magazine photo of actor Bela Lugosi in his role as Count Dracula, with the words 'WANTED, UNDEAD OR ALIVE', in red marker written across it. From there it had gone from annoyance to aggravation, insensitivity to insult, and finally to the straw that snapped the proverbial camel's back – seeing what the situation had done to her partner, Detective Sergeant William Moseley.

Poor Bill. God knew – Jen knew – he'd done his best to remain loyal, to ride out what, for him, must have been a bumper car ride of nonstop workplace Hell. She'd heard him joke about it, had witnessed his attempts to act as a protective shield, launching a string of witty counter-quips at their smug, holier-than-thou colleagues. But you don't spend the amount of time they'd spent in one another's company – a more than three years, five sometimes six days a week; eight to frequent sixteen plus hours a day association that went beyond mere partnership – without getting to know that person, in the deeper (though non-Biblical) sense of the term. And Jen could both see and sense that the situation was taking its toll on him.

Today it finally boiled over during their lunch break stopover at the Gold Star in a confrontation between Moseley and a mouth, opinionated prick from the Robbery Division – probably the same dick responsible for the garlic necklace and cross – that came to within an inch of a head-to-head brawl.

Thankfully, in one respect at least, it was a slow day. With no major incidents or cases to work on, they had the day to allow the emotions caused by the blow-up to settle. But just before they clocked out for the day, Bill had come to her to announce his decision to file for a transfer.

Could she blame him? In all honesty, no.

Did it hurt? God yes, it did. With everything else she had been going through over the past few weeks, it may not have been the last straw, but Jen was definitely felt the pressure. The dogs of impending defeat were snapping at her heels. And after a day like today, she imagined she could almost feel the heat of their combined breath on her ass.

Dogs.

Damn dammit! Jen froze as she slid behind the wheel of her car. Sudden recollection directed her to the glovebox and a folded slip of yellow notepad paper. A grocery list, as memory dictated, written the night before. And sure enough the sixth item on the thankfully short list . . . dog food.

She and her hubby normally alternated on the shopping chores – both of them worked jobs whose schedules were anything but predictable – but in the last week things had been slower for Rick and he had taken on the task for both of them. A relatively smooth process for Rick, inasmuch as his office was only a block away from a Safeway supermarket. For her, on the other hand, it called for a trip to one of the city's Alberstons. The nearest of which on Bothell way, was still six blocks off her usual route.

One of the things Jen always found amusing during her forays into the shopping realm – supermarkets especially – was the people. Her fellow shoppers. Their actions, attitudes and a plethora of dress styles that ran the gauntlet from drab, bland and downright ugly to the eccentric and extremely bizarre. And tonight's crop were far from the exception.

Two that were particularly noteworthy.

The first was a woman – dirty-blonde, late-to-middle forties – in a studded black leather jacket, a knee-length white Minnie Mouse t-shirt, green tights, and fuzzy brown house slippers. *Motorcycle Mama ala Domestic*, Jen laughed to herself.

And the second, a bizarre 'blast from the past'. A throwback to the days of John, Paul, George, and Ringo; Mick and Keith; Granny glasses and the Grand Exalted Goddess of the supermodel set was a little British girl who probably weighed ninety pounds soaking wet. And with this one, Twiggy was alive and well – bobbed hairdo and beret, thigh-high mini-dress, coloured hose, calf books, the whole nine yards.

Bizarre may have been more of a ricochet than an on-target hit. The woman's counter-culture, retro attire more eccentric when compared to the styles of the current period and excessive in terms of their location. But one thing was undeniable: she stood out among her drab and unremarkable fellow shoppers like a whore in a church. A fact that might have become accepted, become accustomed to, and ignored by most of the supermarket's patrons – Jen included – eventually. But for Virginia Frost the cop, the red flags rose higher when, within the first five minutes of her arrival alone, the Carnaby Street cos-player either strolled past the aisle ahead of her or entered the aisle in front or behind her. And what's more, pushing an empty shopping cart.

Coincidence? Jen didn't believe in them. Which is why when it happened again, moments after she entered and moved down the cereals aisle, she stopped to take up a strategic position mid-aisle under the pretense of perusing the ridiculous variety of *Cheerios*. She calmly and covertly slid her hand into her right-hand pocket, to her still-holstered gun, and waited for the suspected – *what? Nutjob? Stalker? Relative or girlfriend of a former collar bent on payback?* – perpetrator to make her move.

It took a minute or so – the woman in the Mary Quant garb seemed to be deliberately taking her sweet time – but soon she wheeled by. And for a moment it looked as if she would continue down the aisle. Jen continued to track her, eyes only at first, but gradually turning as she moved out of visual range.

When the move came, it was almost unexpected. In fact, there was a brief blur of motion and suddenly she was standing directly to Jen's rear, their bodies less than a foot apart, with the other woman facing in the opposite direction.

"That's not necessary, you know," she finally spoke after waiting for a trio of their aisle-mates to pass and move out of hearing range. "The gun in your coat," she resumed, and this time Jen caught a distinct accent – British, possibly. "If I wanted to hurt ya, I could've done it outside in the car park. Less witnesses."

"That's comforting," Jen replied. She kept her hand on the gun, however. "Alright. You got my attention."

"Got a present for ya. Look in your cart, luv."

Hesitating for a five-count, Jen swung outward in a half-circle that would keep her beret-clad 'suspect' in sight and made a quick visual inspection of her shopping cart's interior. A task she had to do twice, in jerky snatches, before she finally spotted the small manila envelope nestled between her two cans of French roast coffee. Too small to be a bribe or pay-off, Jen thought. And not big enough to be a bomb. At least one that would do any significant damage. Still, in these times of terrorists/Jihadist activities, one never knew.

"You might wanna keep in mind, my gate only swings one way," Jen remarked. "So if that's some little trinket – a ring, bracelet, pendant – of your undying affect-"

"Let's get into your gate another time, luv," Beret chuckled. "Right now," she nodded to Jen's cart, "it's a locker key. The Greyhound Station, 503 South Royal Brougham Way."

Jen shrugged. "And why would I want what's in it?"

"Boy… boy oh boy!" This time Beret launched a full on peal of laughter that, strangely, sounded as though it issued out of two separate throats and sent an icy chill up Jen's spine. "Play hard to get, if it suits ya, Detective. It's no skin off my nose. *But* . . . you're the one who's been making noises about high level secret cover-ups and hidden agendas. I thought maybe, just maybe, you might want 'em answered."

"And you have the answers?"

"I got what you need."

Both paused, approached from both directions by a parade of other shoppers, and Jen took the opportunity to take a close, more analytical look at the woman before her as the newcomers filed by.

She was an undeniable paradox. First impression – her smooth, unblemished complexion bespoke of a girl of no less than nineteen, no older than twenty-one. But the voice, the vocal inflection, her bearing and attitude marked her as someone as worldly as Jen herself. Someone who'd lived and seen far too much beyond her years. And *that* alone was enough to raise a few more red flags.

There was, of course, another possibility.

"They put you up to this, didn't they?" Jen said, a knowing smile gradually dominating her features. "That . . . asshole, Clevenger and his toadies in Robbery. It's them, right? They sent you after me, to get me all worked up. I buy into your little lure and show up at the bus station where they're all wait—"

"The Pagans – Romulus and Rema," Beret cut in, prompting a smile of her own in response to Jen's brow-hiked reaction. "Real names Sisko Taggart and Kira Cahill. The media nicknamed them the 'Star Trek Bandits'. First off, because their folks were huge Star Trek fans . . . *Trekkies* . . . and named them after characters from one of the shows – Deep Space Nine, I believe – and also because they robbed sixteen all-night gas station minimarts in Star Trek costumes .
. .

"And, oh yes," she added. "They also shot and killed twelve of the sixteen cashiers, kidnapped, raped and murdered four customers. They were finally caught a few hours after robbery-murder number seventeen, in Room Sixteen of the Casa Bonita Motel on Interstate 5. All that happened two years *before* Detective Clevenger and most of his crew joined the SPD.

"Heard enough, or shall I continue?"

Jen gave a head-tilting nod.

"Let me give you a recap of what occurred next – the official version versus the cover up. Three days later, while awaiting arraignment on the charges for their crimes, Kira and Sisko escaped from the country lockup facility. Officially, they had inside help and several members of the night shift guard crew were suspended pending an investigation. *Unofficially*, no one had the slightest notion how they got out of cells with electronically locked doors and got out of the facility without being recorded on security cameras.

"Their bodies were discovered a week later, in a hunting cabin in the woods near Bremerton. The cause of death was officially ruled as murder-suicide. Unofficially – and I believe your partner, Detective Moseley, can confirm as he was a member o the team from Seattle brought in by the Bremerton PD to consult – the bodies of the two eighteen-year-olds, in addition to being completely nude, had been severely savaged, post-mortem, by animals. . . covered in teeth and/or fang bites, and were completely drained of bodily fluids. Bodies so badly mutilated that the weapon used to bring about their initial deaths could not conclusively be determined. And the fact that there wasn't a single drop of blood left in their bodies—"

"Alright, alright! You made your point," Jen almost barked, self-consciously scanning their immediate area for curious and unwanted bystanders. "So what you're implying, what you want me to believe is that someone entered into, and helped Taggart and

Cahill escape from a highly secure corrections facility, just to take them out into the woods and kill them?"

Beret nodded, smiling. "Though the point – points, plural, I should say – is *how* they were *how* they were killed and *why*. Let's go with the why first. On their last robbery, the cashier they murdered was, shall we say, connected . . ."

"Now we're talking gangsters, Mob, cartel, right?" "You could say that, Detective. The *ultimate* cartel. World-wide, in fact. And this particular cashier, though he had no idea, was connected by blood . . . by ancestry."

"You're losing me now," Jen snorted. "What, if anything, does any of this have to do with—"

"My God, you *are* a sceptic!" Beret interrupted again. "What is the one thing the deaths of Taggart and Cahill have in common with the family in Ravena, with all the others that came after in your case in involving the children a few months back . . . with *Teresa Bennion*? Wait, I'll tell *you* – extreme blood loss, bite marks. You know where it leads. Say the word . . . Say it, Detective."

"That is absurd. It's not possible," Jen shook her head in disbelief.

"Go to the bus station. Check out what's in the locker. Then try to deny it."

Jen took a lengthy pause, still struggling with what she was hearing. "Okay. Let's say, for the sake of argument, that I believe this crap. My question is – what's your part in all this? Why do *you* care?"

"I could ask you the same questions, Detective. And I can guarantee you I'm not the only one who's asking. Your own people – the higher ups – you got them sweating blood and bullets, luv."

"Good," Jen said, with obvious satisfaction.

"Don't get too big-headed, Detective," Beret warned. "They're watching you, do ya know that? Right now, there's a couple of brush-cut brutes sitting in an SUV out in the car park. They have been following you all day . . . the past week, matter of fact. And they probably have your home and landline bugged. These people are nervous, scared, and that makes 'em dangerous."

"Okay. If that's the case, then why are *you* helping me?" Jen asked.

"Maybe because I agree with you, luv. Because it's time the truth be revealed. There are things happening out there. People being killed . . . murdered. Savaged by creatures, *monsters* that until now everyone believed were creations of Hollywood. And a faction – *two* factions – of supposed protectors have been covering up for decades."

"And you," Jen had to know. "How is it that you know so much about . . ." Jen's question trailed off out of both embarrassment and uncertainty.

"About the monsters?" Beret offered, her amused grin sliding leftward, as did the rest of her body, in something Jen was certain had to be a trick of the senses – her eyes – as the woman in the retro attire blurred away. In an instant, the spot in which she had stood was empty, occupied only by her empty shopping cart. And in the next instance, Jen felt the girl's warm breath at her ear.

"About the monsters," the girl repeated Jen's query. "Because I'm one of them."

Jen reflexively swung in the direction of the voice, only to find the space empty. The girl in the beret was nowhere to be seen.

"Oh, Jesus," Jen hugged herself against any icy wave that washed over her from top to bottom.

GLOSSARY

CHARACTERS

Arletta Chambeau – Human. Shadowfall's Chief of Medicine.

Brother Custos – Pureborn. A member of the *Cabal*

Cameron – Shadowfall's Chief Mechanic and Head of Transportation

Eayann Ó Beolláin - Elder Statesman of the House of Sasul.

Eden Walker - Missing sister of Rowan Walker.

Elsbeth I'Ane Dasmalle – A Pureborn. Wife of *Lord Zuron*, mother of *Taz I'ane*

Fallon Wylde – Formerly a 17ᵗʰ Century Pirate. For the past five centuries a mercenary/soldier for hire and member of the *House of Sasul.*

Gayle Hunter – A Halfblood. *Kane's* adopted daughter and General Manager of Shadowfall's food, beverage and entertainment venues.

Hamish Satori – Lord of the House of Satori and Commander of the *Necuno*

Hannah Satori – Wife of *Hamish*

Kane Thoth – The Egyptian. Uber-wealthy entrepreneur and owner of Club Shadowfall. More than 5,000 years old and dark celebrity within the Vampire Nation

Kayla Monroe – Human. Local Seattle television personality and intimate associate of *Taz I'Ane*

Koo - Kate Chan of the House of Sasul.

Knox - Information Merchant extraordinaire.

Marjean Sălbatica - Lady (Leader) of the House of Sasul.

Morganna Satori – Assassin for *House Nikaris*

Pantera Rydel – A Member of *House of Sasul*, she is Shadowfall's Chief of Security

Qetsiyah Anastasia Camlo – Pureborn. Queen of Seattle's Rroma Czerny Clan and of the *House of Camlo*. Also known as "Kizzy"

Rowan Walker - A fiesty young (Human) woman struggling to locate her missing sister.

Taylor - Eden's boyfriend.

Tigr - A Shadowfall bartender.

Taz I'Ane – Heir Apparent to the throne of the *House of Nikaris* and the son of *Lord Zuron*

Virginia "Jen" Frost – Human. Detective Lieutenant, Seattle Police Department, Special Crimes Unit

William Moseley – Human. Detective Sergeant, Seattle Police Department, Special Crimes Unit

Zuron I'Ane Dasmalle – A Pureborn. Current Lord of the *House of Nikaris* and the father of *Taz I'Ane*

VAMPIRE HOUSES

House of Nikaris

Founded: Date Unknown
Founder: Nikaris the Cimmerian – Scribe, Scholar, Shaman and Master of the Mystic Arts

Oldest and most powerful of the Houses. Little is known about the Cimmerian, but what is documented is that he was the first to organise his followers and *progen* into first, a cohesive tribe and then a House – even before the Great Retribution. Often called the Grand Architect of the Vampire Nation.

House of Belaur

Founded: Date Unknown
Founder: Queen Belaura – Student and (some believe) consort/wife of Nikaris. Sorceress of the Dark Arts.

An off-shoot of the House Nikaris. Belaurans are fiercely xenophobic, contemptuous of human beings AND other vampires. They practice Black Magic in all it diverse forms and believe that vampires, as the superiors of human, should rule the world public and not hide behind a façade.

House of Paladin the Warrior

Founded: 1809 A.D.
Founder: Guerrier alias Paladino alias Paladé; an alleged minor officer in Napoleon's army Sired during the Battle of Corunna.

Paladins are martial. Chiefly, though not exclusively sired from the ranks of the military, law enforcement, street gangs, outlaws, etcetera.

House of Sasul

Founded: 1510 A.D. Hungary

Founder: Vlad Sasul, and not Vlad Tepes, as some believe. Called "the Changeling" because of his ability (a curse by some accounts) to tap into his inner *animus* and become his "spirit beast". Pure propaganda, of course.

It was the House's current leader some say, Lady Marjean Sălbatica, who whispered in Bram Stoker's ear while he slept and sparked the dreams which inspired the writing of Dracula. Deliberately misleading, it gave the legendary vampire the abilities which formed the universally accepted Vampire mythos.

House of Machiavel

Founded: Date unknown

Founder: Unknown. But the House was supposedly inspired by the works of Italian philosopher and writer Niccolò di Bernardo dei Machiavelli.

Power brokers. Political corruption; corporate espionage, in both the human and vampire realms.

House of the Abyss

Founded: Date unknown

Founder: Unknown.

Abyssians court mayhem, murder, chaos, and madness and are drawn to them… and their perpetrators like moths to flame.

House of Molochi

Founded: Date unknown
Founder: Malachi.

Molochi, whose name is variation of their founder, are vampires who may have spawned the mythology of Medusa. They are so beautiful that anyone who looks directly at them are instantly enthralled and, in most cases, reduced to raving maniacs.

House of Sybarite

Founded: Italy, the Renaissance period.
Founder: Unknown.

Hedonism. Art. Creativity. Sybarites dance within the arenas of entertainment, fashion, creative expression, and carnal excess.

The Rroma Alliance

Founded: 1800 A.D.
Founder: Unknown.

A loose coalition of Romany families, tribes, and clans spread across the globe, each lead by a King or Queen, or both. Rromas... "Gypsies"... like their human counterparts, excel in the realm of larceny, deceit, and the grifting arts. They are also widely used by several of the larger more organized Houses for various and sundry unconscionable tasks.

House of L'élite

Founded: Date unknown
Founder: Unknown.

Also referred to as "The Elite". This House consists of vampires from various Houses and clans, but all members share 'blue blooded', Pureborn heritage. Most are titled— Prince/Princesses, Duchess/Dukes, Earls, Counts/Countesses, Barons/Baronesses. They are the vampire Jet Set.

House of Maggio

Founded: 1780 A.D. Southern Italy
Founder: Salvatore Maggio.

As much a vampire Mafioso family as a House. They have several sub-houses, run by Maggio-sired "sefu" (or Dons) and is credited with being the spawning ground for several vampire cartels. Most notable the Purple Brotherhood.

ABOUT THE AUTHORS

L. Ann lives in Derbyshire, UK with her partner, children, and the many imaginary voices in her head.

L. Gene Brown lives in Central Point, Oregon, USA for sanity as well as for the sake of continued literary inspiration.

ONE LAST THING...

If you enjoyed this book, we would be very grateful if you'd post a short review on one of the many review sites. Your support really does make a difference and we read all the reviews personally so we can get your feedback and make our books even better.

Thanks again for your support!

Made in the USA
Columbia, SC
05 October 2020